The Dreaming Prophet

By

Susan Davis Sandberg

SusanDavisSandberg@gmail.com

ISBN (print): 978-1-939577-04-7
ISBN (kindle): 978-1-939577-05-4
ISBN (epub): 978-1-939577-06-1

Cover design by John Sandberg
Cover photograph © by Triff, Shutterstock.com

To

My son John

For giving me the
fruition of a dream

Chapter 1

"We're having our next baby at home," Aleta Praetzel announced as soon as she was settled in the back seat of Chief Lyle West's car.

West slipped into the front seat, smiling. Stanley settled in the back seat next to his wife and baby. Little Gerard was only two hours old.

"Can we get this one home before we make those arrangements?" Stanley queried, knowing full well his auburn-haired wife was not going to let the matter be postponed.

"I missed the apple trees blossoming this time. I'm not doing it again," Aleta announced firmly.

"You missed a few other things as well," Stanley announced. "I made some changes to the house."

"Without asking?" she asked both surprised and dismayed.

"I knew you would fret if you weren't there," he ventured.

Lyle drove through his town of Arborville slowly. When his car crossed the border into Willow Glen, Police Chief Tom Milani got the report immediately. He radioed Lyle.

"Was Chesney right this time?"

Lyle laughed. Dr. Chesney had told him just a few months prior that he was going to have a girl. Lauren had unexpectedly given birth to a healthy boy in the Praetzel's guest room during a party.

"Aleta and Stanley have a boy."

"Who won the pool?" Lyle asked.

"You'll never guess."

"What pool?" Aleta asked from the back seat, temporarily diverted from getting Stanley to accept her decision.

Lyle filled her in. "When the baby would be born and it's sex. Go ahead, Tom, tell us who won."

"Jocelyn."

"Jocelyn's too young to bet!" Aleta declared. "You didn't take her money, did you?"

"Bertha said it was her allowance. She could lose it if she wanted.

"How much did she win?" Aleta asked.

"Two hundred and fifty dollars in our pool. I think she entered two others as well. Nice return for three investments of ten bucks. She evidently takes after her grandmother in more ways than one."

"She's not a prophet!" Aleta declared.

Tom laughed. "I hope not. If she is, I'll lead a petition to get that subdivision moved into Arborville. Lyle has only one prophet. He deserves more."

"I already have the hospital," Lyle put in. "Half of the incidents take place there as it is. You keep the boundaries where they are!"

"As if the town council would ever let go of that jewel," Tom grumbled affably.

"Aleta wants to have the next baby at home," Lyle reported.

"When is that going to happen?" Tom inquired facetiously.

"When the apple trees are in bloom," Lyle replied.

"Stanley has agreed?" Tom asked surprised.

"He hasn't a prayer," Lyle said. "Aleta's determined."

"This time Jocelyn doesn't get to enter our pool," Tom announced firmly.

Stanley leaned over and whispered in his wife's ear. "I'm not planning the event so far in advance."

"You always plan everything months ahead," Aleta quipped. "I need to put my two cents worth in early."

"Well, you're already too late. My mind was made up two hours ago," Stanley retorted. "We aren't scaring Gerard to death."

"Your mother will take him."

"My mother's a sitting judge. She always has a full calendar. I didn't even call her to tell her Gerard was born."

"Jocelyn will obviously be able to tell her when to take the day off," Aleta grinned. "Now tell me what you changed in the house."

"I put a new door into the bedroom."

"Good."

"I gave your grandmother the furniture in the blue guest room."

"Good. All the furniture in her guest room was destroyed in the fire."

"I had Bertha move the bassinet into our bedroom," Stanley said relaxed.

"Stanley, no!" Aleta protested immediately.

"He can live in his crib during the day when Bertha's here."

"He can't be in our bedroom."

Lyle smirked as he left the tree-lined streets of Willow Glen and entered the farmland beyond, dotted with the estates of the rich. It was horse country, and while Stanley had purchased his acreage with no thought of ever having horses, despite having a barn, he now had six and an ancient horseman to care for them.

The fields were green with new growth, the trees fully leafed, huge pink peonies and purple iris were in full bloom.

"I want those," Aleta exclaimed. "Those big pink ones. They're gorgeous. What are they?"

"You didn't have peonies in California?"

"No. We had irises though and I love them too."

"And lilacs?" Stanley asked pointing at a row of bushes with large flowers.

"I think so, but they didn't have blossoms like those."

"They need the ground to freeze in winter," Lyle said.

"How come you know that?" Stanley asked.

"I talked to our gardener a lot when I was growing up."

"That's what we need next," Aleta declared. "We need to plant a garden."

"I like the fact that our place is simple," Stanley said. "Gardeners cost money."

"The baby can't sleep in our bedroom," Aleta declared, suddenly switching back to her earlier protest.

"Why not?" Stanley asked as Lyle drove up the rise just before their modest appearing house came into view.

"You know perfectly well why not," Aleta declared. "We aren't going to be doing anything for a month."

"I will not be watched when I change."

"He's two hours old! He can't even see yet."

"I will not have him seeing me unclothed," she declared.

"You're breast feeding!" Stanley gasped.

"Who are all those people?" Aleta exclaimed as Lyle's car reached the rise in the road.

Lyle was on the radio. "Tom, how did news get out? We need crowd control at the Praetzel place."

"It's four o'clock!" Tom protested. "What are they doing there?"

"Send a couple of units," Lyle said.

"How many people are there?" Tom asked.

"Sixty-three," Aleta answered from the back seat. "Why are they here?"

"Either because you're a prophet or because you're the lawyer who can pull rabbits out of the hat."

"But Justin's articles about the trial were months ago."

"Milani has been shooing people away from your house every day since. You being in the hospital eventually reduced the members to only a few. But how did the news that you were coming home get out?" Lyle asked puzzled.

As he started down the driveway, Aleta made him stop.

"Aleta, you aren't getting out!" Stanley exclaimed.

"Don't forbid me," Aleta replied tersely as she handed him the baby.

"Wait for Milani's men," Lyle urged.

"That woman needs a ride," Aleta said. "She can sit up in front with you, Lyle."

Lyle turned in his seat and addressed Stanley.

"What do you suggest I do?"

"Give the old woman a ride to the house, I guess," Stanley said.

As Aleta led the elderly woman around the patrol car, both men noticed she limped badly and relied heavily on her cane. Her plump face was uneven, one side drooping listlessly while the other side smiled in response to whatever Aleta was saying.

Lyle opened the door an Aleta helped the crippled old lady into the car.

"Gentlemen, Mrs. Dorothy Gonski of Arborville," Aleta said. "Chief Lyle West and my husband, Stanley, holding Gerard."

The woman mumbled several unintelligible words. Aleta smiled. "Two hours. His name's Gerard."

More sounds came out.

"My father-in-law named him," Aleta said. "I liked the name he gave his own son so I left the naming of his first grandson in his hands."

Both Chief West and Stanley had witnessed Aleta interpreting the jumbled speech of stroke victims in the past, but both believed the ability had been replaced by another gift.

This time when Mrs. Gonski turned and said, "Pret... ba..." it was difficult not to believe that this time Aleta was simply just listening carefully and guessing at the words. Both men relaxed.

"He looks like his mother," Lyle said.

The old lady cackled. "Goo... ving..."

"Yes," Stanley agreed. "Only Aleta wants one that looks like me."

"Yuvs you," came the almost unintelligible response.

Stanley watched as Aleta turned away and went back to the row of people.

"Lyle, what is she doing?"

Lyle didn't respond as he had already stopped the car and was out the door.

Aleta was eyeing a young man in shabby clothes. Lyle appeared at her side in time to hear her say bluntly, "I don't give interviews to deceitful men. Leave at once or I'll have you arrested for trespassing."

"You can't just arrest me," he blurted out.

"I can have whomever I want arrested," Aleta declared. "Don't tempt me. Just leave."

"I dare you!" the young man challenged.

Aleta didn't even turn around. She gave the order with her eyes still fixed on the reporter.

"Chief West, arrest him. I'll press charges."

The man found himself spun around, handcuffed and moved over to the car marked Arborville Chief of Police just as one of Willow Glen's patrol cars drove up.

The old man who'd been standing in front of the reporter drew back fearfully.

Aleta put her hand on his shoulder. "Come with me. Let's have a cup of coffee and talk.

The old man mumbled incoherently and struggled to pull an envelope from his coat pocket. He finally managed to extract it and hold it out.

"I know you can't speak so anyone can understand you," Aleta said, taking the envelope. "Was it a stroke?"

The old man nodded and pointed at the envelope.

The man standing in front of him said, "He's been garbling like that since we got here. Now I can tell you plain and easy what my case is about. He's a waste of time."

Aleta eyed him coldly. "You, Sir, are obviously quite capable of finding another attorney. He isn't."

"So you won't take my case? I was here first. It's a big case. I want to sue..."

"Stop right there. That's not anything I'm interested in," Aleta said.

"But it'd mean big bucks for both of us."

"Not interested," she replied and walked on guiding the old man toward her front door.

Lyle saw Milani drive up and went over to speak with him. He told him Aleta had selected some people she evidently planned to help. One man she had him arrest for trespassing because he wouldn't leave.

"If the others don't go, I think you're going to have to arrest them," Lyle finished.

"For heaven's sake!" Tom sputtered. "How big a jail does she think we have?"

"Then be your usual persuasive self and just threaten the hell out of them."

"Why'd I ever let Peets leave?"

"Because he deserved the Oakwood chief spot."

"Yeah, I know, but why'd I do it. He was so damned good at stuff like this. All he had to do was just stare at someone and they'd fold."

"She's pulling another one out of line," Lyle observed aloud. "Doesn't she know she just had a baby?"

"She laid in that hospital bed for two months. I think she was penned up too long," Milani said. "And if I don't hurry she'll come back and pick out a few more. If ever I needed Peets, this is the moment."

"Tell Aleta how Martha Cook handled it."

"How did she? That was before my time."

"Mine too," West said, "but I understand she had the police arrest anyone who bothered her and she used that word 'bother'. The chief had to be creative with the charges and most were released after being booked and fingerprinted. A second offender spent time in jail. Martha meant to preserve her privacy."

"Is that Stanley in your car?"

"He's holding the baby."

"Leave it to Aleta," Tom chuckled. "Can I take a peek?"

"He'd love it," Lyle said. "It's a little redhead. Looks like the mom."

"Why on earth did she want it to look like Stanley?" Tom asked getting out of his car.

"His genes may dictate the next one. She's already talking about it."

"So soon. It took Rachel two years before she'd even consider another pregnancy."

"Took Lauren about a year," Lyle said as they reached Lyle's car. Tom leaned in.

"Looks like Aleta," he observed.

Stanley grinned. "There are times when I give in."

"She still wants one that looks like you?" Tom asked.

"Aleta is determined," Stanley said. "You do know that she thinks Bulldogs are gorgeous, don't you?"

"Lyle told me about that."

"I guess you can get used to anything."

"As I remember it, she liked you from the very beginning," Lyle said.

"We were there, you remember," Milani added.

"Well, I thought she was the most beautiful woman I'd ever seen," Stanley said.

The Dreaming Prophet   9

"You'll get no argument from either of us on that," Tom said. "She was a looker and now that her injuries have healed, she's back to being that again."

"So what exactly is Aleta doing?" Stanley asked Lyle.

"I have no idea whether she's hired you some more servants or taken on five new cases."

"My word!" Stanley exclaimed. "Stop her."

Lyle's jaw dropped. "Me?"

"My hands are full!" Stanley spouted. "Drive me the rest of the way. What is it with you two? You just let her go ahead and... and..."

"And be herself?" Lyle said. "Only you can order Aleta to do anything. Why didn't you stop her?"

"She forbid it," Stanley reported testily.

"What do you want me to do with all these people?" Milani asked.

"Hey, I'm not in charge anymore it seems," Stanley quipped. The baby began to fuss and he looked at him. "You'll need to get used to it, Gerard. Mommy is like that."

Tom trotted up to the front door while Lyle slipped into the driver's seat and drove behind him.

Once inside the house, Stanley told Aleta they needed to talk.

"Bertha, please serve my clients some coffee," Aleta said. "I'll be out in a minute."

She followed Stanley into their bedroom and let him hand her the baby.

"Sit!" he ordered. Aleta sat down and rocked her baby.

"Hush," she said. "Your daddy needs to yell at your mommy."

"I'm not yelling!" Stanley shouted.

"Everyone in the kitchen can hear you," Aleta responded quietly.

Stanley lowered his voice, "You can't take clients, Aleta. You just had a baby."

As he looked at her holding the baby so tenderly, his annoyance vanished. "Tom says he's handsome."

"He is, you know."

"He looks like you."

"And that pleases you, doesn't it?"

"I couldn't be happier!" Stanley admitted.

"Then you know why I also want a son that looks like you."

"No, I don't."

"I love you," Aleta said. "That's why."

"You're making no sense. Why would I want to have a son who looks like me?"

"Ask your parents that question," Aleta said.

"They love me," Stanley said.

"Exactly," she replied. "Now, I told Tom that he was to invite the rest of the people to leave and arrest any who wouldn't."

Stanley nodded. "That's what Martha did years ago. So what's with the group in the kitchen? Why them?"

"The man in the blue coat is our new gardener. He's been falsely accused. The woman with the child is Bertha's new helper and her daughter needs you. The woman needs me. The old lady just needs an interpreter. She's Lyle's case. And the old man is here on a mission."

"You got a vision, didn't you?"

"Not really. Just a feeling and then when I needed to know, the words came."

"We aren't going to get shot at, are we?"

"I didn't sense any danger, except from the reporter and I packed him off to jail."

"Can I give Milani a heads up?" Stanley asked.

"Yes," Aleta said rising slowly and putting the baby into the bassinet. She covered him with the soft blanket hanging over the edge and followed Stanley out of the room.

Stanley headed for the front door and as he opened the door he saw Lyle driving down the driveway.

"Call him back," he ordered Milani. "Aleta wants to see him. She's had..." He stopped when he realized two of Milani's men heard him.

Milani spoke into his radio. "Chief West, someone needs you."

"I don't change diapers," West quipped. "I'm taking on the role of godfather with the same caveat Stanley put on his acceptance of being godfather to my son. No diapers!"

"You need to tell Aleta that," Tom jibed. "She's the one asking for you."

Lyle backed up the driveway.

Bertha opened the door and ushered Chief West into Stanley's study where Aleta was waiting with the short, plumb old lady from the line.

"Have a seat, Chief," Aleta said. "Mrs. Dorothy Gonski wants to file a criminal complaint."

West held out his hand. The old woman shook it and smiled.

"Mrs. Gonski has a problem. A crime has been committed and she can't tell anyone, that is, she couldn't until now."

"Are you here as her lawyer or interpreter?"

"Both," Aleta said. "Mrs. Gonski, tell him your story and I'll translate for you."

"Do you have a tape recorder?" West asked.

Aleta pulled one out of the drawer, took out the tape and inserted a new one. While she was doing that the old woman was digging in her handbag. She pulled out a worn bottle of pills and handed them to the chief. West read the label. The date showed them to be expired.

"I don't understand," he said.

Aleta set the tape on the desk and the old woman began mumbling. Aleta translated for her as she went.

Her story unfolded slowly. She was so grateful to be understood that all her frustrations poured out alongside her problem with her medicines, but because neither of her listeners showed any impatience with her ramblings she began to focus on what had been done to her. Someone had been switching her medications and a stroke had been the result.

"I could have died," she said through Aleta, "I want my great nephew arrested for attempted murder."

Chief West looked at Aleta. "Let me check out a few things. How can I reach Mrs. Gonski?"

The old woman shook her head and mumbled a long string of unintelligible sounds.

"She left the Home. She thinks he has a partner at the Home. She's too scared to return," Aleta said, eyeing Lyle with curiosity. "But then you knew that, didn't you?"

"Yes."

"How?"

Lyle avoided answering. "Has she been staying at the Homeless Shelter?"

The old woman shook her head.

"There's a missing person's report on her, isn't there?" Aleta guessed.

"Yes," Lyle said.

"She can't stay on the streets," Aleta determined. "She needs to be in protective custody."

"Jail?"

Dorothy Gonski struggled to her feet.

"Wait!" Aleta said.

The old woman hesitated.

"Lyle, put her in the same motel you housed the homeless men when you had them in custody. Dorothy, it's a nice hotel. It has a restaurant next door."

"She can't speak," Lyle protested. "How can she order food?"

Aleta opened a drawer in Stanley's desk and rummaged around in it. Then she closed it and opened another. "Now where would he put them?"

"Put what?" Lyle asked his curiosity overtaking his surprise at her being distracted.

"My new business cards," Aleta said. "I know he ordered some. He does everything way before it's needed. He knew I'd pass the bar."

"Maybe in that box on the shelf behind you," Lyle said.

Aleta ripped open the wrapping and took out a card. She wrote a brief note on the back and handed it to Dorothy. The old woman read the back and nodded.

"She's all yours," Aleta said to Lyle. "I expect results in a week."

"A week?"

"It's a simple case," Aleta said. "What else have you got to do?"

"Run a police department?" Lyle suggested with what he thought was a rhetorical question.

"French does that," Aleta smirked. "Oh, and Dorothy, I'm sending over a woman named Beatrice to take you shopping for clothes."

"Have you asked Beatrice?" Lyle queried.

"I know her. She'll love doing this."

West gave in. Smiling at the old woman, he offered his arm. "Come on, Mrs. Gonski. Let's get you a room with a shower, a bed and a TV set."

She mumbled a few sounds.

Aleta smiled. "You're welcome."

When the door opened, Stanley walked in. "The baby needs you."

"I'll take care of him. Take Mr. Ledgewood out and introduce him to Mr. Hubbs and show him our property."

Stanley closed the door.

"I don't really want a gardener."

"He's a teacher. This is new territory for him."

"Why are we hiring him?"

"He can't ever go back to teaching. He loves plants."

"What don't I know?"

"We're his defense attorneys."

"On what charge?"

"Something to do with child pornography," Aleta replied calmly.

"Oh, Aleta! No!" Stanley protested vociferously, "I'm a child advocate. I deal with children who have been abused or molested all the time. I can't defend a child pornographer."

"He's not," she replied quietly. "He's accused of visiting such websites."

"Even then," he declared.

"Are you telling me I can't defend him?" her voice still matter-of-fact.

"Yes. I see a conflict of interest."

"Talk to him," Aleta said. "Be honest with him. You have the final say in this."

"I never have the final say," Stanley muttered.

Aleta rose and came around the desk. "Thank you for the business cards."

She put her arms around him. "I love you more each day."

"Is the choice really up to me?"

"It is," Aleta said. "Now kiss me."

He bent over and did as he was bid. His heartbeat accelerated. From watching the monitors in the hospital for two months he knew hers did as well.

When they parted, he said, "Are you setting me up?"

"Yes," she murmured, "however, he really isn't your client. He's mine. That little girl in our kitchen is yours. Her mother is mine."

"A custody case?"

"Of the worst kind."

"She's not her mother?"

"Well, yes and no."

"Aleta, either she's her mother or she isn't."

"Kiss me again. I can't get enough of you."

"We are making no decisions after we go to bed," he determined. "You always win."

"The only decision we're going to make in bed is when we're going to have our next child."

"Why the hurry?"

Aleta switched the focus. "By the way, you have night duty."

"Me? When was this decided?"

"It's a given."

"Since when?"

"Since I decided."

"We share!" Stanley declared.

"Okay. I take him during the day. You take him at night."

"Bertha's here to help you during the day."

Aleta laughed. "I'm just lucky I guess."

"You're breast feeding."

"Okay, so I'll help out at night." Aleta grinned. "Do I get another kiss?"

Stanley embraced her and slowly gently brushed his lips across hers. He felt her tremble slightly. Buoyed up by her response, he let his passion take over.

When they parted, he said, "Let me interview Mr. Ledgewood in here."

Aleta glanced down. "I can still stir you, can't I?"

He went behind the desk and sat down and grumped, "We've been too long without sex."

"We have one more month to go," Aleta commented.

"I know. You had a lot of stitches," Stanley said. "I won't complain again."

"After tonight, you won't have to."

"What's happening tonight?"

"We're moving Gerard to his room. And Dad's moving into the guest room."

"Dad? You mean your Dad?" Stanley gasped.

"He has to vacate the RV," Aleta said as she breezed out the door and called, "Mr. Ledgewood, my husband will see you now."

"Your husband?" Gordon said his smooth brow wrinkling and his dark eyes pleading with her to say it wasn't so.

"If you're going to work for him, you need to find out why he hates formal gardens."

Ledgewood brightened. He smiled as he walked into the study and extended his hand. Stanley didn't rise but he did offer his hand and bid Mr. Ledgewood to sit down.

"You have a lovely wife," Ledgewood said. "How old is the baby?"

Stanley looked at his watch and Ledgewood tensed. He was going to be given five minutes.

"Exactly two hours and forty minutes old," Stanley said, then looked up quickly to catch the surprised look on the stout man's face."

"Short labor?"

"After she finally told us, it was short. We were at a party in her honor and she didn't want to leave until it was over. It was a mad dash to the hospital. We almost didn't make it."

"This house shows no signs of a party."

"It was in the new physical therapy wing of the hospital. She was sworn into the bar. She's only been an Illinois lawyer since noon."

"She defended Shakir Aloman and, according to the paper she won rather gloriously."

"You read an early edition of today's paper, I see."

"Every word."

"So why the questions?" Stanley asked.

"Just making conversation."

"My wife doesn't defend liars."

"Who says I'm a liar?"

"We all are. It's human nature. Being a social science teacher, you've learned that if nothing else from your study of history."

"I'm innocent of the charges," Gordon Ledgewood declared. "I have never even logged onto an adult pornographic website let alone one dealing with children."

"Who is accusing you?"

"If I'm not hired as a gardener, I won't be able to pay."

"Have you any experience?"

Gordon hesitated and remembered what Stanley had just said. "Absolutely none."

"Do you like plants?"

"I'm not sure," Gordon Ledgewood hedged.

The door opened and Scooby bounded in. Gordon turned and greeted the dog. "What a beautiful fella you are. Do you like plants? I bet you'd dig up half those I plant and nibble the rest down to their roots."

He ruffled Scooby's ears and the chocolate Lab pup put his front paws on Ledgewood's lap and stared at him.

"What do you want, Boy?"

"His name's Scooby," Stanley said. "And he wants more petting. Aleta says he's insatiable."

"He's a show Lab, isn't he?"

"Why do you say that?"

"Broad head."

Bertha poked her head into the room. "Sorry, Sir. The door must've been unlatched."

She called him and Scooby dropped off Ledgewood's lap and trotted toward her.

"What a good dog you are," she said.

"Nice lady. She's a good cook too," Ledgewood said.

"She's my future mother-in-law," Stanley said. "Aleta's father and she are marrying as soon as his divorce is final."

"Mine will be final in August," Ledgewood said. "When these charges were leveled, my wife threw me out. I have a public defender. He wanted me to plead guilty after the preliminary hearing, but I won't do it. My son is sixteen. My daughters are thirteen and ten."

"Who turned you in?"

"My wife."

"How strong is the prosecution's case?"

"They have records of me logging on to child pornographic websites on both of my computers. And my credit card was used to pay the charges."

"Was the card stolen?"

"No."

"How do you explain it?"

"Some sort of identity theft. I still have the card in my wallet."

The door opened and Aleta walked back into the room. "Gerard's all changed and comfortable."

Ledgewood rose quickly, "Here take this seat. I can sit over here."

Aleta sat down. "Dad's here. I told him he was moving. He will do it as soon as he and Bertha are done fussing over Gerard."

"It's a computer violation," Stanley said. "Mr. Ledgewood says he didn't visit the sites."

"So what's the decision?" Aleta said.

"No conflict really. You can take the case," Stanley said.

Aleta smiled. "Mr. Ledgewood come by tomorrow at nine. I'll tell you what I want planted."

"Don't you need to know more about my case?" he said, taking issue with her cavalier approach.

"You told Stanley the facts, didn't you?"

"Just the bare bones," he quipped dourly.

"I don't need any more until after I see what the prosecution has," Aleta said. "I expect you here every week day at nine o'clock. You plant my flowers and I'll dig up a good defense. When's the trial date?"

"Next week."

"I'll ask for a continuance," Aleta said. "Stanley, write up a contract--gardening in exchange for legal services."

"Why am I writing up your contracts?"

"Because I just had a baby and I have two more clients to see."

"Why not just stop with Mr. Ledgewood?"

"Can't," Aleta said. "God told me I need to handle the four I chose plus one. So you need to help."

"I have a secretary, you know," Stanley quipped.

"Call her," Aleta said. "She can give the contract to Robert tomorrow and he can bring it by at lunch. Working here includes lunch, Mr. Ledgewood."

She took one of her new business cards and wrote the word "gardener" on the back and handed it to Gordon Ledgewood. "This'll get you past the guards tomorrow morning. Show it to Chief Milani on your way out."

She then told Stanley to help Robert move and show the new housekeeper her new quarters in the RV.

"Does Bertha know you've hired a new person without consulting her?"

"She's temporary so Bertha can concentrate on her wedding and enjoy her honeymoon."

"Does she understand English?"

"She understands enough. I don't know how well she speaks it yet. She's Lithuanian."

"You speak Lithuanian?"

"Evidently, I do today."

"Are we going to get shot?"

"That's the second time you've asked me that today."

"Well, it happens to us a lot whenever you take a really nasty case. And I suspect the lady's case is that kind."

"Show in the old man. I absolutely must see him today."

"Then we talk."

"Then we talk," Aleta said.

The old man entered the room and sat in the chair offered. Stanley left and closed the door.

"You can understand me?" the old man asked.

"So far, I can. God has given me the gift today. He took it away not too long ago; so, I am mindful that it is His gift and can be withdrawn at any moment. It was for that reason, I was planning to see the Lithuanian woman next; however, I was told to see you first."

"Do you know why I'm here?"

"No. I need to be told."

"I'm here for my friend Denny Middlebourne."

Aleta wrote the name down.

The old man watched her intently. She turned the pad toward him. "Did I spell his name correctly?"

"Yes."

"Go on."

"Just like that." The old man sputtered. "Know why he ain't here himself?"

"I assumed you'd tell me," Aleta answered.

"Denny's my friend. He's got ALS. He's pretty crippled up with it."

He paused and watched her write "ALS" on her pad.

"You know what that is?"

Aleta nodded. "It's short for amyotrophic lateral sclerosis. People often refer to it as Lou Gehrig's disease."

"He said you were smart after we read about that trial with the Arab. And he liked that you didn't give up when the judge put you in jail for contempt. I was worried they'd put you back there straight from the hospital. How come they didn't?"

"My husband served those six days while I was in the hospital."

"And the judge went for it?"

"Stanley said that we were a team," Aleta replied. "Stanley is a very persuasive litigator."

"But Denny wants you!" the old man exclaimed. "Not some kid's lawyer. He ain't no kid."

"Go on with your story," Aleta said evenly.

"Denny said I shouldn't plow into the middle. I was suppose to tell you up front that he can't afford you but he wants you to be his lawyer anyway. He told me to come down here personally. He said that was his only shot at living out his life on his own terms."

"It was a good decision," Aleta said. "I chose only three people in that line of sixty-three. I can't handle more than four cases."

"You said three."

"One is coming."

"Well, Denny don't want to sue for money. He has enough to last him, except for hiring you. He asked me if you could ask for them to pay your fee if you win."

"Possibly."

"Well, that'll make him rest easier," the old man said. "My name's Sid, by the way, Sid Palermo. Denny and me, well, we go way back. Used to be neighbors before he sold his house and gave each of his sons a piece of the pie and then plunked down 160 grand to buy into that retirement center. Said it was a church sponsored place and they wouldn't mess him over."

"Who exactly is he planning to sue?"

"Why the place, of course. They call it a continuing care retirement community. It's even got initials: CCRC. They sent him an eviction notice yesterday. That's what's in that envelope I give you. He's got thirty days to leave."

"Leave?"

"Not the whole place. Just his apartment with all his stuff--you know, books, records, photographs, even some trophies from when he competed."

"In what?"

"Shooting."

Aleta laughed and Sid Palermo eyed her quizzically. "I'm sorry," she said quickly. "My husband asked me twice if we were going to get shot."

"His guns aren't loaded."

"He's got guns?"

"He collects them," Sid replied. "Can't take guns where they want to put him. You can't take anything. It's not like Denny isn't being cared for. He's got aides that come every day. And it don't cost the group a cent."

"Who's paying for the aides?"

"His sons. They love him. They want him to live the rest of his life like he wants it. And it's all they can do to pay for his aides. They'd hire you if they could afford it. They ain't moochers."

He paused and reached into his back pocket and pulled out a worn leather wallet.

"He give me this to give you," the old man said extracting a ten-dollar bill. "He says the usual amount for telling a lawyer he's hired is a dollar; but he says you're worth ten times what a regular lawyer is."

"I need to see the contract," Aleta said.

"He gimme his copy," Sid said taking out another envelope. "Do I tell him you're his attorney?"

"Yes. My secretary will deliver a contract tomorrow. I need that signed by him in order to act on his behalf. First I'll get the eviction delayed to give us time to prepare our case. Then we'll work out a strategy. I see several approaches. I will discuss them with Mr. Middlebourne next week."

"He ain't got long."

"I want to be prepared when I see him. That takes time."

"He said you'd do that," Sid commented. "I figured you'd get the eviction notice stopped and then drop it. He said you wouldn't."

"He's right," Aleta said. "When I see him I'll be ready to move."

"It was nice meeting you, Ma'am," Sid said as he rose. "I'll go back and tell him right now."

"God go with you, Mr. Palermo," Aleta said.

"He usually does, Ma'am."

Stanley popped in as the old man left.

"A client?"

"Not him. His friend."

"Big case?"

"Gigantic."

"Money?"

"Pro Bono," Aleta said. "Can you take the last case? I'm not feeling well."

"Aleta, all the woman does is nod. She doesn't speak English as far as I can tell and her child is just four. The child has no idea why they are here."

"Does she like the RV?"

"Yes."

"I'll talk to her in the morning."

"I could just send..."

Aleta shook her head. "What I don't understand is why God wanted me to do so much and then took away my strength."

"God didn't take away your strength," Stanley countered his voice softening despite his exasperation over being unable to stop her from dealing with clients only a couple hours after giving birth. "You could have made appointments to see these people tomorrow."

"And send Mrs. Gonski out to roam the streets until tomorrow?"

"Well, maybe not her, but how about the old man?"

"Mr. Palermo is going to die tonight," Aleta said calmly.

"Murdered?" Stanley asked taken aback.

"Massive stroke. He literally gave his life for his friend."

"Can we do anything?" Stanley asked obviously unsettled.

"It's his time," Aleta said.

"What about Ledgewood."

"I had you interview him," Aleta smiled. "I think maybe I'm not supposed to do more today."

Stanley came around and helped his wife to her feet. "I couldn't agree with you more."

"What are you doing?"

"I'm not letting you do another thing."

"You can't carry me!"

"Watch me!" he said lifting her off the ground.

"I'm too heavy."

"You're two people now. And Gerard is being sensible. He's sleeping in his bed. He knows being born is an exhausting event."

Aleta kissed him. "You are special, you know. But you can't do this. Everyone will think I'm really sick."

"Good!" he puffed as he went through the door.

She laid her head on his shoulder.

As they passed the woman and her daughter in the kitchen, Aleta said, "We will talk in the morning. Bertha will ask you to help. Please do it."

In the bedroom, Bertha put the baby back in its bassinet and rushed over to help Aleta.

"She overdid it," Stanley said laying her on the bed where Bertha had hastily drawn back the covers.

"I'll get her ready for bed," Bertha said. "Take Gerard into the nursery. Jocelyn is staying at a friend's house. I'll sleep here tonight. I'll take care of the baby."

"She's breast feeding," Stanley pointed out.

"I'll mix formula for tonight. Mrs. Praetzel needs her rest. Besides her milk's not in," Bertha said. "Trust me."

"Bertha, I do," Stanley said picking up his son. "Daddy's turn, Gerard. Let's take a trip."

"Don't worry. A good night's sleep and she'll be fine," Bertha predicted.

"Your parents will want to see the baby," Robert said.

"Aleta doesn't want him in our room," Stanley said. "Bring the bassinet. They can visit him in the nursery."

Robert picked up the bassinet and followed Stanley.

"Have you set the wedding date yet?" Stanley asked Robert as they settled Gerard in his bassinet.

"My divorce should be final in a day or two, so we're planning for June first, that is, Bertha is planning for it to happen that day."

"Is it still a secret?"

"From me it is."

"She is going to tell you when and where to show up, isn't she?"

"I hope so."

Stanley laughed. "Don't fret. She wants to be married to you as much as you want to be married to her."

"Why is she surprising me?"

"You surprised her with your proposal?"

"Payback?"

"The good kind," Stanley smiled. "She loves you after all."

Chapter 2

Aleta awoke at five the next morning, almost twelve hours after Bertha had put her to bed. She looked over to where the bassinet had been. Before she could wonder where her baby was, she heard his cry.

She rose and went into the nursery. Bertha was changing his diaper. The chunky housekeeper turned and smiled.

"He's ready to nurse."

Aleta sat in the rocker and Bertha handed her the baby.

"I'll fix you a glass of warm milk," Bertha said.

"I overdid it, didn't I?"

"Yes, Ma'am, but no harm was done. The baby had a good night. He's a wonderful baby."

"Did Stanley's parents get to see him?"

"They were quite taken with him, Ma'am. I think their words were 'What a beautiful baby!'"

"He is, isn't he?"

"Absolutely!"

"I'm expecting both doctors this morning for a short visit."

"After you feed the baby, it would be best if you went back to bed for a few hours."

"Whatever you think is best," Aleta said demurely, "I'm going to need you to stay here, aren't I?"

"Yes, Ma'am."

"Until June first, right?"

"Yes, Ma'am."

"What about Jocelyn?"

"Mrs. Luther said Jocelyn could stay with her for the next few weeks."

"Grams was here last night?"

"Yes, Ma'am," Bertha replied. "She said you'll have to try again. This one looks just like you."

"You don't think Stanley is homely do you?" Aleta asked abruptly.

"I like his looks, Ma'am."

"He is so worried we might have a baby that looks like him."

"Yes Ma'am."

"He had a hard time growing up."

"Yes, Ma'am."

"But I want a baby that looks like him. Do you think that's wrong?"

"To want a baby that resembles a man you love? No, Ma'am," Bertha said. "And, Ma'am, if I might say so, your whole family loves him too."

"Yes, they do, don't they. All except my mother. I'm almost glad she's not speaking to me."

"She didn't applaud your choice, Ma'am?"

"Bertha it's five in the morning," Aleta said warmly. "How about we agree that you're my nurse and housekeeper from eight until six. The rest of the time you're my mother. And even though you aren't married to my father yet, I think I'll call you that. So, Mom, did you feed him last night?"

"Twice," M... er, yes, two times. His weight is good."

"You weigh him?"

"He should be weighed before and after each feeding."

"But you didn't weigh him before this feeding."

"Your milk's not in yet, M... er Aleta. I'm not sure I can do this."

"You're his gramma. He is not calling you Bertha."

"We're blurring the lines."

"If we raise your salary, can we blur them completely?"

Bertha sat down. "I don't understand."

"We have a housekeeper now. Teach her how to be formal and be my mother."

"I... I... don't know what to say."

"Talk it over with Dad. I call him Dad at the office even though he's a partner in our firm, so why not call you Mom here?"

"Stanley calls him Robert."

"That's his choice," Aleta said. "But I love you. I choose you to be my mom."

Tears began to roll down Bertha's plump cheeks.

Aleta rose and walked into the guest room, carrying Gerard with her. "Dad! Dad! You've got to get up!"

Robert rolled over and sat up abruptly. "What's wrong? Do you need to go to the hospital? Where's Stanley?"

"Bertha needs you."

Robert reached for his robe and followed his daughter back to the nursery.

He found Bertha sobbing and went over to her immediately and kneeling down asked her what happened.

Instead of telling him, she put her head on his shoulders and cried.

"Mom, I'm putting Gerard back in is bassinet. I'm going back to bed. Stanley and I aren't to be disturbed for a couple hours."

She laid the baby in the bassinet and added, "He may need to be changed."

Aleta's father stared at her. "What is going on?"

"She's been promoted. I've raised her salary."

"You called her 'mom,'" her father pressed.

"That too," Aleta smiled. "She'll explain that part."

When Aleta crawled back in bed, she snuggled up against Stanley.

"Everyone loved the baby, didn't they? You did such a good job."

"I did?" Stanley responded sleepily. "I know it's too early in the morning for this. My brain's foggy, but did you look at him. He doesn't look like me at all."

Suddenly, her hand slipped along his hip and down his thigh under his pajamas.

"Aleta, we can't," he whispered. "The house is full of people."

"Then I guess you'll have to lay very quietly won't you?" Aleta whispered. "I'm about to thank you for giving me a beautiful son."

"We can't. The doctor said... Aleta, are you listening?"

"Yes," she said. "I know what you can't do. So relax. This is my thank you."

And Stanley lay quietly and reveled in her thanks. He'd forgotten how good she was.

"I want to start our day early today," Aleta said.

Stanley was thinking how nice it was just lying next to his wife in the quiet as the dawn arrived. He didn't want to move.

"I'm still tired. I was up entertaining company last night."

"Your parents and Grams and Claude aren't company. They're family," she said. "And I've added a new member."

"He was the reason for the company."

"I mean another besides him."

"We are not adopting that child. Besides you said that was temporary."

"It is and we need to plan how we're going to do this."

"Do what?"

"Take the case."

"What's the problem? And who did you add to the family."

"Bertha."

"She's not an addition. She's been here all the time."

"I'm calling her Mom now."

"You mean when she's working here?"

"Yep."

"I thought we agreed."

"She likes your looks too."

"What's that got to do with anything?"

"Everything."

"Why are we discussing my appearance?"

"Because you still tell people I think Bulldogs are gorgeous."

"Well, you do."

"But I don't like you disparaging yourself like that."

Stanley turned toward her. "Aleta, I am what I am. I know how I'm seen by the general populace. I'm what's generally termed as homely. Let me handle that my way."

"I haven't changed my mind, you know. Your face has character. And you are a person of great sensitivity and depth. At least give others a chance to react honestly. You might be pleasantly surprised."

"I've been pleasantly surprised by honest reactions enough. Do you remember when we first met?"

"She was an idiot!"

"The first words out of her mouth were, 'Don't you think he needs a nose job?'"

"And you don't want your child to ever be hurt that way, right?"

"Yes."

"But look at the consolation prize you got."

"Any other woman would have agreed with her," he declared.

"Some other women," Aleta said. "Exactly how many women do you need to think you're the most attractive man on the planet before you're satisfied?"

Stanley laughed. "None, but you. But I'm still reminding people you think Bulldogs are good looking."

"Speaking of which, our Bulldog puppy has been born."

"How'd you find out?"

"Lyle told me."

"He didn't tell me."

"It was born same day as our son. Don't you think that's propitious?"

"When is she coming?"

"Two months from now. I'll be pregnant by then too."

"Aleta!" he gasped.

"There's no way I won't be," Aleta grinned as she kissed him. "Unless..."

"Unless what?"

"Bertha told me that nursing mothers usually can't get pregnant."

"Really?" Stanley asked, a lilt in his voice.

"Could be an old wives tale, but we'll test the theory, won't we?" Aleta said.

Stanley gave in. She would do what she would do and he'd go along. He loved Gerard already. The idea of another was actually a pleasant thought. He'd always wished for a brother or sister.

"I love you," he whispered. "And I don't want to get up yet. And yes we can have a baby whenever you want. Now can I go back and sleep a little longer?"

"You can do whatever you want. Who's stopping you?"

"Wake me in two hours," he said closing his eyes.

At seven, Stanley woke up at the butterfly touch of her hand on his most sensitive body part.

There are ways to wake up, he thought, but Aleta always managed to do the least mundane. He wondered if she would do more than just touch him lightly once. He soon found out.

He heard the shower in the other bathroom. Her father was awake. Was the door open? Sounds came from the kitchen. He hadn't heard these sounds before. He realized the new door brought sounds into the bedroom that the solid wall had kept out.

If sounds could come in, he reasoned then sounds made in their bedroom could be heard outside. He resolved to tell Aleta later.

Suddenly the baby woke up and began crying. The speed with which Aleta stopped and rolled out of bed startled him into blurting out, "You aren't going to finish?"

"I'll pick up where I left off tonight," she replied as she pulled on her robe.

"Aleta," he scolded. "I'm not a book you can put a bookmark in to mark your place."

"Of course you aren't, Dear. I would never do that. Besides I can remember the page we're on without one," she said kissing him lightly on the forehead.

"You can't leave me in the middle."

"The baby needs me," she said as she went to the door. "I'll schedule another playtime later if you want."

"I don't want to schedule sex!" he declared.

"Don't be silly. We do it all the time."

"We do not!" Stanley charged. "And every sound travels through that door."

"I thought it was the baby monitor."

"What baby monitor?"

"The one next to your ear," Aleta said. "Turn it down if you like."

Stanley fell back on his pillow and listened to Aleta enter the nursery and coo at their baby. He listened to her chatting with him as she changed him. What a happy voice she had. His crying lessened as she cared for him. When it stopped, he knew she was sitting in the rocker feeding him. Suddenly, he wanted to be there. He grabbed his robe and took the new door from his bedroom to the nursery. Somehow it seemed okay to travel in the bedroom wing in his robe. Always before he'd exited from the master bedroom into the living room with its giant picture window and had felt compelled to be dressed.

The window overlooked the path past the orchard, now in leaf to the newly restored barn, a wedding gift from his father-in-law and Ed Ornstein. Ed had been Aleta's companion when she flew from California to Illinois to oversee the transfer of the assets of the huge Tontine Trust. Stanley had been chosen to be the Illinois lawyer for the Trust.

It was completely out of his bailiwick, but Martha Cook had insisted. She and Harriet Locke, Aleta's grandmother, who managed the Trust, had cooked up a matchmaking scheme. Neither Aleta nor Stanley were aware until much later that they were being thrown together purposely.

At thirty he had given up hope of marriage and begun the remodeling of the old farm house he'd bought when he was in college. It was surrounded by seventy some odd acres of flat Illinois farmland. His parents lived in a large colonial house next door complete with manicured lawns, formal gardens and a plethora of servants.

Having given up on marriage he'd designed his house for a single person, hence the door from the bedroom straight into the living room. He only planned three rooms. Aleta had changed all that. They now had a family room attached to the kitchen, a guest bedroom, a nursery, a study and a second bath.

He entered the nursery and sat down and watched his wife nursing his baby. It was a pleasing sight.

"There are limits to the number of children we can have, you know," he said because one had to rein in Aleta early.

She looked at him and smiled. "Yes, I know."

He looked surprised. "You do?"

"Eventually I'll be too old to have children."

"Aleta!" he exclaimed. "We are not having twenty!"

"I guess that is too many," she said soberly. "How about nineteen."

"Not nineteen or seventeen or eleven or nine or even seven."

"So we're having six?"

"I was just protesting large numbers."

"You stopped," Aleta determined. "Six is a good number. After that we can talk."

"No talking! Not six! I agreed to two. That's as far as I go."

"Don't be silly, Stanley. You want more than two. You want a brother for Gerard and a sister and a sister for his sister, now don't you?"

"Stop being reasonable! We can't plan like that. Look at Lyle. He's got one girl, three boys."

"Exactly. That's why we probably need to look at six. Then we won't fret over the sex of each one. It won't matter."

"You get one more. And that's that!"

"Six is a good number. We'll need more bedrooms."

"Aleta. I said one more. And they can share!"

"Probably should have your architect draw up plans for six more bedrooms."

"You've got one too many, Aleta. We already have one."

"And a playroom."

"We already have one," Stanley mentioned.

"This room?"

"Yes."

"It's going to be a second guest room."

"We don't need two guest rooms. With that many children we won't have any guests at all."

"Well, we do have the RV although I was hoping to use it for dog shows."

"Then why did you fill it up with that woman and her child?"

"Because we need a housekeeper while Bertha's gone."

"No we don't. We can manage."

"You're right," Aleta said suddenly. "Well, let's get on with her case then."

"And we find her a new place to live, right?"

"After."

"After we take her case, right?"

Aleta rose and put the baby in Stanley's arms. "I need to get dressed. I can't interview clients dressed like this."

Stanley looked at his son in his arms and exclaimed, "I need to get dressed too."

"You need to hold Gerard. Bertha's busy."

"But..." he protested as she left the room.

Robert came through the door. He went over and grabbed a cloth diaper and put it over his shoulder. "Go get dressed," he said. "I'll hold the baby."

When Stanley entered the kitchen thirty minutes later, Robert was sitting at the table still holding Gerard.

"Good, you're here. I need to be off to work," he said handing Stanley the baby and putting the diaper over his son-in-law's shoulder.

"Why didn't you put him down?"

"Aleta is talking to a client. Bertha is serving breakfast," Robert said. "And Gerard doesn't want to be put down. He's a redhead, Stanley. There are different rules for redheads. If I were you, I'd make sure the next one isn't."

"Aleta is planning on six," Stanley blurted out, not fully cognizant of why he did that.

"Nice number," her father said. "You'll need more bedrooms."

"She's already told me to call my architect."

"Paul might do a preliminary design for you and that won't feel like a commitment, but it'll satisfy Aleta."

"He's so far away."

"Claude and Mother will fetch him. She wants Paul's family to visit when school is out. And they'll all want to see Gerard. Paul will come if he can combine business and pleasure."

"Does Aleta's mother know about the baby?" Stanley asked her father. The divorce had been acrimonious and Robert had given Marian all his assets except for a large trust fund for each daughter.

"Aleta won't want her to come while you're away," Stanley added.

"It might even be better if she did come when we're gone," Robert said. "I know her. She would be rude to Bertha."

Stanley sat down. "As long as I'm holding Gerard, anyway, Bertha, I'll take breakfast. Don't worry, Robert, considering how she feels about your mixed heritage, I can't see her wanting to see this grandchild."

But Stanley was wrong. Marian Locke had snagged the last open seat on a direct flight from San Francisco to Chicago. She would arrive five hours later.

Meanwhile on the outskirts of Northridge, an exclusive suburb north of Chicago, the minister of the First Fundamentalist Church was pacing his study.

His wife, a woman considerably his senior, thin with withered breasts and bony hips, entered and he turned. "Any news?"

"They aren't in the hospital or the morgue," Dorthea reported. "She has no friends. She barely speaks the language. Where could she have gone?"

"Did you yell at her?" the Reverend Bertram Amend pressed.

"No more than usual."

"Did you punish the child?" he asked.

"I only scolded her. She was impertinent." Dorthea said. "Emerita was there and she scolded her too."

"I don't understand why we must wait two days before we can report her as missing."

"Maybe we shouldn't report her at all."

The minister, whose aquiline nose dominated a face balanced by heavy brows and a strong chin, frowned, "Why would you say that?"

"I think the foolish woman has run away."

"I want the child."

"Not the woman?" Dorthea asked her eyes seeing beneath the mask of piety her husband wore even at home.

"You are enough woman for me. But the child is ours."

"May I suggest another way?" Dorthea said slyly. "One that won't jeopardize the network." She knew he wanted Emerita back, but this action on the young Lithuanian's part would ensure her immediate departure from the household.

"Go on," he replied fiercely.

"A private investigator."

"He would be expensive."

"He would report only to us," Dorthea said. "Meanwhile you could keep Teodora. She, at least, doesn't mock me every day with a child."

"I want the child!" he stated with a fierceness that made Dorthea quiver.

"So do I," she said. "But I don't want her mother here. Soon Nina will listen more to Emerita than me."

The minister stroked his chin thoughtfully. He looked down his long nose at the withered old crone he had wed and, as usual, caved in to her demands.

"We'll do it your way," Bertram Amend said. "As usual, your path is wisest."

Dorthea smiled. She knew exactly whom to call.

Chapter 3

"Where is our new helper?" Stanley asked.

"In the study with Aleta... er, Mrs. Praetzel."

"It's okay. Bertha, Aleta told me this morning," Stanley said. "So you've been promoted."

"In more ways than one," Bertha smiled.

"Aleta always manages to sweeten her requests, doesn't she?"

"Is Emerita going to be a new addition to our staff?"

"She's temporary, Bertha. Actually, I'm hoping she leaves immediately."

"If she needs a place to stay, she could have the spare room in my house. It has a double bed. I'm sure the child would want to sleep with her mother in a strange house. I would like having someone there while I'm away. She could house sit starting today if you like. I think I should stay here at night for a while. I can sleep in the nursery. Or Robert could move back into the RV."

"I like having you two here in the house. Let's not move him again."

"I'll clean the RV when Emerita and Nina move to my place," Bertha said. "Mrs. Praetzel wants to use it for dog shows."

"You are going to trust that woman? We know nothing about her."

"Let me have the baby while you go find out whatever you need to know," Bertha suggested.

Stanley handed over the infant. "Should he be held this much?"

"He'll tell us," Bertha smiled as she took him.

"He's not even a day old. Isn't this when we tell him?"

"He's a redhead. They're born knowing what they want."

"Are we spoiling him?"

"No. We're loving him."

Stanley knocked lightly on the study door and when Aleta told him to come in, entered.

"Dr. Cook's here," Aleta announced. "Stanley, persuade Nina that we need to draw blood to do a DNA test."

"But we don't," Stanley said going to his desk and taking out a packet. "No needles in my kit."

He broke the seal and removed a cotton swab. "Emerita open your mouth," he ordered. He deftly rolled the swab along the inside of the mother's check while the child watched. He put it in the container that came in the kit.

"Now you, Nina. Open wide."

The little girl opened her mouth and Stanley put her swab in a second container and marked it as well.

"Aleta, why are we doing this?"

"Emerita wants to keep her child. She says that Reverend Amend might not be Nina's father; but first we have to prove that Emerita's her biological mother. Her name's not on the birth certificate."

"If Amend is the father and his wife's name is on the birth certificate, the child is legally theirs."

"It's a mess," Aleta agreed.

"Bertha has offered a temporary job to Emerita as her house sitter," Stanley said, "but I believe the child must go back."

"No!" Emerita shouted.

"Aleta, did you ask the hard questions?"

"In the presence of the child?"

"Yes."

"No, I didn't," Aleta admitted. "I thought you could interview the child while I take Dr. Cook in to see the baby."

Stanley sat in the desk chair Aleta had just vacated and rolled it around the desk right up to the chair the little girl was sitting in. He smiled at Emerita.

"Nina, let's talk about your home, okay?"

The child nodded.

"Where do you sleep?"

"In my bed."

"And where is your bed?"

"In my room."

"Whose room is nearest to yours?"

"Nobody's."

"Where do your mother and father sleep?"

"Away."

Stanley changed the subject smoothly. It was as if the two subjects were connected.

"What toy do you like the best?"

"Susie Q."

"Is she a doll?"

"Uh-huh."

"Did you bring her with you?"

The little girl shook her head. "I want her."

"You love her, don't you?"

"Uh-huh."

"Who else do you love?"

"Pooh Bear and Pluto and Fuzzy."

"What person do you love as much as Susie Q?"

The child hesitated. A frown appeared.

"Don't answer that," Stanley said.

The child appeared relieved.

"Let's talk about something else. Okay?"

"Okay."

"Do you go to the park?"

"Uh-huh."

"What do you like to play on?"

"Monkey bars."

"Better than swings?"

"Uh-uh. Swings."

"Better than the slide?"

"Uh-uh. Slide."

Stanley smiled. "I like them all too."

Nina returned his smile.

He rolled back to the desk and opened a drawer. He pulled out a piece of paper and a box of crayons.

"Can you draw?" he asked.

Nina nodded.

"Take this into the kitchen and draw me a picture and color it. Okay?"

Nina took the paper and box of crayons and Stanley walked her to the door.

"We'll be waiting to see your picture," he said.

Stanley closed the door.

"Why don't you think this child is your employer's?"

"I met a man before."

"You must have more to go on than that."

"No more children."

"He didn't use a condom?"

"He came at me all times."

"The child must go back," Stanley said.

"No!" the woman cried, tears welling up in her eyes.

"Do you want to keep her forever?"

"Yes. Yes." The young woman sobbed. "But she not go back, break bargain."

"Wait a minute," Stanley said. "You need to explain to my wife."

He exited and walking into the kitchen glanced at Nina's drawing.

He pulled up a chair and sat down. The drawing was crude but the stick man had three legs. He asked Nina to tell him about her picture.

When Aleta exited from the nursery she noticed that Stanley was engrossed in a conversation with Nina.

"He's working," Aleta explained as she quietly led Wayne and Yancey Cook to the door. The Cooks understood and left quietly.

When Stanley finished talking with the child, he asked Bertha to watch Nina. Bertha suggested that they take the dogs for a walk. Stanley asked Nina if she would like that.

"We have a barn with horses," he added.

"Emerita come," the child said.

"Emerita will wait with us. We will watch from the big window, okay?"

The child nodded and took Bertha's hand.

Stanley fetched Emerita and told her they were going to watch Nina from the living room window.

Bertha stopped after about ten feet and told Nina to wave at Emerita.

Emerita waved back.

"Explain the bargain," Stanley said.

Emerita spoke rapidly in Lithuanian and Aleta listened without translating. Stanley could tell nothing from his wife's face. It was receptive to the story, but not reactive.

When Emerita had finished, Aleta asked a few questions and turned to Stanley.

"What did the child tell you?"

"Nothing, but her drawing told me volumes and when I asked her to explain it, the explanation was--well, horrendous."

Aleta looked at the drawing.

She turned to Emerita. "Does she watch Pastor Amend urinate?"

She repeated her question in Lithuanian, but Emerita was already shaking her head.

"You didn't tell me everything, did you?"

Emerita nodded her head vigorously. "But I did! I did!"

Aleta showed her the drawing.

Emerita gave a long explanation in Lithuanian.

Aleta turned to her husband. "She doesn't know anything about this. She said he promised."

"Promised what?"

"To leave Nina alone if she would do what he asked and say nothing. He told her she had no claim on the child even if she could prove Nina was hers. He would say he'd arranged with her to carry a child for him and his wife and the law was on his side. That's why she came here. She said she heard I was a prophet of God and a lawyer."

"You know that people lie to their lawyers, don't you, Aleta?"

"Well, Mr. Aloman thought he was protecting his son."

"Emerita is hiding something," Stanley avowed. "They have to go back."

Aleta spoke rapidly to Emerita in Lithuanian. The women went from shaking her head in protest to nodding her acceptance of whatever Aleta was saying.

"Take her now with the child," Aleta said. "I am her lawyer and you are her child's advocate. Make certain that Mrs. Amend knows that."

"Not Reverend Amend?"

"I don't see him," Aleta said. "Please go. Now!"

"Aleta, I..."

"I'll call Milani," Aleta promised.

Before Stanley was at the end of the drive, Aleta had punched in Tom Milani's number. When Milani answered, Aleta told him she sensed trouble. He told her he'd be right there.

His men were there, he knew, so it was something bigger than people lining up to ask a favor either of the prophet or the lawyer, both of which were housed in the body of one young, slender auburn-haired woman.

Once she disconnected from Milani she called Justin Conway and told him to come over. She didn't understand her urge to call a reporter, but as she hung up, she told herself she could ask him to write something about the police turning away people. That might slow down the influx of seekers.

Mr. Ledgewood arrived and Aleta was dismayed.

"You told me we'd talk this morning," he spat out petulantly.

"You can't be seen on my property," she declared.

His jaw dropped.

"What in the world..."

She opened a drawer and took out a purse. She withdrew two large bills. "Go buy plants."

"But I don't know what to buy," he lamented.

"I want flowers that don't need a lot of care. Ask the man at the nursery. Don't come back for at least two hours," she ordered. "We'll talk then."

"This is crazy!" he spouted. "I need an explanation."

"You will do exactly as I direct or you will be fired and I will not be your lawyer."

"I'm not moving until I know what's going on," he declared obstinately.

"You're fired!" Aleta said with authority. "The money is your severance pay. If you don't leave now, I'll have the guards escort you off the property."

"I deserve an explanation," Ledgewood insisted.

"I don't explain," Aleta returned.

She went to the door.

"Guard, escort Mr. Ledgewood off the property now. If he won't go, arrest him for trespassing."

"You can't."

"Sir, let's go," the guard said as he took him by the arm. "Is this your truck?"

"Remember peonies," Aleta called after Ledgewood.

"How'd you piss her off?" the guard asked as he opened the truck door and signaled Ledgewood to get in.

"I wanted her to explain," Ledgewood replied as he climbed into his truck. "Is that so unreasonable?"

"Mrs. Praetzel's not your regular person. She reasons differently."

The guard slammed the door shut, stepped back and motioned at Ledgewood to move on out.

Ledgewood started the truck and drove down the driveway. He didn't have a choice.

What did she mean 'remember peonies', he wondered. Did she leave the door open a crack?"

To hell with her, he decided. "I'll go have breakfast.

Aleta told the guard that Justin Conway was invited to visit.

"No other reporters," she added.

"Yes Ma'am," he replied.

"Chief Milani is also invited.   You can let him through," she grinned.

"Yes Ma'am," he replied smiling.

Aleta ducked back inside. "Bertha we're going to have visitors. Serve coffee and rolls. I'm going to be nursing the baby."

"Yes, Ma'am."

"Milani's coming. Put out the jelly ones if there are any left."

It was surprising how quickly Aleta and she had reverted to their old habits of familiarity, Bertha ruminated.

She went to the door at the first knock, louder than Milani usually made. Three men were standing there. One was wearing a police uniform.

"We're here to see Mrs. Aleta Praetzel," the uniformed Northridge cop announced.

"She's nursing the baby," Bertha said.

"Call her to the door immediately!" the policeman ordered.

The siren of an approaching police car caused all three to turn around. Immediately, Bertha shut the door and locked it. She went back to the nursery.

"Mom, what is it?" Aleta asked.

"Aleta there's a strange policeman at the door demanding to see you."

"Is Tom here yet?"

"I heard a siren. They turned. I locked the door."

"Tell Chief Milani no reporters except Justin," Aleta said. "Tell them they can either wait outside until I'm done or they can come in and have a cup of coffee while they wait."

That said, Aleta turned back to her baby.

Bertha hurried back to the front door. This time the knock was familiar.

"Good morning, Chief," Bertha said. "Mrs. Praetzel is feeding the baby. She will be right with you. She said to serve you coffee and those jelly rolls you like."

"We're here on business!" the Northridge policeman announced. "I have a warrant to search the premises."

Milani snatched the warrant from his hand and read it.

Justin Conway's car rolled up, and he leaped out of it, and after few long strides, the black reporter was at the door.

"What are you doing here?"

"He's invited, Chief," the guard said. "Mrs. Praetzel said, 'no other reporters'."

"Then he needs to go," Justin declared, pointing at one of the three men.

Milani looked at the uniformed Northridge officer. "You brought a reporter?"

"So?"

Milani got on his radio. "Which one of you let the reporter through?"

"He was in the police car, Chief."

"Well, get your butt up here and escort him off the property."

Milani turned to the other gentleman. "Who are you, Sir?"

"The Reverend Bertram Amend of the First Fundamentalist Church of Northridge and I have reason to believe that Mrs. Praetzel is harboring the kidnapper of my child."

"That's a pretty serious allegation, Sir," Chief Milani said. "Bertha, did you say there were coffee and rolls waiting?"

"Yes, Sir."

"I'm for some," Justin said, stepping in.

Bertha eyed the two frowning faces and said, "Mrs. Praetzel said you could wait outside or inside and she will see you when she is done feeding the baby."

The two stepped in.

"She could be sneaking them out as we're standing here." Amend warned the cop. "Execute the warrant."

"I suggest you don't open the door to the nursery," Bertha said. "All the other doors are open."

The cop headed straight for the closed door.

"Wait," Milani ordered. He called through the door. "Aleta who is in the room with you?"

"Just the baby."

"No one else?"

"No."

"No need to look in there," Milani said.

"You believe her?"

"Aleta doesn't lie."

"Hogwash!" Amend charged. "Everyone lies."

"God doesn't like it she says," Milani reported.

"Well, I know that!" Amend declared angrily. "That doesn't stop anyone."

"It stops her," Milani claimed staunchly.

"She's a saint and we're all sinners, is that it?" Amend scoffed.

"Come back in the kitchen and wait. When she's done nursing, she'll get dressed and we can talk to her then."

"I've talked to mothers nursing babies before," the minister said.

"Tell Mr. Amend to stick his lasciviousness in his pocket and keep it there. I will see him when I am finished feeding my baby."

"Gentlemen," Milani said. "I suggest we wait."

Back at the table in the kitchen, the aroma of the freshly brewed coffee beckoned to all of them.

"French roast?" Amend asked.

"Grind the beans for each pot," Bertha replied.

"I think I'll have a cup."

Shortly afterward, a properly dressed Aleta showed up in the kitchen. Bertha poured her a cup of coffee as she sat in the single empty chair at the table.

"Mr. Amend," she began.

"Reverend Amend," he corrected her.

"Sir," Aleta returned. "I am informing you that I am Emerita Balta's attorney. Stanley Praetzel is Nina Amend's child advocate."

"Where are they?" Amend demanded.

"Mr. Praetzel took them both back to your house thirty minutes ago. Call your wife if you'd like to check."

Amend turned to the Northridge officer. "I want Emerita arrested for kidnapping."

"I wouldn't do that," Aleta cautioned smiling at Justin who took out his notebook surreptitiously.

"She same to consult with me yesterday afternoon," Aleta said. "I took ill before she could tell me why she came. I didn't find out who she was until this morning. I sent her home immediately after I had talked with her."

"She speaks Lithuanian," Amend inserted.

"Yes, I know," Aleta replied.

"Why didn't you call?"

"I had other things that took precedence," Aleta replied.

"Are you telling me you were sick all night and you miraculously recovered?"

Aleta smiled.

Milani recognized that smile.

"I gave birth yesterday afternoon," she said. "Have you ever given birth to a child? No, of course not. So you wouldn't understand."

"I'm a minister. I've seen women after they've delivered."

"You're telling me you've seen them exit from the delivery room and go home? And you've seen them interview clients with their infant less than two hours old? Are you telling me that is what you witness regularly?"

"No, but obviously you..."

Bertha broke in harshly.

"Mr. Praetzel had to carry Mrs. Praetzel into the bedroom. She was barely conscious when I dressed her for bed."

"Who took care of the baby?" the minister charged.

"I'm a nurse," Bertha said. "I did."

"Emerita still should have called," Amend insisted.

"Does she know your telephone number?" Aleta asked.

"She had no identification with her," Bertha said.

Amend eyed Aleta's housekeeper coldly.

"In my house servants know their place."

"As they do here," Aleta stated icily.

"Emerita shouldn't have taken the child with her," Amend declared vociferously.

"Are you telling me you wanted her to abandon Nina in the park?"

"No. I'm not! She should have brought her home and then gone."

"Were you home?"

"No, we were out."

"So she was to leave a four-year-old alone in the house. Is that what you're saying?"

"No I'm not. But she shouldn't have gone anywhere with her."

"Does she get days off to conduct personal business?"

"She's a full-time nanny."

"Meaning she doesn't get days off, correct?" Aleta queried matter-of-factly. "When is she supposed to conduct personal business?"

"She doesn't have any personal business."

"Everyone has personal business," Aleta stated unequivocally, adding, "and there are laws."

"She doesn't know the language. We take care of all her needs."

"As I said before, there are laws," Aleta said. "I assume since she is a full-time employee that you have filed a wage report with Social Security."

"She's not a citizen."

"Do you even pay her?"

"We provide food and shelter as payment for services."

"So you don't pay her, correct?"

"What we provide is just compensation for her services."

"For all her services?"

"What did she tell you?"

"That she is your mistress. Your unwilling mistress."

"That's a lie!" Amend said rising.

"Sit down, Sir," Aleta commanded.

Her tone was bereft of any weakness. Its very steeliness shocked the man who was used to leading groups of leaders. He bowed to no one, let alone a woman. Still, he sat.

Amend couldn't understand why he did so, but he counseled himself to calm down. This lawyer couldn't prove anything, but, he had to know what she knew.

Aleta studied his face, usually so controlled, struggling to remain passive.

He would be believed, he assured himself. He forced his features to take on their beneficent look. It was well practiced and the slight smile turned up the corners of his mouth while his forehead lines moved from angry to quizzical. He had but to deny everything. The puzzled look began to disappear slowly as the auburn-haired lawyer sipped her coffee.

He watched the lawyer's servant take the cup of coffee from which she was obviously savoring, from her and substitute a glass of milk.

Aleta looked at the servant and smiled. She took a sip of milk and set down the glass.

She had used the pause to rethink her line of attack. She decided to switch her approach.

"Well it's your word against hers, isn't it?" Aleta said. "I assume there were no witnesses."

"I didn't rape her," Amend put forth.

"Interesting choice of words," Aleta said.

"That's what you're inferring," he stated firmly. "But we had no sexual intercourse at any time."

"You do know how babies are conceived, don't you?"

"Don't be insolent. Respect me as the leader of a Christian congregation if you are unable to treat me in a civil manner as a man."

"You say Nina is your child. Emerita claims she is hers."

"Oh, that," the minister brushed off casually. "She was a surrogate mother. She was impregnated artificially."

"With your sperm?"

"Of course. Unless the sperm bank or the doctor made a mistake. Even so, legally, she is my child."

He kept his face serious, but Aleta read his eyes. He thought he had her.

"Ah well, we will see, won't we?"

"I forbid you to take a sample of Nina's DNA," he charged resolutely.

"It's been done and is on its way to the lab."

"Stop it."

"Stop the US Mail? Even I haven't that kind of power," Aleta returned lightly.

Amend looked down his long nose at her. "It only proves she's the mother. But she has no standing in the court. The child is ours legally."

"As I mentioned earlier, the child's welfare and placement is in my husband's hands. Emerita is my client," Aleta reiterated. "She wishes to be released from your employ."

"She has no money. She has nowhere to go. I will not be pictured as a heartless taskmaster who throws a helpless girl out into the streets penniless."

"So you plan to reimburse her for her last two weeks of work, less room and board?" Aleta asked.

"Two hundred dollars," Bertram Amend stated flatly.

"Hmm," Aleta said. "Ten hours a day, seven days a week at five dollars an hour equals approximately three hundred fifty per week. You are taking out two fifty for room and board. Bertha, is that about right."

"Mr. Hubbs doesn't cost that much."

"Who is Mr. Hubbs? And what's he got to do with this?"

"He's our horseman. He lives here and takes all his meals here."

"She's a young woman. She eats a lot," Amend declared.

"And her room has its own bathroom?"

"She shares with Nina."

"Both room and bath?"

"She's her nanny."

"She has a corner of your daughter's room?"

"She's her nanny," he reiterated.

"We'll credit you fifty for the room and one hundred for food per week," Aleta said. "I'll take a check for four hundred dollars for two week's severance pay. Make it out to Emerita Balta."

Aleta watched the minister write out the check and saw him note 'two weeks severance pay.' She picked up her cell and punched in Stanley's number.

"He has released Emerita from his employ," she said. "Bring her here so she can pick up her check and start her new job."

Amend looked up with a start. "She's working for you?"

Aleta smiled benignly. "Now what kind of business woman hires her own client? She has a job elsewhere."

"Doing what?"

"Housework is my guess. Ask her employer," Aleta said nodding at Bertha.

Amend stared at the chunky woman who'd been waiting on them.

"A little housework is included," Bertha said.

"Here, of course," Amend said.

"Not here. Bertha is expanding her business," Aleta said.

"What business?" the minister asked.

"Cleaning houses. This is her first employee. She already has three jobs lined up."

Bertha managed not to look surprised. With a quick excuse, she rushed out to check on the baby.

Aleta never lied. Who wanted houses cleaned regularly? She had no idea. Here she thought Aleta couldn't surprise her anymore and then she does.

Her own business. What a good idea! Her mind began to work. She knew a lot about housekeeping. It would be fun to run such a business. There were already such businesses up and running, but she didn't need to have a large base to begin with. She had already tested eight applicants for Aleta. Two who'd been rejected because they were a bit insensitive, were good workers. Three spots. And the woman could help her here. She'd get a real feel for her strengths and weaknesses. In fact, she'd test them all here. Her mood was buoyant when she entered the nursery.

"You're awake, you precious darling," the people sitting around the table in the kitchen heard her say. "Come on, let Gramma change you and then we'll rock a bit."

Aleta flipped the monitor to send rather than receive. Bertha could now hear them.

"Gramma?" Amend observed aloud, his tone rife with suspicion."

"Mothers usually like to be called that by their daughter's children," Aleta replied. "She's my adopted mother, but my mother nonetheless."

"So she's not married to your father?" Amend pressed. This was one quirky lady.

Milani couldn't resist entering in.

"Is the wedding still scheduled for June first?" he asked.

"Dad's not sure, but he plans to be available all day," Aleta said gaily. "I'm dying to know what Bertha's planning. She won't tell me. She's sure I can't keep a secret."

Amend smiled. So this little demand of Aleta's for four hundred will be the end of it.

He rose. "Since our business is done, I'll take my leave."

"Tom, Justin, please stay," Aleta said.

Amend turned. "I hope none of this sees print." His tone was ominous.

"Justin is here on another matter," Aleta said. "The world doesn't revolve around you."

Bertram Amend stormed out.

"Why exactly am I here?" Justin asked.

"Didn't you get any ideas from the conversation?"

"Loads," he grinned.

"Stanley will bring Emerita back here. You can get her story then."

"She doesn't speak English."

"Record it.   Get it translated," Aleta said.   "She understands English."

"You know the INS will be on her the minute she reaches this place," Justin predicted.

"You can take her to a bank to cash her check," Aleta said, "only it'll be one I write. I need this check for her court case."

"What court case?"

"She'll be suing for back wages."

"Now that will make this story fly!"

"Now that I've done you a favor, I need one from you. Will you write a short piece about Chief Milani turning people away from my house? He's arrested several. You can interview him right now."

"Is that why I was called," Tom said. "Not that I didn't appreciate the jelly roll."

"You were here to protect me," Aleta said. "I had to promise Stanley I'd call you. If you're upset, scold him."

Justin butted in.

"You switched tracks in the middle of your confrontation with Reverend Amend. Why did you decide not to go for the jugular? I could see you pulling in your claws."

Aleta looked shocked. "I don't have claws!"

"You're as mysterious, beautiful and wary as a cat," Justin said.   "And every bit as sharp.   You're up to something."

Aleta laughed. "Stanley says that all the time. Must be that Afro American blood in me. We're a sneaky lot, you know."

Standing at the front door of the Amend residence, Stanley snapped his cell phone shut and announced, "Mrs. Amend, your husband has just released Miss Balta from your employ. I will wait while she goes to her room and gathers her belongings."

"She has none!"

"She has the clothes she arrived in."

"I threw them away."

"Miss Balta, you are to go to your room and take one item of clothing equal to what you had when you arrived. Did you have a suitcase?"

"Yes, but it was taken too," Emerita said sadly.

Stanley glared at Dorthea Amend.

"It's in the attic," Mrs. Amend confessed.

"Mrs. Amend, have one of your servants go with her," Stanley said.

"You don't trust her?" Dorthea asked with a depreciating laugh.

"It is a wise bit of protocol," Stanley returned evenly.

"Nina?" Emerita asked apprehensively.

"Help her pack too," Stanley said.

Nina darted under Dorthea's arm and ran up the stairs. Emerita followed.

"The child stays here!" Dorthea exclaimed.

"No, she doesn't," Stanley countered. "I have the authority to remove any child from any home for cause."

"What cause?"

"Nina has been sexually molested by your husband."

Dorthea's eyes flooded. "Don't be a fool. He would never do such a thing. Emerita is a born liar."

"Emerita doesn't speak enough English so I can understand her."

"Then how?"

"I had Nina draw a picture. I intended the task to be busy work because we needed to talk with her mother..."

"I'm her mother!" Dorthea decreed.

"Legally, yes, you are. And as such, I will hold you equally liable for what happened to her."

"Nothing happened to her!"

"Let me finish," Stanley pressed firmly. "I asked Nina to explain the picture. The man had what appeared to be three legs. Two were pink. One was brown."

"So the child has a fanciful imagination."

"Well, I don't," Stanley said. "It seems your husband encouraged Nina to engage in fellatio with him. The brown color represented chocolate."

Dorthea's face drained of color. Her jaw dropped. Her eyes widened in shock.

"He... he wouldn't..." she stammered. "He's not... Oh, my God! Tell me you're lying."

"So you suspected?"

"Not that. Honestly. Not that. I knew he was doing the servants but not... my God... the women were tempting he said.   He couldn't help himself.   They wore no undergarments even though I bought them some. But Nina is... Why didn't Emerita stop him? What kind of mother would allow that? Surely she knew... How could she not have known?"

After a pause in which Stanley allowed Dorthea Amend to gather herself, he said gently. "You need to decide where you stand."

He watched her pull herself up, take a deep breath and declare, "I am a very wealthy woman. I can hire the best lawyers. You would be wise to leave Nina here and forget this whole matter. I will guarantee her safety."

"Nina is probably not your husband's child," Stanley stated without emotion.

Dorthea was quick to take the offensive. "She is legally ours. My husband is listed as her father. I am his legal wife. Read up on the law!"

Stanley swallowed hard, but his voice remained calm, "Nina's custody is for the court to decide. I am the child's lawyer. I will not be on the opposing side in a custody battle. Emerita's lawyer is Aleta Praetzel."

"Never heard of her."

"Your lawyers probably have."

Emerita and Nina came running down the stairs with two old suitcases and a plastic bag bulging with toys. A house maid followed them.

"Well?" Dorthea demanded of the maid. "Did you watch them?"

"Yes. Ma'am. They never left Nina's room. I fetched Emerita's suitcase from the attic myself."

"She has two suitcases," Dorthea pointed out, vexed.

"I found an empty suitcase and I brought it down for Nina," the maid said. "It's an old case. I didn't think you'd mind."

"You aren't paid to think!" Dorthea screeched.

"Yes, Ma'am," the maid said. "Should I return it to the attic?"

"No! No! Let it go. It's just an old case. But don't think again."

"Yes, Ma'am."

Stanley took Nina's hand and walked toward his Lexus. Emerita followed.

Dorthea watched the three enter the car and wondered briefly how come a child's advocate was driving such an expensive car. Her first thought clung like a barnacle to a ship. He was on the take.

Chapter 4

By the time Stanley arrived home with Emerita, the house was already full of people. Justin Conway, Tri-City Register's hot young reporter was unfolding tables with the help of Claude Luther, Aleta's new grandfather.

Bertha was busy in the kitchen thawing rolls and hamburger patties. Harriet was holding the baby and talking to Bertha. Dorothy Gonski was sitting at the kitchen table sipping coffee and nibbling on a fresh-baked sweet roll. Beatrice was stacking plates and silver on the kitchen table, ready to set the tables.

"Exactly how many people are we feeding?" Stanley asked.

"Fifteen or so," Bertha replied. "Aleta's a bit vague on the exact number."

"Aleta's never vague with numbers," Stanley returned. "Where is she?"

"Talking with a client," Bertha replied. "Oh, Emerita, can you work half a day today?" Bertha asked. "I need help."

"Yes, Ma'am."

"Follow me," Bertha said, leading the way into the master bedroom. "Two of our clients are here today. So do your best because you will be doing their houses. Both of them will allow you to bring Nina to work."

"Thank you," Emerita said, her voice breaking with emotion."

"I'll get you started," Bertha said. "Don't worry. We've all been in bad places."

"Mrs. Praetzel?"

"Her more than anyone," Bertha said taking out fresh linens. Emerita stripped the bed and the two began remaking it. "If ever she gives you an order, follow it without asking why."

"Why?"

"Because that's the rule in this house. Hubbs does it. I do it. Mr. Ledgewood didn't do that this morning and she fired him."

"She will fire me?"

"You work for me, remember?" Bertha smiled. "And I am telling you to obey her no matter what."

Emerita mumbled something in Lithuanian.

"No," Bertha said cheerfully, guessing what she'd said, "she's not a dictator. She has reasons for her orders, but she never explains. She's a prophet and when she gives someone an order it's because she senses danger or even death. She has special gifts. That's why she can speak your language."

"Speak in tongues," Emerita murmured.

"I guess that's as good an explanation as any."

"Worship her?"

Bertha reacted vehemently.

"Of course not! That would be blasphemous!"

"Yes," Emerita said.

Bertha gave her a few more instructions and left her to complete the task in the master bedroom suite.

Stanley, meanwhile, entered the study.

"Good timing," Aleta said. "We're just about done."

"How many people did you invite to lunch?" Stanley charged.

"The number keeps changing. We're up to seventeen. Tell Bertha, will you?"

"Seventeen!" Stanley exclaimed. "That's practically a party!"

Aleta laughed lightly. "It is, isn't it? Tell Claude we need one more table."

"For heaven's sake, Aleta. You can't entertain. You aren't well enough yet. Did Dr. Chesney check in yet?"

"Evelyn's bringing the pies. They're coming for lunch."

"Seventeen is too many! Uninvite some."

"Don't be silly. Bertha said she could handle it."

"You'll wear her out."

"Most people will leave at one. You have an appointment at one thirty. Dr. Chesney has to get back to the hospital. Justin is going to interview Emerita. Beatrice is dropping Mrs. Gonski back at the motel to rest and going shopping for clothes for Emerita."

"Without her?"

"Emerita has to work. Bertha needs help."

Stanley threw up his hands. "I give up! I'll go tell Bertha to expect seventeen."

"Now Mr. Ledgewood, are you ready to go to work?"

"I apologize for my..."

Stanley paused. "Go to work?"

"He's going to plant bushes in our yard. Bushes that flower."

"I told you I didn't want gardens."

"Mr. Ledgewood understands it's to look as if the plants just popped up there."

"I like my land unpopped," Stanley retorted.

"Whatever you don't like, we'll redo, okay."

"I like it as it is now."

"So do I," Aleta said. "I love this home you've built for me. And I'm not really going to change it. I just want to have flowers to pick. We'll let you approve every single hole before we plant. Okay?"

"There won't be enough work for a gardener," Stanley said. "Sorry Mr. Ledgewood."

"That's okay," Aleta returned. "Mr. Ledgewood is hoping to return to teaching."

Shocked, Ledgewood burst out, "I thought you said I had to think of that part of my life as over."

"That's because I was thinking too narrowly," Aleta confessed. "Think about the garden and you'll understand."

As everyone gathered to pile their hamburgers high with lettuce, tomato, ketchup, mustard, pickles, bacon, cheese and onion, then grab a handful of chips and a piece of fresh fruit, Stanley looked around.

"Aleta, your count is off," he announced.

He was still upset over the flurry of activity that had robbed him of what he had envisioned as a quiet time of being with Aleta and his first born. He'd watched Lyle and Lauren enjoy Locke's birth in their guest room and planned to experience the same joy.

It hadn't happened.

"One more will come," she replied.

"You were wrong," Stanley pressed. "Admit it."

Laughter greeted his statement and he withdrew bewildered. Harriet leaned over and whispered, "Aleta never admits error. Don't you know that by now?"

"Sixteen is not seventeen!" he insisted.

"Stanley, I know what you want," Aleta said. "And I promise you one whole day with me and Gerard alone. Well except for Bertha and Dad, of course, only Dad will be at work. Bertha needs a day to finish her wedding plans."

"No other exceptions?"

"None," Aleta promised. "I'll take a day off to be with you."

"My, you make us all feel welcome," Harriet laughed.

"I could use the day," Bertha commented. "I can return in the evening."

"We could go out for dinner," Robert said. "We haven't done nearly enough of that."

"Well, Bertha has promised that Emerita would come to my house tomorrow and I'll need to be there," Harriet said, "so I can't come anyway."

"It'll be a couple of days before I have anything to report," Ed said.

"See, Stanley," Aleta said. "Everyone loves you even when you're cranky."

"I'm never cranky!" he protested, and then suddenly realized he had been. "Well, I guess there's a first time for everything."

Ledgewood spoke up. "I'll put the pots around where I'm going to plant them and you can look at them and I won't need to disturb you at all tomorrow."

"Mr. Ledgewood, did you sleep in your truck last night?"

"It's okay. I've done it before."

"Use the RV tonight."

"It's not been cleaned, Ma'am," Bertha said respectfully. "I'm not sure there's time to do it today."

Ledgewood laughed. "Have you seen the cab in my truck?"

Bertha glared at him.

"I can keep the RV nice," he said.

"It's clean," Nina said. "Emerita cleaned it. Emerita cleans good."

"Thank you, Emerita. I appreciate that," Bertha said. "After work today, I'll take you to my house."

"Stanley do you have four hundred dollars on you?" Aleta asked.

"I have," Claude said reaching for his wallet and pulling out four hundreds.

Aleta took the money and handed it to Emerita explaining in Lithuanian that she needed to use her severance check in the court case.

Emerita replied in Lithuanian and the two conversed as the other guests listened raptly to Aleta speaking a language all of them knew she had no knowledge of.

Just as they were finishing, the front door flew open and Aleta's younger sister burst into the living room. She rushed straight into the kitchen calling for her father.

She interrupted her headlong rush when she spotted the food spread out on the kitchen table.

"Bertha, can I have a hamburger?" she said. "I'm starving!"

"What are you doing here?" her father asked. Harriet put her hand on her son's arm, so he didn't rise.

Bertha quickly loaded a hamburger with everything.

Jocelyn watched Bertha without turning around. "More sauces, Bertha, I want it to ooze out," Jocelyn ordered.

"How did you get here?" her father demanded.

"A guy from school gave me a lift," Jocelyn said. "Chill out, Dad. We've got an open campus. You can get me back in time for fifth period."

She took a huge bite and turned around. She almost choked when she saw the number of people staring at her. She bent over and Bertha shoved a plate under her hamburger and told her to chew and swallow.

"What are all these people doing here?" she blurted out.

"Chew and swallow," Bertha repeated handing her a glass of milk.

"I want cake."

"Drink," Bertha ordered.

Jocelyn took a big swallow and then finished her query. "Aleta, are you having a party?"

Aleta laughed. "Just lunch."

Jocelyn looked around. "She's not here. I'm in time."

"Who's not here?" Aleta asked.

"Mother."

Aleta paled. "She's coming?"

"Didn't she tell you?"

"No."

"So this isn't a party to welcome her."

"It isn't a party at all," Aleta said. "When is Mother coming?"

"She's practically here."

"Did she call you?" her father asked.

"No," Jocelyn said. "Dad, you've got to take me on your honeymoon."

Her suggestion was greeted with group laughter.

"The rest of you stay out of this!" Jocelyn ordered. "Dad, you've got to."

"Jocelyn," her father said calmly, "honeymoon's are for..."

"Yeh, I know," she interrupted. "Sex!"

"As I was going to say," Her father said sternly, "honeymoons are a time for newly married people to get comfortable with each other."

"And have sex," Jocelyn added. "Look, I know that's what's going to happen. Can't you get a room with two bedrooms and I can be in the other one?"

"You are not coming with us!"

"Dad, she's going to take me back," Jocelyn cried.

"She can't," her father declared.

"You'll be with us Jocelyn," Harriet said. "We'll protect you."

"That's where she's going to get me," Jocelyn said. "Dad, please. I can leave the room whenever you ask. I can go shopping, or to a movie or buy lunch or feed the birds in the park. Please, please don't leave me here."

The room full of people was silent. This wasn't a spoiled child demanding attention. This was a terrified girl.

"You can come with us," Bertha said. "We'll work it out."

"Bertha!" Robert said dismayed.

"What if you stayed here?" Aleta offered. "Bertha will be gone. You could help with the baby."

Jocelyn shook her head.

"Did your vision change?" Harriet asked.

Jocelyn nodded her head.

"And she still took you?" Aleta asked.

Again Jocelyn nodded.

Bertha nodded. "She comes with us. Jocelyn from the moment after we kiss you never leave your father's side or mine until we reach our honeymoon suite."

Jocelyn burst into tears. "I'm ruining your life."

Bertha embraced the young girl. "You are not ruining our life. You are one of the reasons it's going to be wonderful. Both of us would be devastated without you. I have no idea how your mother plans to do this, but I believe you."

"You can kiss Dad as much as you want," Jocelyn said. "I won't say 'ugh' not even once."

Bertha chuckled. "That'll be a nice change. Now sit down. We have pie for dessert."

"Real pie?"

"Yes. Not the fake stuff you buy. Evelyn baked it."

Jocelyn plunked herself in the only empty chair she saw and wound up sitting next to Mr. Hubbs. She looked at Bertha and said, "You are the best mom in the whole world!"

The entire group applauded.

Then she told Mr. Hubbs that when she was with her parents on their honeymoon, nobody was to take her horse anywhere. He nodded. Two of the horses under his care had been taken by schoolmates with serious consequences. It would not happen again. He had a direct line to the chief of police. And this time he'd use it.

The guard at the gate announced the arrival of Marian Locke by phone to Stanley.

"She's here," Stanley announced, rising.

"Bertha, how about us taking the dogs for a walk," Robert suggested. "Emerita can clear the table."

Ledgewood rose as did Hubbs. Both mumbled something about going back to work.

"Finish your pie, Gentlemen," Aleta said. "Dad and Bertha need a bit of time alone."

The two workers lowered themselves into their seats as Bertha and Robert ducked out the back door with the two young dogs.

Stanley opened the door and the cabbie brought in two large suitcases.

"You have company," Marian said disdainfully. She had noted the large gathering of vehicles surrounding the house. "I would have thought you'd have more consideration for your wife."

"I agree. Aleta should have more consideration for herself."

"You didn't tell me the baby had arrived. I had to find out from Andrea."

"We knew she'd tell you," Stanley said. "Most people found out from others."

"You told your parents right away I'll bet," she scoffed.

"No I didn't. Mother was in court."

"Surely, she would have wanted to know immediately," Marian snapped.

"I don't think she would have," Stanley said evenly.

"Where's Aleta?"

"In the family room with our guests," Stanley said. "Would you care for a cup of coffee and perhaps a piece of pie?"

"Aleta shouldn't be having coffee if she's nursing," Marian declared walking into the family room and looking around. "Really, Aleta, you shouldn't be entertaining."

"Hello, Mother," Aleta said politely. "We didn't know you were coming or we would have set a place."

"I see you have a new maid," Marian said nodding at Emerita who was clearing the table. "So Bertha decided she was too good to work for you, did she?"

"Bertha is still my housekeeper. Emerita works for her."

"Your housekeeper has servants?" Marian asked, shocked at the concept.

"My housekeeper has staff. She is starting a cleaning service."

"Well, you give a person a chance and they leave you for greener pastures. Happens every time. Aleta you were far too familiar with her. See where it got you."

"She's permanent," Aleta said. "As is Mr. Hubbs. Mr. Ledgewood is temporary. He's here to plant some bushes."

"Surely not where he's put them?"

"As a matter of fact, yes. Stanley doesn't want a formal garden."

"That's ridiculous! His parents have lovely gardens. Are you sure he just doesn't want to pay a gardener. You get what you pay for, after all."

"Why did you come, Mother?"

"To see my grandchild of course," Marian said looking around. "Where is he?"

"He's sleeping."

"I'd like to see him."

Jocelyn spoke up. "She's here to see if Jayline has to worry about our Negro blood showing up."

Aleta's eyebrows shot up.

"Jayline knows?"

Again Jocelyn spoke, "Jayline doesn't know. Mother wants to be sure Jayline won't be surprised with the truth."

"Mrs. Locke, Gerard looks like Aleta," Stanley said. "He has reddish hair and a nice nose."

"Well, thank heavens for that. You could still do something about yours, you know," she said, confident in her own reasonably balanced features. She'd lost weight and her hair was lighter and carefully styled.

"And have my children wonder where their noses came from?" Stanley asked with a studied politeness.

"You can tell them. You don't have to show them," she snapped.

"Then they would feel they were flawed," Stanley returned, still the gentleman.

"Well, they would be right," she retorted.

"Mother, I think it's time for you to leave," Aleta asserted. "Ed, since you and Beatrice are taking Mrs. Gonski back to the motel, perhaps you would take my mother there too."

"I'm staying here!" Marian exclaimed, her voice sharp.

"No, Mother, you are not," Aleta proclaimed.

"I'm here to help with the baby."

"Bertha helps me perfectly."

"She cleans toilets!" Marian spit out.

"She's a nurse," Aleta corrected.

"Stanley can drive me," Marian decided abruptly.

"Stanley has a one-thirty appointment," Aleta replied.

"Then Harriet can drive me," she resolved.

"She and I need to talk with Jocelyn before she needs to return to school," Aleta said.

"How about him?" Marian said pointing at Claude.

Aleta turned to Ed Ornstein whom she'd asked to drive her mother to the motel.

"Ed, I apologize for my mother's rudeness," Aleta said. "I will call her a cab. And Beatrice, I think Dorothy's dress is lovely. Thank you so much for helping her shop. Mrs. Gonski, I'm so glad you could stay for lunch. I'll be in touch day after tomorrow."

Mrs. Gonski took her hand.

"Thanks so much for all you've done," she mumbled.

Aleta noticed Marian moving toward the hall.

"Mother, where are you going?" Aleta asked.

"To see my grandchild, of course."

"He's sleeping. No one is to go in there now."

"Don't be ridiculous, Aleta. I didn't travel over a thousand miles to be shunted off to a motel."

"Your attitude is one I won't tolerate in this house," Aleta announced. "Your rudeness to my husband has been inexcusable. I have no wish to hear your remarks about my baby at this time. You are leaving. Oh, and Stanley and I are not receiving visitors at all tomorrow. You may call for an appointment the day after."

"Call for an appointment?" Marian gasped. The double chin had been tucked up and the lines around her eyes were gone. She looked much younger. Her anger, however, was laying down new lines in her face. "I'm not going. I'm your mother. I'm staying in your guest room."

"Dad is sleeping in that bed."

"With Bertha, no doubt," Marian sneered almost inaudibly.

"She sleeps in the nursery," Aleta said. "Not that it's any of your business."

"Well, I'll sleep there and Bertha can sleep wherever she wants," Marian declared. "She can even go home."

"I need her here," Aleta said.

"I'll sleep in that RV outside."

"My gardener is using it."

"Where's Jocelyn living?"

"With me," Harriet replied. "And Claude and I are not prepared to entertain more than one guest right now. We're still on our honeymoon."

Marian wrinkled up her nose. "That's disgusting."

"Actually, it's okay," Jocelyn said. "They really love each other. Too much kissing. They're as bad as Dad and Bertha, but Stoney keeps them in line until they shoo him out and then he whines and so they lock him in the guest room. He's quiet then. He likes that bed really well. I guess it's got lots of nice smells from all the people who've used it."

"Your cab is here," Stanley announced. "Claude, would you give me a hand with Mrs. Locke's bags."

"Who called the cab?" Marian demanded.

"I did, Mrs. Locke," Stanley replied. "Aleta needs to rest now. With the baby sleeping, she'll have a chance to nap."

"You're shoving me out!" Marian complained bitterly.

"We're helping you relocate to a place where you'll be happier," Stanley said.

Marian switched her tack.

"Jocelyn, you and I will go shopping tomorrow," Marian resolved. "I'm sure there's new tack you've been eyeing."

"I have school," Jocelyn declared staunchly.

"You can miss one day," her mother said.

"No, I can't."

"After school then?"

"No," Jocelyn answered sharply. "I have homework. Dad won't let me go out until it's done. Neither will Grams."

"Harriet, surely..." Marian beseeched.

Harriet smiled. "Absolutely not. Robert is quite firm about that."

"I see. A solid front," Marian surmised. "I do have visiting rights you know. My lawyers will be in touch."

Having delivered that warning, Marian spun around and left.

Dr. Chesney approached Aleta and bade her sit down. He took her pulse and smiled. "Your body handled that well. I assume you were mentally prepared."

"I guess I was."

"That woman is bad news for you as a nursing mother. I recommend you keep her visits down to five minutes or less."

Aleta looked at him askance.

"Or you'll lose your milk," he predicted.

"Five minutes, huh?"

Immediately after her mother left, Aleta led Jocelyn and her grandmother to the study.

"I told Stanley I had one more case," Aleta began. "I didn't know what case it was until now. Jocelyn, Stanley and I are going to be your lawyers. Stanley will be yours, I'll be Dad's."

"Why?"

"First, let me do something. I want to test our DNA-- yours, mine and Grams'."

"Mine?" Harriet queried, surprised.

"I can't explain now. But it's not a matter of not trusting Dad. It's a matter of knowing what will be needed."

"I don't like needles," Jocelyn admitted, "but I'll do anything to stay here."

"No needles," Aleta said. "Cotton swabs. I'll have Hawk run the tests."

She pulled open the drawer and took out three kits.

"Was Stanley going to test the baby?" Jocelyn joked.

"You know that's not a bad idea," Aleta said, reaching in and pulling out another kit. "I'll do him too."

"But you know who the father is," Jocelyn said.

"Open," Aleta ordered.

When she returned the swab to its container, she said, "The baby won't mind."

"You see some sort of trouble, don't you?"

"Not really. I just got the feeling that it would be a good idea when you joked about it."

"Are you doing Robert too?" Harriet asked.

"No. It's not necessary," Aleta replied. "Now, Jocelyn, Grams and I need to know how you knew Mother was coming."

Jocelyn hung her head.

"If Lettie told you, it's okay," Harriet said. "I know you and Lettie are best friends. I've long ago gotten over what you two did."

"Claude will hate me and not let me stay with you."

Harriet took her granddaughter's hand. "Claude didn't hate you then and he doesn't hate you now. He's not that kind of person."

"We didn't think anyone would read our email."

"So how did you know about Mother's coming?"

"It's worse than you think," Jocelyn said.

"No one told you," Aleta guessed.

"Yeh, that's the truth. It was so real. I mean one minute I was standing staring into my locker and the next minute I saw myself agreeing to go home with Mother. And I don't know why. It all happened so fast."

"We believe you," Aleta said.

"Does that mean I'm a prophet too?"

"We don't know, but God warned you that we do believe. He told me I had another case coming after I picked three people out of the line. I told Stanley, but I didn't have any idea if what I was saying was real or not."

"You have doubts?" Jocelyn gasped.

Harriet spoke up. "It is important you not tell anyone."

"Don't worry!" she exclaimed emphatically. "They think Aleta is crazy now. I wouldn't have any friends at all if anyone found out."

"I'll take you back to school now," Harriet said. "We'll pick you up. Don't go home with anyone else."

"What if something happens to you?"

"Then Stanley or your father or Bertha will fetch you," Aleta said. "Jocelyn, trust yourself."

By the time Marian Locke had entered the Praetzel house, Robert and Bertha had reached the barn. They sat down on hay bales and Robert put his arm around his intended bride.

"I don't want Jocelyn on our honeymoon. I want it to be just us."

"Your ex-wife is planning something," Bertha said. "I believe Jocelyn was honesty terrified. If we left her now, we wouldn't enjoy ourselves. If anything happened to her, we'd never forgive ourselves."

"You're right," Robert conceded, "but I feel as if I've waited forever."

"We could follow your mother's example."

"You mean fly to Vegas and get married?"

"I was thinking of before," Bertha said. "When they exchanged personal vows before God and then made love."

"Bertha, I can't."

"Why?"

"I don't want to ruin anything. I love you too much."

"Harriet and Claude love each other," Bertha commented softly. "You have the same fire in your belly your mother does."

"But we've waited for so long."

"Your divorce wasn't final. You couldn't marry me before. Now you can."

"You mean exchange vows, just you and me?"

"Why not? We can do it for others on June first. That's what Harriet and Claude did. Aleta and Stanley had two weddings too. Of course, theirs were both in church each for a different part of the family."

"I know. I was at both."

"If we just exchange personal vows, we could have our first night to ourselves."

"We can't spend that night at Aleta's house," Robert pointed out.

"Of course not," Bertha said. "Besides, they want tomorrow to themselves. I have shopping to do for the wedding and you have court, but we're meeting for dinner."

"It's such a break from tradition," Robert murmured reluctantly.

"And taking a sixteen-year-old on a honeymoon isn't?"

"I'm not cut from the same cloth as my mother and daughter. I'm a traditionalist."

"That's one of the things I like about you," Bertha said. "I just want to make you happy. I want that more than anything in the world."

"So if, we just have dinner, that'll be okay?" Robert said.

"A romantic dinner will be wonderful," Bertha responded honestly. He kissed her lightly. Then he kissed her passionately.

"But let's get our marriage license tomorrow," Robert said. "I want you to know that even though I turned down the most wonderful offer a man could receive, I'm barely able to contain myself I'm so in love with you."

"We can get it tomorrow," Bertha said. "We may not get another chance we're both so busy."

"And you are going to invite me to our wedding, aren't you?"

"I'm thinking about it."

Chapter 5

Hubbs entered the barn while Bertha and Robert were discussing how to handle having Jocelyn with them on their honeymoon.

"It's going to be awkward," Bertha said. "If we accept that, it will work out okay."

"We can't send her off anywhere alone," Robert commented, "but I want to be alone with you."

"I guess we can make use of those headphones she wears most of the time," Bertha said.

"And blindfold her too?" Robert suggested facetiously.

"I guess we could use the bathroom."

"Bertha, the floor is hard as a rock."

"Who said I was going to be on the bottom?"

"As I said, the floor is hard as a rock."

Hubbs came up upon them laughing.

"The witch is gone," he announced. "Miss Aleta done threw her out."

The two gasped simultaneously.

Hubbs went on. "Yep. She gave her a what for and told her she couldn't come back tomorrow."

Robert was the first to recover. "How did Mrs. Locke take it?"

"Pretty pissed. She tried to cover it by asking Jocelyn to go out with her, but Jocelyn wouldn't do it. How come you ever hitched up with her?"

"She wasn't always like that."

"Hey you can paint stripes on a horse but that don't make him a zebra."

Robert smiled. "She doesn't like it when things don't go her way."

"You two is divorced, right?"

"Yes."

"Why is she got herself a lawyer then?"

Robert frowned silently as he thought about his ex-wife.

Then, he blurted out, "Oh, my God! I know what she's going to do."

As the two rushed back to the house, Bertha pleaded, "Tell me, Robert, please."

"She's going to take Jocelyn's horse. Yudi, the one Jocelyn brought from California. The papers are in Marian's name."

"Yudi's retired. Jocelyn is planning to compete with Royal."

"But Jocelyn loves Yudi. And Marian knows that. On top of that, Marian has no liking for the horse."

"Oh," Bertha said.

"It's worse," Robert said. "Jocelyn gets to choose the parent she wants to live with. She knows we'll take care of Royal. Marian is going to force her to return to California with her."

"Can we hide the horse?"

"She'll get a court order," Robert said.

Bertha and Robert returned to the house to find Aleta alone and agitated.

"Mother called after Stanley left," Aleta said, pacing the floor. "I picked up the phone without thinking.

"She said that Conan Lloyd said the baby was his and he's going to file for custody."

"A red herring," her father said, glancing at his watch. "Bertha, tell her what's really going on. I've got to get to court."

He kissed his daughter on the cheek and hugged her. "It's a lie meant to distract you. No one here will believe it for one minute."

"But I don't want her to even... don't you know... oh, Dad..."

"Gotta go," he said. "Listen to Bertha. I love you."

Bertha took the handoff as if Aleta were a football. She led her to the couch and sat down with her.

"Don't be angry with him," Bertha said. "He really is late and he can't afford to get caught up in what we're going to be talking about the rest of the day."

"Talking about?" Aleta said bewildered. "I can get Stanley's DNA tested and that should end it."

"But you don't think it will, do you?"

"No. Someone sleazy will find the accusation newsworthy. Even rumors would hurt both our reputations. We need to stop her."

"I disagree," Bertha declared. "What we need to do is not think about this at all!"

Shocked, Aleta spouted, "You're wrong. You're so wrong! This is important."

"As important as your father losing Jocelyn?" Bertha asked bluntly.

"Of course not," Aleta returned, thoroughly shaken, "but he has custody."

"There's a loophole. Your mother has found it," Bertha replied gently, realizing that Aleta was even more upset then before.

"Tell me," Aleta ordered, her attention completely engaged in the truly significant threat.

And Bertha did.

When Stanley arrived home late that afternoon, Nina ran to her mother and shouted, "He's got fish, lots of fish, lots and lots, all over."

Stanley explained, "I have large fish tanks in my office. Children like my fish."

Emerita picked up Nina and hugged her. "You had fun?"

"Can we go tomorrow?" the child asked.

"Not tomorrow," Stanley said. "Tomorrow we are going to a place with three big dogs. Next day, we will go see the fish again, okay?"

"Okay, Emerita, please!" Nina begged.

"Yes," Emerita said. She'd worried when Stanley had taken her daughter even though Aleta had explained what the reason for the visit was.

She still didn't believe he would protect her as she would. Now she was wondering if he was able to do it even better.

"You can do the guest room now," Bertha said. "You and Nina can chat while you work. It hasn't been properly cleaned for a week."

Nina followed her mother down the hallway and Stanley noted that Bertha was fixing baby formula.

"Isn't that a lot of formula for one feeding?" he asked a bit apprehensively.

"Your wife lost her milk today," Bertha told him. "This will take you through tomorrow in case it doesn't come back."

"Robert told me what Marian is planning," Stanley divulged. "I took care of Conan Lloyd from the office."

Bertha smiled. "Aleta said you'd go there before you came home."

"Is she napping?"

"Yes."

"Show me how to make this formula," Stanley said.

"You can buy it in a can; but I couldn't leave Aleta.

"Write it down in case I can't either."

She opened the cabinet door over the counter she was working on. "I taped the instructions to the back of this cabinet door."

"Is there no hope her milk will return?"

"Not really. Her milk was coming in just before lunch. It was early, but once it starts, it's in. She has none now."

"Tell me everything else I need to know," Stanley said. "I still want you to take tomorrow off. I won't leave her side."

"Well, that's nice to know," came Aleta's voice from the living room. "But, I'm okay. My body reacted to Mother's threats and I couldn't will it not to. I rather enjoyed the exclusivity breast feeding gives, but maybe I need to share the pleasures of nighttime feedings with Stanley."

"I knew I'd come out on the short end of the stick," Stanley quipped.

"I need my energy if I'm going to work."

"And I don't?"

"You won't be pregnant."

"If I'm too tired, you won't be either."

Aleta grinned. "You win. Is Gerard's bottle ready?"

"Try him on the breast first," Bertha said handing her the bottle.

"I have good news," Stanley said following her into the nursery.

He waited until she had the baby settled at her breast before he spoke again. He enjoyed watching her care for the baby. She was so gentle.

"I called Conan Lloyd."

"You had his number?" she asked, surprised.

"It's two hours earlier there. I called him at work."

"That he wouldn't like."

"He didn't like what I had to say either," Stanley pronounced. "I told him his case was facetious and that if there was even a hint of it being considered, I'd counter sue for defamation of character, libel and emotional damage to my wife. And I added that I had deeper pockets than he."

"I had a DNA sample taken of Gerard today," Aleta announced casually. "And one of Jocelyn and me and Grams."

"Whatever for?"

"Mostly it was done to prove Jocelyn's heritage."

"Why didn't you include Robert?"

"Jocelyn didn't want him to think she didn't believe he was her father."

"Why Gerard's?"

"Jocelyn suggested it. I went with it."

"What don't I know?"

"About us?"

"Not that. I know you. You are and always have been exclusively mine. As a matter of fact, you were mine before we even met," Stanley asserted.

"I don't know why I included Gerard. Then when Mother called, I was glad I did. I thought that we'd need it in court."

"You know we couldn't let it go to court, didn't you?"

"I knew Mother wouldn't back off," Aleta said. "I couldn't bring myself to call Conan. I was too furious."

"I'm glad you didn't," Stanley said. "Conan knew it was a spurious claim. He's pulling out."

"Mother isn't thinking straight," Aleta commented.

"Or else..." Stanley began and paused so Aleta could catch up.

Aleta's puzzled wrinkling of her brow lasted only a few seconds.

"You think she's been plotting this for a long time, don't you?" Aleta concluded. "And we played right into her hands, didn't we?"

"She baited you," Stanley said.

Tears came to Aleta's eyes. "How could she be so cruel? I'm her daughter too."

"This isn't about you or Jocelyn," he replied. "This is about hurting your father."

"No wonder Jocelyn is terrified," Aleta said. "Mother will take all her wrath out on her or her horse which as far as Jocelyn is concerned it the same thing."

"Dad is coming over to talk with Robert tonight. Are you up for a legal brainstorming session?"

Aleta looked down at her baby. "I wish I could nurse him."

"No milk still?"

Aleta sighed. "I had such hope when I sat down. And yes I heard Bertha, but still..."

She sighed as she picked up the bottle and offered it to the baby. Gerard spit out the nipple and turned his head away.

Stanley laughed.

"It's not funny!" she retorted, pushing the nipple back in his mouth.

Gerard spit it out again and turned away.

"Here, let me try," Stanley said reaching for the baby and the bottle. Aleta handed him over reluctantly.

"Why do you think you can succeed where I can't?"

"Because I'm used to dealing with redheads. You're just used to being one," he said, his voice soft because he was looking at the baby as he spoke. "You're just like your mother."

Slightly piqued, Aleta watched Stanley tease the baby with the nipple until the tiny one's head was following the nipple trying to grab hold. Within minutes, Gerard was happily nursing from the bottle.

Stanley sensed Aleta's displeasure at his success in what she considered her bailiwick and sought to alleviate her distress. "What you don't understand is that you're his mommy. He wants breast milk from you. I'm not his mommy, so he'll take whatever I offer."

He saw her smile at that explanation and knew it sat well with her.

"But we let him nurse on you first," Stanley said. "I'm not ready to give up yet. I haven't lost all hope."

Aleta brightened immeasurably. Stanley realized that for all Aleta's seeming acceptance of the fact that she couldn't order her body around, she still yearned to nurse her first born.

"You can opt out of tonight's discussion if you want," he said. "Everyone will understand."

A soft knock on the door interrupted them. Bertha opened the door.

"I'm going to drive Emerita to the bank so she can open a checking account. She has a temporary address so she can get one now."

"Good idea," Aleta said.

"I'm giving her a sign-up bonus and today's wages. I want her to know what to do with a check," Bertha continued. "Then I'm taking her shopping for groceries and then to my house."

"In the bedroom, on the chair are some bags of clothes Beatrice bought for Emerita this afternoon. Have her try them on tonight. We can return any she doesn't like," Aleta told Bertha. "I called the INS. I think I can get her visa renewed. Go into the study. Give her one of my cards."

"Yes, Ma'am."

"See you later, Mom," Aleta said.

"Supper's in the oven, Aleta," Bertha returned. "I've set the timer. It'll be ready at six. Enough for you two. And your dad and me. Don't invite guests."

Aleta laughed. "My, you slipped into the mother role fast."

Bertha closed the door softly. Aleta had made it easy to do that, she realized.

Bertha didn't notice a car pull out of a side street only a block from the Praetzel place. He followed her easily.

He was a pro. She wouldn't spot him.

First came the bank stop. Then the threesome went grocery shopping. Finally, he tailed the old car to a small bungalow in Arborville on one of the tree-lined streets that dated back about a century.

Bertha and her husband had raised three boys in that house. One had died in an auto accident when he was seventeen. The other two had married and moved away, Earl to California, Bob to New York. There were no grandchildren. She saw them rarely. She'd told both about the wedding; but neither had responded to her invitation.

She opened the door for Emerita and showed her around. Nina bounced on the bed in the room Jocelyn had used. The curtains had been changed to fluffy tiebacks. The spread was a wild orange-yellow-green mix. There were stuffed animals and books on the shelves.

"Can I sleep here?" Nina asked.

"Yes, you may," Bertha said turning to Emerita and explained how she'd fallen on rough times a year ago, how her husband had just died and the insurance company had refused to pay on the policy and she'd been fired and until she met Aleta Praetzel, she couldn't get another job."

"But you're good," Emerita commented and Bertha realized she had a rudimentary knowledge of English.

"Maybe some other time I'll explain," Bertha finished. "What I was trying to say was that I'd packed up what I valued most because I planned to ship them to my son in California."

"They are here?"

"They're at my new house," Bertha said. "Robert and I may need to take some of this furniture for that house. But we won't take much. Most of the furniture will stay here. I'm asking you to care for this house until I decide what to do with it. Meanwhile, it's yours to live in free."

"Three beds?" Emerita noted.

Bertha guessed instantly where Emerita was going.

"You may rent out a room, if you like," she said. "You may keep the money."

"You are... noble," Emerita said.   "You are noble woman."

Bertha smiled.   "I do believe that is the nicest compliment I've ever received."

"Does Mr. Ledgewood know this place?"

"I told him," Bertha said. "He's coming for supper, isn't he?"

"To teach me English," Emerita responded. "That is bargain..."

"Let me show you how the stove works and where the pans are."

Emerita picked up the bags in the front hall.

"Not those," Bertha said. "Those are clothes Beatrice bought for you."

"Gifts?"

"Yes."

"Thank you."

"Beatrice gave them to you. She wants you to try them on. She'll return any you don't like."

"One does not return gifts," Emerita said clearly.

Bertha looked at her askance. "How much English do you know?"

"I taught Nina."

"Tell Mr. Ledgewood what you need to learn. Don't waste his time," Bertha said. "He is a nice man. And he is a real teacher."

"He is gardener," Emerita said.

"And you are a maid," Bertha said. "But he is not really a gardener. And you aren't really a maid. He is a teacher. You are a student."

"Thank you," Emerita said.

"You need to change clothes," Bertha said.

"What is right?" Emerita asked.

"Students wear jeans and shirts. Maids wear uniforms. Women who go out to dinner or to church wear dresses."

"Tonight I am student."

Bertha opened the closet door and shoved her clothes to one side. She took out a dressy blouse and a dark skirt and told Emerita that she'd come over on the weekend and take the rest of her clothes.

Emerita protested quickly, "I have not many. There is room."

Bertha went over to the window and drew the drapes. She spotted the man sitting in a car parked across the street. He was a stranger.

She opened her cell and punched in the number for Chief West.

"She's one of Aleta's clients," Bertha explained. "She's going to be living in my house on Cherry."

"I'll take care of it," West said.

When Bertha left, the man was gone.

The brainstorming session among the family lawyers started at seven. Bertha had dessert and coffee ready. Aleta told her to join them.

Everyone took turns bringing Hubert up-to-date.

"You're sure she baited you?" Hubert said.

"You wouldn't believe how rude she was," Stanley said. "She attacked me repeatedly. She knew eventually Aleta would make her leave."

"Why would she act like that before she saw Gerard?" Hubert asked.

"Coming to see Gerard was her excuse," Aleta reasoned. "She doesn't really care about this baby. She was sure Dad would be here, but he'd taken Bertha and left."

Stanley drew in a deep breath. "That's why I got both barrels. She intended to attack Robert."

"Where were you?" Hubert asked Robert.

"Out in the barn kissing Bertha," he grinned.

"So she doesn't know you're taking Jocelyn with you on your honeymoon," Hubert mused. "Let's keep that under wraps."

"We had seventeen people for lunch!" Stanley exclaimed.

"Don't worry about it," Hubert said. "No one will believe you'll actually do it."

"What do we do about Jocelyn's horse?" Robert asked. "Marian does legally own Yudi."

"Yudi never came up," Hubert said, "because he wasn't your property and you thought of him as Jocelyn's horse. Sorry about that. I assumed the horse was Jocelyn's. Your ex-wife can claim the horse."

"And we can't do anything?" Aleta asked. "Mother doesn't even like horses."

"Would Jocelyn agree to go back to California if her mother had her horse?"

"Yes," chorused Aleta and her father.

"Well you can't sell the horse. Marian owns him."

Everyone nodded in agreement with Hubert's deduction.

"You can't kill the hose, Jocelyn loves him."

Again everyone nodded.

"You can't hide the horse. That would be illegal."

"So what do we do?" Aleta asked.

"You let her have the horse," Hubert concluded. "Now because it's a ploy to woo Jocelyn away from her father who is the parent she chose, we devalue it."

"Jocelyn won't do that," her father said. "She'd be afraid Marian would call her bluff."

"How exactly would Marian do that?" Hubert asked.

"Sell the horse or kill it," Robert said.

"She can't sell it as a show horse," Aleta put in.

"Does she know that?" Hubert asked.

"No, but the buyer would find out quick enough and demand his money back," Aleta said.

"Then what would she do?" Hubert pressed.

"Complain," Aleta said, "and one of her friends would come up with the name of a trainer who'd whip the horse into shape. There are good trainers and bad ones. Either way the trainer would hand Yudi back as an untrainable animal and recommend he be put down."

"He's that bad?" Hubert asked.

"Not here. Not now," Aleta explained. "But he can't handle another cross-country trip. He was pretty messed up by the last one. And that explosion a few months ago completed the job. He is too unstable for the show ring. He's barely rideable."

The room was silent. No one had any ideas. Then Bertha spoke up.

"Emerita said something interesting," she started. "She said one doesn't return a gift. She said it as if it were a rule. Aren't there rules governing gifts?"

"I guess there are," Robert replied, "but, as a parent, you can take back a gift given to a minor."

"Wait a minute," Aleta said. "Didn't you pay for the horse, Dad?"

"Of course, but your mother's name is on the paperwork."

"Don't you have some record showing that the two of you gave her the horse?"

"I guess it could be considered half mine."

"Stay with me, Dad," Aleta said. "Didn't Mother know the horse was being moved here?"

"Of course."

"Why didn't she object then?"

"I was broke. She thought the burden of supporting the horse and Jocelyn would break me."

"And what was the arrangement made with us in order to use our barn?"

"Jocelyn had to care for Stanley's horse as well as her own."

"And who paid the vet bill after the explosion and the blacksmithing fees and the worming?"

"I did," her father said catching a glimmer of where Aleta was leading.

"So, Mother took no responsibility for the horse, after he left California," Aleta concluded. "So by her action she deeded her part ownership to you and you took full responsibility for the horse's care. I need to look up case law."

"We need to have the horse evaluated," Hubert said.

"Can we have it done off the property?" Aleta asked.

"What are you thinking?" Hubert asked.

"I want to move Yudi to a training stable the day before the wedding," Aleta said.

"Will that be early enough?" Robert said.

"I'll ask Ed to check and see when she's ordered him picked up," Aleta said. "And I'll make arrangements for the move the day before he's to be shipped."

"She'll press you for his whereabouts," Hubert said.

"And I'll refuse to tell her."

"She'll get a court order," Hubert pointed out.

"And I'll get a restraining order, citing that the ownership of the horse is in question. Then we can go to court."

"She might very well win," Hubert countered. "Courts like paperwork."

"Then we'll have to go to our backup plan."

"Which is?"

"No idea."

The private investigator reported to Reverend Bertram Amend that same night. Northridge was only twenty minutes from Arborville.

"You found them?" the minister asked almost rhetorically. The man wouldn't be ringing his doorbell at night if he hadn't.

"They're living in a house on Cherry in Arborville. But, before the cop chased me away I saw a red truck drive up and park in front of the house. I got a shot of the guy going in. I checked him out. He was recently convicted on a child pornography charge. He's out while his case is being appealed."

"And he went into the house?" Amend asked.

"Yes."

"Well, she is a pretty child," Amend commented. "And she won't even have to be trained."

"You into that?"

"Me? No! Her mother taught her. That's why I want her back," Amend declared. "To protect her."

"You want pictures?"

"I thought you took one."

"Just got his face. Don't connect him to her."

"Why didn't you take more?"

"A cop chased me off."

"Go back. Get me proof."

Chapter 6

The following evening, as Robert drove the two of them up to his daughter's home, Bertha protested, "Stanley and Aleta wanted to be alone until late this evening."

"But I forgot something," Robert said.

"You never forget anything," Bertha remarked.

"Look! Stanley's parents are there. We won't be interrupting anything. They won't mind. I'll only be a minute."

"I'll wait in the car."

"I have a present for you. I want them to see me give it to you."

"Will I be embarrassed?"

"I'm not giving you a negligee if that's what you're thinking. We said we were waiting until we were married," Robert informed her. "I have not changed my mind."

"I'm sorry I even thought about it," Bertha murmured contritely. "I thought maybe you'd changed your mind."

"And that I'd insisted we get a marriage license to prove I was still planning to marry you," he concluded, smiling at her.

"Something like that," Bertha confessed.

Robert leaned over and kissed her. "Stop trying to guess and get out of the car."

She obeyed meekly, slightly embarrassed, not at her conclusion but at her wishing he would break tradition just tonight. She respected him more for not and herself less for her desire.

Aleta opened the door dressed in a lovely dinner dress.

"Just stopped by to fetch a gift for Bertha," Robert said.

"You didn't tell her what it was," Aleta queried softly.

Bertha stepped inside. Everyone was dressed for dinner. "Are you going somewhere?" she asked, not only curious but a bit nervous. She usually knew Stanley and Aleta's plans almost the moment they made them.

"To a wedding," Stanley said.

"You all look very nice," Bertha replied still wondering how she hadn't known.

Robert took her hand and turned her toward him. "To our wedding, Bertha."

Her shocked look gave him a chance to continue.

"When I turned down your loving offer yesterday, I know a part of you thought I didn't want you and you wondered if I would marry you on June first. And then today even though we bought a license, you still had doubts. I want you to know I'm coming to our wedding on June first and just so you can be sure of that, I'd like to marry you tonight in a civil ceremony. None of our plans need to change except maybe for our after dinner plans."

"You planned all this so we could have a night alone?"

"I need this, Bertha, and I thought you would like it."

"Like it?" Bertha gasped. "Like it?"

She took off the chain around her neck. "Who holds this?"

"I do," Stanley said. "Robert will put it on your finger.

She handed Stanley the ring, chain and all.

"You separate them while I kiss this wonderful man," Bertha said. As she did so a camera's flash went off.

Judge Davis donned her robe and told the pair where to stand. Aleta stood beside Bertha, separating Robert's ring from his chain. Hubert stood to one side holding the baby and a camera which flashed several times as everyone was getting ready and then stopped.

The ceremony was brief but properly formal. When they kissed at the end, Hubert managed to get two shots off.

As they completed their kiss, Robert said, "Remember we have to get through dinner."

Bertha laughed. "You are sweet."

Robert then kissed her again. "I'm not being sweet. I'm so crazy about you I can hardly stand it."

Aleta piped up, "Use our house. We'll go out to dinner. We're all dressed."

"Good idea," Stanley said. "Aleta and I need an outing."

"Not necessary," Bertha said. "He can wait."

Robert groaned. "Oh, Bertha, you are so wrong. Thank you. We'll use the guest room."

"Robert, you're embarrassing me," Bertha whispered.

Stanley laughed. "Now I know whose genes Aleta got. Welcome to the Locke family, Bertha. Aleta may have taken my name, but that's all. Have a good night."

Hubert grinned. "The Lockes have been the best thing that ever happened to the Praetzels. Have fun. We're out of here."

Suddenly the four were gone.

"Are we really married?" Bertha asked inanely.

"Everyone signed," Robert replied. "We're official."

"You really couldn't wait."

"I still can't. Come back into the bedroom with me."

I'm a bit frumpy, you know," she said not moving.

"I know."

"Dowdy, even."

"I love everything about you," he said. "Everything."

He took her in his arms and kissed her. When he finished he slowly began to unbutton her blouse. She stood unmoving, not certain what to do.

He threw her blouse to one side and embraced her again. The skirt was next and he had her step out of it.

Surely, he'll stop, she thought. He'll see what I really look like and it'll all be over.

To her surprise he left her slip intact and undid her bra and pulled it out from underneath.

"I love the feel of a slip," he murmured as his hands roamed her body. "You are the most sensual woman in the world."

Before she could say a word of protest, he kissed her again. This time she believed him. He didn't see her as she saw herself. She couldn't understand it but she finally accepted it.

"Oh, I do love you," she whispered.

"I know," he replied. "You just haven't loved yourself for a long time."

"But you're changing that," she murmured.

"May I escort you to the bedroom," he offered, "or should we do it right here?"

"I love you," she giggled.

And to her surprise, he lowered her to the floor. She became so caught up in his ministrations and her response that she didn't realize until they were in the final stage that even a carpeted floor was a poor choice.

As they lay, satisfied, she whispered. "You win. Next time we use the bed."

"Then we better hurry," he quipped.

"You're kidding!"

"We've only just begun," he whispered.

"We have dinner reservations," Bertha reminded him.

"Not until eight."

Later at dinner, Robert said. "I didn't plan to pounce on your like that. I intended to be much more considerate."

Bertha smiled at him. "You were perfect! If you'd been considerate, I'd have thought you were just being kind. I needed your passion more than I've ever needed anything in my life."

"I didn't offend you?"

"You know you didn't."

"You didn't think it was sheer animal lust driving me?"

"Oh, you had instinct driving you alright, but I never once felt used by you. I felt loved."

"You realize we have just one night," he said a little sadly.

"And then in a week, we'll have the other nights," Bertha said, her practical side emerging. "By the way, Aleta stuck a card in my purse. She said it was a wedding gift. Should we open it now?"

"Now would be a good time," Robert said. "I really hate the thought of only one night. I think maybe we made the wrong choice."

Bertha opened the card and a slip of paper fell out. Robert picked it up. "It's a gift certificate to the furniture store in Willow Glen."

"I didn't know Willow Glen had one," Bertha said, reading the card silently.

"Custom furniture only. Very exclusive."

Bertha looked up.

"For how much?"

"Enough for the living room, dining room and our bedroom," Robert breathed. "My word. All this time I kept thinking about what I could leave her that would be... there is nothing..."

"You gave her Stanley's barn back after the fire made it a hazard. And now she has horses in it and she's told me over and over how important it was to have the barn restored."

"She does love it."

"They both do," Bertha said. "This is from both of them to both of us. You've raised a beautiful daughter and she chose a special man."

Tears welled up in Robert's eyes. "It's true, isn't it?"

"You need to read the card," Bertha said.

"My eyes are... well... read it to me."

Bertha read the sentiment and then said, "She stuck in a post-it note. That's what I wanted you to see."

"Tell me what it says," Robert pushed.

Bertha looked around. "Well, I guess I can. It says, 'Please feel free to use the guest wing as your own special place. Wear your wedding bands and enjoy your secret honeymoon.'"

"I don't know if..." Robert began skeptically.

"There's a P.S. She says, 'The baby monitor will be turned off.'"

"What does that mean?"

"We're on nursery duty at night and they won't leave their room."

"So we'll have a baby on our secret honeymoon?" Robert asked. "And a sixteen-year-old on our regular one?"

"Looks like," Bertha chuckled.

"Could be worse, I guess," he sighed.

"We could have none at all," Bertha reminded him.

"How quiet is the baby?"

"Think of it this way," Bertha proposed. "Every time he wakes up, you can say, 'Well, as long as you're awake, let's...'"

"Really?"

"That's what honeymoon's are for."

"Where'd you learn all this?" Robert asked.

"From your family," she paused, "well not exactly from your family. More from the people who married into your family."

"Claude and Stanley talked to you?" he gasped.

"Not exactly," Bertha smiled. "As Harriet told Aleta my first day on the job, 'forget about having secrets with full-time servants.' I'm like the woodwork."

"I never thought of you that way," Robert said.

"I don't listen, you know. I just hear."

"Ever hear me?"

"No, you were always conscious of my presence."

"Were you really surprised earlier?"

"Absolutely. It was the one scene I didn't even imagine."

"Are you going to tell me about our June first wedding?"

"No way."

"Not even a hint?"

"Do you have a bathing suit?"

"You're kidding!" he gasped horrified at every image that question brought to mind.

"Stop asking questions then."

"Now I'm really worried. You have layers I didn't realize you had."

"Keep thinking that."

"If I make love to you enough, will you move away from whatever you have in your plans that's bizarre?"

"That sounds like a good plan."

"Will it help?"

"You never know," Bertha responded with a sly smile.

"You're enjoying my discomfort, aren't you?"

"Maybe just a little," she admitted. "Here's a clue. I think maybe you should learn how to ride a horse."

"You don't ride," he retorted smugly.

"I used to," she said.

"I've never been on a horse," he wailed.

"I know. Your daughter told me. I think it would be fun, don't you?"

"You're teasing me, aren't you?" Robert said a note of desperation in his voice.

"Now will you leave it be?" Bertha asked. "The first time you make love to me the bathing suit idea goes down the tubes."

"And the horses?"

"That'll take most of the week."

"And then it'll be a regular wedding?" he asked hopefully. "You know—in a church, minister, flowers, organist?"

"Nope. You'd be disappointed."

"I won't, honest."

"You want flowers?"

Robert eyed her suspiciously. "Yes, but remember I listed other stuff too. I like church weddings with the bride dressed in white coming down the aisle while an organist plays and flowers all around."

"You get the bride part," Bertha said.

Robert gave up. "I guess that's really the only part that matters."

"Let's take our dessert to our room," Bertha said. "Aleta packed my nightclothes, didn't she?"

"Yes, why?"

"I only have flannel gowns."

"You won't need a gown. I ordered a room with heat."

"We can't sleep without..."

"We can do whatever we want."

"I've never..."

"Tonight we can."

"Yes," she murmured. "Tonight we can."

Chapter 7

The next morning Bertha and Robert arrived at the Praetzel house at seven thirty. Stanley was sitting in the kitchen reading the paper and holding the baby. The empty bottle of formula was on the table.

"Aleta is still sleeping," he informed them. "Her milk never came in."

"Poor Aleta," her father murmured. "For her this is a major setback."

"I know," Stanley said quietly. "I hope you two had a pleasant evening."

"Wonderful would describe it," Robert said as Bertha hurried to the nursery to change.

"I don't want her mother to visit," Stanley said. "She hurts Aleta when she attacks me. Aleta doesn't need that."

"She will come," Robert said. "I no longer have any influence with her."

"I don't believe it's your problem anymore, as if it ever really was. We are none of us responsible for the actions of others."

Aleta came down the hall.

"You're telling Dad that he didn't make Mother who she is, aren't you?" Aleta surmised. "Don't fret, you two.

She's done her damage, but at least Gerard isn't really going to suffer. Look at how he loves his father's arms."

Robert smiled.

"So are you two going to have a baby in nine months?"

"Aleta!" her father gasped, shocked and dismayed.

"We did."

"We're older."

"Bertha's not too old you know."

Robert paled. He spun around and rushed down the hall, met Bertha coming out of the nursery and taking her arm steered her into the bedroom and closed the door.

"Can you still have children?"

"I'm a little old," Bertha said calmly.

"Are you too old?"

"What do you mean?"

"I mean can you become pregnant?"

"I don't think so."

"What's that mean?"

"I guess it's possible, but highly unlikely."

"How highly?"

"Very."

"99%," Robert asked.

"Close to that."

"I didn't use any... did you?"

"No. You caught me by surprise."

"You mean you would have otherwise?"

"Well, yes. I'm a careful person," Bertha said. "I thought you'd bring it up if it mattered."

"Of course, it matters. We're too old for children. We're grandparents."

"Don't worry, Robert. Nothing happened."

"You're sure?" he asked fervently.

"Would it be terrible if it did?"

He sat down hard on the bed. "I'm panicking for nothing. Do you know what was the first thought that popped into my head?"

"That you didn't want a child?"

"Actually, that possibility appeals to me now in retrospect, but all I could think about is that Jocelyn can count."

"Robert, we're going to tell her anyway," Bertha said. "Just not until we are all on our honeymoon."

She sat down beside him. "Just think of it this way, if ever there was a love child, ours would be it."

"I'd feel foolish."

"I'd feel blessed, as if I was being given a second life-- a complete life."

"You want a baby?" he asked quizzically.

She stroked his face tenderly.

"With you, yes."

"I wouldn't really mind, I guess."

"There's not much of a chance, you know," Bertha said. "I'm not even having regular cycles anymore. I'm probably not even producing eggs."

"It's just that Aleta brought it up," Robert said.

"Aleta?"

"As a joke," Robert assured her.

"And you rushed right back here," Bertha laughed. "Well, if they had any doubt about how we spent our night, they don't now."

"I think the unmade bed told them," Robert pointed out.

"We weren't thinking straight last night," Bertha said. "Can I go to work now?"

"Work? I almost forgot." He looked at his watch. I'm late."

In the kitchen, Stanley eyed his wife with amusement. "You almost gave your father a heart attack."

"She's pregnant."

"Oh, come on, Aleta," Stanley said. "You've never been able to predict that."

"What did you say?" Aleta asked.

"I said you've never been able to predict that."

"What?"

"Pregnancy."

"Who's pregnant?"

"You told me Bertha was."

"Bertha?"

"You don't remember?"

"Because I didn't say it," Aleta declared. "I have to go see Mr. Middlebourne today."

"I thought you weren't going until next week."

"I need to go today."

"Better get dressed then," Stanley said.

"How could I know Bertha was pregnant?" Aleta asked. "She and Dad only got married last night."

"I know what I heard."

"And I said Bertha?"

"No, you just said 'she's pregnant', but you said it after I mentioned your father."

"I don't remember saying it. I could have meant someone else."

"That's possible," Stanley said. "But it's weird all the same.

"I wish I could remember saying it because then I'd remember who I was thinking about."

The knock on the door was soft.

The two looked at each other, surprised.

Bertha rushed past them and opened the door. "She's not here," they heard her say. "But maybe you'd better come in."

A slender young woman entered and suddenly clapped her hand over her mouth.

"Hold it!" Bertha ordered, rushing her past the two in the kitchen, straight into the bathroom. She emerged in a few minutes.

"Morning sickness," she announced. "She's pregnant."

Stanley and Aleta exchanged glances. Now they understood the strange prediction. Both relaxed.

"Who is she?" Stanley asked.

"Friend of Emerita's. That's the only word I understood."

"Have her wait," Aleta said. "Feed her or maybe don't feed her. Just have her wait. I need to get dressed."

Stanley looked at Bertha and said, "I'm not pregnant. I can eat."

"Did the dogs have their run?" Bertha asked, pulling out the frying pan.

"A short one."

"I'll take them out later," Bertha said. "Thanks for watching King. Will Mrs. Praetzel be taking breakfast?"

"Why are we being formal?"

"We have a visitor."

"Yes," Stanley replied to her query. "Aleta is going to stop for breakfast if we have to stand at the door with it."

Bertha chuckled remembering back to the beginning of her employ when she and Aleta stood at the door with a tray and Aleta insisted Stanley eat before leaving for work.

He not only took breakfast now, since Gerard's arrival, he left his bedroom in his robe and slippers. The baby's head was curled under his ear and he was sucking his fist loudly.

When Robert strode in, Stanley rose and handed him the tiny bundle.

"I need to dress."

"I'm late for work."

"Hold him and eat," Stanley ordered. "Enjoy one of your wife's breakfasts as a husband. You two shouldn't go around avoiding each other. You'll give yourselves away."

"He's right," Robert said.

"We'll stay in the pattern," Bertha agreed.

"I don't want to go to work at all," he confessed when Stanley left. "You don't suppose I could play hooky?"

"No, you can't," Bertha said. "Bury yourself in work, only come home for lunch as usual."

"You are a taskmaster!" Robert exclaimed.

She kissed him on the forehead. "I am indeed. Sorry you married me?"

She ducked away before he could grab her and kiss her.

"We have tonight," she said, putting a plate of eggs and bacon in front of him. The toast popped up and she put the slices on a plate and slipped it beside the other two.

The aroma of the bacon stirred his stomach to demand attention. He ate with one hand, holding Gerard against his shoulder. Bertha came over and buttered his toast, but that was all. She left him hampered by the baby.

Aleta arrived before he finished.

"Practicing?" she asked.

"You are teasing, aren't you?" her father asked.

"Bertha, make an appointment with Dr. Chesney."

The two started.

"Why?" they chorused.

"I think our visitor's been raped," she replied.

The two relaxed visibly.

"Are you two still worrying?"

She grinned as the two flushed.

"You are married, you know."

"You're upsetting your father, Ma'am," Bertha said matter-of-factly."

Aleta leaned over and kissed her father on the forehead. "Just look at all the experience you've had."

"I'm too old, Ma'am," Bertha commented.

"I would never tease you if it weren't a possibility. That would be cruel."

"We are taking no precautions, Aleta," Bertha said, switching to the familiar, "because none are needed."

"You are pregnant already," Aleta announced.

The two stared at her in shocked silence.

Aleta's next words were Lithuanian.

"And I believe you've been raped."

Bertha and Robert spun around and noticed that the young woman had emerged from the bathroom and entered the kitchen holding her stomach with both hands.

Robert handed Aleta the baby. Bertha walked him to the door.

"Just because we feel young again doesn't mean we are," he whispered.

"We're young enough to enjoy sex and old enough not to have to worry about complications."

Robert kissed her lightly. "Whatever happens, we've got each other now."

"Nothing's going to happen."

"How soon could you tell?"

"Three days."

"Pregnancy test?"

"No. Morning sickness. It's one hundred percent accurate."

"And how are you feeling?" he asked, half serious.

"Fine," she replied smiling. "See you at noon."

But at noon Bertha was escorting Teodora into Dr. Chesney's examining room. Aleta had carefully explained what was going to happen. At first Teodora had looked distressed, but, as Aleta talked, Teodora relaxed and began nodding her head.

Robert arrived at the house and ate lunch with Stanley who was again holding the baby. Aleta had spent the morning in the study looking up case law on the Americans with Disabilities Act and the federal Fair Housing Act in preparation for her meeting with Dennis Middlebourne at one o'clock.

"What's she going to do when you go back to work?" Robert asked.

"Well, I did take paternity leave, so it makes sense to Aleta that I use it to be paternal."

"She still feels guilty, doesn't she?" Robert asked. "The question was more of a statement than a question.

"That's why I don't want her mother to come."

"Did Marian call?"

"Not yet."

"She's keeping you waiting on purpose. Waiting used to make her nervous."

"Aleta's too involved to have even noticed the passage of time," Stanley said. "I have a favor to ask of you. Since Bertha may not be back, would you drive Aleta to see Mr. Middlebourne at the Safe Harbor Retirement Community northeast of Willow Glen? I need to take care of Gerard."

"She can't drive yet?" Robert asked.

"My choice. I'm worried about her."

"It'll give me a chance to offer the help of our new law clerk."

"Aleta is a hands on type of lawyer," Stanley said.

"Territorial," her father said.

"Her mind shoves into high gear when she reads arguments on other cases. You know her. She was born contentious."

"She is handling not only two potentially huge cases but a personally critical one. I think she needs to share the load," her father said.

"You're the one handling the office."

"I'd like to hire a new clerk just to help her."

"You've been interviewing?"

"Along with the rest of the legal world."

"Aren't we a bit late? Haven't all the top people been snatched up? Recruiting began in March."

"I've been looking under rocks."

"Small schools?"

"Less prestigious schools. They put out some high caliber people too," Robert said.

"You've been looking at minority candidates."

"I actually hooked up with two who took the bar with me. When I mentioned our firm, both became interested because they want to work with Aleta."

"Nothing like having your daughter be the drawing card, is it? I think we've already been eclipsed by our newest partner."

"Does she know it yet?" Robert inquired. "I mean officially."

"She dug out the business cards I made up for her. Not that either of us had any doubt."

"Except when she had that offer," Robert reminded him. "We aren't the only one to recognize her talent."

"But we are the only ones that will let her practice law without constraints," Stanley said. "Which of the two men will Aleta like?"

"Both."

"They'll want to come in as associates," Stanley mused aloud. "Either of them interested in child advocacy cases?"

"That's the down side."

"We'll let Aleta decide then. I can't spend the rest of my life in child care."

"Wanna bet," Robert chuckled.

"I know. I know. Six. But she could change her mind."

"Hold out for two," Robert advised. "She likes to feel she's won a tough battle."

Aleta entered the kitchen.

"You're talking about me, aren't you?" Aleta said.

"Don't sneak up on us!" Stanley snapped.

"And miss what my two favorite men are saying about me?"

"Your father's going to drive you."

"I can drive."

"He wants to talk with you about interviewing two candidates we are thinking of bringing on as associates."

"You've been recruiting?" she accused.

"He met them at the bar exam."

"Hardly a stellar qualification--passing the bar," she quipped. "They did pass, didn't they?"

"If they hadn't, we would have offered them positions as clerks," Stanley replied tersely. "Why are you so against us hiring anyone? You've been pushing for a new clerk and secretary."

"We don't have the work."

Stanley and Robert looked at her.

"Chief Milani is still turning away thirty or forty people a day," Stanley said.

Robert interjected his idea. "We could let our interns interview them instead of just shooing them off your property. Those they connected with they could do the legal leg work on."

"I was hoping we'd hire a woman."

"One's black," Stanley said.

"The other's Chinese," Robert added.

"And you like them," she asked her dad.

"More to the point, they want to work with you."

"They aren't interested in child advocacy?"

"No," the two men chorused.

"You're hiring two to help me?" she asked surprised.

Both men nodded.

"Okay. Three months," Aleta said.

Stanley smiled. "Tell them they're permanent. Pay the going rate for a good associate. And tell them they get Aleta as their mentor if they have a legal problem."

Aleta grinned. "I know. You're a child advocate and these aren't children. Is Dad joining your branch of the firm?"

"We have enough child advocacy work for both of us," Robert said, "but I'm willing to catch any spill over you might have, Aleta."

"Tell me about them on the way over to see Mr. Middlebourne."

Robert opened his cell. "Alice, set up appointments with both candidates for three this afternoon... Yes, both at the same time. Aleta will be interviewing them together."

"How did you know that's what I'd do?" Aleta asked her father as they headed for the door.

"Because you would never do it the ordinary way."

"I want to see how they treat each other," Aleta said. "In an office as small as ours, that's important."

Behind her Stanley rose and carried his infant son into the nursery. Aleta was wise. She had her finger on the most important quality in an associate coming into their tight little group.

Then he laughed. The baby stirred. As he put Gerard in the crib, he explained his outburst to him.

"You know, Gerard, I just hired two men whom I've never met and whose names I don't know and I offered them an associates wage. That's ludicrous."

The baby gurgled and Stanley thought he saw him smile.

"You agree. Well, you have certainly changed me, but your mommy has really done all the spade work. She has great instincts about people. It runs in the family, you know. I think I trusted her father intuitively. He married a great woman, you know. She's the one that cares for you when the rest of us are sleeping.

"Your mommy kidded them about becoming parents. She really shook them up. I was surprised. Bertha is a bit old for that."

In Dr. Bernard Chesney's office, Bertha was sitting opposite the desk wringing her hands.

"Go ahead and ask," he urged. "It stays here."

"Can a woman going through menopause have a child?"

"You know the answer to that one, Bertha. Of course she can."

"Will she carry a healthy baby? I wouldn't want a child with Down's Syndrome."

"Are you pregnant?"

"I can't be, can I?"

"If you had unprotected intercourse, you could be."

Bertha reddened. "It's a secret."

Dr. Chesney spoke softly. "I'm not your judge, Bertha. I'm your doctor."

"Judge Davis married Robert and me last night. And afterward... well..."

"I thought you were getting married June first."

"We were. We still are. This was just a civil ceremony. We both had the night off and... Oh, this is embarrassing."

"Bertha, do you know how unlikely it would be that a woman your age would conceive a child as a result of only one night of sex?"

"We had a lot of sex," Bertha mumbled.

"That's what newlyweds do," Dr. Chesney remarked. "But why are you so concerned. You know how remote the possibility is."

"Aleta joked about me being pregnant."

"She didn't say you were, did she?"

"Actually, she did. Only there was another woman in the room and everyone believed she was speaking to her, but I'm not sure."

"Do you and Robert want children?"

"We never gave it a thought," Bertha said. "But he warmed to the idea immediately."

"So what's the problem?"

"I don't want to give him an unhealthy child."

"There are tests we can do if you are pregnant," Dr. Chesney told her.

Bertha shook her head. "No, I don't think I want those."

"You wouldn't be committing yourself to an abortion," Dr. Chesney said. "You'd just be preparing yourself in advance for decisions that might need to be made. It is a wise move for a person your age."

"You talk as if I'm pregnant."

"Aleta didn't tell you she wasn't speaking about you, did she?"

"No, but I didn't ask her."

"Let me examine you in two days. How long has it been since you have a gynecological exam?"

"Years."

"You're due."

"What about sex."

"Enjoy it."

"No one knows about the marriage," Bertha said, "except the Praetzels."

"Not even Harriet?"

"No."

"I do understand you know. I was at the luncheon when Jocelyn invited herself along on your honeymoon."

"We needed the initial moment to be private," Bertha explained.

"How about Monday at one?"

"Monday's Memorial Day."

"Tuesday. That's only two days before your wedding. Can you manage it?" Dr. Chesney added.

"I'll be here."

"Whether or not you think you're pregnant."

"Yes, Doctor," Bertha promised. "Whether or not."

At exactly one o'clock, Aleta was ushered into Dennis Middlebourne's single story house. She'd walked up the wheelchair ramp, which she noticed only one other home in the cluster of small domiciles had in place.

She noticed that the door was unusually wide as she stepped into a spacious hallway.

The thin man whose head was held erect by a neck brace greeted her from his wheelchair as his aide closed the door behind her.

His words were slurred and barely understandable.

"He is welcoming you," the aide informed her.

She nodded at the old man, "I am so sorry to hear about your friend's death. I know you will miss him."

The old eyes tears as she spoke.

"Mr. Palermo visited often," the aide said.

The old man spoke and the aide repeated his words. "Sid was a good friend."

"I imagine he understood your speech better than anyone," Aleta remarked. "That's because he knew how you thought."

The old man blinked.

"One blink means yes," the aide said. "Two means no."

"Mr. Middlebourne, do you have a room where we can speak privately?"

The old man blinked once.

"Please escort me there."

The man turned the motorized chair and led the way to a small room in front that overlooked the courtyard around which the tiny homes of the residents were clustered.

The aide followed.

Aleta looked at him quizzically.

"I'm just going to set up his computer screen. It reads his eye movements and there are words and phrases it will speak for him."

"We can manage without it," Aleta said.

"But he needs to communicate with you."

"Yes, he does, and I will call you if I need your assistance," Aleta stated firmly.

The aide left and Aleta put her briefcase on the floor and sat in a chair opposite the old man.

"I can understand you," she said. "It is not an ability I want generally known which is why I sent your aide away. You were counting on me being able to do that, weren't you? That's why the remark about my legs when I entered. It was a test wasn't it?"

The old man blinked.

"You can speak. I can understand."

"I can't even form the words anymore," he mumbled.

"I evidently only need your effort to do it."

"You can read my mind?"

"No, I can't. I can only understand what you put into speech, however slurred," Aleta responded. "And for this hour we have together, you will be able to communicate as you used to."

Tears flowed down the old man's cheeks.

"I know," Aleta said. "To have things to say and no way to say them. I had a stroke this past year. I lost my power to utter the words I was thinking. It was a terrible experience. It was not of the same magnitude as your situation, but I do remember the frustration. Now let's talk about your case."

"I want to die in my home surrounded by my books and trophies of my life. I want to be listening to Bach when I draw my last breath. The end is coming. I don't want to be lying in a hospital bed with a few photos on the night stand or even a wheelchair in an impersonal day room with the television set turned to some inane soap opera. I want to read my books and look up from the printed page and watch the birds light on the tree in the courtyard. I want to hear the strains of Beethoven or Handel or Bach depending on my mood. I want to watch tapes of shooting competitions that my sons bring me. You shoot, don't you?"

"Not in competition."

"Hunting?"

"Yes,"

"Tell me a hunting story."

"Now?"

"You said you were staying an hour."

"I wanted to discuss our approach," Aleta said.

"You're going to base my case on either the federal Fair Housing Act or the American with Disabilities Act or the fact that my civil rights are being violated. The Constitution guarantees me the right to life, liberty and the pursuit of happiness or is that the Bill of Rights?" Before Aleta could reply, he rushed on. "I'm sure that forcing me to leave a home that I love because I am too disabled in their eyes to live a normal life is a violation of my rights. I'm physically disabled, but I have aides that allow me to move and communicate. My brain works. My eyes work. My ears work. And thankfully so does my bladder, at least, so far. I need a respirator at night, but not during the day. I can't feed myself and I have trouble swallowing. Eventually, I will need to be tube fed. Just when one thinks there is nothing more that will go wrong, another system breaks down. When that happens, you adjust. But I harm no one by living here. I have capable help which my sons pay for. The CCRC isn't out a dime on my account. Still they are making a unilateral decision to move me."

"I can stay your eviction until we go to court," Aleta said.

"I don't want only that," Middlebourne said. "I want you to keep going even after I'm dead. I want them to lose in court, not to have my death resolve the problem."

"I brought another contract with me," Aleta said. "It spells out your wishes in case of your death."

"I knew you were the right lawyer for me," Dennis Middlebourne exclaimed. "I told Sid that."

"And he believed you," Aleta said. "And he convinced me."

"You aren't going to say that we could lose?"

"Why should I? We both know it could happen."

"But will it?"

"Let's just say I will keep at it until we win."

"You need a witness," Dennis said. "We can do that at the end of your hour. Tell me about duck hunting. Did you use a dog?"

"Oh, I need to tell you about Stoney," Aleta said her eyes lighting up. "He's my grandmother's dog. She taught me to shoot. My mother didn't like that she did, but Dad was okay with it."

"Stoney is a Lab?"

"A Chessie."

"Your grandmother hunted with a Chessie?"

"Trained him too," Aleta said, her voice buoyant. "And she let me show him in dog shows. He's a breed champion and a master hunter. We went everywhere with him until I entered law school and the year after that. But now we're back showing and hunting."

"How good a shot are you?"

"Almost as good as my grandmother."

"Do you know Lyle West?"

"He's my husband's best friend. His wife Lauren is mine."

"He hunts with his Lab Morgan."

"I know."

"He's a superb marksman. He won competitions when he was younger. He was the best marksman I've ever judged."

"He's still a great shooter," Aleta said. "He doesn't dare lose his touch. Morgan has this disgusted look he gives a person if they miss. Lyle's hunting partners complain because the dog expects perfection. Now tell me more about your judging."

The talk went on for two hours. The front doorbell reminded Aleta that the purpose of her visit was to discuss the case. She apologized profusely.

"We got to know each other," Dennis said. "That was my agenda. You don't know how great it was just to talk."

"We will talk again," Aleta promised. "That's my dad at the door. I'm supposed to interview a couple of men applying as associates."

"Are they going to be working on my case?"

"They will help. You've broadened the scope of my approach to a point where I need help, but I'm representing you myself."

"I will sign the contract now," Dennis said.

"Before we do that, I need to warn you. This ability of mine is a special gift. It's been taken away before. I may not have it the next time we meet."

"But you had it today. And I said what I wanted to say," he mumbled. "And we're now friends."

"Yes, we are," Aleta affirmed.

Chapter 8

Early that morning, Rollo Travick had followed the red truck that picked up Emerita and drove her to a house inside a gated community. The road was winding and the houses few, but he drove up a road that ran alongside the outside of the fence and stopped at the top of the rise. He spotted the red truck travelling the road on the other side of the small lake. It disappeared and reappeared behind several houses before it didn't reappear. When it did reappear, it was going in the opposite direction minus the woman and child.

He had reported to Amend, received specific instructions and returned to watch the house. He saw Stanley drive his gold Lexus behind the house. The man drove back down the road minutes later. Rollo surmised that Stanley was still alone in his car.

The child was buckled into the back seat and her head barely showed above the window ledge when she was sitting up. Stanley had given her a book to read and she was bent over sounding out the words as her fingers pointed to each one.

"You are a good reader," he said when she'd finished.

"I know words," she replied proudly.

"Did you mommy teach you how to read?"

"No. She's too busy. Emerita teached me."

They drove along chatting.   Stanley had his tape recorder running.   He didn't ask her much about her situation. He asked about her new home and what she liked about it.   Comparisons were a natural outcome.

Rollo Travick saw a car depart from the target house immediately after the gold Lexus. He glanced at his watch. His plan was to enter the gate when the crews from the sites under construction left the grounds.

Still, the householder was gone now. Emerita and Nina were alone. It would be an easy snatch now.

Travick had his suspicions as to why the minister didn't want to involve the police. The curly-headed blonde child didn't look like either parent. He assumed it was an adoption gone awry. It didn't matter. The pay was good, the job easy, and the risk minimal. The nanny didn't speak English. Also, she wasn't a citizen. Non-citizens rarely called the cops and they never pressed charges.

He drove up to the gate, still undecided as to what to do. He'd just begun to back up when a car approached from the other direction.   He shoved his gear in first and approached the gate and stopped.   The gate opened automatically for the exiting car. Rollo slipped through the gate as it began to close.

He parked in the driveway and approached the back door. He heard the vacuum cleaner near the other end of the house.   He heard both a washer and dryer going. As he turned the knob, a dog barked. He jumped back. He leaned over and peered through the window. Inside the room were the washer and dryer and three crates, each containing a dog. There was a large tub with steps leading to a waist high counter top and then to the tub. Plastic aprons hung on hooks just outside the dog washing alcove.

The vacuum kept going.   It was then he realized that the dog's barks were loud to his ears because only a window separated them. The woman was at the far end of the house.

She didn't hear the barking. Or if she did, she was ignoring it. He slipped into the house unseen and, as far as he was concerned, undetected.

Next door Harriet's Chessies, however, heard Topaz barking frantically. All three stood up and growled. They moved from one door to the other pacing in front of each in turn, always facing Evelyn's house.

Claude called up the stairs, "The dogs are upset, Harriet."

She left her task and came down the stairs. One glance and she headed for the fireplace and took down her gun and shoved two loads into the breech and shoved it shut, closing the aperture. Claude was only seconds behind her.

"I'll take the back," Harriet said. "Stoney, heel."

"I'll take the front," Claude said, opening his cell and punching in Milani's number.

Rollo, meanwhile, had moved stealthily through the hallway leading through the kitchen family room into the living room. He surveyed every inch of the rooms as he moved through them looking for the child.

He decided she must be upstairs. He rushed up to the woman whose back was to him and grabbed her from behind. He put his knife to her throat.

"Call the child," he ordered.

"Nina not here," she choked out.

"Call!" he insisted.

She yelled her daughter's name. There was no answer.

"When is she coming back?" he growled.

"Don't know."

"Well, I guess we'll just wait," he decided. He told her to lie down on her stomach. She complied at once. He yanked the vacuum's cord from the wall socket and used it to tie Emerita's hands behind her back. Then he had her bend her knees and wound the cord around them as well.

"Please, no," she cried. Her voice spurred the dogs into more barking. He took the dust cloth and shoved it into her mouth.

"Leave it there," he said, "or I'll cut out your tongue."

Emerita's eyes widened in fear.

Rollo smirked. "I see I got your attention. Now stay quiet."

Emerita nodded. She had to stay alive. If she died, her daughter would become the minister's new mistress. Maybe not right away. There was always Teodora to occupy him until Nina grew up.

Poor Teodora, she thought. She thinks I got away. She will try. He will not let her go. She is with child. Not his, but he will claim it. She will sign the papers just as she had. She will not understand.

Yet Teodora understood a little. She had brought down her suitcase from the attic too and begged Emerita to take it too.

Emerita had been afraid but Teodora had pleaded with her. She'd taken out her nightgown and a sweater and they'd laid two of Nina's dresses on top along with her favorite pajamas. They'd put play pants and tee shirts in the sack with the stuffed animals.

Nina had insisted that they take all her favorites. The sack bulged but no one had noticed the clothes on the bottom. The soft forms of the stuffed animals were easily discernable.

Emerita had pressed the remainder of her money into Teodora's hand and told her how to take the bus to Willow Glen and what road would lead her to the Praetzel house. She had not believed she would see her again, but she told her she would keep her suitcase forever. She knew it held her pictures from home.

It was for the sake of the keepsakes that she had agreed. If she should die, the suitcase would be thrown out.

She began to cry. It wasn't the suitcase itself that was important. It was what it represented. It held their hope for the future. Teodora had sent it ahead. She planned to follow.

Amend would send this man after Teodora. Or some other man. Mr. Praetzel had to save Nina. Could he do it if she wasn't there to claim the child?

He had been happy with the first meeting with the psychologist. And Nina had come home happy. He would care for Nina. She could die. Nina would be alright. Nina knew the suitcase belonged to Teodora. She would tell them.

But this man mustn't grab Nina. Mr. Praetzel would be bringing her home. He might be killed. That couldn't happen.

Ever so surreptitiously she shoved the dirty rag toward the front of her mouth.

She heard footsteps on the back steps. The dogs began barking furiously. They were here.

Rollo grabbed the rag from her mouth and pressed the knife into her neck. "Tell her to come in here."

The door opened slowly. The knife drew blood.

"Nina, come to Mommy," Emerita called. She hoped Mr. Praetzel would know something was wrong. Nina didn't know she was her mother.

"Should we let the dogs out?" a male voice asked.

Again the knife was pressed into Emerita's neck.

"Tell her you ain't done cleaning," Rollo hissed.

"No, Nina. Cleaning not done."

Police sirens could be heard approaching. Rollo shoved the cloth back into Emerita's mouth and unlocked the front door.

He heard a dog growl on the other side of the door and he opened it a crack.

A rifle was shoved in his face and he backed up pulling the door shut. The rifle barrel held it open and he took a step back, his knife ready to plunge it into the arm of the rifle bearer.

The blast of the rifle caught him completely by surprise. He wasn't in its line of fire, he thought in the microsecond between the sound and the realization that he'd been hit by a bullet. He hadn't connected the pieces in any logical sequence. His knife dropped to the floor.

He grabbed his arm.

"Back up!" the woman ordered as the police sirens pulled up outside.

"You didn't warn me!" he shouted grabbing his arm. "I'll have your badge!"

"Lay down and spread your arms and legs," Harriet ordered.

"I've been shot."

"I still have two loads in this gun. You want me to use them on your legs?"

And for some unfathomable reason, Rollo leaped at what he saw as an old lady and grabbed at her rifle.

Harriet backed up one step, lowered the gun and shot him in the foot.

"You shot me!" he screamed.

"Down!" she ordered.

The dog at her side dropped instantly. Rollo hadn't even seen him until he did that.

"I can't," he cried.

The next shot hit him in the leg. He fell instantly.

"I mean to be obeyed," she said.

Rollo lay on the ground screeching about police brutality when the police burst into the house. Claude put down his rifle and held his hands up. One officer kept a gun on him as he leaned against the wall and was patted down.

Harriet handed her gun to the first officer through the front door. And when Chief Milani entered, he saw Emerita trussed up like an animal, a rag in her mouth and a stranger bleeding on Evelyn's new carpet.

"You couldn't somehow manage to shoot him outside?" Tom asked. "This carpet's brand new."

He leaned down and took the rag from Emerita's mouth. "Sorry about this."

He untied her. Harriet went over and led her to the couch and put her arm around her. "Claude we need a cup of tea in here."

"As soon as this man lets me move, I'll fetch it."

Milani looked over and told his officer that he was one of West's deputies. The gun was withdrawn instantly.

He turned to Harriet. "Did you warn him?"

"He had a knife. He was going to stick it into me. Claude didn't want him to do that."

"He's all shot up," Milani said. "Did any of you guys call an ambulance?"

Three men talked into their radio at once.

"Man, I miss Peets!"

"Are these all new men?" Harriet asked.

"I didn't think there'd be any crime on the streets this week. Aleta just got home after all. How come there's a crime wave over here?"

"Aleta's new case," Harriet said. "One of them."

"The reverend?" Milani assumed aloud.

The look on Rollo's face told him he'd guessed correctly.

"I assume he was after the little girl," Milani said. "She's okay, isn't she?"

Claude approached with a mug of hot tea. He handed it to Emerita. Then he called Stanley on his cell and told him not to bring the child home for another hour at least.

"We've had an incident," he said and then hung up.

Milani turned to two of his men, "Did either of you arrest this man?"

The two shook their heads.

"You, big guy, what's your name?"

"Tim, Sir."

"Okay, Tim. Arrest him and read him his rights."

"Rollo Travick," Tim began.

Milani interrupted him. "You know him?"

"He's a P.I.," Tim replied. "He's got an office at the northernmost corner of the county."

"Go on," Milani said.

Tim heard the ambulance siren, so he hurried his spiel. He managed, however, to cite three violations including two assaults with a deadly weapon.

Milani looked pleased. "Tim, stick to this man like glue. If they operate on him, make sure you are close enough to see the rifling on the bullet."

"Yes, Sir," Tim snapped.

"Did I hire you?"

"No, Sir. I'm on loan from the County Sheriff."

"And your partner here?" Milani asked, nodding at the man standing beside Tim.

"I'm a loaner too, Chief. The sheriff says you can teach us a lot."

"I'm not a training academy," Milani spouted.

"You didn't know about this Tom?" Harriet asked.

"Peets talked about an officer exchange before he left. That was months ago," Milani replied. "Who knew he'd pull it off?"

"Will these men follow your orders?" Harriet asked.

"Yes, Ma'am," Tim said. "We've been told the chief shoots anyone who doesn't."

"Who told you that?" Milani charged.

"The desk sergeant."

"It's true," Harriet said. "The man limps to this day."

Milani burst in. "He doesn't limp. He just has a little scar. And I saved his life!"

"He disobeyed a direct order," Harriet put in.

The two country men were properly shocked.

"So what am I going to do with Emerita and her daughter?" Tom asked which he wouldn't have done if he weren't ruffled.

"I have an idea," Harriet said, rising and motioning to Claude to calm the trembling Emerita. She led Milani onto the utility room off the back hallway.

"Why are Evelyn's dogs in crates?" Tom asked.

"That's my idea. There is a three day show this weekend. Evelyn leaves this evening. It's only a couple hours drive from here."

"Please tell me West is entered."

"He and Lauren are going," Harriet said. "So are Beatrice and Ed. I entered Scooby when Aleta was in the hospital. I wasn't sure everything would turn out with the baby and well, I thought she might need to get away. Anyway Claude and I are going. We're going to break in our new RV. They can travel with us. We can sleep four."

"I suppose you want your rifles back?"

"You don't need them. We might."

"Try not to shoot any more... What's he doing here?" Milani said looking past Harriet through the window overlooking the road. "Damn it! He's got the TV crew with him."

Chapter 9

Aleta Praetzel found her two aspiring candidates in Stanley's office staring at the fish.

"That one's Mrs. Cook," she said. "Martha liked its tail."

"They have names?" the short-statured, Chinese lawyer asked.

"Yes, they do. And Stanley can remember them all. I only know some. That one he named for his mother. And those three are named for the police chiefs."

The shorter man turned and offered his hand, "Mrs. Praetzel, it's a pleasure meeting you. My name is Roland Chin."

"Andrew Jackson," the taller man said. "And, yes, my mother did name me for the president. She has high aspirations."

"You'll never make it working in this office."

"I beg to differ, Ma'am. This is exactly the office I need to work in."

"Why would you say that?"

"Because you're always in the news," Andrew replied.

Aleta grew thoughtful. Her silence disconcerted both men standing in front of her.

Andrew finally broke the silence. "Did I say something wrong?"

Aleta stirred herself back to reality. "Well, when you become the president, remember to appoint me to the bench."

Roland Chin spoke up. "You have it backwards Ma'am. When you become president, we'd like to be appointed to the bench."

"This office doesn't need a diplomat. Stanley handles that quite well. Now tell me, Mr. Chin, what qualities in Mr. Jackson do you like best?"

"He's forthright and bright and down to earth."

Aleta turned to the black man, "Mr. Jackson, what qualities in Mr. Chin would you value?"

"He's a diplomat and no office has too many of those. He's shorter than me, so he'll look up to me. And what else can I say? He's obviously quick on his feet. Quicker in fact than I am."

"Well, Gentlemen, you're both hired," Aleta said.

"You don't want to see our resumes?" Andrew Jackson asked.

"They're good, aren't they?"

"Yes," both chorused.

"My dad likes you," Aleta said. "I like you, what more is there to know? What is the top salary given any associate graduating from your law school?"

Each named a figure and Aleta said, "We'll go with the top one. I assume you are accepting our offer."

Both men nodded, broad smiles on their faces.

"We have two major cases, Gentlemen," Aleta said. "I want you both on both of them. My notes are at home. I want you both to come with me so I can introduce you to the guards."

Her father knocked and then entered. "There was an attack on Emerita a few minutes ago. Claude and Mother shot the man. He was after Nina. Evidently, Amend means business."

"That's one of our cases, Gentlemen. Emerita was imprisoned and raped for almost five years. She escaped with her child. Her slave owner wants the child back. He claims she was a surrogate mother and the child is his. Stanley is the child's attorney. We are representing Emerita Balta and Teodora Popova who was sold to a friend of Amend's, impregnated and returned and then raped by Amend. Teodora just finished being examined by a doctor and we're hoping for proof of the rape. She escaped this morning."

"Mother wants to talk with you right away," her father said.

Aleta excused herself and called her grandmother. "Grams, are you alright?"

"We have a plan," she said.

Aleta listened until she finished.

"Mr. Ledgewood is living in my RV. I have a new client, Teodora Popova. She's Lithuanian. Same story as Emerita. And she doesn't speak English. Scooby hasn't been washed. I'm not packed. I just got two new associates..."

"You're coming?" Harriet asked.

"Of course, I'm coming."

"You can't. It would be too risky for the baby and I know you and Stanley won't leave him."

"He can stay in the RV. I won't pass him around. I'll have Bertha and Teodora clean it before we leave."

"What about Ledgewood?"

"He can house sit Bertha's place," Aleta said. "Emerita and Nina will be at the show."

"What about Teodora?"

"She has to come too," Aleta said. "She and Emerita will be good company for each other."

"I will come over and fetch Scooby. We'll wash him here at Evelyn's. I'll get Beatrice to pick up clothes for Teodora. Is she the same size as Emerita?"

"Don't bother. I'll loan her some of mine," Aleta said. "Is there an RV space reserved for me?"

"Yes," Harriet said.   "We can caravan to the fairgrounds.   You, Beatrice, Evelyn and us.   And Lyle, of course.   Madge and Nathan are leaving in the morning. They don't show until two.   Julia and Jason are already on their way."

"What about Jocelyn?" Aleta asked.

"I guess she could stay with her father," Harriet suggested.

"No!" Aleta cried. She can't."

There was silence on the other end of the phone.

"I'm sorry I yelled," Aleta said contritely. "We can't leave her here. I have two gigantic cases and..."

"Aleta don't mislead me," her grandmother said.

"She can't stay here," Aleta said. "I can't explain."

"Since I have the Lithuanians," Harriet responded, "Jocelyn will need to bunk with you."

"Pick up Teodora when you come for Scooby."

Aleta shut her cell phone and turned away from the window to find all three men staring at her.

"Dad, you and Bertha have the house for the weekend. Andrew, Roland, you need to come with me and get my notes on both cases. "Who's got a car?"

Three hands went up.

"Dad, we can't all fit in your truck. Andrew, we'll take yours. It's bigger."

"Am I a stereotype?" he quipped.

"No, just taller," Aleta said. "You wouldn't fit in a small car."

"Why did you assume his car is smaller?" Andrew pushed.

"Roland would select one that gets good gas mileage."

"You don't know that," Andrew pressed.

"His suit tells me he's careful with money."

"What's wrong with it?" Andrew asked.

"Roland was right about you. You are forthright. You want to know if I've hired you to prove I'm not prejudiced," Aleta responded. "You do know I'm part Negro, don't you?"

"African American," Andrew corrected.

"Don't correct me," Aleta quipped. "I will decide my heritage my way."

Andrew was immediately contrite. "I'm sorry. I overstepped myself."

"Actually, you have every right to test the waters. You were chosen because my dad was drawn to the two of you, also because it's late in the hiring season and we know that to get talent so late we had to look at graduates from less prestigious law schools. Neither of you is a token anything. My dad and I take care of that all by ourselves."

"My suit," Roland mentioned slightly abashed. "It is not correct?"

"It is perfect," Aleta said, "but is very expensive and for a tailor made suit, it doesn't fit exactly which means you bought it second-hand. It fits as well as any suit off the rack only I recognize the touches of a tailor. I believe a good tailor could make the minor adjustments needed and it would be worth your while. If you buy your other suits with a tailor to fit them to you, you will be well-dressed at one third the cost."

"Take me with you next time you shop, man," Andrew said.

"My pleasure," Roland beamed.

"Let me tell you about our other major case," Aleta said. "The two of you will have to work this weekend. Mr. Locke will be working on Nina's case. You are to help him if he needs it. Nina's custody case is top priority. Staying Mr. Middlebourne's eviction is top priority. Keeping Emerita and Teodora in this country and free of whatever contracts they signed is top priority."

"What order should we handle these assignments?" Roland asked.

"No order. All are equal. There are two of you. You have three days before we can move legally. Hammer out the briefs."

"Briefs?" the two chorused.

"I prepare briefs in advance," Aleta said. "Anticipate the rulings."

The two drew in collective deep breaths.

"You didn't think I was going to expect you to be this involved this fast?"

"You're taking three days off?" Andrew asked.

"I will be with our clients. The cases will go with me. I will be back Monday afternoon. We will touch base then."

Two hours later, Scooby had been washed and dried, Evelyn had recovered from the shock of the huge blood stains on her new carpet, Emerita and Teodora had had a tearful reunion, both had received several outfits suitable for the casual dress at a dog show, Nina's toys and play clothes had been fetched from Bertha's house, Mr. Ledgewood had been moved, the trailer had been cleaned, the bassinet and sundry baby care essentials had been jammed into the RV, and Bertha had added several bottles of fresh formula and half a dozen cans of canned liquid formula.

Evelyn and Beatrice packed extra food, as did Lauren. Madge promised to bring fresh baked goods the next day. Claude added more meat for the barbeques to his coolers.

By six that evening Robert and Bertha found themselves alone in the house.

"I can't believe they're gone," he said.

"Let's not assume they are for a couple of hours," Bertha said. "I'll make supper. Mr. Hubbs needs to be fed."

"I'll take King for his evening walk and tell him we'll eat in half an hour," Robert said. "If I stay here, I'm not sure I'll behave."

"I went to see Dr. Chesney today," Bertha said as she pulled a frozen casserole from the freezer and put it in the microwave. She began making biscuits.

"Yes, I know. You took Teodora."

"He said the chances of my being pregnant were extremely remote."

"You told him?"

"I was worried."

"About what?"

"About whether at my age I could bear a healthy child."

"You believe Aleta was speaking to us, don't you?"

"Yes,"

"But both times Teodora was in the house--well, in the case of her telling me, she appeared right after Aleta spoke."

"She never said I wasn't."

"She mentioned that you were too old. Maybe that was her way of telling us it wasn't us."

Bertha began to cry.

Robert put his arms around her. "You wanted it to be true, didn't you?"

She nodded her head which was buried in his shoulder.

"There's a time for everything, Bertha. Our time has passed. We're grandparents now. And you're working here where you will be helping raise our grandchildren. We are singularly blessed."

Bertha pulled away and wiped her eyes with the hem of her apron. "I'm fussing over nothing."

"Losing one's ability to bear children is not nothing," Robert said. "Mother told me that."

"You didn't tell her about us, did you?"

"She guessed when Aleta was so adamant about not leaving Jocelyn here with us," Robert said. "I told her what Aleta had said about you being pregnant. She said that Aleta's saying it would stir up old feelings of loss."

"Does she think it's possible?"

"She doesn't think there's much possibility. She has known of change-of-life babies and she says all those she's known have been healthy."

"Dr. Chesney is going to do an exam on Tuesday."

"What for?"

"He's an OBGYN man. They love to do yearly exams, pap smears and the like. I'm overdue. He caught me at a weak moment. I hate pap smears."

"I don't know how to help you."

"Just make love to me," Bertha replied.

"I hate to see you sad," Robert remarked.

"It'll fade. Go get Mr. Hubbs."

He kissed her lightly, then embraced her and kissed her again. "I love you. I didn't marry you because I wanted more children. I married you because I want to spend my life with you."

"Aleta awakened something is all," Bertha replied sadly.

"She should think before she speaks!" he declared.

"No!" Bertha said. "She shouldn't. She didn't wound me. She simply opened a door I'd closed too soon. This sadness will pass."

When Robert walked toward the barn, one of the guards accompanied him. He asked him why he did this.

"I'm not a target," he stated.

"The chief wants no surprises to be waiting for the Praetzels when they return. He has men stationed at your mother's house as well."

"And Bertha's house?"

"West has his men watching that one."

"They're taking no chances," Robert said.

"We've learned the hard way."

"Do you think Aleta should hire private security?"

"No, Sir. She couldn't find a private security company that's as good as we are. And we're not guarding jewels. We're guarding a person."

Robert chuckled. "She is that."

Chapter 10

After supper Robert lit the fire and wondered briefly when Bertha had found the time to prepare it. When she joined him on the couch, he put his arm around her and together they watched the fire, reveling in each other's company.

"This is our real honeymoon," he whispered, kissing the tip of her ear.

"You missed," she joked.

"Don't you want to watch the fire?"

"Too bad we can't do both."

"Who said we can't?"

He rose after telling her to wait and when he returned he had an armful of bedding.

"The drapes are open," Bertha said.

Robert dropped the bedding in a heap, walked over and drew the drapes. On his way back, he locked the door.

When he returned Bertha had spread the blankets and folded them so they made a thick layer of padding.

"That's just in case," Bertha said.

"Just in case of what?" her new husband asked tongue-in-cheek.

"In case you get lucky," she quipped. "It's not guaranteed you know."

"Come and sit next to me and let's watch the fire," he said.

"That's all?"

"You said there was no guarantee, so I plan to start slowly," he said putting his arm around her and kissing her.

She snuggled down in the crook of his arm and whispered. "I didn't mean it, you know. I'm just embarrassed."

"Aleta said the house was ours," Robert responded slowly unbuttoning her blouse.

He slipped it off her shoulders and stroked them. "You have such soft skin."

"That's not the only place I have soft skin," she said reaching back and unsnapping her bra. She, however, didn't remove it.

He slipped her blouse down further and kissed her upper arm. "Just as soft," he whispered.

She drew her arms out of her blouse and it lay crumpled around her waist. He slipped the straps of her bra down her arms, and then suddenly he pulled it off and tossed into the fireplace.

Shocked, she cried, "What are you doing?"

"Getting rid of the blasted thing. And you better not replace it until Monday.

"I need it."

"Why? Where are you going?"

Bertha sank back. "I'm not young, you know. I sag a bit."

"It inhibits me," Robert said. "And this is our honeymoon, after all."

"Yes, it is," Bertha agreed softly. "Next thing I know all my clothes will wind up in the fire."

"Hadn't thought of that. But now that you mention it..."

"What can I do to prevent that?"

"You could lay down on the bed in front of the fire."

"That's all?"

"That's just the beginning."

"Clothed or unclothed?"

"As you are."

"And you won't burn up anything else?"

"I'm going to burn everything."

"Why?"

"I want you naked all night long."

"Oh, Robert. I'm not beautiful."

"I'm a lot like Aleta. I like Bulldogs too."

"That's what I look like?" Bertha gasped.

"That's what you think you look like," Robert said tenderly. "But to me you are a beautiful woman and I want to enjoy every curve of your body."

"Really?" she murmured.

He kissed her and undressed her. One by one he threw her clothes in the fire. And she watched them burn. Bit by bit her inhibitions followed their smoke up the chimney.

He sat beside her while she lay naked on the blankets before the fire. He didn't even take off his tie. His fingers traced every curve of her body with a light touch. His caresses soothed her and excited her both.

"You aren't going to make love to me?" she asked quietly.

"I am," he said quietly.

And she realized he was, in a way she never dreamed of. Every touch told her he prized her. She began to tremble.

"Please," she whispered.

And he complied.

A loud banging on the front door woke Bertha and Robert. Robert jumped up from the floor and pulled on his pants.

A rough voice called, "Police. Open up. We have a warrant!"

"Coming!" Robert shouted, swiftly gathering his clothes and the bedding and shoving them at Bertha. "Throw these in the laundry room and take a shower. Turn on the water and get in."

She rushed off as Robert went to the front door yelling, "I'm coming! I'm coming!"

He looked back as he put his hand on the dead bolt. Bertha was disappearing around the corner. He heard a police siren in a distance. Milani had probably been called as soon as the men saw the patrol car.

"Show me your badge," he yelled.

"Tell him," he heard the rough voice order the Willow Glen officer.

"Sir, he is a Northridge police lieutenant," a familiar voice said.

"Okay, then I'm opening the door," Robert said. He heard the water running in the shower.

Briefly, he hoped it wasn't too cold.

He slid the bolt and opened the door.

"Do you have a warrant?" he asked. One was shoved in his hand. He scanned the face quickly and stepped back. Two officers entered.

"You may look everywhere but the bathroom where Bertha is taking a shower."

The siren drew nearer.

The Northridge lieutenant headed straight for the bathroom where Bertha was.

"You touch that door and I'll have you up on charges. No one is in there but Bertha."

"I need to look."

"Give her a chance to get out of the shower then," Robert said. He then shouted, "Bertha, you have to open up now."

"The house is empty, Sir," the Northridge officer reported.

The shower was turned off and after a long minute the door was opened. Bertha was in a white terry cloth robe wiping her face with a towel. Soapy water was dripping onto the floor from under the robe.

The lieutenant stepped in and pushed his hand into the shower.

"Can I finish now?" Bertha asked.

The lieutenant backed out and Bertha slammed the door and threw the bolt.

"Where is everyone?" the lieutenant asked Robert.

"Some are gone. Some are here," Robert said as he heard the shower water running again."

Chief Milani came through the front door. "Where's Bertha?" he asked. "They didn't hurt her."

"They interrupted her shower," Robert replied. "And now they're leaving."

"We aren't leaving," the lieutenant shot back. "We want answers!"

"I'm Nina's layer," Robert replied coldly.

"You aren't her lawyer!" the lieutenant charged. "Stanley Praetzel is. Now where's he taken her?"

Chief Milani took charge.

"He can't tell you. After the botched kidnapping attempt and the assault on Nina's mother, we put them both under police protection."

"We want the child."

"Your warrant only allows you to search this house and Bertha's house," Milani said. "That's it. You're done. So leave."

"I'll be back."

When he left, Milani said, "French gave me a heads-up. They hit Bertha's house first."

Bertha left the bathroom and ran to the back bedroom. Milani raised one eyebrow.

"We're married," Robert said. "A civil ceremony. Only a few people know."

"What about June first?"

"It's still happening," Robert said. "We wouldn't have done this if Jocelyn..."

"I was there, remember?" Milani put in then added, "He'll get a new warrant."

"I guess I'm going to have to work today after all," Robert said. "I need to get a few court orders myself. Bertha can whip you up some breakfast if you like."

"I'm not staying," Tom said. "Call me if you need me."

"Thanks, Tom."

A few minutes later he entered the bedroom to find Bertha sitting on the edge of the bed upset.

"I was planning to wear that uniform today," she said morosely. "My other uniforms are in the wash. Now what do I do?"

"Wear my sweats."

"They'll be way too big."

"The pants have a drawstring."

"The legs and arms will be too long."

"Cut them off."

"And ruin them?" she gasped horrified at the thought.

"Much as I'd like you to run around naked, the house is going to have too much traffic for you to do that," Robert said as he pulled a clean part of sweats out of his drawer. He pulled the shirt over Bertha's head while she protested that she couldn't cut up a good outfit.

He looked at how long the arms were and then pulled the top off, took out a pair of scissors and cut the bottom of the sleeves off. Then he stuck the top back over her head and put her arms in the sleeves and found the three quarter length perfect.

He had her step into the pants next and measured them. He removed them and made straight cuts on both legs. She put them on.

"These are comfortable," she murmured.

"You look great!"

"I look like the Pillsbury Doughboy," she countered.

"I see we need another lesson in believing your husband," he said lifting her up and sitting her on the bed.

"There's no time," she cautioned. "Hubbs needs his breakfast..."

He kissed her quiet and she let him undress her again.

Chapter 11

When Stanley emerged from the tiny back bedroom in the RV, he asked Aleta where Jocelyn was.

"Outside pouting about being forced to come along and spend three whole days with a bunch of old people watching a bunch of dogs running around a ring."

"Same attitude as last night, huh?"

"No amount of reasoning will charge her. She couldn't see any reason why she couldn't have been left behind with Dad."

Stanley kissed Aleta lightly on the cheek. "We left two happy people behind at the house."

"They are getting their honeymoon after all," Aleta said.

"Three whole days and no visitors."

"And no work. Court is shut down for three days."

The RV door was thrown open. Jocelyn stormed in. "There's no one to talk to."

"I told you before, Jocelyn. If you're going to grump, do it outside. This RV is too small."

"You make no sense at all sometimes."

"Go for a walk," Aleta said. "Cool off. Everyone found out last night how much you didn't want to be here. Now it's time to be civil."

"I could be riding."

"Are you going to give Bertha and Dad this treatment when you join them on their honeymoon?"

"No."

"Well, there is that," Aleta responded simply. "Go have a miserable time outside. And stay away from Grams and me until lunch. We're both showing this morning."

"I don't know why you even came. Scooby's too young to win anything. I heard you guys last night."

"He might take Reserve," Aleta explained. "That would be a judge's stamp of approval on a promising pup. That would make Ed feel good. This is Emma's first litter and she's not a show dog."

"I'm surprised you got a pup that wasn't from two champions."

"Championships are hard to get on Labs, for one. And Emma is a quality Labrador with a special temperament."

"Scooby's sister is here," Jocelyn said. "Are you competing against her? I wouldn't think that would make Ed too happy if he loses with his dog."

"Bitches and dogs are judged separately," Aleta explained.

"You showing that Bulldog I keep hearing you talk about?"

"No, she just had a litter. We'll be getting one of her pups," Aleta said. "I'm only showing Scooby this trip."

A knock on the door brought the conversation to a halt. Aleta opened the door and stepped outside. Jocelyn glanced at the baby being changed and decided to leave as well. She was determined she wasn't going to be stuck in the RV babysitting.

"Tom!" Aleta said surprised.

"Is your husband here? I thought I'd ask him to step into the ring for me. Unless, of course, you're free. Congratulations on your son, by the way. I was surprised to see you here so soon."

"Grams signed us up when I was in the hospital. She thought I might enjoy getting back into the swing of things."

"You heard that Maggie had her pups."

"Born the same day as Gerard. Stanley's changing the baby now. Let me get him."

"Are you showing today?"

"Just my Lab pup."

"Think you might be up for group this afternoon? I have two that should take the breed in Non-Sporting."

"The Frenchie," Aleta said. "Who else?"

"A Shar-Pei," Tom said. "My assistant will take in the Poodle if he wins."

"The Shar-Pei is new, isn't he?"

"He has a few points, but what he needs is a Group win."

"Is he good?"

"Yes."

"So who do you want me to take in?"

"The Shar-Pei."

"Not the Frenchie?"

"I'm committed to showing him. The owner got upset when I started taking Maggie in and I told him Maggie was going to be bred soon. My assistants do well with the Poodle and the Shar-Pei but the Frenchie is always on."

Aleta chuckled. "So you're beating yourself?"

Stanley stepped out of the RV with the baby. "Aleta can probably do Group for you, but nothing else. I could tell by the lilt in her voice she was going to say yes, so I thought I'd say no to the rest for her."

Tom smiled. "So this is the little one. He is a handsome fellow."

Aleta's genes won out," Stanley said. "Her grandmother says he's the spitting image of her dad."

"How can she tell?" Tom asked.

"I guess women can judge babies the way they can judge litters. It's in the genes."

"Stanley, I wonder if you could help me out at eleven."

"I only showed those two dogs I watched Aleta show," Stanley protested.

"I thought maybe you'd take in the Shar-Pei. He's the only dog entered. My assistant is taking in my Frenchie because I'm on the Afghan."

"I guess I could do that," Stanley said. He noted Tom looking at the baby. "Don't worry. Aleta takes care of Gerard once in a while."

"Grams is here," Aleta said and both men laughed.

As Tom was talking to Aleta, Jocelyn noticed a young man about her age hanging on every word. Tom finally introduced him.

"This is Kevin Slingsby. He's in Junior Showmanship."

Aleta introduced Jocelyn and mentioned that she showed horses."

"Really?" Tom said. "Dressage, Trail, Jumping?"

"Jumping."

"How long?"

"Three years," Jocelyn said. "I have a new horse. He's quite good. In fact, I should be home working him instead of here watching dogs run around the ring."

"You show too then?" Kevin asked, finally speaking. His voice wavered between high and low. Jocelyn was then sure he was her age.

"What's Junior Showmanship?" she asked.

"It's where the handlers are judged, not the dogs."

"Cool!" she exclaimed. "I'd like to see that."

Aleta and Stanley glanced at each other.

"The Lions are putting on a pancake breakfast. All you can eat for three bucks if you're a junior," Kevin said.

Jocelyn scowled.

"Under sixteen," he said. "I think they charge more if you're twelve though."

Jocelyn laughed. "Guess we don't have to worry about that!

"Aleta, I need money," Jocelyn said.

"No you don't," Kevin said. "I've got enough."

"I'll pay tomorrow. They will be here tomorrow won't they?"

"Every day," Kevin said.

"Tell me about this showmanship thing," Jocelyn said as the two walked off.

Aleta and Stanley smiled at each other. They looked at Tom who was grinning.

"I tell you," he said. "As bad as dragging along a teenager that doesn't want to be here is being the mentor of one who watches your every move."

"You planned this," Aleta accused. "Did you really need me or Stanley to show your Shar-Pei?"

"Kevin was driving me nuts," Tom said. "He wanted to show one of my dogs in Group."

"You said he was good," Stanley pointed out.

"I can't put one of my dogs on a Junior. Besides Aleta has beaten me before. My client will appreciate my choice."

"A group One on a class dog, a Shar-Pei no less. You are expecting a miracle," Aleta murmured.

"From you? Always!" Tom returned, and then he softened his approach. "You'll show him well. The owners will be ringside. Make the cut and that will satisfy them."

"Does the judge know Shar-Peis?"

"Not really. But tomorrow's judge does. There are two points in dogs tomorrow. I'll take him in tomorrow," Tom said. "See you at the Lab ring."

Aleta turned to her husband. "You know, Stanley as long as you need to dress for the ring anyway, why don't you take Scooby into the ring, too?"

"I don't understand," Stanley responded obviously puzzled. Aleta lived for showing. She hated watching.

"Just a hunch," she said. "But since there's no competition in the Six-to-Nine class, you can get ring experience. I'll take him into Winners."

"You're going for the points?"

"Always."

"I don't know anything about stacking a dog."

"One doesn't stack puppies," Aleta said. "You'll do fine. I need to watch him in the ring before I take him in."

"I have no idea how to show a Lab," Stanley protested.

"Chessies show before Labs. You can watch Grams."

"That'll be a lot of handling of the baby."

"Grams will be there."

"With three dogs!"

"She can give them to Claude."

"You need to feed him if I have to change."

"Isn't it nice to be away from the turbulence of daily life?" Aleta commented taking the baby from Stanley.

He stared at her. "Aleta, you bring it with you."

"Stop fussing," Aleta returned. "You love being a participant."

She heard him grumbling about that not being true when there was a baby in the mix. She smiled. It was important that he not be the relegated baby sitter. Grams would love to hold Gerard and Claude will be delighted to be managing three Chessies. They were, after all, a man's dog.

Almost the entire Arborville-Willow Glen group was there to clap when Harriet's male Chessie champion took the Breed. They'd come out mainly to watch Stanley. Aleta sat at ringside holding the baby when he went in. Her eyes were glued on the pup when her grandmother eased herself into the seat beside her and gently lifted the baby out of her arms.

Stanley's pace was perfect," Aleta whispered to her grandmother. "How did he know?"

"Watched me, I guess," Harriet remarked.

"You moved faster."

"No, I mean he watched how the dog was suppose to move."

"You think he caught that nuance?"

"He's pretty sharp."

She watched Stanley politely thank the judge for his blue place ribbon with a respectful demeanor. He took an extra second and she saw the judge smile at his words. She wondered what he'd added.

He refused to tell her.

Well, it couldn't be bad, she reasoned. Judge Garren Johnson had smiled. There was one entry in Bred-By, one in American Bred and four in Open. Seven in many breeds would mean major points. In Labs it meant just one.

When Aleta entered the Winners class there were three other dogs. It was almost a foregone conclusion that the Open Dog would win. He'd already beaten three in the ring. The American Bred was too light in bone and slightly spindly. The Bred-By wasn't in the best shape. On top of that there was a handler on the Open Dog and he was a yellow which was a color preferred by many judges. Chocolate was the least favorite color.

The judge walked down the ring past the dogs eyeing each carefully. When he came to Scooby he stopped and smiled. The gentleman had been correct. This dog was considerably more alert with the wife. He asked her to move the dog down and back.

Flawless, he thought. What a beautiful animal.

He moved him up to the front and then had the Open Dog move.

Not bad, he judged. Not quite as good.

He asked the two to move around the ring together. The handler on the Open Dog didn't crowd Aleta because that would have broken his dog's gait. Thus both dogs moved smoothly.

The handler spent a few seconds adjusting a back leg as Garren Johnson stepped back to view both in profile.

Aleta moved the pup back and then forward. He fell into a natural stack, his tail going furiously, his ears perked as his nose smelled the liver bit in her fingers.

The judge studied the two for a long minute.

"Winners," he said, pointing at Scooby. The crowd at ringside cheered. Judge Johnson smiled. It was always nice to make a popular choice.

When she left the ring, she asked Stanley again what he said to the judge. He refused to tell her.

"Can we have a picture taken with the two of us since I won his first ribbon?" Stanley asked.

"That would be neat!" she responded. "Glad you thought of it."

Beatrice took in Scooby's sister, Minx, a lively black Lab whose movement matched her brother's. She took Reserve.

"There are two points in bitches," Lauren whispered to Aleta as she got ready to take in Holly, her chocolate champion. Lyle was in line with Morgan and Tom Wilson had Morgan's black son Banner. The champions filed in first, followed by the Winners Dog and the Winners Bitch. In the ring were two chocolates, two blacks and three yellows.

Aleta had won over a yellow under a judge, earlier despite the fact that Dr. Garren Johnson preferred yellows but would occasionally put up a good black. Until Scooby he'd never put up a chocolate. Lauren had debated entering Holly, but Lyle had told her Scooby was entered so she decided to enter too. They could commiserate later as chocolate Lab owners do.

The judge looked at the yellows hoping to find one as good as the two blacks. Tom had been doing a lot of winning with his black, but he'd heard about the owner of a big black that showed rarely, so to speak, and always gave Tom a run for his money.

As Judge Johnson went over Morgan, he could see why. The dog was magnificent. Balanced, muscled and smooth moving. He'd heard this singular dog had won a couple Best in Shows and he decided to let him go for another.

Johnson decided he liked his yellow Winner's Bitch. She was almost as good as the chocolate bitch champion in the ring. He wasn't fond of chocolate; however, when he looked at Scooby he was again taken with what a superb pup he was.

I wish you were yellow, he thought and then brought himself up short. Was he that prejudiced?

After he gave Scooby Best of Winners, he found out the chocolate pup's father was Morgan, his breed winner.

A photo was taken with Morgan and Scooby, Lyle and Aleta in addition to the individual shots of each dog and handler.

It was the judge who told Aleta what Stanley had said. He'd done it as more of an affirmation than a revelation.

"Your husband said the pup thought you walked on water," Garren Johnson chuckled. "He's the first chocolate I've put up."

"Lots of firsts," Aleta said. "First time in the ring for Scooby, first time either of us has shown our own dog."

"Is that your baby that was at ringside?"

"It's his first show too," Aleta said.

"Starting him early, aren't you?"

Stanley laughed. "You have no idea."

"How old is he?"

"Three days," Stanley said. "We needed the rest."

The judge roared. "You two just made my day."

"And you made ours," Stanley returned.

Lyle received a call from Tom Milani in the midst of the barbeque. He called Stanley over and told him what had happened that morning. He said that Robert had gotten hold of a juvenile court judge and wrangled an order to leave the child under police protection until an emergency custody hearing Tuesday afternoon.

"That's terribly short notice," Stanley griped.

"Robert had to do some fast talking not to have an emergency hearing today."

"I wanted one more psychologist to examine her," Stanley said. "If I have three, the judge is apt to accept their findings without ordering more, especially as two are well-respected in our area."

"You know that Lab judge we had this morning is a doctor. I think he's a shrink."

"I need a child psychologist."

"Maybe he knows someone," Lyle said. "But you have to wait until after Group to ask him."

"No one knows where we are, right?"

"Robert had to tell the judge," Lyle reported. "It was part of his pitch. Why not let the child have a good time?"

"The judge wasn't worried about undue influence?" Stanley asked.

"She said she had no intention of asking the child to choose. She told Robert if he had asked the temporary custody be given Emerita, she would have refused. But the fact that Nina would be sharing a room with a female deputy made the order defensible."

"Aren't you glad you deputized Harriet and Claude when you mounted that rescue mission?" Stanley queried smiling.

"They need some instruction in police procedure according to Tom."

"They didn't shout 'Police!' did they? They just shot."

"Tom said it was a righteous shoot."

"It will always be that," Stanley predicted. "So, are we in any danger?"

"Do you have your gun and badge with you?"

"Yes."

"Harriet and Claude have their rifles.   Ed always carries a piece," Lyle counted aloud. "We need to have Aleta somehow caution the two women to stay with the group."

"You think they're the targets?"

"They're the accusers."

"Actually, Emerita isn't. She's refusing to talk."

"What is she afraid of?"

"The point is that Amend probably doesn't see her as a threat. And he wants the child."

"You think he'll go for Aleta?"

"She told him she was Emerita's attorney," Stanley said. "And she speaks Lithuanian. That was something he hadn't counted on."

"So, all he has to do is take out Aleta and Emerita will fold."

Stanley grew silent as he considered Lyle's conclusion.

"I just thought of something," Stanley said. "Teodora and Emerita together point to a larger issue here. If that's true, Aleta is in even more danger. Amend could get the two women deported, if Aleta weren't in the picture."

"I'll call French and have him bring down a couple of men," Lyle said. "They can stand guard at night."

"I think I'll forbid Aleta from taking any more cases."

"You plan to be celibate the rest of your life?"

"I won't be. She wants six children."

"So you have six nights of pleasure between your months of celibacy."

"She wouldn't!" Stanley declared. "Would she?"

"I'm just saying that I wouldn't forbid her anything."

"She has me tied around her little finger."

"Join the club."

That afternoon Aleta walked into the Non-Sporting Group competition with a Chinese Shar-Pei and after taking her place near the end of the line, she looked up into the judge's face as he came down the line only to find the Lab judge smiling back at her.

When it was turn for the Shar-Pei to be individually examined, Aleta walked him into a stack. The judge examined him and as he stood back for one final look, he said. "Is it your mission in life to shake me up?"

"You have to forgive Toby for making you think outside the box."

"A triangle," the judge said genially.

The pace was perfect. The Shar-Pei moved true, his feet converging as Aleta picked up the pace. When she turned to show his side movement, he saw at once the reach of his front legs and the drive in his rear. He was a movement judge first and foremost.

When Aleta returned, the judge held her there for a moment while he mentally checked the dog against the picture of the standard he had in his memory. Wrinkles, not superabundant as in puppies but on this dog limited to the head, neck and back as they should be. He had the correct bite, the bluish gray tongue, the short, harsh coat and the dip just behind the withers. This young woman handler was wise to self stack this dog. Stretching it might level the back. She had presented him just right.

The judge sent her around to the back of the line and stepped out so he could watch the side movement again. When she stopped his eyes were still on her. The dog halted in perfect profile. He realized she'd turned the dog just slightly to get that effect. It was a risky move if the dog had certain faults. For the repeat winners this was commonly done, but this was a class dog.

He had never given a class dog a first in Group and here was this young woman fighting to break down yet another of his traditions as he called them. The rest of the dogs were good, Tom Wilson and his Frenchie were outstanding. The Poodle up in front was a show stopper as was the Chow. The Lhasa was a beauty. But his eye kept going back to the strange dog that broke all the rules and the young woman showing him who insisted he stand regally the entire time. When he finished examining the last dog, the handlers brought their dogs into perfect stack. Aleta and the Shar-Pei didn't move a muscle.

His eyes roamed down the line. Did he dare? No, he told himself. He was mesmerized by the woman. He didn't know the breed that well. Better to go with the dogs he knew. If it was a champion, he could take a chance, but to give it a major. An unthinkable act.

He pulled out the Poodle, the Chow, the Shar-Pei, the Bichon, the Frenchie and the Lhasa. He asked them to move around the ring once. And his eyes followed the Chinese Shar-Pei. What a smooth mover.

Aleta took first; the Poodle, second; the Lhasa, third and the Frenchie, fourth. The cheer from the gallery told him that either this young woman had brought her own cheering section or the gallery liked the queer, little brown dog.

"Broke down another one of your rules?" Aleta asked smiling.

"Eventually, I won't have any rules left. Then how will you win?"

Aleta laughed. "I have no idea."

After the photos were taken, Aleta took Tom Wilson aside. "I'm running on empty. I can't show anymore today."

"Don't worry about it," he said kindly. "Getting that major was a gigantic feat. And I know how much energy that took. You just go sit down and relax."

"Thanks Tom."

"It's me that owes you."

"I enjoyed showing Toby.

"If he takes the Breed tomorrow, I might ask you to take him in again."

"Ask me tomorrow."

Aleta came over and sat down with Stanley and took Gerard from him.

"Miss me?" she asked as she cuddled him.

"You were pretty spectacular," Stanley said.

Behind her Aleta heard a woman say in Chinese, "That's her. The one with the beautiful baby."

Aleta turned around and replied in Chinese, "It is your dog that is beautiful."

"Thank you for showing him so well," the woman said again.

"He showed himself. He won because he is a good Shar-Pei."

"You had much competition," the man said in English.

"You are correct," Aleta responded in English.

"You will show him tomorrow, yes?"

"I believe Mr. Wilson plans to show him in the class competition."

"You won five points for him today."

"It was a big win," Aleta agreed.

"We would prefer you do it again."

"It would be unusual to win twice like that," she said in English then seeing the puzzled frown on the woman's face reverted to speaking Chinese. "I will show him tomorrow in the afternoon. Mr. Wilson will show him in the morning. But one does not win the same prize twice."

"Never?" the woman asked.

"Almost never," Aleta replied. "You will be disappointed."

"No, the woman said. "He looked regal. He looked as he should--bowing to no one. We want him to look like that. We will take judgment we are given."

"I understand," Aleta said. "I have not much energy. I cannot take him into the final competition today. I will only be able to show him once tomorrow. You pick."

She heard them arguing quietly in Chinese. The man spoke next. "Into Group where everyone watches."

"Yes," Aleta said. "I can do that."

"Thank you," they both said.

Stanley leaned over and whispered into Aleta's ear. "Are you sure?"

"We will go back right after the Sporting Group. I want to see Lyle and Grams."

As the Sporting Group began filing into the ring, Aleta turned to Stanley and whispered, "We must leave right now."

"Give me the baby," he said as Aleta began to rise.

"No time!" she said. "We must go now."

He bent down to pick up the diaper bag and by the time he looked up, Aleta was well down the path leading to the RV's. He hurried to catch up.

She headed straight for her grandmother's RV, opened the door and disappeared inside it. He followed her.

"Bring Babe and Keeper inside," she said.

"What is it?" he asked.

"Just do it," she ordered, her voice strained.

Stanley sat the diaper bag on the table and went out. He left the door open. When he opened the pen, he said, "In."

The two dogs bounded into the RV. He followed them.

"Close the blinds," she said. He did as she bid.

She slid into the booth behind the small table and clutched her baby to her breast.

He could see the tears ready to spill out.

"What is it?" he repeated. "Please tell me."

Her voice was shaky as she replied, "Peter French dove in front of me and the baby and he was killed, but Peter French isn't even here. But it happened right where we were," Aleta cried. "I didn't know what to do except not be there."

Stanley sat down on the bench beside her and put his arm around her. He could feel her trembling. "Peter French is here," he told her. "Lyle called him earlier. He has two other Arborville officers with him. They are all in plain clothes."

"Who wants to kill me?" she cried.

"Hush," Stanley said. "It's okay. He didn't die."

"Who is it?" she persisted. The baby began to fuss. Stanley took the bottle from the diaper bag and set it in a pan of hot water.

"Your father and Bertha had a visitor this morning. He had a warrant," Stanley said. "Robert went to work and got an order keeping Emerita and Teodora and Nina in police custody until the custody hearing Tuesday afternoon."

"Why would Amend come after me now?"

"Lyle and I think you've touched the tip of the iceberg. We have two escaped indentured servants, possibly slaves, in custody. You speak their language. You are a big threat. This proves it. Amend hasn't this kind of reach on his own. He hired one inept private detective to fetch back Nina. The man botched the job royally. Now we're dealing with true professionals. Your vision tells me that. Amend's associates have stepped in."

"They shot me at a dog show," she moaned. "Right out in the open."

"I think you were too tempting a target just sitting there. Especially with everyone's attention focused on the dogs in the ring. I'm guessing the shooter used a silencer. There is a line of trees along the edge of the ring area. He could have hidden behind one and been out of sight by the time any of us looked around."

"Is the bottle ready?" Aleta asked.

Stanley got up and took it from the water, turned it over to let a few drops fall on his wrist and then handed it to Aleta.

She put it in the baby's waiting mouth and Stanley began to settle in the chair opposite the table when Aleta asked him to hold her. He again squeezed onto the bench which was spacious for one but tight for two, especially when Aleta was cradling the baby.

He could feel her tremble and he balanced himself on the edge of the bench and embraced her. She laid her head under his chin and he could tell she was weeping.

"I'm so scared. I've never been so scared."

"You've been a target before."

"This time I have a baby."

"This time God had you hide. But why here?"

"Hush," she whispered.

The two Chessies rose and growled. The door handle was turned. The two humans crowded together and held their breath.

Keeper's growl was loud.

"Wait!" they heard a male voice say. "Did you hear that?"

"What?" questioned a second voice.

The door opened partway.

Both Keeper and Babe stood side by side at the level above the inside step. That put their heads at the height of the man's head as he turned to enter.

Huge growls rose from the throats of two Chesapeake Bay Retrievers, but the man's eyes stared straight into the gigantic bared teeth of a pair of angry dogs.

He froze in place, the blood draining from his face as if to escape the inevitable bite. It raced toward his heart which beat frantically to redistribute it. His eyes fixated on the teeth as his brain screamed at him to close the door.

Inside, neither Aleta nor Stanley moved a muscle. Stanley's grip which had tightened when he heard the voices, stayed firm and unyielding as if by holding his precious wife he could keep her safe.

The baby sucked on the bottle oblivious to the threat facing his parents. His quiet sucking noises were masked by the deep growling of the two dogs that stood between the young family and the strangers threatening to enter.

It was the fear generated by the people behind them that set the dogs teeth on edge. As the second man came around the half-opened door, and put his hand on its edge, Keeper decided that more of a warning was necessary.

Barking would have been the reaction of most dogs, but these two had never been rewarded for barking, only for growling. Still, Keeper felt compelled to do more.

She snarled as she moved in. When the man didn't move, she bit him in the face.

He howled in agony and fell back. Chessies, not being Bulldogs, didn't hang on. A bite was a bite.

Keeper snarled again as her jaws snapped a second time. This time the face was gone. Babe, however, zeroed in on the hand still holding the door open. Her teeth closed on the knuckles. Her powerful jaws crunched down and pulverized skin, tendons and bone. The howl of agony could be heard at ringside.

The hand was snapped back. A foot kicked the door shut.

"Let's get the hell out of here," one of the voices shouted.

"Damn dogs!" spat out his partner. A string of curses followed.

Neither Stanley nor Aleta moved although both began to breathe more normally, and Stanley's grip loosened. Neither spoke. The men were still outside.

"Look through the back window," the second man shouted. "Why didn't you wait?"

"My face is bleeding."

"Stop griping and do it!" the second man ordered. The words were forced out through gritted teeth.

"If they're in there, we're taking them out now!"

Stanley clutched his wife, drew in his leg and pulled Aleta back toward the wall. The kitchen counter shielded the baby from view.

The RV bounced slightly as the man scrambled onto the rear bumper.

"Anybody in there?" called a voice muted in pain.

"No. The place is empty except for the dogs at the door."

"Sure?" growled the leader.

"Come 'n look yourself," came the indignant response.

Stanley and Aleta felt the RV bounce again as the second man used the back bumper to climb up and peer through the back window and down the aisle way to the driver's seat. Stanley resisted the temptation to peek and held onto Aleta with a new fierceness.

Suddenly, the RV bounced and they knew both men were again on the ground.

"Someone's coming," they heard one man hiss. He was just outside the open kitchen window.

"I want them to pay!" the leader barked.

"They ain't here!" he shouted. "My face is burning. We gotta go!"

"You think my hand don't hurt like hell."

"We can come back," the second man pleaded.

"What're you waiting for?" snapped his exasperated companion.

Stanley and Aleta heard the footfall of two men running away.

Suddenly, they heard a strong male voice shout, "Police. Stop or I'll shoot."

The footsteps stopped.

"Hands up!" they heard a familiar voice order. Peter French was outside their RV.

"Stay still," Aleta whispered.

"Why?"

"Do it," she said softly.

Stanley did as he was bid.

"You should arrest them dogs," one man said. "They bit us."

"What dogs?" French asked.

"The ones in that RV," said the leader.

"And why did you go into that RV?"

"To look around," the leader said. "We was looking for somebody."

Stanley and Aleta heard Peter call for back-up.

"The rifle," Aleta said, pointing at the rack on the wall.

Stanley stood up and plucked the rifle from the rack. He opened it and shoved two shells into the breach and then clicked it shut.

"Don't move!" Peter ordered.

Gun pointing upward, Stanley opened the door.

"Stay," he hissed at the dogs. He crept down the two steps, shut the door quietly behind him and crept along the side of the RV.

He dropped to the ground and looked out from under the RV. He could see the two men slowly moving apart. He raised his rifle and as the one man reached behind him, Stanley shot once, hitting his elbow.

The man howled as the bullet penetrated. Peter aimed directly at the second man.

"By the barrel," he said. "Drop it."

The gun fell on the ground.

Stanley rolled over and got up, his rifle still pointing at the man he'd just shot.

"Thought you could use a bit of help," he said.

"So what do we have them on?"

"Attempted breaking and entering. Attempted murder. Resisting arrest. Attempted shooting of a police officer.

"We didn't do any of those things!" the man with one crushed hand and one arm hanging limply at his side.

"That's why I used the word 'attempted'," Stanley said. "Lieutenant French, you better read them their rights."

French began the litany. By the time he finished, both his fellow Arborville officers arrived and, at French's command, began searching both men. Two hidden guns were found.

"Quite an arsenal for people not planning to do anything," he noted.

"We ain't saying nothing. And we're charging them dogs with assault," the man with the torn face said.

"What dogs?" Peter asked.

"The two in that RV," said the torn-faced man pointing toward Harriet's RV.

Stanley turned around as he brushed himself off. Both Keeper and Babe were back in their outside pen. Harriet was putting Stoney in with them.

"That's him!" the man with the torn face shouted.

Harriet clipped the lead back onto Stoney's collar and walked toward the two men in police custody. "This dog?" she asked. "Are you sure?"

"I'm sure. He bit me in the face."

"And he bit me on the hand," said the other.

"Sorry," French said. "He'll need to be quarantined."

"Really," Harriet said smiling. "He has an alibi."

"An alibi?" French laughed.

"He made the cut in the Group ring," Harriet explained. "I have a couple dozen people who saw him with me for the last twenty minutes including Lyle who beat me out for fourth place."

"Then it was them other two," the torn-faced man shouted.

"Which one?" French asked.

"One of them. How do I know which one? They both look alike. Shoot 'em both."

"I'm not shooting a dog just because you think he looked like the dog that bit you."

"It's gotta be them!" the torn-faced man screeched.

"They're in the pen outside," French said.

"That's where I left them," Harriet put in.

"They were in the RV when I opened the door," the torn-faced man said. "And then one of them bit me in the face."

"He growled at you first," said Aleta walking up carrying the baby. "Why didn't you shut the door and leave?"

"He had big teeth."

"Why didn't you shut the door?"

"He had his hand on it."

"Me?" the man with the injured arms exploded, his pain driving his utterance to the guttural level. "It's my fault? You dumb ass! I told you to wait."

"You didn't say why?"

"You opened the damn door."

"You put your hand on it so's I couldn't close it."

"You weren't moving."

"Well, it's your own fault your hand got bit. That was dumb."

The man with the crushed hand grimaced as he ejaculated, "What a shithead!"

"Who were you looking for?" Aleta asked the man with the torn face.

"You know who."

"Why were you looking for me?"

"To talk to you."

"You didn't go to my RV. Why?"

"Oh, we went. You wasn't there. We looked."

"It was locked."

The torn-faced man laughed. "It ain't no more."

His partner scowled at him.

"What did you want to talk about?" Aleta said, still focused on the man with the shredded face.

The torn-faced man looked at his companion for the first time.

"Our boss wants you to lay off," said the man whose crushed hand was bombarding his brain with pain signals. "I need a doctor."

"Lay off what?" Aleta persisted.

"Get me a doctor!" he shouted furiously. "You can't question me. I got rights."

"I can question you," Aleta said coldly. "That's my right."

The man looked at the cop. "She can't, can she?"

"She's not a cop," French said. "She can ask questions."

"So what was the message?"

"To lay the hell off," he growled.

"The trade in women or the molesting of children?"

"We don't know nothing about no molesting," the torn-faced man said. "We don't touch kids."

Aleta mused aloud. "So it is the trade in women slaves I'm to lay off."

"You got it!" the torn-faced man said.

"Shut the hell up!" the other shouted. "Keep your damn mouth shut!"

"The cop said she could ask."

"We don't have to answer."

"Oh."

The ambulance pulled up quietly. Two police cars drew up beside it and local uniformed police exited their cars.

French showed them his badge and told them he was a member of a special police unit sent to guard a little girl. He produced the court order. He then explained what happened.

"Where are the dogs that bit them?"

Aleta pointed to the pen. "There."

"We have to take them in," the officer said.

"The dogs have had rabies shots," Aleta said.

"Animal Control still needs to quarantine them."

"Not if I can get a vet to certify that they don't have rabies," Aleta said.

"I don't know nothing about that," one officer said.

"I'm a lawyer. I do," Aleta said. "But here comes a police chief. He can tell you."

"What did these men do?" the officer asked as Lyle drew near.

"They confessed to two counts of breaking and entering," Aleta said. "Also, they should be charged with three counts of attempted murder, resisting arrest and an attempted assault on a police officer.

The paramedics loaded the two into the ambulance and French told his men to go with them.

One of the officers protested. "It's our case now."

"Are you going with them?"

"They're injured and unarmed."

"Until these two are in jail or under guard, my men will stay with them," Lyle said. "That attempted murder charge is too serious not to call for a serious response on your part."

Stanley spoke up. "I suggest you accept his offer of help or you will find your department embroiled in a lawsuit. I do not want these men to kill my wife. Am I clear?"

The two local officers glanced at each other.

"Tell your chief to call me if he has any questions," Lyle added.

The ambulance left with two Arborville officers inside.

"Stanley, hold the baby. I need to go."

"Go where," he asked. "Aleta, where are you going?"

"You can't go," one uniformed cop said.

"We need statements."

"It's almost time for Best in Show," Lyle said. "Explain it, French."

"He's a police captain!" the local cop protested.

"I don't understand it either," Peter French said, "but they'll be back. Meanwhile, you'll want to bag these guns and check out the lock on the RV. And you can get my statement and Harriet's...where did she go?"

"She took off after them others," one cop said.

"This Best whatever must be pretty important," the other put in.

Chapter 12

As Aleta came into view, Tom Wilson spotted her and hurried toward her. "Please say you'll take Toby in. My Afghan owner showed up. I have to take him in."

Aleta smiled. "That's why I'm here."

She turned to Stanley who was carrying the baby. "Do I look okay?"

"Beautiful as always."

She approached the Chinese couple holding the tan-colored dog.

"Fortune smiles on us today," the woman said.

"You are correct," Aleta replied. "I have the strength."

She walked into the ring with six other dogs. Even though she didn't recognize them, she sensed that they were all well-known handlers. Tom Wilson was at the head of the line with his fast moving Afghan. The German Shepherd lined up behind him. The English Setter and the Standard Schnauzer were both in front of her. Behind her were the Fox Terrier and the Pug.

The judge surveyed the group. All the dogs were familiar to him except for the Chinese Shar-Pei and all the handlers were familiar except for the young woman handling the Shar-Pei. He'd put up three of the dogs lined up before him and watched two more win under other judges. The Pug had taken multiple groups. He was definitely due for the top prize.

The judge moved the group around once. Smooth moving dogs, he assessed. Interesting that the Shar-Pei fit right in. He began his individual judging. The Afghan was flashy as usual and the judge looked at him for a long time. Tom Wilson was showing him beautifully. The judge relaxed. He had his winner.

The Setter and Shepherd put in flawless performances but Tom's hound outshone them both. The Schnauzer was slightly off. His had been the group judged just before Best in Show. Some dogs needed a respite.

He watched the young woman walk the Shar-Pei into a stack. Then she just stood there. Doesn't she know she's supposed to do something, he wondered. Every other handler had adjusted a foot. He looked back at the dog. He was in a perfect stack. She lucked out, he thought, as he approached to go over him. Good broad muzzle with a fold over the nose. He liked that. The sharp dark eyes stared seemingly unseeing until the judge realized they were focused on the woman who was whispering some words foreign to him. It sounded as if she were speaking Chinese.

The dog stood rock still as the judge examined him. He acts as if I'm paying homage to him, the judge thought. The little prick!

He smiled inwardly. He'd heard a tale from his friend about this woman. She will make you come alive again as a judge, he'd said.

The dog was everything a Shar-Pei should be. He'd heard a fellow judge telling the Group judge that he was a great specimen of the breed.

Aloof, the standard said. Regal.

Now why did those words pop into his head? Could it be that this handler knew not to touch him? Only a seasoned pro knew or a rank amateur did that. She was no rank amateur.

He had her move the dog and when she stopped and the dog halted one foot slightly turned, she backed him up and brought him in again. He heard her words this time. They weren't English. He looked down at the dog. The stack was perfect. She'd even kept the dip just behind the withers while showing the angulation in the rear legs.

He watched her move to the end and thought about her and the brown dog, full of skin folds, which stood like a monarch.

The Fox Terrier's liveliness almost seemed disrespectful in the wake of the Shar-Pei's sense of worth. The Pug was not his usual engaging self and the judge dismissed him from consideration.

He went over and looked at the Shar-Pei again. Then he walked to the front of the line and studied the Afghan.

They weren't alike. The Afghan was beautiful with a flowing coat and a confident bearing. The Shar-Pei was ugly in comparison yet there he stood, proud of who he was.

The other handlers knew which dogs the judge preferred but they kept working their dogs. Judges had been known to switch at the last minute.

Aleta knew she was being considered. It was all she wanted. She spoke softly to the dog in Chinese and he cocked his head slightly. She tipped her head the other way and he straightened out.

It was such a small thing, but it decided the fate of the two dogs. The king had bowed to the queen. Aleta saw the judge go over to the table, mark his book and pick up the giant rosette. He walked to the middle of the ring, his decision made.

"The Chinese Shar-Pei," he announced.

The clapping told him he'd made no enemies. Tom Wilson rushed over and hugged Aleta. The judge heard him thank her and wondered until he called the diminutive Chinese couple into the ring and told them they should be in one of the pictures. Then he realized the Shar-Pei was one of Wilson's string.

"It is proper?" the woman asked in Chinese.

Aleta answered her. "We will take two photos. One for you to send to magazines; one for you to frame and look at. It is proper."

"Thank you," the man said in English.

"You do speak Chinese," the judge said. "I thought that's what I heard."

"You spoke Chinese to the dog?" Tom queried.

Aleta laughed. "He's a Chinese Shar-Pei. Of course he understands Chinese. It does help that his mom speaks to him only in Chinese."

"I can never manage that," Tom groaned.

"He's bilingual," Aleta informed him tongue-in-cheek.

"Where'd you learn Chinese?" Tom asked.

"College roommate."

"I thought I had this one," Tom said.

"It was close," the judge admitted. "You and your dog never looked better."

"But you were intrigued by her," Tom said. "Don't worry. You've got company."

Later that night, Aleta snuggled next to Stanley and said, "I feel safe tonight."

"I so want you to give Emerita's case to a large law firm. We are too small and too vulnerable."

"And Nina?"

"We won't get killed over her."

"And if we prove Amend raped the two women?"

"We won't get killed over that."

"Someone should fight the evil."

"Weigh this case against the others. Those people are important too," Stanley said. "I'm not certain we are suppose to sacrifice ourselves on the altar of this one case."

"Can I pray about it?"

"When have I ever objected to that?"

"Never," she murmured. "Just hug me and hang on."

We're on a roller-coaster? Stanley asked silently as he held her in his arms and began to pray himself.

I don't know if you want to hear this, God, he prayed without uttering a sound, but I don't want her to die for an evil that will continue to thrive after she is dead. Men have always made slaves of men. But then you know that.

In fact, you know what my heart wants, but I'll ask it anyway. I want to keep Aleta. And I want her to honor You as she's been doing. I now understand why Jesus prayed for the cup to be passed from Him. His was a bitter death. And He prayed with a pure heart. And I pray with a sinful one. But, this world needs a love such as Aleta's. I need her love. Our child needs her love. I would not have been able to let my son make the sacrifice You asked of Yours. I don't want my wife to make such a sacrifice.

I know there are hundreds of thousands of people less blessed than me asking that a life be spared. But I'm asking for Aleta's life.

His mind wrestled with whether he could end his prayer with Jesus' words.

I can't do it, God, his heart said. I can't.

Aleta stirred in his arms and how precious she was to him enveloped him. How could he let her go? What if God took her? Would he denounce Him?"

Aleta kept saying that her ability to understand people's garbled speech was a temporary gift. While she had it she used it. When it was taken away, she was startled, but accepted it.

When she was given a new gift she was upset because it meant she had lost control of her thoughts.

And here he was trying to think of someway to control God. Trying to come up with some ploy that would persuade God to heed his cry and grant his prayer.

How ludicrous, he thought. He had no idea what challenges awaited them tomorrow. God knew. And He knew about the next day too.

Still he hung on wanting autonomy. He wanted to be master of his fate. He clung to the law because it was a system of reasonable rules the society of man chose to live by. He represented children because they were innocent and he could use the rules to help them.

Aleta wasn't like him. She waded in dangerous currents while he waded in still waters. He wanted to pull her over to his little pond where it was safe.

She wanted to be in charge of her words, yet that had been taken from her. She hadn't fully accepted that yet.

He found it easier to accept than she did, but that's because she was on the inside. It had happened to her.

God, I'm so tired. This is too much for me. I can't let go of my desire to spend my life with her.

It was the last thought he had before sleep overtook him.

Chapter 13

The baby woke at three and cried.

Both parents woke up.

"I'll go," Stanley said. "You sleep."

"Thanks," she murmured.

As he was pulling his arm from under her, she said, "He gave me the talent."

"Yes, I know," Stanley replied, sitting up and planting his feet on the floor.

"He protects me."

"Yes, He does," Stanley responded, rising. He bent over and kissed her cheek. "Whatever God decides, I'm okay with."

As he walked away, he wondered why he had said that. It was a lie.

"God, forgive me," he breathed.

He couldn't bring himself to try to explain away his words to God. How does one face God with anything but the truth?

"I don't know why I said that..." he began and stopped short.

He knew exactly why he'd said it. He wanted to soothe Aleta. He sensed she was still struggling with the proposition he put to her before they went to sleep. The words just came.

I wish they were true, he thought as he put the baby's bottle into a pan of hot water to warm. He rolled Gerard over and began changing him. The cries softened as the baby recognized he was being cared for.

When he was changed, Stanley picked him up and began to walk the floor, patting him gently.

"Aleta says you can drink it cold," he murmured in the tiny one's ear. "She says that would be like eating ice cream, but I don't agree. I think you need warm milk. Now if you agree with me, you have to learn a little patience. I'm preparing your bottle right now. Trust me. I love you."

As Stanley spoke the last words, it occurred to him that those would be the words God would say to him. Trust me. I love you.

He shifted the baby from his shoulder to his arms and the baby's crying ceased and he looked at him.

"I don't even think you see me clearly," Stanley said and then chuckled. He'd read the Bible when he was younger.

"The whole Bible?" Aleta had gasped when he told her. She'd skipped a couple of books in the Old Testament. Afterward when he occasionally referred to a passage during a conversation with others, she'd bragged about his accomplishment. It hadn't been a religious journey for him. He had just wanted to know what it said. His memory had retained much of what he read as it habitually did. The religious aspect had crept up on him after he fell in love with Aleta. Being married to a prophet jolted one out of complacency.

Now as he gazed into the eyes of his first born, he realized how much he wanted him to see and know his mother.

"I could never explain her," he whispered. "You need to experience her."

The baby gurgled and Stanley smiled at him. "So you want it halfway between warm and cold. What a little diplomat you are!"

He plucked the bottle from the water, dried it off and offered it to the baby. He'd asked Aleta why they didn't have a bottle warmer and she'd told him that she wasn't planning on bottle feeding the baby for one thing, and, if she did, she wasn't warming it. So he was stuck with sticking the bottle in a pan of hot water.

"You know," he had argued, "if we open a can and put it right into the bottle, it'd be room temperature."

He remembered her response. "Open a can with a baby in my arms. Don't be ridiculous."

"You could open it before..." he'd started but she'd cut him off. "We will have bottles ready in the refrigerator."

"Your mother sometimes makes decisions based on whether or not she's losing an argument," Stanley said as he offered his baby the lukewarm bottle.

Jocelyn who was asleep in the bunk over the driver's section, stirred.

"No more jabbering," he whispered.

As he sat cradling his baby, he thought about how the two of them had dashed around all day the day before handing the baby off continually. Must have been unsettling for you, he thought. Your world before birth was so contained and so safe.

Peaceful water, he thought, and now Gerard you're travelling down the river.

"Okay, God, I get the picture," he said aloud.

Jocelyn woke up. She raised her head and stared at Stanley. Suddenly, she rolled over and climbed down crying as she did so.

"We've got to do something!" she exclaimed, her voice panicky. "Mother and some men are loading Yudi into a trailer."

She grabbed her suitcase and opened it.

"When?" Stanley asked, not moving.

She pulled out a pair of jeans.

"Close your eyes," she ordered.

Stanley did as he was bid but he continued to talk. "Tell me what's going on?"

"Don't you understand? There's no one there to stop her but Bertha," Jocelyn rushed on. "Are your eyes still closed?"

"Yes," Stanley said. "When is this happening?"

"Bertha's in Dad's clothes. What is she doing in Dad's clothes? Where's Dad? Why is Bertha even there? It's Sunday morning. She goes to church on Sunday mornings."

"Today?" Stanley asked. "They are coming for the horse today?"

"What time is it?"

Stanley opened his eyes and looked at his watch. "3:20," he said.

"We can still make it," Jocelyn said moving over to him. "I'll hold the baby. You drive."

Stanley didn't move.

"Jocelyn, sit down. We aren't driving anywhere."

Jocelyn collapsed onto the floor. Her action startled Stanley. Then he realized she was sitting.

"I'm sitting," she announced as if he couldn't see that. "Now can we go save my horse?"

"We will save your horse," Stanley said.

Jocelyn began to rise, "Good!"

"...But," he continued, "We can't do it your way."

"She'll take him."

"She has the law on her side," Stanley explained. "She owns the horse. We are going to argue your right to him in court. It's the only way."

"But he'll be gone."

"Jocelyn, how much do you know?" Stanley asked. "Why is your mother shipping your horse?"

"Yeh, why?" Jocelyn said calming down. "It sure seemed real. But it was a dream, right? I mean, Dad wasn't there but Bertha was. And she was wearing his clothes. And what would Mother want with Yudi. She doesn't even like him."

"Why don't you go back to bed?" Stanley said. "We can talk in the morning."

"Please no," Jocelyn begged. "I don't know why I told you. Please don't tell Aleta."

"Okay," Stanley said. "I won't."

"Promise?"

"Yes."

"Can I trust you?"

"I keep my word. I won't tell your sister about your dream."

Jocelyn sighed with relief. "Thanks."

She climbed back into bed and pulled the covers around her and hugged her pillow. "It was a scary one though."

"Yes, it was," Stanley agreed.

The phone startled Bertha and Robert awake.

"Who?" she said, a bit frightened.

Robert got up. "You just stay there. I'll get it."

He traipsed down the hall, glanced at the clock and answered the phone.

"Stanley!" he exclaimed. "What's wrong?"

Bertha heard only one half of the conversation; but when she heard who it was, she slipped on the sweat outfit Robert had fashioned to fit for her and which he was pleased to find her wearing when he finally got home at five.

"Of course, you woke me. I'm not in a different time zone. It's 3:30 here too."

Bertha put on his slippers because she couldn't find hers and padded down the hall.

"What's she wearing? Is this a joke?" Robert asked irked.

Bertha stopped, her mouth agape. Stanley was asking that?

Robert answered him and Bertha was glad she'd put something on.

"She's got on a sweat outfit of mine and my slippers... What do you mean Jocelyn knew?"

Bertha, by now, was completely undone. She flushed and sat down in the chair Robert pulled out for her. He put his hand on her shoulder as he listened to Stanley.

He squeezed her shoulder and she looked up at him. He smiled at her and mouthed the words, "It's okay."

"Just a minute," she heard him say. "Bertha's upset."

"Jocelyn had a vision. This is what you were wearing."

Bertha giggled. "At least I was dressed."

Robert laughed at Stanley's next remark and commented, "No, she's not actually. It's me that's like Aleta. She just wants to please me."

Bertha looked up at him and smiled, he smiled back, but his attention was riveted on what Stanley was saying.

Suddenly, he asked her, "What time do you usually get up?"

"Five thirty."

He repeated the time and listened again. Finally he said, "I agree. We'll do that."

"Do what?" Bertha said when he hung up.

"Take Yudi over to Bessie Dobbins place. Make Hubbs a nice breakfast and a thermos of coffee. He's going to horse sit for a couple hours."

"Are you going to tell me what's going on?"

"Marian is coming for the horse this morning."

"Her visit yesterday..." Bertha began.

"Right," Robert said. "We have to hurry."

"Breakfast," she repeated. "And coffee."

Robert disappeared into the bedroom as Bertha began with the coffee. Her brain was a bit foggy and she was trying to think what kind of breakfast one could eat cold.

When Robert reappeared, the coffee was in the thermos and the aroma of sizzling bacon was filling the kitchen.

"I hope you made extra," Robert said snatching a piece from the paper towels she'd laid there to drain.

"I don't want to be here when your ex-wife gets here."

"Go get dressed then," Robert said.

"I can't wear my work uniform and everything else is at my house," she lamented.

"Come as you are. We're only going from one barn to another. We aren't going to visit anyone."

"You're sure?"

"That's why Hubbs is staying, so nobody has to worry about the horse until it's time to walk him to the horse ranch next door. It's too early to take him there directly."

"So we're just driving over and back."

"And settling the horse. We may have to clean the stall."

"I guess I'm dressed for that."

"I'd put on shoes," Robert said. "I'm going to wake Hubbs. We'll load Yudi and pick you up."

"Should we leave the house?"

"The two guards will be delighted to have something to guard."

"I should have made rolls."

"You made some yesterday. Warm them and the guards will be happy," Robert said. "Stop worrying. It's not as if she's an invited guest or even a desired guest."

"You're right, I guess."

Robert saw her worried expression and took her in his arms, "Bertha, she's coming to steal a horse. She doesn't expect rolls and coffee."

Bertha managed a small smile, before a frown reappeared. "I know I'm being silly but..."

"No buts. She and I aren't married. You and I are."

"Hubbs..."

"So we'll tell him. Who's he going to tell?" Robert said. "Besides he already suspects."

"How?"

"Your car never left the property."

"Oh."

With that, he kissed her, his hands ducking under her sweat shirt and stroking her back.

"Don't," she whispered, "or we'll never get away in time."

He broke off. "The getaway! I almost forgot. Don't change, please. We'll pick up where we left off when we get back."

The dawn was breaking when Hubbs and Robert unloaded Yudi at Bessie Dobbins place. Yudi had put up such a fuss loading that Hubbs suggested they load Sterling into the other stall in the trailer. Once Sterling was in place, Yudi walked right in.

When they arrived the barn lights were on and Bessie Dobbins emerged from the house with her new friend, Eunice Rivers. The two women watched them unload Sterling followed by Yudi and listened to the explanation.

They were surprised to see Bertha with them and insisted she join them for coffee and fresh rolls that Eunice had baked once she heard they were going to have visitors.

"I'm not really dressed," Bertha said. "We didn't want you to fuss."

"Fuss! Why not? This is exciting!" Bessie Dobbins cackled. "Is there any chance that they could stay on my property instead of being shut up in that smelly old barn next door?"

Eunice chuckled. "Bessie is putting the worst spin on it she can. The smell is just the smell of horses. Horses don't mind. Even Bessie doesn't mind. She wants to paint a horse in her pasture."

"Two would be better," Bessie said.

"Hubbs can't go back and forth," Bertha pointed out.

"Not much care when a horse is in a pasture. No stalls to muck out," Bessie argued.

"It might not be a bad idea. How about it, Hubbs?" Robert asked.

"Yudi would do okay if Sterling was here, but I'd wanna check on them."

"Can't," Robert said. "My ex-wife would follow you."

"I know horses," Bessie said. "And Hank is just over there if I need help."

"Well," Hubbs said, "Yudi would do better with just Sterling."

"We'll set the two of them up in the barn and Hubs will check the fence."

Bertha followed the two ladies into the house. When they entered the lighted kitchen, Bertha apologized again. "Robert's ex-wife was coming. I didn't want to be there."

"Why are you staying there with the Praetzels gone?" Bessie asked.

"Who says I'm staying there?"

The two women just looked at her. Bertha blushed.

"Sharing the honeymoon with Jocelyn move things up a bit," Eunice suggested.

"It did," Bertha admitted.

"It's okay," Bessie said. "We won't tell anyone."

"It's not as if you're not going to be married in a week," Eunice put in. "So you have your honeymoon first. Who can blame you?"

"Robert wouldn't do that," Bertha declared.

Bessie grinned. "I knew it! He married you, didn't he?"

"Judge Davis married us on Tuesday. Robert wanted... well we needed... we only figured on one night... You know to get the awkwardness out of the way and then Aleta and Stanley took off to the dog show."

"What about your wedding?" Eunice asked. "I was looking forward to it."

"We only had a civil ceremony. Robert says he wants a religious ceremony too, so we're still getting married on the first. Almost no one knows although Harriet guessed."

"She wasn't there?"

"We didn't want to tell Jocelyn."

"Anyone else."

"Hubbs guessed, so we told him on the way over."

"And now us," Bessie gloated.

"Chief Milani caught us too," Bertha said. "I'm not too good with secrets."

Bessie laughed. "I am so happy for you. I love Robert. He's such a gentleman. I'm so glad I was right about him."

"I'm not as much of a lady," Bertha admitted glad to have a couple of women to talk with. "I was ready to do it as Eunice here thought we had, but he said no. I was crushed. I was so ashamed of myself. He wasn't though. He loved me for it."

"This new outfit," Eunice asked. "His idea?"

"I wasn't packed. Aleta decided to go on Friday and they just left and there we were. And all we could think about was that we were alone. We didn't expect to be active."

"Or was it that you were too busy?" Eunice teased.

"I thought I'd give away our secret," Bertha said.

"To whom?"

"West has a guard on my house."

"And your not coming home at all—that doesn't clue anyone in?" Eunice joshed.

Crestfallen, Bertha reiterated, "I'm not much good at stuff like this."

Bessie reached over and patted her hand. "Bertha, you're good where it counts. Just look at the man you landed."

"I'm sorry," Eunice said. "I shouldn't have teased you. We wouldn't have even known if you weren't more concerned about Jocelyn's horse than yourself."

"And if you'd insisted on staying in the truck, we'd have been hurt," Bessie said. "You're always thinking of others. You only told us because you didn't want us to think badly of Robert."

"Tell us how the wedding plans are coming. Can we help?" Eunice asked.

"I've had to change them," Bertha said. "I will need help."

"Tell us," Bessie urged.

Aleta woke at seven thirty when the baby cried. She looked over at Stanley and said, "You want me to take this feeding?"

"Yes, please," he murmured.

"I have the answer," she said.

"I know. God told me," he murmured, burying his head in the pillow.

Aleta arose and went into the kitchen. She saw the pan sitting in the tiny sink. She didn't want to throw out the water. They were a long way from a place where they could empty their waste tank. She put the pan on the stove and taking a bottle from the refrigerator, stuck it in the pan and then turned on the burner.

Then she changed the baby and rocked him gently as she stood waiting for the water to heat up. He rooted around when his cheek touched her breast and she thought, why not try. He'd at least get a bit of suckling in.

She opened her pajama top and offered the baby her breast. He latched on happily and she could feel the pull deep inside. She'd heard that mothers loved this sharing of themselves and wished she could do it.

She stood watching the water in the pan and was reminded of the adage that a watched pot never boils. With her baby still sucking, she lowered herself into the nearby chair.

She wondered briefly why the baby kept sucking on a dry breast; still, she was glad he was happy. It would be a while before the water heated the bottle. She was content. She could wait.

When he finally let go of her nipple, he fussed. She stood up and looked inside the pan. The water wasn't boiling. Then she noticed the burner behind the one she'd set the pan on was red.

Even though Aleta planned to give the baby cold bottles, she refused to be defeated by the stove. She moved the pan to the back burner.

The baby continued to fuss as he rooted around searching for her nipple.

"Let's try the other side," she said, shifting him onto the other arm.

He latched onto her breast and began sucking anew.

Again she sat down. As she held him she wondered again at his enthusiasm. She felt the pull deep inside her breast.

"If I had any milk," she murmured, "you'd sure get a tummy full. But at least you can suck to your heart's content. It's better than a thumb any day and I don't mind.

She leaned back and thought about what Stanley had said. He'd talked to God. What did he mean he knew? She didn't know. When she said she had the answer, she meant the way to find out what God wanted her to do, not that she knew.

Why would God tell Stanley and not her? He didn't work that way, she reasoned and then chuckled deep inside her mind.

How ridiculous, she thought. Who knows what ways God chooses to impart his responses?

Well, at least, I can stop worrying, she concluded. He'd told Stanley.

The baby continued to suck vigorously and the water began to boil. Aleta let her mind wander into exploring the answer she was certain God had given.

She remembered what she'd said when Stanley rose to feed the baby in the middle of the night. He'd reply that he knew, but she could tell by his response that he was unhappy. Yet this morning he was content. What had changed?"

Did Stanley take her words and accept them? That made sense. God had given her the talent. He always wanted people to use the talent he gave them. He even wanted them to take risks. And He protected her. That is so far.

Suddenly, she was frightened. How did that thought get there? Wasn't going after the slave traders what He wanted?

She tensed and began to rise to pace the floor as she habitually did when she was worried.

The baby lost the nipple and cried. Aleta looked down. What was she doing?"

She sank back into the chair and let him find the nipple again. He latched on and began to suck. She could feel the sensation in her whole body. It was as if her body was telling her this is what she was made for.

Tears streamed down her face. They dropped on the baby's blanket and she let them flow.

Suddenly, quietly a thumb brushed them away.

"Why are you weeping?" Stanley asked.

"Because I want to nurse this baby and I can't."

"You are."

"I'm just letting him suck until his bottle is warm."

"You didn't hear the pan boil dry?"

"It didn't!" she cried. "I already put it on the wrong burner. How many mistakes can I make?"

"Gerard doesn't view this as a mistake."

"He likes to suck."

"Did you give him both breasts?"

"Yes, why?"

"Well, I'd say we should get through the entire morning of showing before you'll need to nurse him again," Stanley said taking the baby from her arms.

"What are you talking about?"

Stanley put the baby on his shoulder and patted him gently. The baby burped loudly.

"I'd recommend you burp him when you switch sides," he said smiling. "Your milk is in."

Aleta looked down at her breasts. "It can't be. They're empty."

"He took it all," Stanley told her.

"He got nothing," Aleta insisted.

"Well in four hours we'll give him more of your nothing."

"You mean I fed him?" Aleta asked completely overwhelmed.

"You didn't notice anything?" Stanley asked as he cradled the baby.

"I can't fight the slave traders. I need to feed Gerard."

"I do believe you'll have free time in between nursings."

"No, I mean I can't risk my life. It was a crazy way to get an answer," Aleta rushed on. "But I'm sure that's what it was."

"As you said last night, God will protect you."

"Not if I don't do what He wants."

"He gave you talents. I'm certain he wants you to use them."

"So am I," Aleta asserted. "So am I, but He wants to choose where I am to use them. I hadn't asked Him. He had to speak to me through you."

Stanley drew in a breath sharply.

"Through me? What did I say?"

"That I was sacrificing myself as if I were Joan of Arc, that I had people who needed my help and a family that needed me. I wasn't given all these responsibilities to shirk them. Emerita needs me to plead for her and to set her free. So does Teodora. They are only two, but they are people He cares about. Bringing the traders to justice is not my job.

Defending Ledgewood is my assignment. Fighting for Middlebourne's rights is my assignment. Make sure Jocelyn stays where she will be loved and can develop her gifts is my assignment and..."

Jocelyn broke in. "You told!"

"No, Jocelyn, I didn't."

"Then why am I on her list."

"Because I forgot what big ears you have. Now what was Stanley not suppose to tell me?"

Jocelyn eyed her brother-in-law skeptically, "You didn't tell?"

"I didn't tell your sister. I did tell your father."

Jocelyn tumbled out of bed.

"You're dressed?" Aleta noted, surprised.

But Jocelyn was too furious to respond. "That's as bad as my sister."

"Yudi has been moved."

"I told you it was only a dream!" she bellowed. "Why did you call him? Now he'll think I'm some wacko kid."

"Yudi is safe," Stanley repeated calmly. "Now your nightmares will stop."

"You had a nightmare?" Aleta asked. "Do you need to talk about it?"

"It was suppose to be forgotten, but big mouth here had to blab it to my father. "I'm never going to forgive you!" she fumed. "Never!"

Having said that she slipped on her Nikes and, without tying the laces, she stormed out of the RV, slamming the door behind her.

"Good thing she was dressed," Aleta joshed.

"Should I go after her?" Stanley asked.

"And do what? Apologize? You kept your word," Aleta replied. "She had a vision is my guess. Don't say anything. I'm not asking."

Chapter 14

"Am I going to show Scooby again?" Stanley asked.

"Do you want to do the whole thing?" Aleta asked. "I think I'd like sitting and holding the baby and watching you."

"You love to show," Stanley said.

"Scooby has a good chance today. This judge likes chocolates."

"All the more reason for you to show him," Stanley said.

"I'd rather you have the experience," Aleta reasoned. "There's a chance you could win."

"I'm not as good as you."

"Well, I would hope my years would count for something," Aleta commented wryly. "Stop worrying. Puppies don't have to act like adults. Beginners don't have to look like pros. Judges like both."

"Will you get dressed just in case?"

"In case you get cold feet?"

"Yeh. In case of that."

"Okay I can do that."

When they headed for the ring, Tom Wilson stopped them. "Who's showing Scooby today?"

"He is," Aleta said.

"We both are," Stanley corrected.

Aleta scowled at him. "You're showing him. You'll be fine."

"I have an Irish Wolfhound puppy in nine-to-twelve and I have a conflict. Labs will be done, but Frenchies won't be."

"What would you do if we weren't here?" Aleta asked.

"Grab Lauren or Lyle," Tom smiled. "But I saw you first."

"How can we resist such a proposal?" Aleta asked. "We'll be there."

When they walked on Stanley asked, "What do you mean 'we'?"

"Have you ever seen an Irish Wolfhound?"

"I guess. Why?"

"They're huge. You need the experience. I'd like to handle one, so we'll each take a crack at it."

"I don't know how to show one."

"It's a puppy, Stanley. You're a beginner. The combo is perfect."

"Suppose there's competition?"

"So?"

"I do better when there's not."

"You do fine when there is."

"I haven't watched these Wolfhound things being judged. I won't know what to do."

"Well, I wouldn't try to put him on a table."

"Don't tease me," Stanley retorted. "I'm being thrown into a race without having been taught how to swim."

"I'll tell you what," Aleta compromised. "If the dog needs to be stacked, I'll take him in. I don't expect you to know how to do that--yet."

"I gather I'm getting a lesson today."

"What else have we got to do? Scooby has the afternoon off. You can practice on him."

"I thought maybe we'd try to figure out how to tell whoever's ordering these hits that we got the message."

"That's taken care of."

"When did you do that?"

"When you were dressing."

"Who'd you call?"

"Dad and Justin."

"The reporter?"

"How many Justin's do we know?"

"What do you expect him to do?"

"Put our decision in the paper," Aleta said. "He's coming down to the show."

"Why?"

"To interview me. That's why I'm dressed."

"I should have known!" Stanley quipped.

Aleta change to a new topic.

"Dad says Yudi is settled at Bessie Dobbins place. Yudi insisted Sterling go along and Bessie offered them the pasture behind her place."

"That could be better," Stanley said his focus turned away from the interview. "I was worried she'd find Hank with a week to search, but now I hope she does. Hank will tell her that Yudi is scheduled to arrive on May 31st and he doesn't know where he is."

"Won't we have to tell her?"

"Yes, we will, but I'm hoping Robert will have a court order in place by Tuesday. My guess is that he and Bertha will avoid her until then."

"Do you have liver?" Aleta asked.

"What?"

"We're here," Aleta announced. "Put the chair here. I'll hold Scooby while you pick up your armband. You'll be the first dog in the ring."

"Just like yesterday?"

"Yes," Aleta said, sitting down with the baby cradled in her arms. He snuggled close to her and didn't waken. Lauren set her chair up next to Aleta and sat down. She didn't speak because Stanley had just entered the ring.

Together they watched Stanley take Scooby around the ring. The dog moved true and then came into a nice stack with good angulation apparent. He wiggled when the judge went over him, then turned to watch the man whose hands were moving down his back.   Stanley waved liver in Scooby's face when the judge took hold of the tail. The pup focused on the tidbit. The judge adjusted his rear legs and Scooby kept them where the judge had put them when Stanley whispered, 'stay'. When the judge handed Stanley his blue ribbon, Stanley thanked him for his help.

"You did very well," the judge returned.

Stanley left the ring smiling. He didn't join Lauren and Aleta, but stood on another side of the ring.

"What's he doing?" Lauren asked.

"Studying," Aleta said.

"You aren't taking Scooby into Winners'?"

"Not today. Why?"

"There's a major in bitches today. And the judge likes chocolate."

"I told Stanley he was taking him in. I can't take him back now."

"Do you know how hard it is to get a major on a chocolate?"

"I can tell from your tone it's very hard. But Scooby's a pup."

"How can you be so calm?"

"My milk came in this morning. And I took home the big one yesterday."

"You're on a hot streak."

"Well, Tom asked me to take in a Wolfhound, so it isn't as if I'm not showing at all."

"Tom never hands over a dog unless he's the only one in the class."

"You got it."

"Oh, Aleta, sometimes I don't understand you."

"You know how much fun you and Lyle have at shows," Aleta explained. "Well, I want to have the same with Stanley and I won't if I always go for the points."

"He's just a beginner. And there's a major at stake," Lauren protested.

"And Scooby's a puppy! Aleta reiterated. "He can fumble a bit with a pup and not look bad. Besides I'm feeling really good right now."

The two then watched the various adult classes.

"Why is there a major in bitches?" Aleta asked.

"The owner of a nice chocolate bitch only needs a major to finish. She's had everyone she knows enter. She built the major."

"Poor Minx. No Reserve for her today."

"Lyle's handling her," Lauren said. "Beatrice is in with her Scotties."

"Ed's here," Aleta observed.

"He's afraid he'll miss the class. Madge is helping Beatrice."

"Nathan's here."

"Ed needs support too."

"We're here," Aleta commented.

"Ed needs lots of support," Lauren said.

"Remember how scared we were when we showed our first dog."

"I threw up this morning," Lauren said.

"And you asked me why I gave Scooby to Stanley."

Lauren laughed.

Stanley entered Winners at the end of a line of six dogs. The Open classes were divided by color and there was a mature chocolate dog in the ring.

The judge came down the ring slowly and Stanley looked back at his dog and saw that the rear legs were slightly askew. He draped the lead over Scooby's shoulder and told him to stay and moved to the rear and set Scooby's back legs as the judge had done.

The judge noticed the movement and stopped his walk and stepped back and watched Stanley who once the legs were properly positioned moved back to the front of the dog and picked up the lead.

A titter from the audience told Stanley he'd made an error. The judge watched to see what he would do. His next moved surprised him even more. Stanley let go of the lead and stepped back and viewed his dog. He did it quickly and then satisfied that the dog was stacked well picked up the lead and reminded his pup to stay.

The judge finished his walk down the row and then went back to the open chocolate and moved him. He did the same with the open black dog. Then he had Stanley move Scooby. He told Stanley to bring his pup up behind the open black and then he put the open chocolate in front and had the three circle the ring.

When they stopped, no one touched his dog. Lauren and Aleta knew the judge had told the handlers to free stack their dogs. Aleta breathed a sigh of relief when she saw Stanley not attempt to straighten out Scooby. There was a lot she needed to tell him, she told herself.

The judge looked at each of his three choices again and then looked down the line. Then he said, "Take them all around."

"He's putting up the black," Lauren whispered as the dogs circled the ring one last time.

Stanley saw the finger point at him and then at the black in front of him. He knew what that meant. He went over and stood where the first place sign was and accepted the purple ribbon.

"An unusual way of stacking," the judge commented.

"My wife hasn't taught me the proper way yet," Stanley responded.

"When does she plan on doing that?"

"This afternoon."

"I'd have her do it before the Breed," the judge said.

"Yes Sir," Stanley replied.

He passed Lyle on his way out and was congratulated. But the man didn't say a word about his faux pas for which Stanley was grateful. He just said, "See you in Breed."

Stanley headed straight for Aleta. "The judge says you need to teach me how to properly stack him before the Breed."

"Grams will do it," Aleta said. "Gerard is sound asleep. I don't want to wake him."

Harriet laughed when she heard her assignment.

"Is it hard?" Stanley asked.

"It's tricky."

"Just teach me the back legs then."

The bitch classes took an hour. Stanley was back in time to see Lyle enter Winners with Minx. Ed barely contained his excitement. The small black bitch showed beautifully. Beatrice had done a lot of work with her. The judge had the whole group face front. He walked down behind the line comparing the rear, then back up doing the same comparison with the fronts. Lyle handled the changes smoothly while Stanley stood outside hoping he'd not have to do that and knowing deep down that he would. Major points were on the line. More dogs were involved. Every nuance counted with so many vying for the top prize. There were seven bitches in the line. It was practically a class by itself.

The judge pulled out three dogs again: the open chocolate, the open yellow and the six-to-nine puppy. He had those three circle the ring. The owner of the chocolate was standing outside the ring smiling. This judge rarely chose a yellow over a chocolate and the black was a puppy. Ed, on the other hand, was trembling. Stanley put his hand on the short, rotund man's shoulder.

"She looks great!" he said. "Just like Emma."

Those words relaxed Ed a bit. Beatrice had told him she was just a pup and not to expect a miracle. The three came into a free stack at the end of the run and the judge walked around them. While the handler moved the chocolate slightly as he was looking at her, the judge caught the fault he was trying to hide. Just to be sure, he moved the three up and back. This time he saw the fault. It was a common fault, one that frequently accompanied extreme rear end angulation. The bitch was slightly cow-hocked. The yellow bitch was every bit as good as the chocolate. He studied her face when she returned. She had a light eye. It was a minor fault but he didn't like it. The pup moved up and back with the same correct parallel movement he'd seen in the chocolate male pup. He wondered briefly if they were littermates. Her thick coat matched his as did her balance and thick otter tail. A lot of Labs were being bred without the hallmark of the breed and he was sorry to see that go. The tail was as important for a dog bred to swim as were the webbed feet.

Two pups, he thought. Still, she was black. And she was the best of the three today. She might not mature well, but today she was what he liked.

Minx took the major.

Stanley came over to Aleta. "I can't go against Lyle."

She smiled at him. "Lyle's taking in Morgan. Beatrice is taking in Minx. Now go get the major."

Her grandmother sat in the chair Lauren had vacated. "I'm surprised you aren't taking over."

"Grams, my milk came in. You have no idea how good I feel. I want to just sit here and hold him. Besides Stanley is fun to watch."

Harriet chuckled. "He is that. But he's upset that you threw him into a race without preparing him properly."

"I'm preparing him properly. I'm giving him experience with a pup under a judge who likes beginners."

"So you do know what you're doing."

"At this moment, yes. It would hurt him if I took over now. That's not worth the win."

Harriet put her arm around her granddaughter. "Am I ever going to get to hold him again?"

"We're showing a Wolfhound for Tom. You can hold Gerard the whole time."

"What's Stanley doing?"

"Taking him into the class. I'm taking him into Winners."

"You're tired from yesterday, aren't you?"

"A little," Aleta admitted. "And I don't want to lose my milk."

"Is nursing that important to you?"

"For some inexplicable reason, it is."

The dogs entered the ring and stood in a line, five champions, the winner's dog, winner's bitch and a veteran.

"What's Stanley doing?" Aleta whispered.

"I told him to adjust Scooby's back leg whether or not it needed it, so the judge would know he heeded his advice."

"It looks better."

"He has a good eye."

The judge examined the dogs one by one. The big black was handsome. He noticed the handler on him was the same person who had handled the puppy bitch. When he watched him move he saw the same movement she had.

The black dog stayed in his mind as he went over another black almost his equal with Tom Wilson on him and a chocolate male who didn't come up to the two blacks. The black bitch was nice, but the chocolate was outstanding. She had a dark eye, a sweet expression and that otter tail he loved.

He compared his two winners. The novice handler had done as he suggested and this time his positioning of the wayward back leg was expertly done. Someone was teaching him well. He wondered why they hadn't taught him the rudiments before he even stepped into the ring. Stacking was the first thing usually taught.

He moved his two winners. They moved alike. He was again reminded of the big black he'd looked at first.

He thought about his choices. He hankered to choose chocolate over blacks which he'd traditionally done. He looked at Scooby for a long time. His head reminded him of the big black's head. He pulled out the four. He was curious. All four handlers stood in front of their dogs and he found that consistency interesting. He moved them around together. Surprisingly the smaller chocolate champion bitch matched the larger black. The pups didn't have quite the reach of the two adults but they moved smoothly. He noticed that the novice handler didn't try to speed his dog up but kept him at his own pace.

Lauren's Holly took the Best of Breed, Lyle took Best Opposite with Morgan and sandwiched between the two was Scooby. The judge asked Stanley who sired his dog. Stanley pointed to Morgan.

The judge asked Lyle if the Winners Bitch was out of his dog as well and when he nodded, he said he certainly stamps his progeny.

"It was close between you and the breed winner," he said, "but when you moved, she kept up with your dog."

"Holly doesn't like to be beaten," Lyle said.

"She's not the mother of these two."

"She's the mother of the other black that was in the ring. Banner is also a Morgan son."

"He's a fine producer," the judge said and Lyle left the ring a happy man.

Chapter 15

Justin Conway arrived on the show grounds just as Labs had finished. He sought out Aleta and she told him he could set up anywhere he wished. He looked around.

"Can I do it here? I'd like the dogs showing in the background."

Aleta looked back. She saw her grandmother enter the ring with Babe.

"It'll be perfect," she said.

Aleta rose and walked ten feet from the ring. Aleta was taller than the average, but Justin bent slightly as he questioned her.

He asked her about the attack the night before. She talked about how she and Stanley had let her grandmother's Chessies protect them. She turned and waved toward the ring. "That's one of them in the ring now."

The cameraman zoomed in on Harriet and Babe as she moved Babe singularly around the ring.

Aleta pointed out Keeper standing beside Claude. Justin asked about the bigger dog.

"Stoney was in the Group competition at the time," Aleta said. "He's even more protective than the two girls."

Aleta spun a fascinating tale of the event and Justin followed up with the question he knew would be uppermost on his audience's mind.

"So what do you plan to do about the threat?" he asked.

"I intend to take it seriously," Aleta replied.

"Exactly how are you going to do that?" Justin asked vaguely aware that Aleta was leading him.

"I do not intend to pursue any investigation into the modern day trade in slaves. I'm going to let the press and law enforcement do that."

"You are abandoning these women?"

"Only insofar as going after the group that enslaved them," Aleta said. "I intend to fight for their right to become citizens and for the payment of back wages."

"Back wages? They were brutally treated, even raped."

"Nothing I can do can give them back what was taken from them. They were violated. They were innocents who suffered at the hands of evil men. I cannot restore their souls. I am not God. He told me that. What I can do is to be their lawyer and exact from their employers the wages due them."

"That seems like a weak response," Justin accused.

"It is," Aleta said. "But it's all I am prepared to do."

"I do not understand," Justin pressed.

"The battle against slavery goes on as it has since the time of Moses. God has not given me the directive He gave him. He is preparing others to fight this battle. He has told me not to."

"Are you saying God doesn't want you to fight evil?"

"He wants me to obey Him. That is His prime directive. The evil I see is too big for me to fight alone. I will die and then all the good I could do will die with me."

"You are predicting your own death?" Justin asked aghast.

"If I pursue these people at this time, I will die," Aleta said. "I chose to live at this time. That is God's plan for me. I will die if and when He asks me to."

Justin was stopped by Aleta's last statement, she smiled at him and said, "Thank you for coming."

Justin started and quickly finished off the interview by signing off.

The cameraman observed aloud, "The tape doesn't even need editing."

"You're right," Justin said. "Thanks again, Aleta. You are always good copy."

"I need this to get out today," Aleta said.

"I'll be able to make today's paper if I hurry. We should be able to get this on the TV noon news."

The cameraman interrupted. "The station will take it now as live feed. I told them it was breaking news."

"It's not that major," Aleta protested.

"It's that interesting," the cameraman said.

Chapter 16

When Stanley saw the Irish Wolfhound pup, he exclaimed, "He's no pup. He's a giant. A giant, scruffy, gangly dog."

Aleta laughed. "He's all of those, but he's beautiful."

"Where?"

"Everywhere," she said gazing at the huge animal with the rough wiry coat. And he likes me."

"All dogs like you."

"That's not a given," she argued. "Don't you want to take him in?"

"Aleta, I'm worn out. Can't I just hold Gerard?"

"Grams has Gerard. I promised her."

"Just one class, right?"

"I promise."

Stanley took the dog in and Aleta watched him begin to relate to the big dog as he showed him.

"He's just a puppy," he said when he exited the ring.

Aleta took the big pup in against the winner of the open class. It was a slightly smaller Wolfhound with a little less bone. Her pup didn't have as deep a chest as he would have as an adult but it was deep enough. What he had was a presence.

He took the points. There was only one bitch so Aleta wound up back in the ring for the breed competition almost before she'd caught her breath.

The woman handling the bitch whispered to her, "Slack off a bit will you. Share the points."

"Sorry," Aleta said and turned away.

The judge had everyone circle the ring and the woman started off before Aleta. That movement placed her between Aleta and the judge. Aleta turned her dog and trotted back a few paces.   Then she turned again and let her dog go. The big dog extended his front legs and clearly outreached every dog in the ring. When Aleta tried to reinsert herself into the line in her proper place, the woman crowded her. The judge was already going over the first champion, so Aleta did the unthinkable. She turned her dog around and stepped back. She bumped into the woman and apologized.

"Turn around," the woman hissed.

"Sorry," Aleta said. "But this direction is longer." Her voice while soft was distinct. The judge turned and stared at Aleta and the big dog that was facing the wrong way.   He motioned to the bitch owner to move her dog back and, when she did, Aleta turned her dog around.

Aleta took the Breed.

Tom rushed up to her when she left the ring. "You put major points on Tank. I knew you could do it."

"That woman was rude."

"Forget her," Tom said. "How about taking Tank into group?"

"Sure," Aleta said. "All I need is three days of sleep."

"Try three hours," Tom said. "Hounds are second to last group."

When Aleta arrived back at the camp, she found people crowded around a small portable TV.

"You made the news," Madge said. "So did Harriet's Chessies. Are you really in danger?"

"Not anymore," Aleta said.

While Stanley watched, Aleta entered the RV to change the baby. When she finished, she sat down and opening her blouse began to nurse him.

Jocelyn stomped up the stairs to the RV.

"You're on television," she raged. "What do you mean... what the hell are you doing?"

"Breast feeding."

"Does Mother know?"

Aleta laughed, but Jocelyn didn't see the humor in her query. She ranted on.

"You're at a dog show for Pete's sake. That's practically in public. You should bottle feed him when you're here."

Aleta picked the baby up and began to pat him.

"Good!" Jocelyn exclaimed, relieved. "You're done."

"I'm just burping him before I switch him."

"Oh God! No!" the sixteen-year-old bellowed.

"We can talk when I'm done," Aleta offered.

"You're doing this to gross me out!"

"I'm feeding Gerard because he's hungry," Aleta said calmly. "And if you don't like it you can leave."

"I'm not leaving!" Jocelyn declared. "You said on TV that you knew you'd die if you did something like free the slaves. Lincoln already did that! Why would you say such a crazy thing?

"Kevin thought Stanley was out of line when he called Dad about my dream. This is going to freak him out."

"You are not responsible for anything I say or do," Aleta said as she moved Gerard to her other breast.

"Stop doing that!" Jocelyn objected vociferously. "I know Mother would say it's wrong."

"I know it's not. Someday you'll understand."

"No, I won't!" Jocelyn declared. "And I want you to stop saying crazy stuff."

"What I said was true."

"I don't care. Just don't say it," Jocelyn demanded. "You aren't going to die. You always get saved at the last second."

"I'll remember your concern," Aleta said.

Jocelyn settled down markedly. "That's all I want really. Just for us not to seem like crazies."

"Stanley did believe your dream was a..."

Jocelyn broke in. "It wasn't. It was just a dream. Nothing else. And I want them to move Yudi back."

"He and Sterling are being models," Aleta said. "Bessie is painting them."

"She is?"

"She thinks they're beautiful," Aleta added, knowing that's how Jocelyn saw them.

"She's a famous painter, isn't she?"

"Pretty famous."

"I guess it wouldn't hurt for them to be models for a while," Jocelyn said. "I'll see you later. Good luck. You did win, didn't you?"

"Yes I won. So did Stanley. Scooby got his first major today," Aleta reported.

"Whatever that means," Jocelyn said. "I'm going to tell Kevin about my horse being a model."

"Just don't tell Mother."

"Why would I tell her?" Jocelyn said. "By the way, Kevin thought you were really lucky yesterday. He said you didn't do much."

"No, I didn't," Aleta said. "I had a good dog."

"You going to show that dog again?"

"Tom's going to show him today."

"You've got to do more," Jocelyn said. "That's what Kevin says."

"I'm showing an Irish Wolfhound in Group today," Aleta told her sister.

"We're going to watch. Tom is showing his Afghan. He wins most of the time."

"Yes, he does," Aleta agreed.

When Jocelyn left, Aleta looked down at Gerard.

"You're draining my contentious nature away," she murmured. "It's hard to be argumentative when I'm feeling so contented."

The baby continued nursing as if she hadn't spoken.

I'm just a milk bottle, she thought, leaning back. Why does that make me feel good?

Stanley found her asleep in the chair, the baby still at her breast sucking lightly. He removed the tiny one and laid him in the bassinet. Then he helped his wife to the small bedroom, removed her outer clothes, and laid her in bed as well.

Then he left to find Tom Wilson.

Chapter 17

Several hours later when the Hounds went into the Group ring, Jocelyn who was sitting at ringside with Kevin, exclaimed, "What's Stanley doing in the ring? Where's Aleta?"

"She flaked out," Kevin commented.

"Well, she's going to get a piece of my mind."

"I want to watch Tom," Kevin said.

"Did I ask you to come?" Jocelyn snapped, flouncing away.

The RV area was nearly empty when she entered. There was one of West's officers in plain clothes sitting in a chair by the pens. Jocelyn knew everyone was at ringside to watch Aleta. And she didn't come, so poor Stanley got roped in.

She was probably feeding that baby. There were bottles of formula in the refrigerator. There was no reason for her sister to opt out of her obligation.

The guard didn't stop Jocelyn. He knew who she was. She charged up the stairs and rushed headlong into the small interior of the one-bedroom house on wheels. She hesitated briefly when she saw the baby asleep in the bassinet.

So she wasn't feeding him. So what.

She stormed into the bedroom and shouted her vexation.

"You said you were going to show an Irish Wolfhound. Stanley took him in. Kevin said you flaked out. It's bad enough you say crazy things on television, but not to show up. Even I know that's the worst thing a handler can do. You have to be dead or something to have an excuse. And you're not, so you don't."

Even though half asleep, Aleta heard every word of her sister's tirade.

"Stanley's in the group ring?" she asked trying to wake up.

"Isn't that what I just said," Jocelyn said as Aleta reached for her clothes. "You don't need to bother getting dressed. You're too late. He was the first one in."

Aleta dressed silently as her sister continued to shower her with scorn.

Why had he let her sleep, she wondered.

Aleta looked at her blouse. It was mussed. Then she remembered she'd nursed the baby. She ripped off the blouse and reached for a fresh one.

"That looks terrible," Jocelyn said, so Aleta changed her skirt.

"Why do you care anyway?" Jocelyn said. "It's not as if you're going to be able to show anything."

"Thanks for waking me," Aleta said heading for the door. "Watch the baby."

"I will not!" Jocelyn declared.

"You woke me," Aleta said. "You made me change clothes. There is a reason. I need to go. Gerard is asleep. Watch him."

Jocelyn was taken aback. This was the old Aleta. When Aleta shut the door, Jocelyn looked in the bassinet.

"You just better stay asleep," she muttered.

As Aleta approached the ring, she noticed that Stanley and the Tank had made the cut.

She watched him move the big dog around the ring and was proud of how well he did. Her grandmother joined her.

"He didn't want to wake you and Tom told him he could do it."

"I'm so embarrassed," Aleta confessed. "Jocelyn is really angry. Kevin told her I was a flake."

Harriet put her arm around her granddaughter. "Tom understood. We gave him a choice: Lyle, me or Stanley. He picked Stanley."

"He likes Stanley."

"He sees real potential in Stanley."

"So do I."

"But you're in love with him."

Aleta smiled. "That I am."

Thrasher Curran, dressed casually in jeans and a tee shirt, sat down next to Kevin. "Your girlfriend told me her sister would be showing now."

Kevin responded without take his eye off the dogs in the ring.

"The bitch flaked out and Tom put some amateur on the Wolfhound."

"I assume you wanted that opportunity," Curran said smoothly, noticing with satisfaction that the kid beside him didn't look at him.

"I could've done a better job," Kevin bragged. "But Tom Wilson doesn't see that."

He scowled when the judge began separating the group.

"Damn!" he said. "The son of a bitch made the cut."

"That's bad?" Curran asked.

Kevin's scowl deepened. "He didn't do anything right. He should have been excused with the rest of the losers."

"Bet you wish your girlfriend was here," Curran mentioned slyly.

"Her? No. I don't want her to see this. I told her he was a dud as a handler and he makes the cut. I'm glad she went to their RV to yell at her sister."

Thrasher Curran slipped away as Kevin was muttering. "He can't place. He can't."

Curran passed the old woman talking with a much younger woman. He remembered getting a quick look at Aleta earlier. Jocelyn had pointed her out--a stunning redhead in a gold blouse and a dark rust colored skirt.

The two women were both in green. They looked like twins except for their ages.

Mother and daughter, he assumed as he hurried toward the RV's.

"I left Jocelyn with Gerard," Aleta said.

"Serves her right," her grandmother said. "You look ready to show. Are you?"

"Yes, I guess I am."

"Tom asked me to take in the Shar-Pei, but I'd rather not."

"Isn't he angry with me?"

"Aleta, don't you ever listen to the good things people say about you?"

"I figure Kevin was only repeating to Jocelyn what Tom said in the privacy of his own camp."

"Kevin is a twit!" Harriet declared.

"He has ears."

"Then offer your services as an apology," Harriet suggested.

Aleta nodded. "Good idea. Look! Stanley got fourth!"

"And Tom took first," Harriet said. "He's not going to be angry at all."

"Who took the Sporting Group?" Aleta asked.

"Your best friend."

"Lauren?"

"She was great!"

"How'd Stanley do?"

"A fourth. I'm pleased," Harriet said. "Tom took a third with Beatrice's Scottie. Madge made the cut with Rufus and Evelyn walked."

Tom rushed up. "Aleta, you're up. How are you feeling? Stanley was so worried."

"I'm sorry."

"I'm not. Stanley did a beautiful job and now I can ask you to take in the Shar-Pei. I know Harriet won't mind."

"I'm not certain I can repeat yesterday's win."

"I don't expect that. Besides I put two points on him today so his owners are satisfied. Just seeing you in the ring with him will be enough for them."

Aleta laughed. "I guess I can manage that."

Thurston Curran had a small backpack slung over his shoulder. He looked innocuous enough with his sandy-hair, matching moustache and large round glasses as he strolled toward the area where the RV's were clustered. He knew the aisle that led to the Praetzel RV but he chose to traverse the next row over.

The Tri City group had positioned their RV's in a semi circle with the dog pens clustered to one side under the shade of the row of trees bordering the RV area. Harriet's rig was closest to the pens and the guard sat next to the pens. It would appear to a casual observer that he was watching the dogs, almost all of whom were outside enjoying the warmth of the spring day under the dappled shade of freshly leafed trees. The Praetzels' RV was in his line of sight.

When Aleta left, the officer allowed himself to doze in the warmth of the afternoon sun. He counted on the barking if anyone approached. Thurston walked between the RV's one row over and saw the man dozing in the chair. The dogs would rouse him if he moved too close. He continued to the exit road and walked down it. It was a well frequented road and the dogs in the pens didn't consider it part of their territory.

Curran looked up and down the road. There was no traffic. There was one more day of showing. He raised his stun gun, aimed and, after taking several large steps, fired just as the dogs began barking.

The guard slumped in his chair.

Even though he withdrew, several of the dogs persisted in sounding the alarm. The RV door was flung open and Jocelyn shouted, "Quiet!"

Behind her the baby awoke and began to cry.

"Now, see what you've done," she shouted, ducking back inside.

The door latch, broken from the earlier break-in, didn't catch and the door hung ajar.

Back at the show ring, enlarged to handle the Groups, Aleta took her place in line with Toby. She spoke to him softly in Chinese and he wagged his tail.

"Tail wagging doesn't look regal," she whispered in English, then in Chinese added, "But I'm glad to see you too."

This switch in language caused a more vigorous response just as the judge was coming down the line. He paused and stared at the excited Shar-Pei to whom he'd given the Breed earlier.

He couldn't remember the woman, but two dogs further down, he saw Tom Wilson holding the lead of the French Bulldog, and then he understood.

His memory had told him when he saw Tom handling him earlier that it was the same Shar-Pei that had won Best in Show the day before and he'd wondered why the young woman wasn't on him during the class competition. Now he realized she was back.

He finished looking at the line. He'd judged most of the dogs in the two days of the show thus far. There were a

number of repeat group winners in the mix and half a dozen
handlers he owed a favor.   While it rarely happened, he
hoped for a few problems to winnow the number to four. He
only had four places he could award. But that didn't happen.

When it was Aleta's turn to present the Chinese Shar-
Pei, she walked the dog into a stack.   He was instantly
impressed.   She then stood like a rock and the dog, eyes
staring at her hand whose fingers were wiggling slightly,
presented a perfect profile. On his own. Naturally. He was
looking better than he had earlier.

When Tom presented the Frenchie, he remembered
how big a winner this small dog was. With his bat ears and
round eyes giving his face an inquisitive look, this small
cream colored dog demanded attention.

He couldn't give Tom two places. The other handlers
wouldn't like that. He pulled out all six plus Aleta. He sent
them around the ring and as he watched the Shar-Pei move,
he thought, he deserved that Best in Show. What kind of
message would I send if I didn't put him up?

Aleta and Toby won their second Group One. Tom
took second with the Frenchie. The Keeshond and the Lhasa
were third and fourth. While the handlers had made the final
cut, it was the dogs who won the ribbons in the judge's eyes.
He could defend his choices.

Thurston Curran fired his stun gun through the RV
door that was swung open by a whiff of breeze. Its firing
pushed those dogs who were watching him in joining the
others in sounding the alarm.

The cacophony of barking reached Jocelyn just as she
had removed the diaper and put it in the covered can. She
was relieved he hadn't soiled it.   She half-turned as she
reached for a clean diaper. At that moment the missile hit
her in the side. She dropped to the floor, the fresh diaper
clutched in her hand.

Curran waited a few moments for Aleta to come to her sister's aid.

That she didn't told him that she was either not in the RV or she was hiding. He opted for the latter. He stepped inside to check. The men the previous morning had been fooled.

He opened the bathroom door and then checked the bedroom. The rust and gold outfit lay on the bed.

Immediately, he knew she was the lady in green.

The baby cried and he rushed back and looked in the bassinet.

"You're naked!" he said.

As if in response, the tiny penis let go its load. The spray hit him full in the face.

Cursing, he jumped back; but he was too slow.

He heard the cacophony of barking coming from outside. He had to leave, but he couldn't leave dripping with urine.

He took off his shirt and looked at the tiny penis, he threw it on top of it. He held his glasses under the water faucet in the sink, wishing he could remove the fake moustache and wig, both urine splattered. He contented himself with splashing water on his face and dabbing his moustache with a towel. He patted his wig with the damp towel, but left it in place.

He stuck his gun back into his pack. When he went to shoulder it, he realized he needed a shirt, he hurried over to the drawers and dug through the contents and came up with a plain tee shirt. He pulled it on as he exited from the RV.

He ducked between a couple of RVs and exited onto the next row of the big rigs. The drawn gun pointing at him stopped him short. The man identified himself as a police officer.

"Hell!" Curran exclaimed, raising his hands. One hand gripped the handle of his knapsack.

"Drop it!" Lieutenant Peter French ordered.

"It has a camera in it. Can I set it down gently? Or I can hand it to you?"

"You and I know that isn't a camera. Now drop it or lose a hand," Peter stated.

The knapsack dropped to the ground.

"Now you do the same," Peter said.

"What's this all about?" Curran asked, dropping to his knees. "I haven't done anything."

French cuffed him, searched him, picked up the knapsack and lifted Curran to his feet and made him move back past the RV's. He pushed him into a sitting position beside the Praetzels' RV and went inside.

When French emerged, Joe reported, "Gary's alive. No blood."

"Stun gun," French surmised.

"Aren't you calling the chief?" Joe asked.

"The dogs have quieted. He knows things are okay."

"I think you should call him," Joe pressed.

"And distract him?" French asked.

"From what?"

"Guarding Aleta," French replied.

The Great Dane entered the ring followed by Tom Wilson on the Afghan. Next were the Collie and the Airedale Terrier. Then came Lauren and her chocolate champion Holly and Aleta with Toby. At the end of the line was a toy Poodle.

Lyle moved over toward Stanley and Harriet.

"French took care of it?" Stanley asked.

"I'm presuming he did," Lyle replied.

"What are their chances?" Stanley asked.

Harriet grinned. "Well if the judge has any penchant for beauty, the pair would catch his eye and keep him locked in."

Lyle and Stanley stared at her in disbelief. That they agreed with her had nothing to do with it.

Harriet moved over toward her husband. "Who are you betting on?"

"Is that a trick question?" Claude asked, knowing his wife's granddaughter was in the ring.

"I think the Dane has the best shot," Harriet said.

"Over the Collie?"

Harriet chuckled. "That answers my first question."

Inside the ring, Aleta had come to the same conclusion. The Dane or the Collie. One of those two were going up. Then it was Lauren's turn and Aleta marveled at how beautiful Holly was. Standing by herself, she was lovely.

When Aleta's turn came, the judge smiled at her. He'd seen her the day before in the Lab ring. He'd given Holly Best Opposite to Morgan. That didn't bode well for Holly, Aleta realized.

Her win the day before worked against her as well. But, she brushed that niggling thought from her mind and set about to show this judge what yesterday's judge saw.

She spoke to the dog in Chinese and the sound of the language of the judge's childhood stirred him. He smiled when he heard her tell the dog that kings weren't always tall and none of them were spotted. He knew she'd decided the Dane was her competition. It was almost a foregone conclusion that the Dane had a presence that wasn't easy to deny.

The judge looked at the tan-colored medium-sized Chinese Shar-Pei with renewed interest.

After going over the toy Poodle, he stood back and looked at his group. The Dane was indeed majestic. He stood out. He seemed the obvious winner. He looked at him for a long time. His handler kept him motionless.

The judge's eyes roamed down the line and stopped at the two brown dogs. He walked up to them for a closer look. The Shar-Pei remained aloof and almost disdainful. The chocolate Lab didn't. Her tail wagged furiously; her eyes lit up at the sight of a second familiar face; her brow wrinkled as if asking him why he didn't like her. He almost said I never put up chocolates.

Yet the day before he'd broken that tradition. And now he was being asked by this perfectly beautiful Lab being handled superbly by an owner why he wasn't going to chose her.

Was he going to tell her that he always gave a pro the Best in Show?

He left Holly and went straight to the table, picked up the Best in Show ribbon and walked down the line and handed it to Lauren.

"Your dog insisted it was hers," he said, smiling. "I never argue with a beautiful lady."

It took a couple of seconds for the crowd to respond. Then the roar was gratifyingly enthusiastic.

French called his chief when he heard the roar. "The baby is crying but he won't take his bottle. The two that were hit with stun guns aren't waking up. And I've arrested a man. When should I call the local police?"

"Don't feed the baby. Aleta is breast feeding him. Call the local police now. I'll bring a doctor with me."

Lyle walked into the ring and told Lauren that he needed the judge to come back to the camp as soon as the photo was taken.

Stanley overheard Lyle's request and questioned him. He said he didn't have much information, just that two had been stunned and they had the attacker in custody.

"You only had one man there," Stanley said. "Who else got shot?"

Lyle didn't answer the question directly. Instead he said,

"French is taking care of your baby. He needs Aleta to come feed him." Stanley rushed over to Harriet and told her that Jocelyn had been hurt.

"The baby?" Harriet asked.

"He's fine. He's hungry. Can we use your trailer?"

"Of course. I'll watch Jocelyn until she wakes up."

Stanley had planned to stay with Aleta but Aleta wanted updates on Jocelyn's condition.

"You didn't do anything wrong," he said as he left to check the second time.

"Tell her I'm sorry. I didn't know there was any danger."

Stanley smiled. "She might actually be glad to hear that."

Stanley entered the RV as the doctor was saying, "I'm a psychiatrist, so I don't practice much regular medicine, but I think it's her slight build. She's little more than a child."

"Can you do anything?" Stanley asked.

"Wait," the doctor replied.

"I'm not sure Aleta will handle that well," Stanley responded.

"Who's Aleta?"

"My wife. She's nursing our baby in her grandmother's RV."

"I'll talk with her if you think that would help."

"It might."

When they entered Harriet and Claude's RV, they found Aleta nursing surrounded by the Lithuanians. Nina was at Aleta's elbow watching the baby with fascination.

"I brought the doctor," Stanley said, "so you can ask about Jocelyn directly."

Aleta looked up and a surprise washed down her face. "You?"

"Judging is my hobby just as showing is yours."

"How's Jocelyn?"

"Alive. I think she'll wake a bit later than you'd like," Dr. Johnson replied.

"But you do think she'll wake up."

The puzzled looks on the faces of Teodora and Emerita caused Aleta to explain in Lithuanian what had happened.

Now it was Dr. Garren Johnson's turn to be surprised. "How many languages do you know?"

"I only know a bit of Chinese. My college roommate was Chinese."

"And this language?"

"Lithuanian," Aleta said without explaining.

"It was your speaking Chinese to your dog that made me look at the chocolate Lab again."

Aleta laughed delightedly. "You are full of surprises."

"My parents were missionaries to China when I was very young."

"You understood me?"

"Yes. And I was planning to pick the Dane, but I hate to be obvious."

"Why the Lab?"

"I refused to give her a place yesterday. I owed her."

"Well, I'd say you paid her back royally."

"She gave me such a look," Johnson mused. "I was being scolded in the Best in Show ring by a chocolate Lab with a good memory."

"Morgan does that to hunters who miss their shots," Aleta returned. "He's the big black Lab you did put up."

"I'm surprised he was beaten."

"Holly has done it a couple of times. She's almost the only one," Aleta rejoined moving the baby to her shoulder and burping him. "Mostly she does it under judges who like chocolates."

Without thinking, she turned Gerard around and offered him her other breast.

"Is that one chocolate?" Nina asked.

Aleta laughed. "We were talking about a brown dog that is colored like chocolate. Mother's milk is always white."

"Oh," said the little girl.

"Nina," Stanley said, "Come outside with me. We need to talk. Dr. Johnson, will you join us?"

His nod told the Lithuanian women to stay in the RV.

Aleta's concerned look matched that of both Lithuanian women.

"I'm a psychiatrist," Garren Johnson said. "Stanley asked me for a favor."

Aleta turned to the women and explained.

"I thought you were not my lawyer," Emerita said.

"You saw the news on TV?"

Both women nodded.

"Let me explain," Aleta said. She chose to do so in Lithuanian. When she finished both women were nodding, their relief obvious.

"We did not want to make big enemies," Emerita said in English.

Teodora nodded. "I will learn much English. I will be good citizen."

"Meanwhile, Mr. Ledgewood will teach you if you rent him a room and make him supper and pay him."

"Money go in circles," Emerita noted.

Aleta nodded then said in Lithuanian, "But that way, you will each know how much what you are bargaining with is worth."

Outside Stanley and Dr. Johnson took a couple of chairs to a spot under the trees behind the pens and Garren Johnson began talking with the little girl, occasionally jotting a note in a little notebook.

An hour later Nina rejoined her mother and Dr. Johnson told Stanley he'd write a report that night while his memory was still fresh.

"Submit your bill to me at the same time," Stanley said. "If I need you to testify..."

"I will do it," Dr. Garren Johnson stated unequivocally. "In fact, I plan to be in the Chicago area on Tuesday. I could be in court that day with little expense."

"Come," Stanley said. "I will get your testimony in."

"Your wife's nursing the baby was propitious," Dr. Johnson remarked. "It would have taken me much longer had my exchange with her not taken place. Should I put that in the report?"

"No," Stanley said.   "Let that come out in your testimony on the stand."

"You intend that the opposing council draw it out."

"You've testified before."

"Yes."

"So you know the judge weights facts brought out by opposing council a bit more heavily."

"I'm counting on it."

Chapter 18

Much earlier that day, Robert, Bertha and Hubbs arrived home after a hearty breakfast at Bessie Dobbin's home. Eunice Rivers was not only a nurse, but a cook and Bessie had invited her to make her visit permanent.

"I'm too old to marry," Bessie said which caused both Bertha and Robert to roar with laughter.

"Older than Martha Cook?" Robert asked. Martha had just wed Dr. Michael Taekman twenty years her junior. He was seventy.

"Older than Harriet?" Bertha put in. Harriet at seventy had just married Professor Claude Luther who was ten years her junior.

Bessie chuckled. "Well, I'm older than Harriet, but Martha has me beat, so I won't give that excuse anymore."

"Tell me, Mr. Hubbs," Robert said. "What would an older gentleman like yourself look for in a woman?"

"Same as you I guess--sex," Hubbs replied tersely.

The group exploded in laughter.

"That'll teach you to ask such questions," Bertha chided her new husband.

But Robert wasn't to be dissuaded from pursuing his quest. "Not good cooking?"

"I kin cook," he returned.

"Beans and soup?"

"More'n that," Hubbs said.

"Like what?"

"Bread. Biscuits. Pies."

Everyone stared at him, flabbergasted.

"We don't know you at all," Robert exclaimed.

"Nobody's what you think," Hubbs said. "I never would've put you two together."

"Robert surprised me too," Bertha said.

"Okay, Bessie, what do you want in a man?" Robert asked. "Don't worry, Eunice's next."

"I guess I'd want someone who wouldn't expect me to cook and didn't watch television all day."

"Oh, come on," Robert scolded good-naturedly. "That's what would turn you off. What would turn you on?"

"Someone who liked me, I guess."

"But what kind of man would you like?"

"I never thought about it," Bessie admitted, "but, I guess he'd have to have a farmer's heart, the eyes of an artist and the ears of a musician."

"Wow!" Robert said. "I don't think there is such a man.

"Sure there is," Bessie said. "Mr. Hubbs is that kind of man."

"The eyes of an artist?" Robert queried.

"He can see the lines of beauty I see in those two horses. He actually told me how to paint them."

"I didn't hear him," Robert confessed.

"I did," Bessie said.

"Okay, I'll give you that," Robert said. "But the ears of a musician?"

"He listens to the wind. The leaves in the trees sing to him," Bessie responded.

"Wow!" Robert exclaimed.

Bertha turned to Eunice, "What about you. What are you looking for?"

"A man like Robert, I guess," Eunice said.

Bertha chuckled. "We won't ask you any more questions. You'll give Robert a big head and he'll never marry me."

"Too late," Robert quipped.

Bessie and Eunice giggled.

"You told them!" he exclaimed.

"I'm not good with secrets," Bertha said.

"Then why can't I find out what kind of wedding we're going to have?"

"Because it's a secret."

"You seem to be able to keep that one just fine," Robert griped.

"Only because you're having so much fun trying to pry it out of me."

"Gotta get back to the other horses," Hubbs said.

"Maybe you could come over for supper the day after the wedding," Eunice said. "Bessie and I would love the company."

"I'll pick you up," Bessie said. "And you can come in your work clothes. I'll be in mine."

"Aleta would be relieved," Robert said.

"Then, okay," Mr. Hubbs said.

The three had returned the trailer to its spot behind the barn, Hubbs had let the horses out to pasture and was cleaning the stalls when Marian Locke showed up.

Bertha, dressed in her uniform, answered the door. Robert had received a call from each of the firm's new associates. Each had left a strange message on Stanley's answering machine.

Robert was on the phone with Roland Chin when the doorbell rang. Bertha had told him she'd deal with Marian.

Marian Locke eyed the dumpy woman standing in front of her. The maid's bra wasn't doing a decent job and Marian decided it was a cheap make.

Bertha read the woman's assessment, but remembered Robert's lesson and thought about Marian Locke naked. That made her smile.

Marian took her smile as a greeting appropriate for a woman obviously from a superior class.

"Is Robert here?" she asked imperviously.

"He's conducting business with Mr. Praetzel's new associates in Mr. Praetzel's absence."

"I wish to see him."

"I will tell him you are waiting," Bertha said starting to close the door.

"Wait!" Marian shouted. "I will wait inside."

"I'm sorry, Ma'am. I have orders to let no one into the house in Mr. and Mrs. Praetzel's absence."

"I'm her mother."

"I will tell Mr. Locke you wish to speak with him," Bertha said shutting the door in the woman's face.

She walked back to the study.

"You were right to dress, Bertha," Robert said. "Both of our new associates received threats this morning. I persuaded them to come here. I need to tell the guards to let them through."

"Marian is waiting outside."

"You didn't let her in?"

"Mrs. Praetzel only allows certain people in her house in her absence," Bertha replied.

Robert gathered her into his arms. "Bless you, Bertha!" He kissed her passionately and his hands lifted her blouse and encircled her back.

"We haven't time," she whispered.

"Chin and Jackson won't be here for at least thirty minutes."

"Marian?"

"She can wait."

"Not in here!" Bertha said.

"I can't wait."

Bertha giggled and Robert kissed her again. They didn't leave the study until they were finished.

When they were done, Robert said, "I know Marian treated you like shit. I'm hoping I erased some of her disdain."

Bertha smiled. "You are a good disdain remover."

"I'm sorry I'll be working most of the day."

"Don't worry, I'll cook up some more dishes for Stanley and Aleta," Bertha responded. Then with a twinkle in her eye she added, "That way I can legitimately wear an apron."

"You really think I'll burn up the rest of your clothes if you put on underwear?"

"I know you will," Bertha stated. "And I know exactly what to pack extra of for our honeymoon."

"I won't do it then!"

"I'm still taking no chances," Bertha rejoined.

Robert grinned at her. "You are fun."

"Marian is probably steaming by now," Bertha reminded him.

"You don't think she went to the barn?"

"She wants to rub your nose in it."

Robert looked at his watch. "I've got about ten minutes for her tirade."

"Just remember our last twenty minutes," Bertha suggested. "I'll bake your favorite pie while you're out there."

"Put on your apron. I'll need that pie."

"Start by telling the guard about Chin and Jackson," Bertha recommended as she walked out of the study with him.

She patted him on the rear as they parted and he turned and winked at her. "You'll pay for that."

"I'm counting on it," she responded gaily.

Robert opened the door.

"It's about time!" Marian shouted emerging from the truck. "That stupid servant shut the door in my face."

"Just a minute, Marian," Robert said turning to the police guard. He lowered his voice. "I'm expecting a Mr. Chin and a Mr. Jackson in a few minutes. They are new associates in the firm. Did you meet them yesterday?"

"No, Sir," the officer replied. "But I believe the officer on the gate did."

Robert turned back to his ex-wife.

"Do you know why I'm here?" Marian asked waving the driver toward the barn.

"No," Robert said calmly. "You know Aleta and Stanley are still away, don't you?"

"Yes!" Marian spit back. To Robert the word sounded like the hiss of a snake.

"I've come for my horse," she announced. She expected shock, dismay, utter confusion or even fury. What she didn't expect was what he did. He turned and walked toward the barn.

"Show me," he said striding swiftly away.

Marian trotted to catch up. "Don't play games with me. Just produce Yudi and I'll be on my way."

"We gave Yudi to Jocelyn. He was our gift to her," Robert replied. "I thought maybe you'd purchased the horse we're boarding."

"I have the ownership papers on Yudi. He's mine."

"Jocelyn considers him hers," her father countered.

"She can still ride him anytime she wants," Marian said, "but she'll have to do it in California."

"Yudi doesn't travel well," Robert said, ignoring the implied threat. "Another long trip could be disastrous for him."

"Jocelyn can fix him. If she can't, I'll buy her a better horse."

Robert decided to lay his cards on the table. Marian had changed his plans.

"Jocelyn already has a new horse. Aleta bought him for her," Robert said. "Aleta owns him."

"What about Yudi? She would never sell him."

"He's retired," Robert said. "In fact, he's not here."

"I see horses in the pasture," Marian said as they approached the fence.

Robert pointed to each and identified it, "The Appaloosa is Aleta's, the roan is Stanley's, and the old mare belongs to Mr. Hubbs, and the other two are show horses. That one is Jocelyn's new jumper."

"I don't believe you!" Marian declared. "Jocelyn would never switch horses. Where is Yudi?"

"At a friend's house."

"I want an address."

"Marian, what you're going to get is a court date," Robert said. "We'll appear in Juvenile Court ten o'clock on Wednesday morning."

"Juvenile Court?" Marian declared aghast. "I'm not a child."

"Jocelyn is," Robert said. "Our dispute affects her custody. It comes under the purview of the Juvenile Court system. Stanley is her attorney. And he has a case on Tuesday."

"She can't have a lawyer," Marian protested. "She's a child."

"Exactly why she needs one," Robert said.

"I'm not going through this charade. The horse belongs to me and I'm taking him," Marian declared. "Where is he?"

"I'm not telling you."

"I'll get a court order," Marian threatened.

"And I'll get a restraining order," her ex-husband countered.

"I have the ownership papers," Marian spat out.

"And I have the receipt showing I paid for the horse," Robert said.

"I will win," Marian said. "You paid for the horse with our money."

"She doesn't want to live with you," Robert said. "Don't do this."

"I won't let you have her. I have nobody."

"I'll fight you, Marian."

"With what?" she scoffed. "I have all the money."

"It's time for you to go, Marian," Robert said. "I'll see you in court Wednesday morning."

"I want to see Jocelyn before then," Marian said.

"She'll be back Monday night. She has school Tuesday. You can see her Tuesday night at my mother's house."

"I'll come here."

"No, you won't," Robert said.

"Don't tell me what I can do. I'll pick her up at school and..."

"You won't do that either," Robert said.

"You don't trust me?"

"Why should I?"

"How long is your honeymoon?"

"Ten days."

"I'll wait," Marian sneered and turned away.

Robert walked into the barn and talked with Mr. Hubbs until she had driven away. He told him Bertha was making apple pie for lunch. There would be two guests for dinner-- young lawyers who'd just joined the firm.

"I want you to meet them," he said.

"I'll come then," Mr. Hubbs said. "That witch ain't coming, is she?"

"No way!" Robert declared.

That evening, when Bertha and Robert were again alone, he repeated the entire conversation.

"So she doesn't know we're taking Jocelyn with us?"

"It would never occur to her."

"It would never occur to anyone."

"But we've had a honeymoon of sorts, haven't we?"

"It's been fun actually," Bertha said. "We've been together," Bertha paused, and then giggled, "in every way possible."

"It's been a bit chaotic."

"What's on your mind?"

"You do know I love you with all my heart."

"It's about Jocelyn," Bertha guessed. "You're afraid you're going to lose her."

"If Marian's lawyers are any good, they will win. Marian will be able to take Yudi back to California."

"Won't Marian be good to Jocelyn?"

"She will have robbed her of her right to choose. I won't be there to protect her. Jocelyn will have to conform to survive..." Robert hiccupped as he choked back his sobs.

Bertha put her arms around him and held him. "We should go see her tomorrow."

Robert was surprised at her suggestion.

"It's our last day alone," Robert pointed out.

"We'll leave early. I heard Aleta say that Labs show at eight o'clock. I've never been to a dog show. I would like to watch Aleta in the ring. You can talk to Jocelyn alone as much as you'd like. I'll have plenty of friends to talk with. Everyone's there."

"We won't be able to be together the way we like," Robert mentioned.

"We have tonight," Bertha said. "We can wear ourselves out if you want."

"We can't. We have to get up early."

"Then we'd better hurry and get the wearing out part done."

Chapter 19

Bertha and Robert arrived at the fairgrounds fifteen minutes before the rings opened. Both were tired and hungry. They'd overslept and had had just enough time to dress. At Robert's urging Bertha borrowed one of Aleta's beige pullover sweaters that she had worn during her pregnancy. The skirt from her uniform completed the ensemble. She complained she looked frumpy and Robert, knowing how sensitive she was, said not a word which turned out to be a mistake.

Finally, Robert was forced to comment. "Marian wouldn't be caught dead in such an outfit. She would have refused to go with me. That's why I'm no longer married to her. That's why I'm married to you. It doesn't matter what you wear, Bertha, the minute you begin speaking everyone forgets what you are wearing and basks in the warmth of your personality."

"Really?" Bertha queried softly.

The trip down had been pleasant after that comment. Now walking onto the grounds, the glow left from her new husband's comment faded fast. Robert put his arm around her waist. He leaned over and whispered, "I love you,

Bertha. Stop fretting. The dogs are being judged not the people."

He could tell she hadn't relaxed.

"For heavens sakes, Bertha. People here like Bulldogs. They like fat dogs that waddle. You fit right in."

That comment tickled Bertha's funny bone. She laughed and her moodiness disappeared.

"Isn't that Aleta with that huge gray dog?" Bertha asked.

"Where's Scooby?"

"That's Stanley standing next to her holding the baby," Bertha went on.

"Let's not tell her we're here until after," Robert suggested. "We can stand over there behind Jocelyn. Looks like she's picked up a boyfriend."

Aleta entered the ring with the big dog and seemingly did nothing but run around the ring with him and stand and hold him.

The two heard the boy standing next to Jocelyn say, "See, she doesn't really show dogs. His foot was out of place and she never straightened it. She wins because the dogs are good, not her."

Robert scowled. Bertha put her hand on his arm and he relaxed. She held his hand after that.

Aleta went in the ring again, this time against two more dogs. This time when she won, there was clapping.

Harriet spotted Robert standing behind his youngest daughter and Robert put his finger to his lips and his mother nodded.

"She won over two dogs," Jocelyn noted. "She must do something right."

"The judge liked her because she's pretty. Some men judges do that."

To her father's dismay, Jocelyn seemed to accept this twerp's opinion.

Aleta took the big gray dog in one more time. Neither Robert nor Bertha had any idea what was going on. Robert saw a man with a French Bulldog speak to his mother and saw her point to him. The man left immediately and walked toward him. He stopped near him and didn't speak.

Kevin, oblivious to the presence of the people around him, was intent on downgrading Jocelyn's sister. "I would not have hesitated before gaiting him. That was a mistake. She should have started out with the others and let the dog overlap them. She hid his best quality."

"Ah, Kevin, have you not yet learned why I give her my best dogs to show?"

Kevin turned startled. "Mr. Wilson, I was just telling Jocelyn what little mistake she made."

"It wasn't a mistake. It was a superb decision," Tom countered. "She knows Tank has more reach. To run up the tail of another dog only shows lack of courtesy. That Kevin is why she's in the ring with my dogs and not you. That and the fact that she is the best handler at the show."

"But she just let's the dogs show themselves."

"Yes, she does," Tom grinned. "I'm trying to figure out how she does that."

"She makes mistakes," Kevin insisted. "A few minutes ago she let the dog fall out of stack and didn't replace the foot."

"Where were the judge's eyes?" Tom asked.

"He was looking at the head," Jocelyn put in.

"If she had replaced the foot, she would have distracted the judge from the dog's best quality which is his head and pointed out a minor fault."

Robert had watched Jocelyn's smile grow as she listened. His daughter still had her eyes on her sister and when she won the breed clapped enthusiastically. Bertha clapped as well but Robert picked up his youngest daughter and hugged her.

She turned, "Dad!"

Robert held out a hand and introduced himself to Tom Wilson.

"We came down to watch Aleta show Scooby."

"She's been letting Stanley show him," Tom said. "She put points on him the first day. Stanley managed to put a major on him yesterday. It was quite a feat."

"I'm surprised she shared him," Robert said.

"She's been busy with the baby," Tom said. "She refuses to exhaust herself. Something about losing her ability to nurse him."

"Her milk's in?" Bertha asked.

"Bertha!" Jocelyn cried. "Don't even talk about it. It's so gross."

Bertha laughed. She put her arm around Jocelyn and led her away. The men watched the two in earnest conversation held at whisper level.

"We're going to be married this week," Robert said. "Jocelyn listens to Bertha."

"Kevin, go get the Shar-Pei."

"Can I?"

"No," Tom said.

"I can win with him."

"The owners want to see Aleta on him," Tom responded coolly. He turned to Robert and told him about the Best in Show. Then he told him about the second Group One. "That's pretty remarkable. There's no chance of a repeat, but it will be easier on me if Aleta loses today and not me."

"Does she know this?"

"She's smart. She knows the odds. However, I told her Stanley could handle him if she was too tired."

"Why not Kevin?"

"Stanley has more talent and while he's got a lot to learn, he is courteous. The judges like him. Kevin's a snob. I agreed to take him on a few junkets but I doubt I'll ever let him handle one of my dogs."

"Have you told him this?"

"That little lecture I gave, I've given before. He doesn't listen. I did it for your daughter's sake. The boy hasn't a clue."

Suddenly, Robert had his eldest daughter in his arms. "Dad! You're here! My milk's in! I won Best in Show Saturday!"

Tom chuckled. "Glad that got in there somewhere."

Robert hugged his eldest.

"Where's Bertha? You didn't divorce her already?"

"That would be quite a feat since we haven't tied the knot yet," her father replied, a caution embedded in his reply. "She's over there telling Jocelyn that nursing a baby isn't..."

"Gross," Aleta finished. "How come you're here?"

"I needed a rest."

"Dad!" Aleta exclaimed and Tom snickered.

"They're married," Aleta whispered.

Robert looked around. "Please."

Aleta defended herself. "I couldn't have him thinking the worst."

Robert smiled at Tom. "Aleta is deeply traditional."

"I won't say a word," Tom promised.

"The wedding is still Thursday," Robert said. "Jocelyn is coming on our honeymoon. She's afraid her mother will snatch her when I'm gone."

"What happened, Dad?"

"Your mother is going to get to take Yudi. We can't stop her. I'm here to tell Jocelyn. We argue the case Wednesday morning."

"Oh, Dad," Aleta murmured. "Is there nothing we can do?"

"Should I have Stanley take the Shar-Pei in?" Tom asked.

Aleta nodded.

The two joined Bertha and Jocelyn.

"Stanley's going to show a Chinese Shar-Pei," Aleta said. "Let's go watch him so he won't know anything's wrong."

"What's wrong?" Jocelyn asked as they began walking.

"That dream you had was a vision," her father said. "Bertha was wearing one of my sweat suits. Your mother came with a truck for Yudi."

"Don't worry," Bertha put in. "He's over at Bessie's place with..."

"I know," Jocelyn cut in. "But how could it be a vision. Part of it wasn't true."

"It was all true," Bertha said. "I was wearing your dad's sweat suit."

"Why?"

"I hadn't any casual clothes with me."

"With you? You have spare uniforms at the house in case the baby spits up on you."

"Well, he did," Bertha said. "And they were in the wash."

"That doesn't make sense. You would have gone home..."

The shaking heads stopped her. Without anyone realizing it, Aleta had led them past the Shar-Pei ring to the empty stables beyond.

"Why are you wearing Aleta's sweater?" Jocelyn asked as they halted between two sets of stables. "What's going on? No, don't tell me. You two decided to jump the gun."

"Sorta," her dad confessed. "We got married last Tuesday and when you all left for the show, we..."

"You went on your honeymoon without me?" Jocelyn charged.

The anger in the accusation stopped her father cold.

"We are getting married on Thursday as planned. The three of us are leaving on our planned honeymoon afterward."

"But it won't be real."

Bertha laughed. "Oh, it will be real. It'll just be the three of us. I won't be cooking for the new associates or catching up on the laundry or helping Hubbs and Robert load your horse into a trailer in the wee small hours of the morning. It'll be a real honeymoon. And the wedding will be real too. Aleta and Stanley had two weddings. Your grandmother and Claude had two. It's traditional."

"Grams and Claude had two?"

"Oops!" Bertha exclaimed.

"Why wasn't I told?" Jocelyn stormed. "Why am I the last one to know anything?"

"You're not," Bertha said. "You've been given several visions. You've been the first to know about things God knows are important to you."

"Why didn't he tell me about yesterday then?" she argued.

"What happened yesterday?" Robert asked.

"I was shot!" Jocelyn declared.

"With a stun gun," Aleta added.

"I was still shot."

"I told you before I only get visions about murder," Aleta sighed.

"It was important!" Jocelyn contended.

"I would never have left you if I had any inkling that was going to happen."

"Yes, you would have!"

"What were you doing when you were shot?" Bertha asked.

"Changing the baby," Jocelyn pouted.

"So Aleta left you with her most precious possession and you believe she knew about the danger coming?" Bertha asked.

Robert studied his daughter's face as it relaxed into acceptance. He would have just hammered her with those facts. He decided to follow Bertha's lead.

"Why do you think we're here, Jocelyn?" he asked.

"I dunno," she responded glumly.

"I had a strong urge to see you," Robert said. "Bertha decided we should act on it."

Jocelyn eyed her father warily.

"You didn't have a vision. We can't all be crazy."

"You aren't crazy," her father said. "Bertha believes in you totally. I'm only just beginning to appreciate what a wonderful person you are."

Bertha broke in. "Your mother and father are going to court to settle who owns Yudi."

"He's my horse. They gave him to me."

"Your mother is named as his owner." Bertha went on, "Your father believes the judge will give her the horse."

"Why does she want Yudi? She hates him."

"She doesn't want Yudi," Aleta explained. "She wants you."

"But I already chose to live with Dad."

"But the agreement allows for you to change your mind," Aleta explained.

"But I haven't."

"Mother is hoping you'll follow Yudi back to California."

"Back to California?" Jocelyn wailed. "The trip would destroy him."

"I told your mother that," Robert said. "She didn't believe me."

"We can't let her do that to Yudi," Jocelyn proclaimed. "We can't."

"You know Robert, Yudi travelled to Bessie's place just fine in Jocelyn's new horse trailer," Bertha offered.

"That's because we loaded him and gave him Sterling as company," Robert put in.

"So why not use our honeymoon to take Yudi to California and settle him into his new place. We can take Sterling along to keep Yudi company."

"Oh, Dad, can we do that?" Jocelyn pleaded. "Please. And we can be sure he's in a good place."

"You won't be able to leave Yudi," her father said. "I know you."

"What if I agreed to spend the summer with Mother?" Jocelyn asked.

"She wants full custody," her father replied sadly.

"I agree," Aleta said. "The horse is leverage. She'll threaten Yudi somehow. She'll take good care of him as long as you're there."

"Oh, Dad," Jocelyn cried. "What am I going to do?"

"I won't ask you to forsake your horse. He needs you."

"Robert, tell her you need her too," Bertha said. "She needs to know you love her. You aren't letting her go because you don't care. You gave up everything you had to have her in your life."

"Dad, she's right," Jocelyn said bowing her head.

Robert put his hands on Jocelyn's arms and waited until their eyes met before speaking.

"I have already been repaid twice over. These past six months with you have been worth every penny. You owe me nothing."

Stanley walked up. "I know this is important, but I wanted you to know it's almost time for Scooby to go in."

"We're done," Robert said. "I need to talk with you and Aleta later."

"Sure. After Scooby shows, we'll be free until after lunch," Stanley said.

"Then let's go," Robert said. "Come on, Jocelyn, let's us enjoy the show for a bit. We can talk more later. You need time to think."

Aleta fell in beside Bertha. "Did you have a quiet few days?"

"Don't I wish!" she exclaimed. "Your dad will fill you in later. There were developments. But we left everything in good shape. Did you know Hubbs can cook?"

"Beans and soup?"

"Think bread and pies."

"Really?" Aleta exclaimed. "Stanley, did you know Hubbs can cook?"

"He likes Bertha's cooking better," Stanley replied, falling back in step with Aleta and Bertha.

"Why didn't you tell me?"

"He'd rather tend horses."

"That's no reason."

Stanley smiled. "Oh yes, it is. You get ideas."

"Bessie already has those," Bertha laughed.

"Bessie?" The two listeners chorused.

"Your grandmother is waving at you," Bertha said. "She has Scooby."

Stanley hurried away.

Kevin joined Jocelyn and asked if he could talk to her alone. Her father let her go.

"About before," he started.

"My brother-in-law is showing his Lab," Jocelyn said. "I want to watch."

"He is a true clown," Kevin said. "What does he do for a living?"

"He's a children's lawyer."

"Can't make it in the big time, huh?"

"He's my lawyer."

"What do you need a lawyer for?"

"Custody."

"Just choose the parent with the most money," Kevin said. "That's easy."

"Custody of Yudi."

"Oh him? He's not your show horse, so what do you care what happens to him?"

"I love him."

"People that show can't afford such sentiment. Their places would be crowded with useless animals."

"Haven't you ever loved an animal enough to keep him no matter what?"

"Nope. And I never will."

A woman rushed up to Aleta. "I'd like you to take my Pug into group. You know him. He was in the Best in Show ring Saturday."

"He's a nice dog," Aleta said. "Your handler does a good job with him."

"You're better."

"No, I'm not," Aleta said. "Stick with the handler you've got. He'll win one of these days. He's an excellent Pug."

"Stupid move!" Kevin exclaimed. "She should've taken the dog."

"My sister doesn't make stupid moves. She's very smart. And you're just too stupid to see it."

"Whoa. Where'd that come from?"

"You spend too much time putting people down. I don't like it."

"Come on. Be honest. I'm only saying what you think."

"Maybe," Jocelyn said. "But I have the good sense not to say it. That way I won't get caught making stupid observations like you did."

That?" Kevin scoffed. "That was nothing. Tom puts me down all the time. It's an ego trip with him. He has to defend his choices."

Jocelyn eyed Kevin quizzically. "You really believe that, don't you?"

"Sure."

"Boy, you are clueless," Jocelyn commented. "Tom's trying to get your attention. Go see what he wants."

"Where?"

"Back there," she said.

"Jocelyn," Bertha said from behind, "Shame on you."

"He ruins things," Jocelyn said. "Dad, keep him off me."

"Me?" Robert laughed. "What makes you think he'll listen to me?"

"Please," she begged.

"Okay," Robert said, "only let me know if you have a change of heart."

"I want to spend the day with you and Mom."

Bertha and Robert exchanged glances. Bertha raised an eyebrow and Robert said, "You mean me and Bertha."

"That's what I said."

"You called her Mom."

"That's what Aleta calls her."

"Hey, guys, I'm standing right here," Bertha chuckled.

Jocelyn threw her arms around her, "I love you, Mom." Bertha hugged her back.

"There goes Stanley," she announced.

The three moved to the ring and watched Scooby gait and then pose. The judge went over him and looked at him a long time.

"That's good," Jocelyn whispered.

Stanley moved him up and back and the judge studied the pup when he returned for another moment.

Stanley glanced down at Scooby's feet but he didn't do more. He accepted the blue graciously. The judge made no comment.

Stanley and Aleta walked over to where her father was standing.

"Where's my mother going?" Robert asked Aleta.

"To get her dogs. Chessies are in after the Labs."

"Is Scooby done?"

"No. He has to go into Winners," Aleta said. "Grams wants to see that class."

"Who's in now?" Robert asked.

"The adult dog class. Scooby will go up against the winners of all the other classes," Jocelyn replied.

"There's a Bred-By competition today," Aleta added. "Scooby's sister will be in that class today."

"Does that have special points?"

"No points. Just prestige and a huge rosette to the Best Bred-By in every group as well as overall. Minx is good enough to be considered."

"No handlers, huh?" Jocelyn asked.

"Some handlers are also breeders," Aleta informed her sister. "But Beatrice is a super handler herself."

"Where's Gerard?" Robert asked.

"Sleeping. Evelyn is watching him. I had to promise to take in Topaz in exchange."

"Isn't that a lot of showing," Robert said. "Tom said you were showing the Irish Wolfhound later. You were really worn out when you came out of that ring."

"I'm also showing the Shar-Pei," Aleta said. "I wish I were showing some dog that doesn't run as fast as Topaz."

"Perhaps I can help?" came a male voice from behind. "My client approached you earlier to show my Pug."

Aleta turned. "I turned her down."

"She told me," he said smiling. "Name's Chuck Rigden."

Aleta extended her hand.

"Aleta Praetzel," she said. "I know who you are."

"Do you work for Tom Wilson?"

"No, I don't work for anyone except my husband. I'm a lawyer," Aleta said. "But you already know that."

"My client would like you to show her Pug."

"I have no chance of winning Best in Show. I might not even place in the Group. Besides I have a full load."

"I will take one of your dogs in exchange. Tom told me you just had a baby this month."

"Try this week," Aleta said gaily. "I don't have my strength back yet."

"Tom really wants you to take in the Wolfhound, but he owes me."

Topaz would be the hardest one to show," Aleta said. "But I did promise Evelyn."

"Evelyn Barnes?"

"You know her?"

"Never let anyone show any of her dogs until you came. Topaz is a beautiful Golden," Chuck said with a beguiling smile. "I'll take him in Breed and Group in exchange for you taking my Pug into Group."

"You've got a deal," Aleta decided.

"You don't need to check with your client?"

"She's not a client, she's a friend," Aleta said. "I'm not paid."

"I'm willing to pay," Chuck said.

"I only show for friends and Tom Wilson because he's a friend."

"Can I be one?"

"Well, you helped me out of a jam, so I guess we're on a friendly footing," Aleta said.

"You are indeed a lawyer," Chuck observed.

"By the way," Aleta said, "I always go for the win."

"Tom told me," Chuck said. "I expect that from anyone I hand a dog over to."

Aleta turned to her husband.

"Stanley, how did it go with the Shar-Pei?"

Stanley grinned. "Finally, I get the question."

"I could tell you took the Breed from the smile on your face," Aleta said. "And you put a point on the dog. What don't I know?"

"I put two points on him. Another dog was entered but didn't make it into the catalog. The superintendent straightened it out this morning."

"I bet the owners were thrilled," Aleta remarked.

"I was thanked in both English and Chinese. At least I think that's what she was doing."

"So, will you take him into group?"

"I'm not sure that's wise."

"I am. But ask Tom. They're his clients."

"You need to reteach me those words. Toby raised his eyebrows as if I was speaking a foreign language."

"How could you tell? His face is a mass of wrinkles."

"I could tell," Stanley declared annoyed.

Chapter 20

Thurston Curran never made it to the local jail.

He started by telling the cop driving him that he wasn't a killer.

"I just bought the damn thing and I wanted to try it out and this door was open and that chick was standing there and I just shot."

"What about the cop?"

"Don't know about him. I didn't touch him. I think he was passed out drunk and those out-of-town guys didn't want to admit he was soused."

"The judge will sort it all out," the cop retorted.

"You don't recognize me?" Curran asked. "I usually have trouble going anywhere because I'm always recognized right away."

Curran saw the cop's eyes flick to the rear view mirror.

"Look, that's why I gotta make a phone call before we get to the police station."

"You can wait."

"Ever see one of these?" Curran said, holding a five-hundred dollar bill against the glass.

The cop was so surprised at the denomination, he didn't think about Curran's wrists being cuffed in front instead of behind the man's back.

"There's a phone booth," Curran said. "Look, the bill's yours for one phone call. I'm cuffed, unarmed and you've got a gun. And I'll bet you're a good shot too."

"You better believe it."

"So, how about it? Two minutes of your time. That's all for five hundred bucks and I'm not even asking you to do anything illegal. I sat outside that RV for over an hour and never moved. I don't want any trouble."

The cop drew up next to the outside phone booth.

"You give me the number and I'll call it," the cop said.

Curran spat out an out of town number.

The cop objected. "That's long distance."

"It's my lawyer. Look you got five hundred bucks on the line. Go into the gas station and get change. I'm not going anywhere."

The cop dug into his pants pocket. "I got a calling card."

"Five hundred bucks," Curran repeated.

The voice that answered said, "Legal services."

"Just a minute," the cop said opening the car door. He had his gun out.

"Okay you got a minute," he said.

"That's all I need," Curran said. He stood up, hands no longer cuffed, deftly plucked the gun from the cop's fingers and stuck it in his ribs.

"We're taking a ride. First open the trunk. I want my knapsack."

The cop was found unconscious, his car in a ditch just past the fairgrounds. He was taken to the hospital.

No report was made to the out-of-state police until mid morning the next day.

Lieutenant Peter French fielded the call.

"We have an APB out on the man. We've searched the fairgrounds. He's left town," the local police captain reported. "He's long gone. There's nothing more we can do."

Peter held his tongue. Lyle had admonished him to play it cool when dealing with local police.

"We're in their territory," he'd said. "Keep your criticism to yourself no matter what happens."

French, however, could barely contain himself. He left the RV area and sought out his chief.

He met Aleta heading toward the RV area and asked her if it was over.

"I need to relieve Evelyn," she said. "She has to get herself and her dogs ready. Stanley took the points with Scooby. Beatrice won her class with Scooby's sister. They're judging the Open Yellow bitch class now. You're in time to see Lyle compete. He has a good chance today. This judge likes blacks."

"I'll walk you back first," French said turning around. It's what his chief would want him to do he knew.

"What's up?" Aleta asked her suspicions aroused.

"Nothing," he said. "I just remembered something the chief told me that I forgot to do."

"Oh," Aleta said softly, accepting his explanation. "You're going to show Evelyn's dog, aren't you?"

"Not any more. I exchanged dogs. I hope Evelyn understands. I did get her one of the best handlers on the circuit to take in Topaz."

"So how many dogs re you showing this afternoon?"

"Two. An Irish Wolfhound and a Pug. Talk about extremes."

"What happened to the Chinese dog?"

"Stanley's going to take him in."

"What if Scooby wins?"

"Against his father? Never! If Morgan breaks a leg, Banner will take it."

Aleta noticed Peter's smile and chalked it up to the man's pride in his chief.

"So are you going back to watch?" Peter French asked.

"Not today. I need to nurse the baby and rest. It's going to be a long afternoon."

"I'll be around if you need anything."

"You don't need to stay on my account."

"I thought the men might enjoy seeing the chief in the ring. I'll catch him in the Group later."

"Good plan," Aleta said as she entered her RV and found Evelyn changing the baby.

"He's been sleeping until just a few minutes ago."

"I traded dogs today. I'm dead tired so Chuck Rigden is taking Topaz into Breed and Groups."

"I was going to tell you not to worry about it. I wasn't going to hold you to your promise," Evelyn said. "So what kind of trade did you make?"

"I'm taking his Pug into Group," Aleta told her and then elaborated.

"The owner will expect you to take him all the way."

"I don't see a problem. Tom will take in the Wolfhound if he wins. And Stanley will stay on the Shar-Pei."

"You did think things through," Evelyn marveled. "Well, I wish Topaz would be in there too, but he's beginning to slow down a bit."

Aleta picked up the baby. "Let's give you your lunch."

Evelyn slipped away as Aleta settled in the chair and opened her blouse.

Thurston Curran, who'd been at the show all day, had picked up not only a bit of the lingo but also the order of events.

He saw her leave ringside alone and decided to follow her. When she was met by Peter French, he turned off and went to his car.

He took out his rifle and a large tarp and carried the two under his arm into the RV section. No one even gave him a second look, mostly because everyone had tarps and the rifle was buried in its folds.

He moved past the last row of RV's and walked to the last one in the line. He remembered that it had a ladder that gave access to its roof top. There were actually three such RVs, but he opted for the one at the end of the line. From there he would have a clear shot into the heart of the group when they gathered for lunch and afterward at anyone who left to take a dog from a pen or walked toward the rings.

It didn't matter when Aleta showed. He'd be ready.

He waited until the occupants of the RV had taken their dogs to the ring and then climbed up the ladder, pulled the tarp around himself and laid down.

He loaded his rifle and peered through the site at the various locations. He found the best ones and actually followed the cop that nabbed him yesterday as he moved around the area encompassed by the RV's of the group he was with.

He knew his target had gone to her trailer. He remembered the baby from yesterday. He was a tiny one. He would need to be fed often.

Curran remembered that Aleta Praetzel was breast feeding her infant son. He was certain that's what she had come back to do.

Even if she had come and gone when he went for his rifle, she'd be back soon. All he had to do was wait.

He pulled the tarp over his head and peeked out from a slit near the bottom. He lay still and watched.

Bertha was the first of the group to leave the ringside. She told Stanley she would check on Aleta. So he didn't rush back.

Ed wanted a picture of Scooby and Minx together as both had taken their respective Winners Classes and earned two points. Scooby had won Best of Winners and Minx had won Best Bred-By, so each had a rosette.

Morgan had taken the breed, so Lyle wanted a photo with Morgan and his two offspring. It would make good copy for the National catalog.

The others lingered enjoying the success of their friends. Then the Goldens went in and they stayed to watch Evelyn's dogs.

Stanley, Lyle and Lauren took the Labs back to their pens and Stanley entered the RV to check on Aleta. He found Bertha changing the baby while his wife lay in bed sound asleep.

"Did she fall asleep nursing him?" he asked.

Instead of replying, Bertha had a question of her own.

"Does she do that regularly?"

"Frequently. Nursing seems to relax her."

"Then she'll need someone with her," Bertha said. "I can't believe she'll roll over on him, but if she's in a chair he could slip out of her arms."

"Any safeguards we can take?"

Bertha smiled at him. "Stay with her until she's done and take the baby."

"I'll have to do all the diaper changing then," Stanley groaned.

"Except when I'm around," Bertha said.

"Now is a poor time for you to go on a honeymoon, you realize."

"How much breakfast did she have?"

"None."

"We have to wake her for lunch. She must eat."

"We'll wake her when the food's ready," Stanley said. "And since both are sleeping maybe now's a good time for you and Robert to bring me up-to-date."

"Robert is with Jocelyn. I can fill you in a little. It seems your two new associates were threatened Sunday morning.   They were afraid to show up at the office so they've been working at your house ever since."

"Sunday morning, huh.   That was before Aleta's television interview."

"Is that important?"

"Did Robert receive a threat?"

"No."

"It would seem that Aleta was believed," Stanley said. "I need to talk with Lyle."

"I'll be here. I don't think the baby's cry will wake Aleta."

"Go back to the show. Lyle is right outside, so I'll be nearby."

Stanley scooped a cupful of dry kibble in a pan and went outside to feed Scooby.

Lyle walked over. "Everything okay?"

"Our new assistants were threatened Sunday before Aleta's interview."

"All quiet since then?"

"I'm sure they know that they're working out of the house, but no more threats."

"Sounds like Aleta was believed."

"But the attack yesterday afternoon?"

"Was after," Lyle mused. "Well, contract killers don't communicate. They take their money up front and they carry out their assignment. But, he's in jail."

"I heard your conversation, Sir," French said. "I was waiting to speak with you."

"It's okay French," Lyle said. "You heard something?"

"He never made it to jail."

"How did he escape?"

"The officer said something about being persuaded to stop and let him make a phone call."

"So he's loose?" Stanley questioned apprehensively.

"Is he in the area?"

"The captain says no."

"So that's why his men were all over the place this morning," Lyle concluded. "Well, French, we do our own search. Stanley and I will watch the camp."

He turned to Stanley. "Where's your gun?"

"In the RV, under the mattress."

"Does Aleta know it's there?"

"No."

"Wear it until you show."

"You think he's around?"

"Oh, yeh. He's around," Lyle said. "We keep Aleta in that RV."

"She shows in Group this afternoon."

"Which Groups?"

"Hound and Toy."

"Who's showing the Shar-Pei?"

"I am."

"And I gather she's not showing Topaz."

"She exchanged Evelyn's Golden for the Pug in Chuck Rigden's string."

"Evelyn didn't lose on that deal," Lyle commented.

"Have we met him in the ring?"

"He was on the Dane yesterday; the Pug the day before," Lyle replied. "He wins about as often as Tom Wilson."

"Aleta won't renege on her promise."

"You could order her."

"No, I can't," Stanley said.

"I don't understand."

"And I can't explain, but she's always in some kind of danger. I don't dare interfere. I might put her in danger without realizing it. I need to trust God."

"You've never said that before."

"I haven't, have I?" Stanley remarked evenly.

"In fact, I remember when you did interfere."

"That was a real situation. This is a possible danger."

"A possible danger that my experience tells me is real," Lyle argued.

"She'll listen to Harriet," Stanley offered.

"I'll talk with her at lunch. But Aleta eats lunch inside today."

"No problem. She socialized all morning," Stanley stated. "Only we don't scare Aleta."

"Or Lauren," Lyle said. "So far she thinks the danger is over and so she's not worrying about me."

"And you want to take Morgan into Group."

"The Group judge is the one who gave him the Breed today."

"He gave Stoney the Breed too," Stanley pointed out.

"So Aleta will be at ringside to watch her grandmother."

"Better catch your man before then."

Thurston Curran began to sweat under the tarp. The sun beat down on the metal roof of the RV and even the metal in the shade beneath him began to heat up.

The fire in the barbeque was lit by the police chief and the husband who'd stayed at the camp while the rest of the cops scattered. He assumed that they had finally been told he'd escaped.

He was glad he was hidden on the roof. These cops had gotten a good look at him yesterday. The locals hadn't which is why he could roam the show grounds freely. He'd discarded the glasses which gave him an owl-like look and the moustache. Today he was clean-shaven. He'd also lost the sandy colored wig and was sporting his darkened thinning natural hair. Today people were being scrutinized closely. A disguise might not pass muster.

He was doubly pleased he'd decided not to wear one as the sweat poured down his forehead. A wig would have been unbearably hot.

He wiped his brow with his sleeve and watched the people straggle back from the show rings. The meat was already on the fire. Steaks. His mouth watered.

He watched the women enter the RV's and come out with bowls of potato salad, macaroni salad, greens, fruit salad and biscuits. Pies appeared on the table as well. A large chest was opened. It was filled with cans of soft drinks buried in melting ice.

Hungry as he was, the sight of the cold drinks made him rue the plan he'd chosen.

The people on top of whose RV he was laying disappeared inside and fumes from their cooking rose up the vent near his nose.

He wasn't waiting. The minute Aleta appeared she was dead. His car was parked on the road nearby with its hood up. It would be left alone.

Stanley entered the RV with a plate of food and woke his wife.

"Bertha said you have to eat or the baby will starve."

"You added that last part," she responded sleepily.

"Okay, the starving was mine, but she did tell me you had to eat. Afterward you can go back to sleep."

"Why'd you bring the food in here?"

Stanley didn't want to tell her the real reason.

"Because then you won't wear yourself out socializing."

"There's only one plate."

"I thought I'd share," Stanley said. "I can always get seconds."

"I like my steak rare. You don't."

"I'll eat the edges."

Aleta rose.

"Boy, am I a wrinkled mess."

She sat down at the small table.

"You have another outfit, haven't you?" Stanley asked.

"Why didn't you hang up my clothes?"

"Because you were sleeping in them?" he offered then asked, "And why am I responsible?"

"Because I said so."

"Well, as long as you're being your usual reasonable self," he said, cutting the steak.

Aleta took a forkful of potato salad and Stanley told her that Chuck had won the Breed with Topaz. Lyle had taken the Breed with Morgan, Scooby won Best of Winners and Minx now had two points. She won best Bred-By and would be in the Bred-By Group immediately following the regular Group. He told her Hounds were the second group followed by Sporting, then Terriers, Working, Herding Non-Sporting and Toys.

"I can come back after Sporting and feed the baby," Aleta said.

"And rest!" Stanley ordered.

"And rest," Aleta repeated. "Who'll watch the baby while I'm in the ring?"

Stanley began to list where everyone would be. "Madge will be in Hounds with Rufus; Beatrice will be showing Minx, in Sporting Bred-By; your grandmother is showing Stoney in the regular Group; Lyle has Morgan and Evelyn will want to watch Chuck show Topaz."

"Everyone is showing," Aleta concluded. "And this is Bertha's first dog show so she can't miss seeing the Groups."

"Why are you worrying?" Stanley said. "I can hold him."

"Gerard will be due to nurse just about the time I finish in the Hound Group," Aleta said. "He could start to cry while I'm in the ring."

"If he does, I'll take care of it," Stanley said. "Don't worry. You just go in and enjoy yourself. You want pie?"

"Cut me a piece for later."

To Thurston Curran's dismay, Aleta Praetzel didn't come out to eat. He saw Stanley take a plate of food into her RV She wasn't going to emerge until later, he realized.

The sun continued to beat down on the shiny metal roof of the RV. After over an hour of squinting and blinking the tears from his eyes, Thurston closed his eyes against the glare. Then he laid his head on his hands and assured himself that when lunch was over, the camp would grow quiet and he'd be able to hear the change in sound level and he could open his eyes and start his watch again.

He fell asleep and while he was sleeping clouds began to gather.

Lyle began to relax when Aleta took the Wolfhound in the ring. The crowd had thinned as people not in Group packed up during the lunch break and started their journey home. The handlers' rigs were still intact. They were the last to leave. Many of the people camped out in RV's had a dog in Group. That area was not as affected as the parking lot where the single dog owners left after their breed finished.

Lyle's men scouted the lot for a car parked early in the day that seemed not to belong to a dog owner. The car parked on the road on the other side of the RV area was dismissed after a glance.

Harriet Luther was relaxed as was Aleta. Lyle took his clue from the two women. One of his men stood guard at the campsite while French and the other kept watch near the ring.

Lyle recognized many of the people and others were dismissed when they were greeted by someone he knew. He stood beside Stanley and watched the Hounds, Morgan at his side.

Aleta flew around the ring with the huge Wolfhound and when she stopped the dog gathered himself quickly and stood waiting for Aleta to praise him. Aleta used no liver after a run. The movement was its own reward.

He was the first to be examined being the tallest of the hounds so Aleta had but to move him forward to the place where the individual examination would take place. She adjusted a back leg swiftly and it was in place before the judge turned around from watching the last dog complete the circle.

The judge saw at once he had a nice Wolfhound. He'd already seen him fly around the ring in a smooth even gait. He went over him carefully. Good wiry coat, correct bite, nice shoulder lay back, great bone, well-muscled. A truly correct headpiece, he thought as he had Aleta move him up and back.

Definitely deserves a place the judge thought watching him sail around the ring to the end of the line.

He turned back to Tom Wilson and his Afghan. When he finished, he'd added a second dog that deserved a place. The Greyhound was another choice as was the Whippet. The little red wire Dachshund was up for a place too, he decided.

When he made the cut he included the Beagle as well. He wandered down the line and looked at those he'd selected. All good representatives of their breed. He moved the Dachshund first and then the Beagle across the width of the ring. He went to the front of the line and spoke briefly to Aleta. She moved down the ring at a diagonal, stood for a moment and then circled the ring to the end of the line. Tom took his Afghan the same route. The Greyhound and Whippet handlers were glad to show off their dogs with a longer run. The judge moved Aleta to the front and Madge and Rufus right behind her. Tom took third and the Greyhound fourth.

The group around the ring was delighted with the placing. Aleta was becoming a legend.

"You put a major on the big boy," Tom said. "Congratulations."

"A class dog?" the judge asked.

Aleta nodded. "He's almost a year."

"A puppy?" The inquiry came with a raised eyebrow. "He shows like a champion."

"He is a love," Aleta said hugging the big gangly-legged dog.

The Sporting Group came next. Morgan never looked better. The judge, a veteran Lab breeder, knew the dog. He'd put him up before. He was still the best he'd ever seen. He was taken with the Chessie as well and for a while it looked as if Morgan had met his match. Stoney took second. Topaz garnered third and the Clumber got the fourth. No setters, no pointers and if it weren't for the Clumber, no specials. The judge loved retrievers and those in front of him were among the best he'd seen.

He moved over to judge the Bred-By entrants and spotted Morgan's offspring immediately. Minx took that group.

That Gerard had stayed quiet surprised everyone, especially Stanley. Aleta went for a picture and Gerard finally announced his presence.

Aleta felt her breasts respond. She dashed away immediately after the photo, her face broadcasting her distress. Stanley realized at once what had happened and hurried back to the RV with her. Gerard by now was crying lustily.

Chapter 21

Thurston Curran, who had slept while the owners of a pair of Pharaoh Hounds packed up their campsite, woke up when the baby began to cry. He opened his eyes in time to see Aleta enter her RV.

"Shit!" he exclaimed softly.

Inside the RV, Aleta used the same word to express her feelings.

"You have another blouse," Stanley said entering the RV and handing the crying baby to his wife who tore off her blouse and dropped it on the floor in disgust.

"Go find Grams. I need to borrow a skirt to go with that blouse."

"The skirt you have on will work."

"Go get Grams!" Aleta ordered curtly.

Stanley took off. He met Harriet rushing toward him. Immediately, he sensed trouble.

"Tell me," she said. "That contract killer is in jail, isn't he?"

"What do you see?" Stanley returned.

"Is he or not?" Harriet persisted.

"Not."

"Get Lyle."

"I need to go back to Aleta," Stanley said.

"You need to obey me," Harriet demanded. "It's critical you leave. Go!"

Stanley took off again. This time he ran. This was all wrong, he thought. He had a gun in the RV. Why didn't she let him get it? Lyle didn't have his gun with him. Why had she specified Lyle? French was armed. She knew that.

When Aleta gave an order like that, if everyone did exactly what she asked them to do, people lived. When they didn't people died.

He remembered not too long ago when the Hepner brothers had started shooting CEO's. All were warned. Those that obeyed lived. Those that didn't, even if they elicited police protection, didn't.

He ran up to Lyle and said simply, "Harriet sent me. She wants you. Only you."

Lyle handed Morgan to Lauren and hurried after Stanley.

"I don't have my gun. Do you?"

"Mine's in my RV," Stanley said. "Are you thinking what I'm thinking?"

"She didn't say we couldn't run, did she?"

"No," Stanley said as the two broke into a run.

They heard one rifle shot.

As soon as Stanley left, Aleta put Gerard in his bassinet and took off her wet bra. She toweled herself off and then picked up the baby and went back to the bedroom. She sat on the edge of the bed and felt a hard lump beneath her.

She reached under the mattress and pulled out Stanley's gun and holster. She threw it off to one side and settled back to taking care of Gerard's needs. She talked to him softly as he nursed.

"You always make me so sleepy," she murmured. "I don't dare feed you in the chair. I'm afraid I'll fall asleep and drop you."

She went on. "But this works doesn't it. When we switch sides, I'll lie down and you can nurse until you fall asleep. That seems like a good plan to me. How about to you?"

Her grandmother's shout startled her.

"Police! Drop your gun!"

Aleta felt the RV shake. Someone had a foot on the step. The latch was broken. Whoever it was could come right in.

She reached for Stanley's gun. It was buttoned in its holster.

The crack of the rifle stopped her.

She felt the RV shake as someone fell inside.

Quickly, she crawled back into the corner, the baby still clinging to her breast. She unsnapped the holster and drew out the gun. She gathered the baby to her and undid the safety. She listened for any movement. She sat perfectly still and the RV didn't shake at all.

She was alone.

Still she kept the gun ready.

Her grandmother's voice came through the door. "Aleta, are you okay?"

Stanley rushed back to the bedroom calling her name. He found her frozen in place clutching the baby, pointing the gun at the doorway.

"Whoa!" he said. "Don't shoot!"

She couldn't respond immediately but she put out the hand holding the gun. Stanley gently pried the weapon from her fingers.

"He's dead," Stanley said. "You and Gerard lay down and finish. You don't want to come out here."

He coaxed her to lie down, and he removed her skirt. Without clothes, she'd say put, he knew.

"The Pug," she whispered.

"I will get you up," Stanley said. "I promise."

He closed the door.

Aleta moved the baby to the other breast and within minutes had fallen asleep.

Gerard nursed vigorously for a long time and then happily fell asleep, the nipple in his mouth. At first he slept fitfully, but the nipple was there to comfort him. He used it repeatedly and his mother slept peacefully. Her dreams were pleasant brought on by the pleasurable sensation elicited by her baby's suckling.

"I identified myself as police," Harriet said. "He turned, but he didn't drop his gun. I don't think he believed I could hit him."

"Where'd he come from?" Lyle asked looking around. His eyes on the RV, which was pulling out of its opening.

The man leaned out the window and shouted, "He was on our roof. He scrambled down as I was backing up. I almost ran over him. After that I heard the woman shout 'Police' and I stopped. Then she shot him. Is he dead?"

"Yes," Lyle said, walking toward him. "Stanley, get paper."

Stanley stepped over the body and grabbed a legal pad.

"Is she really a cop?" the man leaning out the RV window asked.

"She's one of my deputies," Lyle said. "I'm chief of police in Arborville."

"You're not in uniform."

"I'm on holiday."

"I know you. You have that big, black Lab."

"I need your name and address."

The man stripped the armband from his arm. "We have Pharaoh Hounds. Look in the catalog. But we ain't testifying or nothing."

"That's okay," Lyle said. "Stanley, did you get what he said down?"

Stanley handed Lyle a yellow pad with the man's words hastily scribbled on it. Lyle handed the pad to the man. "Just sign it."

The man scribbled his name.

Lyle looked at it and had him spell it as he printed it below the signature.

He went around the RV and handed the pad to the wife. "I didn't see anything," she protested.

"All you're doing is witnessing that he signed the statement," Lyle said printing the word witness on the pad to one side of the man's signature. He drew two lines.

She scrawled her name on one and printed her name below it.

Lyle thanked them and told them they could go. The man spent an inordinate amount of time jockeying his rig around before he drove out. Meanwhile Stanley signed as a witness, as did Lyle himself.

"Where's my guard?" Lyle said looking around.

"There," Harriet said pointing to legs jutting out from beneath a tarp.

"No wonder he took so much time maneuvering his RV," Stanley said.

"No wonder he was in such a hurry," Lyle said stopping the RV coming down the road as Stanley pulled away the tarp. French arrived in time to help retrieve the man from the path of danger.

West called the police and asked for the captain. He would speak to no one else and was finally put through.

"We have your man," Lyle said. "He came back. In fact, he was on the grounds all day. Come get him. Same place as before. No sirens. The perp is going nowhere. He's dead."

After a brief response, Lyle said, "One of my deputies shot him."

When he finished speaking, he shut his cell and turned. "French, you handle things. I didn't see anything. Aleta didn't see anything. Harriet will be available at the end of the show as will Stanley and I."

"He'll be here soon," French said. "He won't want to wait."

"But the coroner won't. It's a holiday," Lyle said.

"And if the coroner gets here right away?"

"Don't let them disrupt the show," Lyle ordered and walked off.

"What did Aleta want?" Harriet asked Stanley.

"She says her one good blouse left doesn't go with her skirt. But it does."

Harriet looked inside the RV. "Does she have another bra?"

"I don't know," Stanley said.

"I'll bring an entire ensemble. I think you can pick up her blouse and bra. The local police don't need to see those."

As Stanley entered the RV he remembered that Aleta was nearly naked. He poked his head out the door still wide open with the body sprawled through it.

"French, don't let anyone come in until we've awakened Aleta and dressed her."

"Yes, Sir," French said. He couldn't shake the image of Stanley with the chief's badge which Lyle had pinned on him in several emergency situations. Stanley now had a regular deputy's badge and technically French outranked him. But still, he was special.

Stanley removed the baby from Aleta's breast and he cried. He quickly gave him the other breast and he sucked for a few minutes and then opened his mouth and released it.

"You don't intend to miss a meal, do you?" he whispered softly as he carried him to the bassinet and began to change him. The cool outside air wafted past the bare tummy of the baby and in response the little penis straightened up. The spray caught Stanley in the face and down his coat, shirt and tie.

"I'm never changing you again!" he declared as Harriet walked in.

She laughed. "I got hit quite a few times before I learned to anticipate."

She handed him a towel. "Don't change until you're done."

"I'm done."

"He's not," Harriet grinned. "Go change and wake Aleta. I'll change Gerard when he's finished."

Stanley splashed water on his face and tore off his damp clothes. His jacket was the main casualty, but he changed everything, folding his soiled clothes and putting them in the drawer beside Aleta's soiled blouse which he had also folded. Harriet watched him with amusement. She'd only half-believed Aleta when she told her of this habit. She guessed the reason their house was always neat was because Stanley saw to it that things were returned to their allotted place.

He dressed in the tiny bedroom where there was hardly room to turn around. Then he woke Aleta.

Harriet picked up the baby and rocked him gently as she waited.

The police arrived as Aleta was brushing her teeth. She rinsed her mouth out, brushed her hair quickly and Stanley helped her and Harriet over the dead body and all three began to walk away.

"I need your statements," the captain shouted.

Aleta spoke up first.

"French, tell him I was hiding in the bedroom, petrified, because they let the killer slip through their fingers yesterday. I saw nothing. The deputy shot him as he was coming for me again. I will give him that statement when I'm done. If he doesn't disturb the show, I won't sue."

"What is she talking about?" the captain said.

"If you let her do her showing in peace, she won't sue."

"For what?"

"My guess is attempted negligent homicide," French said.

"What's that?"

"It means you goofed up yesterday and she's thinking about bringing you up on charges."

"She can't do that. No lawyer would take the case."

"She is a lawyer."

"So what does she want?"

"She wants you and your men to wait until the show's over."

"We're police. We don't wait."

"If I were you, I'd wait. She has TV connections."

One of the men leaned over and whispered in the captain's ear. French guessed he was confirming that.

"We'll wait for the coroner. You're right. She shouldn't have to look at the body," the chief said. He called for a blanket to cover the body.

Tom came up to Stanley with the Shar-Pei exclaiming, "Am I ever glad to see you!"

Stanley turned to Aleta. "You promised to teach me a new word." Aleta whispered in his ear.

"What's that mean?" Stanley asked. "I'm not swearing at the pup in Chinese."

"It's something good. Go on. Ask the owners."

Stanley approached the man. "Aleta taught me a new sentence. Will you tell me if I'm saying it right?"

The man nodded. Stanley repeated the phrase. The woman giggled.

Stanley blushed and the woman giggled again. The man smiled. "Your wife plays a joke."

"She does that all the time," Stanley said. "What am I saying?"

"I apologize. I must refuse," the man said politely.

"Give me a phrase I can use," Stanley implored. "Something that tells your dog I'm proud of him.

The man offered a phrase and Stanley repeated it until he had it down.

"He understands English," the Chinese gentleman said.

"I know, but he perks up when I talk to him in Chinese," Stanley explained.

"We do not expect you to match your wife," the gentleman said. "She said even she couldn't do it. But she said you would show him best."

"She played the joke to make me relax," Stanley said.

"You are relaxed?"

"Yes."

"It is good."

Stanley showed the Shar-Pei well; but the Group was won by a Poodle, with a Lhasa taking second. Tom and his Frenchie took third and Stanley walked away with a fourth place ribbon.

Tom Wilson was pleased.

"I don't think I did much."

"You did enough," Tom reiterated. "In fact, you did well."

Aleta took a Group One in the Toy Group with the Pug and the final Bred-By competitions got underway. Minx sparkled, but a lively, brindle Scottie took the top prize.

The coroner arrived as the Toy Group was in the ring and after he left, the captain became impatient.

French looked at his watch. "My chief is in the ring as is Aleta Praetzel. We need to wait."

"He's in my jurisdiction," the captain spouted. "And I'm not used to waiting."

"You wouldn't stop the Kentucky Derby at the last turn, would you?"

"For chrissake, this is a dog show."

"Say it's a football game and there are two minutes left. The score is tied and your team is in field goal range. And I turned off your television set. How would you feel?"

"Mad as hell!"

"Now do you want one of the most powerful families in Northern Illinois mad as hell at you?"

"I'm not afraid of them."

"Then you are..." French bit his tongue.

"What? What am I?"

"Sir. I apologize. I know your time is valuable. And the man is dead. And he was shot entering this RV to kill Mrs. Praetzel. This man was apprehended by us yesterday and turned over to you. You let him go. He reappeared today and attempted to finish the job he was sent to do. Now let me spell out for you wherein you and your men failed.

"First, after he escaped you not only did not send any units to protect his intended victim, you didn't notify the police who were here.

"Second, after a cursory search of the grounds you declared them safe when, in fact, they were not. Your delay gave the man time to hide.

"Finally, when you do arrive, you come unprepared to process the crime scene. And you believe you have the right to disrupt the lives of people who had nothing to do with this event--your people. Your citizens put on this dog show. They've worked for almost a year preparing this three day event, and you would charge in and ruin its climax because you can't wait fifteen minutes until the show reaches its conclusion, and then quietly complete your investigation. It isn't as though there's any danger or a criminal that needs to be caught. Your fifteen minutes is worth more than the months spent by dozens of your citizens.

"My chief knows what he's doing. He is saving your face."

The men attached to the local police force had gathered and listened awestruck at this dressing down of their captain without a single cuss word. Boy, this Arborville chief had some lieutenant. He would make one hellava chief.

No one said a word when French finished.

Finally, the captain spoke. "They did a lot of work. My people did. It would be a shame to ruin it."

French sat down. "It's winding down now. Everyone will come to you."

The dogs filed into the ring for Best in Show. Tom led the way with the Irish Wolfhound. Chuck Rigden followed with his Great Dane. The Collie and Poodle went in before Lyle and his black Lab. They were followed by the Lhasa and the Pug.

Aleta had shoved deep inside her the sight of the dead body she had stepped over and the fear she'd felt for herself and her baby as she crouched in the corner of the tiny bedroom. The memory would be brought out and dealt with later. Right now she needed to concentrate on showing a small flat-nosed little dog with a black face, large eyes that stared at one without blinking, a compact, muscular body encased in smooth tan coat and a tightly twisted tail. It didn't take long before the Pug's strong presence teased Aleta out of thinking about anything but him. She didn't have to concentrate on showing. Her concentration automatically focused on him.

She wasn't even aware of the competition so captivated was she by this tiny dog with the tenacious personality. She was reminded of Maggie, the Bulldog she showed for Tom, one of whose puppies she was buying.

She looked at the little boy in front of her and decided she'd like a Pug too.

She wondered what Stanley would say.

She stood in the Best in Show ring determined to win. She wanted a Pug.

She looked around and felt that same desire in her competitors. This was important to each of them for various reasons.

Lyle was her biggest competition, but Lauren had won the day before with a Lab. His chance of winning had been reduced by that fact even as her chance of winning was reduced by the fact that she had personally won once in this cluster of shows. The first two handlers in line were two of the top winners in the Midwest. Both had excellent dogs at the ends of their leads.

The Great Dane had almost taken it yesterday. Surely, today was his day. Her eye fell back to Morgan. He did deserve to win. Then she looked at the Pug at her feet. And so do you, she thought.

The judge surveyed the group with knowing eyes. The Wolfhound was new and he hadn't seen the Lab before but he was certain he was the one he'd heard about--the big, black Lab shown by his owner mostly in Illinois between hunting seasons. The Dane had won under him twice. He loved the big, regal-appearing dog. He'd seen the Collie and the Poodle before as well as the Lhasa. He knew their strengths as well as weaknesses which in each case were minor. Tom was on the Wolfhound and the judge knew he was looking at Tom Wilson's special. At the end of the line was the Pug. He wondered why this multiple group winner had never captured the top prize. Today, he'd find out.

The group circled the ring. The Wolfhound and Dane took long smooth strides almost in sync. The Collie and the Poodle were evenly matched. He saw the Lab giving them room and then realized why. He was faster. He had more reach and drive.   As the handlers sorted themselves according to this estimation of their dog's swiftness, he was surprised that the man hadn't inserted his Lab earlier. He realized that Labs were rarely faster than Collies. The Lhasa and Pub moved as two small dogs. The Pug handler gave her predecessor room too. The Pug was slightly faster. He wondered if she wanted to be last.

He began his individual exams. He knew at once why the Wolfhound had made it this far. The Dane was still magnificent. He found the Collie's fault immediately as well as the Poodle's. The Lab he took a bit more time with. Balance, strength, muscle, bone and a superb head. He was a dog to be admired. The Lhasa was good but the spark wasn't there, he realized as soon as he turned and looked at the Pug. He took his time going over him. He'd seen him before and given him a couple of Group Ones. He thought maybe the other Best in Show judges had discovered something he hadn't. If they had, it was a mystery to him.

The seven stood in a line and he stood back and viewed them carefully. His eye settled on the first two. He moved in for a closer look. Both handlers brought their dogs up on their feet, ears forward, eyes alert, muscles tensed.

His eye roamed one last time down the line. The Pug had jumped out of line demanding attention. He walked down the line just as the first drops of rain fell. For some reason he glanced at the Lab. The drops stood like beads on his coat. He hadn't given his coat much thought, but suddenly he remembered why the Lab's coat was so important. He glanced at the thick gently swinging tail, the strong broad muscle and he realized he was seeing this dog in his element.

A thought crossed his mind as he went to the table to mask his choice. This was the Lab's territory. Why shouldn't he be crowned king?"

He went out to the center of the ring and looked at his other choices. All three superb! But today was the Lab's day. He pointed at Morgan.

The applause from outside was matched by those inside.

The judge went over to Aleta. "He will make it one of these days."

"I liked this Pug so much I was going to try to persuade my husband we needed one of these too. It would have been easier if he had won."

"So you were fighting to win," the judge queried.

"With every inch of my being," Aleta replied.

"I believe your zeal was matched by the Lab's owner. The rain did it."

Aleta laughed. "That's a new one.

Tom Wilson came up. "Well, Judge, I see you've gravitated to the new Illinois legend, Aleta Praetzel."

"Tom, I didn't win," Aleta protested.

"Yeh, Tom she didn't win," Chuck Rigden interjected. "She wins with your dogs."

"Not against Lyle and Morgan I don't," Aleta said. "Well, not always."

"She wants a Pug, Chuck," the judge said.

"She can buy this one. The owner's gone sour and has put him up for sale."

"Why?" Aleta said. "Auggie is a great little dog."

"He practically lives with me," Chuck said. "This was his last shot. She doesn't really like dogs, but she likes owning winners."

"I'm so sorry," Aleta apologized. "I let you down."

"Well, buy the dog and I'll forgive you," Chuck joked.

Aleta grew thoughtful.

"Is she asking a fair price?" she inquired.

"It's a bit on the high side," Chuck replied. "Look you don't have to buy him. You did a good job."

"I wonder how he'd get along with my Lab."

"He gets along with everyone," Chuck said. "Pugs are like Labs that way."

"I own a Morgan son. I don't intend to cut him," Aleta explained.

Lyle West joined the group. "Hey, in case none of you noticed, I won."

"Sshh," Tom said. "Aleta's buying a dog."

"Can you sell me his crate too?"

"Does Stanley know?" Lyle asked.

"You will want to talk with your husband first," Chuck suggested.

"Well, of course. He's buying it," Aleta said. She turned and called, "Stanley, I need you."

"Is the photographer waiting?" the judge asked.

"He can wait," Lyle said. "I can't miss this."

"What do you need?" Stanley asked.

"Where's the baby?"

"Grams took him to her RV in case it begins to rain harder. You do know it's raining."

"That's how God arranged for me to buy Auggie."

Stanley looked around. "I gather Auggie is a dog. Tell me you didn't buy a Wolfhound."

"Auggie's a bit smaller."

"A Great Dane is still too big," Stanley said. "Besides we have a Bulldog pup coming in two months."

"We need a Special."

"I thought that's what you were going to do with Scooby when he's full grown."

"Do you have your checkbook with you?

"We don't need another dog. We have five running around the house most of the time now."

Aleta looked at the onlookers, "Grams is a newlywed. She and Claude take mini vacations and she leaves her three Chessies with us."

Stanley relaxed a bit. "So which ever one's selling Aleta a dog, our house is full."

"Chuck, who should Stanley make out the check to?"

Chuck Rigden looked surprised. "Didn't he say no?"

"God picked the dog out. Stanley never says no to Him."

Stanley's mind raced back to her first statement. "You said God arranged for you to buy Auggie. How?"

"He sent the rain just as the judge was coming down to pick Auggie. Auggie shook and Morgan let the raindrops bead up on his coat. So I lost. Then I told the judge I wanted a Pug. Of course, I was thinking of a puppy, but God knew what I wanted was this dog, so He arranged for Chuck to overhear us."

The whole group laughed.

"Is He paying for it too?"

"That's why He gave you all that money."

"Why aren't you buying it? You can afford it."

"Because that would mean I'd imposed my will over yours," Aleta positioned. "And I won't do that."

All eyes turned to Stanley.

"She's right," Stanley sighed. "She is leaving the decision up to me."

He reached into his pocket and pulled out his checkbook. "How much?"

"Let's go to my RV," Chuck suggested. "I have his papers there and his crate and food. The price tag is a little high."

"What do we need to know?" Stanley asked.

"If you'll wait another six months before showing him again, the judges will forget he made it to Best in Show ring but never got the top prize. He's only two. He needs to mature a bit more."

"We can wait," Aleta said. "We have Scooby to finish."

"And a baby," Stanley added. "And a law practice."

Aleta smiled. "We can wait. He'll be easy for me to show pregnant."

"I thought you just had a baby," Chuck commented.

"I did. I'm talking about being pregnant by the time Auggie is ready to show again."

"How many children do you plan to have?"

"Two," Stanley said firmly.

"Six," Aleta corrected. "Maybe more."

"Maybe less," Stanley said.

"Not unless you run out of fuel," Aleta quipped.

"Aleta!" Stanley scolded.

The group laughed and suddenly there was a flash. They turned to find the photographer had taken a photo.

"I want one!" they all chorused.

Chapter 22

Lyle walked back to the camping area with Stanley. "Why did you buy the dog?"

"Because Aleta needs something new to focus on. She was terribly shaken by this last attack."

"You gave her such a hard time."

"Purposely."

"You knew she wanted the Pug?"

"No, I thought she wanted the Wolfhound."

"You were ready to say yes to a Wolfhound?"

"I knew some dog had worked a miracle. The woman that asked me if I had my checkbook wasn't the woman I'd accompanied to the ring. Whatever dog transformed her was welcome."

Aleta had run on ahead, like an excited child. She burst into her grandmother's RV.

"Grams, I bought a Pug," she announced.

When she saw the state of her grandmother, she knelt down. "What's wrong? Where's Claude? Where's Gerard?"

"Claude took the baby to your RV to change him," Harriet said. "I was just weeping because I killed him."

"Grams you saved me from having to shoot him dead," Aleta cried.

Harriet stood up and hugged her granddaughter. "I never thought of that. Better me than you. You might have lost your milk."

"And my life," Aleta added.

Harriet chuckled. "That too."

"God gave me this Pug. Auggie helped me forget."

"I guess He wants you to breast feed Gerard."

"I guess He does."

"You'll have to work out of the house," Harriet reminded her.

"I wish I could help you."

"You already have."

"So you gave Claude diaper duty?"

"I think he was pleased I trusted him."

"You are really scared about facing those police, aren't you?"

"They won't understand."

"As your lawyer, I'll take care of it," Aleta said. "You stay here."

"I don't want to stress you. Where's Stanley?"

"Buying Auggie."

"Maybe he'll be done soon."

"I won't be stressed," Aleta insisted. "Watch Auggie for me."

She handed Harriet the leash and left.

"Well, Auggie," Harriet said, "welcome to the family."

Aleta walked over to the local police captain. "I'm here to give my statement and to represent the deputy who shot the would-be assassin."

Lyle, seeing Aleta heading toward the captain, hurried to join her. He had already dropped Stanley at Chuck Rigden's rig.

"We'll take it down at police headquarters," the captain said.

"You'll take it now," Aleta said. "I'm not making a trip to police headquarters to tell you I saw nothing. I can identify neither the deputy nor the would-be killer. I heard only two things and felt one. I heard my grandmother, Harriet Luther, shout 'Police. Drop your gun!' That was followed by a rifle shot. Somewhere between the two the RV shook because someone had stepped up onto the step. That's it."

"I want you to give me that information properly," the captain insisted. "Down at police headquarters."

Lyle butted in. "French, fetch the pad and write down what Mrs. Praetzel said. Mrs. Praetzel will sign it. Lieutenant French and I will sign as witnesses. Captain, that will stand up in any court of law."

"We are more formal than that," the captain blustered.

"Since when?" Lyle charged. He nodded at Aleta. "Go on."

"Mrs. Luther is not able to give you a statement at this time," Aleta said. "However, I will dictate her statement and have her sign it. Lieutenant French will write it down please."

"I want a formal statement from the deputy."

"That's what you're getting--a handwritten formal statement," Aleta declared firmly.

"This isn't how it's done."

"I don't have much regard for your methods. We will do this correctly."

"Are you saying that I didn't..." the captain began sputtering.

"Yes," Aleta stated coldly, cutting him off. She then dictated a statement and French wrote it out exactly as she said it.

When she finished, Aleta told French to take it to Mrs. Luther and have her sign it. She called into the RV, "Claude go with him and witness the signature. And take the baby, your RV is warmer."

"But I have questions," the captain said.

"I know your question. It is not something I will allow my client to answer."

French waited for Claude to exit the RV. Claude, however, waited to hear this exchange.

"Client, hah," the captain sneered. "Since when?"

"Since last August," Aleta said, "when she put me on payroll."

"So she has something to hide," the captain accused.

"Don't we all?" Aleta asked.

"I want to know why she had a rifle in the first place."

Lyle West replied more quickly than Aleta, "Harriet Luther is licensed to carry a gun. When she returned to her RV, she noticed my man was nowhere in sight. Call it feminine intuition or just plain good police training, but she armed herself before investigating. We had, after all, been victims of an attack and the local police had carelessly let the perp escape. When she exited her RV, rifle in hand she saw a stranger with a gun approaching this RV. She called out 'Police. Drop your gun.' He heard her because he turned toward her. He neither dropped his gun nor stopped his forward advance, so she shot him."

"She should have fired a warning shot," the captain argued.

"Do you think if she had, she or this woman or that baby would be alive today?" Lyle spat out. "This was a hired assassin."

"Then she should have wounded him."

"And left him able to kill his target?" Lyle scoffed. "Lieutenant French, do as Mrs. Praetzel bid. Claude, tell Harriet I will be over shortly. If she signs the statement, that will be the end of the matter."

"You can't dictate to me!" the captain blurted out.

"I can and I am," Lyle said icily. "This has been a harrowing experience for Mrs. Luther and Mrs. Praetzel. It was your fault. I know you don't get it, but you owe them and me. If you want to object, do so in court."

"I can have you arrested for obstruction," the captain threatened.

"Yes, you can," Lyle agreed. "But you won't. You're smarter than that."

The captain was finally stopped.

"Get these rigs out of here!" he ordered.

French came trotting back with the statement. "I had the rest of the people in the RV witness it too."

"Rest?"

"Well, Robert Locke wanted to check it," French said. "I figured it was okay. He is a lawyer, after all."

"Her lawyer?" the captain asked, certain he'd been lied to.

"Her son," Aleta returned. "I'm her lawyer."

"The family wants to talk to you Mrs. Praetzel," French reported.

"Are we done?" Aleta asked politely looking at the captain.

"We're done," he agreed grumpily.

"Thank you for your courtesy. I appreciate your allowing the show to finish."

Having said that, she left.

Lyle noted with satisfaction that she'd neatly taken the edge off the captain's memory of the confrontation.

He turned to French. "Let's help these people pack up."

In the RV, Harriet spoke directly to Aleta, "Robert and Bertha want to take the rest of the day off. They'd like to go out and eat and travel home at their own pace. When do you need Bertha?"

"I don't need her at all," Aleta said. "Since I'm nursing Gerard, I won't be expecting her until tomorrow morning."

"She needs to stay at your house until the wedding," Harriet said. "You filled her place with your clients."

"No problem" Aleta said. "Has she met Auggie?"

A woof from behind Harriet's chair answered that.
Nina was playing with him.

"Jocelyn is riding home with us," Harriet said. "She
wants to be absolutely sure she won't have to change a
diaper."

"Won't you be too crowded?"

"The ladies said it was okay."

Stanley knocked on the RV door and then opened it.
"Lyle said there was a family meeting. Why wasn't I
invited?"

"We weren't discussing you," Aleta said. "Can we tie
our door shut so it doesn't fly open when we're moving?"

"Let me have a look," Claude offered.

"Nina, I need to take Auggie now, so the big doggies
can come in. Okay?" Aleta said.

The little girl released the dog.

"Grams, are you going to be okay?" Aleta asked
obviously worried.

"Thanks for your lawyering," Harriet said. "I feel
much better."

"I missed a lot, didn't I?" Stanley said to Claude as
they headed for Stanley's RV.

"Your wife did a fine job of protecting my wife. And
we both owe Lyle."

"I'm way over my head in debt with Lyle now,"
Stanley said.

"Didn't you and Aleta save his life once?"

"Yes."

"Then you owe him nothing," Claude said. "That's the
way it works."

"You're sure? I don't think Lyle knows about that
rule."

Back in Robert's truck, he and Bertha kissed.

"One more night alone," she whispered.

"And no luggage which means no change of clothes, no razor, no..."

"We have time to buy them," she said. "And I can buy clothes so I have something to wear besides a uniform."

"You wear a uniform at Aleta's."

"But not to go to the doctor's."

"I almost forgot," Robert said. "You haven't had any morning sickness, have you?"

"No," she said sadly. "So I'm sure I'm not pregnant."

"Too bad," he murmured softly; but not so softly that Bertha didn't hear.

Chapter 23

Bertha left for the doctor's office at nine thirty after fixing breakfast for the family and putting both Teodora and Emerita to work cleaning the RV and doing the laundry. They were told to serve coffee and rolls at ten o'clock to the two lawyers and two associates working in the study on that afternoon's custody case.

Nina's case was their main focus. All other matters were ignored. Bertha told Mr. Ledgewood that he would have to wait until the following afternoon. Jocelyn's case was going to be heard the next morning.

Ledgewood took comfort in the intensity with which the four lawyers were attacking Nina's case. He decided to buy and plant a bit more. He had an idea what each of the Praetzels wanted.

In Dr. Chesney's waiting room Bertha was too nervous to read. She opened a magazine and her eyes followed one line of print after another in correct order but the meaning of the words forming the sentences never made it to her brain. It was busy thinking.

Robert wanted a baby. Was there any possible way that could happen? She fretted because she already knew the answer. Still, she was determined to ask. If in vitro fertilization would do it, she was willing to try. She could mortgage her house. Even a modest rent would cover the monthly payments. And Aleta had given her a hefty raise.

That gave her pause. Could she work at Aleta's if she had a baby to care for? It was one thing to help Aleta and Stanley; it was another to be the sole caretaker of a newborn. Suppose her baby needed her when one of her employers or their baby needed her?"

It's a foolish dream, she told herself. Robert and I are starting out late in life to build a life. And we have Jocelyn.

On top of that, she reasoned, Jocelyn might feel displaced. She was having problems with Aleta having a child. Her disgust with diaper changing was normal for a girl who'd never done such a thing. But Jocelyn didn't like the baby crying either. For Jocelyn this wouldn't be happy news.

Despair began to settle in.

Bertha was called in. Her thinking was muddled. She gave the nurse a urine sample, then stripped and waited for the examination.

Dr. Chesney was cheerful when he walked in. "Looking forward to the big day?"

"Yes," she said positively. "Doctor, I'm not even sure I want a baby. Jocelyn seems to dislike being around Gerard. But I need to know if there is any possibility I could have one. Jocelyn will be off to college in two years. Robert wants a baby. There. I've said it all."

Dr. Chesney said, "And very succinctly. I love women who are direct and lay everything out for me. Now, let me examine you and then we can talk."

"Pap smear and all?" she moaned knowing what his reply would be.

"You don't want one?"

"No. Can't you just look and see if everything looks okay. You know, no polyps or anything."

"I can do that," Dr. Chesney said.

Except for the Pap smear, Dr. Chesney gave Bertha a thorough examination and, after she dressed, he had her wait for him in his office.

He entered carrying a bottle of pills. "You need to take one of these a day. And I want to see you in a month."

Bertha picked up the bottle and read the label. "Prenatal vitamins."

She looked at the doctor. "I don't understand. How will these help me get pregnant?"

"They won't." Dr. Chesney smiled. "They will keep you healthy now that you are."

"Are what?"

"Pregnant."

"I can't be. No morning sickness."

"Count your blessings."

"It's too early to tell by examination," she protested.

"I used the drug-store test. We took a urine sample, remember?"

"Doctors do that?"

"Not usually," Dr. Chesney grinned. "Usually my patients have taken them before they even make an appointment."

"I was too afraid. I counted on getting morning sickness and when I didn't..."

"So can you handle Jocelyn's teenage angst or do you want me to talk with her?"

"You. Please," Bertha said.

"Does she know you're married?"

"She knows we're married," Bertha repeated unaware that the doctor had asked the question.

"Twelve thirty today. All three of you," Dr. Chesney said.

"Twelve thirty today, Bertha repeated. She got up, dazed, and walked out.

Dr. Chesney sent his nurse after her with the bottle of vitamins. "Your pills, Mrs. Locke."

"Thank you," Bertha said, staring at the bottle.

"Congratulations," the nurse said.

"Thank you," Bertha said still dazed.

The elevator door opened and the dentist's assistant got out. Bertha stared at the panel in front of her. "Do I press 'one' or 'basement'?"

"Basement," Dr. Chesney's nurse said cheerfully.

When the doors closed, the dentist's assistant said, "What's wrong with her?"

"Mrs. Locke?"

"Yes."

"She just found out she's pregnant."

"At her age?" the young girl questioned.

"It happens," Dr. Chesney's nurse said.

When the dental assistant returned to the office, the phone was ringing. She made an emergency appointment for a Mrs. Locke at one o'clock that afternoon.

When Bertha, Robert and Jocelyn entered Dr. Chesney's office at exactly twelve thirty, Dr. Chesney saw the worried look on everyone's face and that pleased him. They were expecting the worst.

"Jocelyn," he began, "how much do you know about a woman's bodily changes?"

Jocelyn blushed and muttered, "Enough."

"So you know that a woman starts menstruating in her teens and this doesn't stop until she's in her fifties."

Jocelyn nodded. "Can't we skip this part?"

"During the beginning stages as well as the ending stages, menstruation is irregular, more so at the ending stage."

Jocelyn's face remained beet red. Her head hung low.

"Lose your embarrassment, Jocelyn," Dr. Chesney ordered sternly. "This is a natural part of life. There is no shame involved."

Jocelyn's countenance remained frozen in disgust.

"I understand you are having trouble with your sister's breast feeding."

"I was handling it," Jocelyn declared angrily.

"By telling her it's gross?"

Jocelyn shot daggers at Bertha.

"So, I was honest."

"Yes, you were. And that brings us to Bertha's problem. She's very sensitive and she thinks her condition will, as you put it, gross you out."

Jocelyn's face underwent an immediate change. This was about Bertha after all. She was dying. She hastened to assure her.

"Oh, Mom, I won't be grossed out! Honest. I can handle it."

Bertha smiled weakly.

"Is she real sick? Is she dying?" Jocelyn asked the doctor.

"Not dying. Not even sick," Dr. Chesney replied. "But she's in what used to be called a 'delicate condition'."

Dr. Chesney watched understanding clear Robert's brow. He waited for the smile. It was as radiant as he hoped it would be.

"Bertha, you're pregnant!" Robert exclaimed, taking her hands and squeezing them.

She nodded.

The news affected Jocelyn differently. Her face registered shock.

"She can't be!" she protested violently. "She's too old!"

"No, Jocelyn," Dr. Chesney inserted. "She's not."

Jocelyn turned on her father, her fury in full evidence.

"Dad, why didn't you use a condom?" she shouted. "Bertha, you gave me some. Why didn't you give him one? That's what you told me to do!"

Robert looked at Bertha, perplexed.

She gulped. "The girls were asking me questions. I was talking to them as a nurse. I told them to wait, but under no circumstances to have unprotected sex."

"You gave my daughter a condom?" Robert asked evenly, trying to grasp what she was saying.

"My guess is she still has it," Bertha replied without defensiveness. "I believe women need to take charge of their health, to protect themselves."

"Dad, don't gross out!" Jocelyn yelled. Frantically she opened her purse, unzipped a section and took out a wrapped condom. "I haven't used it. See. Neither have my friends."

"Bertha, I don't know what to say," Robert started.

Jocelyn interrupted. "Don't yell at her. She told us to wait."

Robert leaned over and kissed Bertha lightly.

"Thank you," he said.

"Well, well..." Dr. Chesney chuckled. "I have no idea why Bertha was so worried about handling Jocelyn's reaction. She seems to have a real communication going."

Jocelyn began to cry. "Oh, Mom, I'm so glad you don't have cancer. And how could you know Dad's got live sperm. He's as old as you are."

The two men laughed.

Jocelyn shot them an annoyed glance. "Don't laugh. It's not funny.

Bertha spoke up. "Jocelyn, Dr. Chesney was supposed to tell you that in his years of experience each birth is a joy, but that doesn't diminish one iota the love a parent already has for a child. It's because your father finds you and Aleta so delightful, he wants another."

"Yes, that's what I meant to say," Dr. Chesney chuckled. "While you're on a roll, Bertha, why don't you tell them what else I was going to say?"

"I did want to make a promise," Bertha said. "You will never have to change a single diaper."

"You aren't going to breast feed her, or him, are you?"

"It's too early to decide that," Bertha said, "but, I'm thinking not."

Suddenly, Jocelyn's attention was riveted on the doctor. He was reminded of a younger Aleta.

"Is she too old?" Jocelyn inquired. "It seems to me that if God made her able to have a child He should make her able to feed it."

Before the doctor could reply, Bertha spoke out.

"I have a job that might make it difficult for me to do that."

"No, you don't!" Jocelyn objected. "You work for my sister. Her husband can afford to hire someone to do the work and you can direct them. What's good for her son is what she will want for her sister, or brother. What are you going to have?"

"It's too early to tell," Dr. Chesney put in.

"Guess then," Jocelyn said. "Dad shots girl sperm. And Mom's already had three boys. She's due for a change."

"Okay, for now, it's a girl," Dr. Chesney said.

Jocelyn sighed happily. "I'm glad that's settled. Girls don't squirt in your face like boys do."

"I thought you were permanently excused from changing a diaper," Dr. Chesney quipped.

"Oh, Mom didn't mean it. She's going to teach me how because she knows I will want to be an expert by the time I have a baby and she's going to let me practice on... what's-her-name. What are you going to call her?"

"Can we get married first?" Robert asked.

"I'll think of a nice name," Jocelyn rushed in. "Don't worry, you just concentrate on the wedding. Now, Doctor, how do we take care of Mom?"

"No heavy lifting and she should stay off horses."

Bertha eyed Robert, as Jocelyn barreled on, "Can she have sex?"

"Jocelyn!" both parents chorused.

"Well, that's what people do on honeymoons and I know that's how babies are started, but after the baby is begun, can they have sex?"

"Yes, Jocelyn, they can," Dr. Chesney said, "up until the last month."

"Good. Not having sex would ruin their honeymoon."

The men stifled their chuckles.

"Can she eat whatever she wants?"

"Yes," Dr. Chesney replied, "but don't over do it, Bertha. I'd like almost no weight gain in the first six months."

"How much afterward?" Jocelyn asked, not relinquishing the lead.

"Fifteen pounds."

"What about drinking?"

"Jocelyn, I don't drink."

Dr. Chesney answered the question nonetheless. "Everything in moderation."

"Can she still work? She works hard, you know."

"Jocelyn" Bertha cut in, "I won't mess up."

"You do know the baby won't be born until February next year?" the doctor put in. "Nine months from now. In fact, I can give you a date. From last Tuesday, right?"

"What about travelling?" Jocelyn pushed on.

"Airplane trips are out later, but right now your mother can do whatever she feels up to."

"Whew! That's a relief! I thought maybe we'd have to stay home on our honeymoon. That'd be no fun."

Later, after Robert dropped Jocelyn off at school, Bertha said, "You know why she was trying to plan the whole pregnancy in one hour, don't you?"

Robert nodded. "She's afraid she won't be here for it."

"Poor baby," Bertha said. "She loves that horse. Marian has her by the balls, if you'll pardon my saying so."

"Will you come with us to court tomorrow?"

"Why?"

"I plan to tell the judge we're married. It might help," Robert said.

"I will do whatever you think will help you keep Jocelyn."

"Marian could have her lawyer put you on the stand," Robert said. "They could rake up the scandal around your husband's death. It could get ugly."

"I think we can count on that."

Chapter 24

At two o'clock that afternoon, another drama was about to unfold. Emerita and her lawyer, Aleta Praetzel, entered the courtroom of Judge Rosemary Fogle and sat at a table in front of the judge. At a table to the judge's left sat Bertram and Dorthea Amend and their two lawyers. Stanley entered alone and sat in a chair in the gallery behind and between the two lawyer's tables.

The proceedings were underway as soon as the judge summarized the question before the court. She asked all present to identify themselves for the court record.

"Where is the child?" the judge asked.

Stanley stood to respond. "She is in protective police custody at this time, and we request she be allowed to remain there until this court determines where to place her."

"So ordered!" the judge said.

Stanley remained standing. "As the child's advocate, I am ready to present to the court the diagnostic statements of three experts--two child psychologists and a psychiatrist who lives out of state. As the psychiatrist is currently in the area on other business, he agreed to be available today to present his testimony pertinent to the child's current psychological state."

Jeff Lundrum shot up. "Objection!"

"Sit down, Mr. Lundrum," Judge Fogle said. "I will listen to your objections at the proper time."

"I do not want his jaded testimony in the court record."

"If it is indeed jaded, I will strike it. Proceed Mr. Praetzel."

Dr. Garren Johnson took the stand.

"Tell us, in your own words, what you determined to be the child's psychological state," Stanley said.

"First, let me say that the child is only four years old. When I talked with her, I was the third psychological expert to interview her. The men who talked with her before me did not traumatize the child. She still has no idea she was molested, but she was profoundly affected by the experience. She is still trying to put the pieces of the puzzle together in her mind. No one thus far has told her what she was encouraged to do was wrong. I hope that she is never shamed because she followed a trusted adult's directive."

The judge interrupted. "You are being vague."

"I apologize, Your Honor. Bluntly put, Mr. Amend poured chocolate syrup on his penis and had the child lick it off."

"That's a bold-faced insidious lie, meant to destroy the reputation of a man of the cloth!" Amend shouted, before his lawyer persuaded him to sit down.

"Excuse me, Your Honor," Dr. Johnson said calmly. "I'm from New Jersey, so I was not aware that Mr. Amend was a minister."

"Go on, Dr. Johnson," the judge ordered.

The doctor went on to detail his interview with the child and his conclusions and recommendation that the child not be placed under the care of the father that the biological mother was the more nurturing of the two mothers, but neither mother had hurt the child.

Jeff Lundrum began to fire his questions at the doctor. "How come you were called in to examine the child? What special qualifications do you have?"

Dr. Johnson looked at the judge. "May I answer the second question first?"

The judge smiled. "Yes, you may."

"I am a practicing psychiatrist in Bound Brook, New Jersey. It's a small town in the middle of the state midway between New York and Pennsylvania, the home of American Cyanamid Company's chemical research and manufacturing plant. As a psychiatrist, I am a licensed medical doctor which brings me to why I was called in.

"I am also a judge at American Kennel Club dog shows and I had just completed a day of judging when a police chief asked if there was a doctor on site. It appears that a young girl had been attacked with a stun gun. I examined her. It was while giving a report on her condition to her sister and grandmother that I met Nina."

"So you were just a man off the street, so to speak," Lundrum scoffed.

"Hardly," Dr. Johnson said evenly. "I'm a trained observer. I noticed the child because she was inordinately fascinated with the breast feeding of the baby."

"Come now, Doctor. Is that unusual?"

"Only a little," Dr. Johnson said. "By itself it fell into the normal range. Her question escalated it to questionable."

"What question?"

"When the young mother transferred the baby from one breast to another, she asked whether the second breast was chocolate."

"What had you been talking about prior?" Lundrum asked.

"The fact that I had awarded a chocolate Lab Best in Show. I had never put up... er chosen a Lab of that color before."

"So the word chocolate had been bandied around a lot before your interview, had it not?"

"Yes, it had."

"And you don't think that colored her description of what happened to her?"

"Actually, I think it was the reason she was so easily forthcoming. Chocolate isn't an evil word. Our conversation proved that. I believe she felt she could use it freely."

"You don't think she just wanted attention and so asked a question about chocolate to get it?"

"That is a possibility," Dr. Johnson admitted.

"Didn't you just take that question and use it to build your package of prefabricated lies?"

"No, I didn't."

"You believe a four-year-old child's fanciful tale that this man undressed in front of her and poured syrup on his penis?"

"Yes, I do."

"Could it be a lie?"

"No."

"One hundred percent, no?"

"Yes."

"Nothing is one hundred percent," Lundrum said.

Dr. Johnson fished a penny from his pocket and put it on the rail in front of his chair. "This is a penny. I am one hundred percent certain of that fact too."

"You're talking about a story told you by a small child?"

"About an event so traumatic that she remembered every detail including the fact that when she got to the end of the man's penis, she tasted something bitter."

"What did she say she did them?" Lundrum asked caught in his own penchant for probing lies.

"She said she wanted to stop, but she was told she couldn't. She had to finish."

"Where was her mother at the time?" Lundrum asked.

"She wasn't present," Dr. Johnson replied.

"That's a lie! She was there the whole time!" Amend shouted jumping to his feet. "She said she'd taught her daughter a new trick. I was tricked."

The gavel banging continued during the whole tirade and finally the two lawyers pulled the man down and told him to shut up. Aleta meanwhile was speaking softly in Lithuanian to Emerita, telling her not to utter a word.

"May I ask a clarifying question, Your Honor," Stanley asked.

"Go ahead," the judge ruled.

"Dr. Johnson, who in this courtroom is the woman Nina calls, 'Mother'?"

"The woman seated over there, Dorthea Amend."

"It is your testimony that she was not present during the incident in question?"

"Yes."

"Who was present during the penis licking incident besides the Reverend Bertram Amend?"

"The house maid, Emerita Balta."

"Thank you," Stanley Praetzel said and sat down.

Aleta whispered in Emerita's ear again and the woman sat silent. Stanley could see that she was clenching her jaw.

"Anymore questions?" Judge Fogle asked.

"No, Your Honor."

"Well, I have one," the judge said.

"We object," Mr. Lundrum said without thinking.

"To my asking a question?" Judge Fogle inquired.

"Sorry, Your Honor."

"Dr. Johnson, did Nina tell you why she took this action?"

"Her father asked her to."

"What did Emerita say?"

"She shouted, 'Oh, no!' she said and then her father said something and Emerita was quiet after that."

"Did the child ask for Emerita's permission after she shouted 'Oh, no'!?"

"The child was never allowed to ask Emerita anything in the presence of her parents. She was not even allowed to look at her for approval."

"Thank you, Dr. Johnson. You are excused."

"We wish to present our own expert testimony," Jeff Lundrum said.

Stanley stood up. "I have no objection to their having experts evaluate them as parents. As the child's attorney I would recommend such a step. I would also like an expert to evaluate Emerita Balta as a parent."

"So ordered," Judge Fogle said. "Each expert will examine all persons desiring custody."

"Your Honor," Lundrum interjected. "We want to have our expert examine the child."

"Mr. Praetzel, what is your suggestion?" the judge asked.

"The child has been examined by three experts, two regularly used by our court system. Today we heard from someone who did not know any of the parties involved including me. Great care was taken not to traumatize the child. These are not Miss Balta's experts. They are the court's experts. They have never even met Miss Balta."

"But they know you!" Lundrum spoke out.

"Almost every child psychologist used by the court knows me. I am, after all, a children's advocate."

"You want the child to stay with Emerita."

"I want what is best for the child. My job is to present as clear a picture as possible. The judge will decide the placement."

Stanley looked at the judge. "It is my recommendation that the child not be examined further."

"No further examination at this time," Judge Rosemary Fogle ruled.

"Then we want to question the child," Lundrum said.

"You are not cross-examining a four-year-old child in my courtroom," the judge proclaimed.

"But she accused my client..."

"That is enough, Mr. Lundrum. We are not deciding guilt or innocence on the criminal charge. In this court we are dealing with the custody of the child, Nina Amend."

Chapter 25

Aleta and Stanley arrived home in the pouring rain. They entered the house wet and angry.

"You blindsided me!" Aleta yelled tearing off her wet coat and when she missed the hanger letting it drop on the floor.

"You coped superbly," Stanley shot back picking up the coat and hanging it up.

"I thought we were working together! How could you pull a stunt like that!" she said, unzipping her wet skirt and dropping it on the floor.

"Undress in the bedroom," Stanley snapped.

Robert and Bertha stared at the two aghast.

"The skirt is dripping wet. Better one puddle than two dozen," she countered, kicking off her shoes. "And don't change the subject."

"Where's Emerita?" Robert ventured.

"In the car," Stanley replied. "She needs to be driven home."

He turned his attention back to Aleta, "I told you I was a child advocate. Exactly what did you think that meant?"

"Not blindsiding your wife who's representing her mother."

"I couldn't consult," Stanley pointed out. "That would have been inappropriate."

"But you know what a pickle I'm in now."

"I saved the child from any more exams."

"But at the expense of the mother."

"She wasn't my responsibility. She has her own lawyer-- you."

"Everyone knew I was unprepared. Everyone knew you caught me off-guard. It was embarrassing."

"It certainly proved I work independently," Stanley said. "And you needn't feel guilty. I didn't even think of that alternative until that very moment."

"What alternative?" Robert interjected.

"He suggested the parents have psych evals to see who is more fit," Aleta replied.

"Sounds good to me," Robert said, hoping to insert a rational tone.

"Emerita's English isn't good enough to understand the questions. Much will be lost in the translation both ways," Aleta complained. "The judge gave me only ten days to find an interpreter and have the evaluation done."

"That sounds doable," her father commented, injecting a positive note.

"You don't understand!" Aleta exclaimed exasperated. "Emerita won't be truthful even with me. She'll lie to the psychologist. She'll be caught. She'll lose her child! Stanley knows this. Still he made that proposal."

"It's my job to see to the child's interests. I can't do that if I'm looking out for the mother's as well," Stanley contended. "And you're doing that just fine. You've got to stop thinking of us as doing the same job, Aleta. We aren't."

"But you don't have to throw in surprise punches."

"I surprised both sides."

"But I wasn't prepared."

"That was your mistake."

"I won't trust you again."

Jocelyn piped up. "You mean I can't trust him tomorrow?"

No one had given any thought to her hearing the altercation until she spoke.

Aleta was brought up short by the query. "Oh, you can trust him. Dad can't."

"Will he hurt Dad?" Jocelyn asked apprehensively.

"I will do whatever it takes to see that you are protected and have a voice to argue your side," Stanley claimed.

Aleta followed up hastily, "Jocelyn, don't worry. Stanley did his job today. He protected Nina. Even I didn't think he could keep her from having to undergo another psychological exam, possibly an abusive one. But he did. He was quite brilliant. I'm upset because I didn't match him. I underestimated him. You couldn't be in better hands."

"So can we talk? Just you and me? Please," Jocelyn begged.

"I think the baby needs to be nursed," Aleta mentioned.

"That's okay. I can handle it. It's natural. There's no reason to be embarrassed," Jocelyn said. It was almost a recitation.

"We'll take Emerita home," Robert offered. "The dogs need to be toweled dry, Stanley, as long as you're in the dog house and already wet."

"All of them?" Stanley groaned.

"We'll be back in time to eat," Robert said. "Bertha and I need to talk about a few things."

"The baby's been changed," Bertha said as she donned her coat.

"Is our talk private?" Aleta asked her sister.

Jocelyn nodded.

"Let's use the study then, so Stanley can change clothes.

"Can't we use the bedroom? It's really private stuff."

"The bedroom it is," Aleta said, heading for the nursery. Within minutes the doors were closed and Aleta had settled into one of the chairs and opened her blouse.

Jocelyn watched her silently for a few minutes and then asked, "Does it hurt?"

"I've been told it hurts some women, but not me," Aleta explained. "It relaxes me."

"Are you and Stanley going to get a divorce?"

"Just because we argued?"

"That's how it starts."

"No, we aren't. He was right. He was brilliant. In retrospect, I'm proud of him. I'll apologize later."

"And make love?"

"I'm out of commission for a while."

"I guess I can tell you."

"Tell me what?"

"Dad's pregnant!"

Aleta's jaw dropped.

"We went to see Dr. Chesney this afternoon and he told us we're going to have a baby. You and I are going to have a sister."

"Bertha is pregnant?"

"Good thing they're married, huh? Old Marian would make her look bad if they weren't."

"How far along?"

"We've got nine whole months to go. Dr. Chesney counted from last Tuesday."

"The night they were married," Aleta mused.

"They're going to have a girl. We decided."

"That's not how it works," Aleta said. "It's too early to tell."

"I can't call the baby an 'it', so we decided it's a she since I don't want to be squirted in the face."

Aleta laughed. "Little boys do that."

Suddenly, Jocelyn sobered.

"The chances aren't good I'll even get to change a diaper, are they?" she asked. "Mom's going to win, isn't she?"

"I'm afraid she's going to get to take Yudi. Whether she takes you is up to you."

"If I don't go, you know what will happen."

"I'm as afraid for Yudi as you are," Aleta said. "But what I'm more afraid of is how she'll blackmail you into doing what she wants if you do go."

"You mean like when I refuse to do something, she'll threaten Yudi somehow."

"Yes.

"Or she won't let me visit him unless I do whatever she says no matter what it is."

"By going you give her power over you," Aleta pointed out.

"But only until I'm eighteen, right?"

"Actually no," Aleta said sadly. "She can refuse to sign Yudi over to you for however long she wants."

Tears welled up and Jocelyn blinked them away.

"But if I let her have him, she'd neglect him. He'll die of a broken heart wondering what he did that made me turn on him," she choked.

Tears streamed down Aleta's face when she envisioned the probable fate of the horse if there was no one to protect him.

She picked Gerard up and burped him, wiping her eyes on his blanket. There was no sense both crying. There had to be something they could do.

"There are always alternatives," Aleta started.

"Stay or go Yudi loses. If I go and be just like Jayline, then things will be good for my horse anyway."

Aleta switched Gerard to her other breast.

"A couple of years is one thing," Jocelyn went on, "but forever? When do I get my life back?"

Tears streamed down her face. The future looked bleak.

"Let's start there," Aleta said. "The court could order her to sign the horse over to you when you're eighteen. You can make a case for that. You've taken good care of him."

Jocelyn wiped her eyes on her sleeve. "That would only mean fourteen months. The baby will only be a little over a year. She'll even be in diapers still."

Aleta brightened. "You need to tell Stanley what you want. He'll see that you get it."

"It'll be fourteen months in hell, but I can do that."

"There are always options," Aleta repeated.

"Yeh. Obey and Yudi lives a good life and I don't. Disobey and Yudi is punished."

"Let's think. What would Mother do? We've both lived with her a long time. If anyone knows her, we do."

"Kill him," Jocelyn suggested and shuddered at the thought.

"The court can order her not to put him down," Aleta said.

"She could make him so sick, he'd suffer and I'd beg her to put him down and she'd say I tied her hands and she wouldn't."

"You think she'd go that far?"

"Oh yeh," Jocelyn assured her sister. "Suppose I started dating a boy like me--part black?"

"You're right. She'd pull out all stops."

"Suppose I threatened to tell everyone about our heritage," Jocelyn posed. "Suppose I refused to live the lie."

"Oh, Jocelyn!" Aleta cried and burst into tears.

Jocelyn ran into the bathroom and grabbed a towel. She brought it back and Aleta cried into it.

"Won't your crying stop your milk?" Jocelyn asked, worried.

Aleta couldn't stop however.

Jocelyn laughed. "Look at him suck! He's not going to let it, is he?"

Aleta looked down and smiled weakly. "He is determined isn't he?"

"He takes after us," Jocelyn said. "So, what will Marian pull that we can prevent?"

"She'll find a way around every barrier," Aleta responded, swallowing hard.

"Eventually," Jocelyn said. "But not right away."

"Let's think about Yudi first," Aleta said. "He needs food, proper shelter from rain and sun, regular vet care... what else?"

"Not to be ridden," Jocelyn added. "And he should be in a pasture with other horses, not shut up in a stall."

"And the place has to treat the animals decently," Aleta said. "And have good pasture land."

Jocelyn nodded. "There are a lot of bad places. Can I be allowed to choose? Can we get the judge to order that?"

"Stanley probably could. It's a reasonable request and you know your horse. I don't think Mother will object to that in court."

"She'll lie to look good," Jocelyn said. "Will I be able to get her to comply?"

"Dad will fly out and see that she does. He's a lawyer in both states."

"Yudi can't go back in a regular horse trailer. We need to take him. I wish I could leave Sterling with him."

"We can arrange that," Aleta said. "We'll pay for Sterling."

"That would make his stay okay," Jocelyn said. "But I need to visit him regularly. Can the judge order that?"

"Stanley can try. It's a reasonable request. How often?"

"At least once a week," Jocelyn said. "I will ask for three days and Mother will take away two of the days to get me to toe the line and Yudi can handle that.

"I need to be able to visit Dad and you and Royal. Can the judge order visitation? Can I pick the days?"

"Most of that Stanley can get."

"How about visits to Uncle Paul and Lettie?"

"You're right. Mother will cut off that association."

"We should have Stanley in here."

"No, not yet. I can tell him after you and I decide," Jocelyn said. "Look at Gerard. He's settled down. He's not so frantic."

Aleta smiled. "I guess he likes his milk unstirred."

"I think Bertha should breast feed. She's worried about you."

"Me?"

"I told her you wanted your sister to have the same advantages as your son."

"She'll have it better than we did. She won't have Mother," Aleta commented. "By the way, you can't call her Marian. It'll infuriate her."

"She's not being a good mother doing this!" Jocelyn declared heatedly.

"She's fighting to get you back," Aleta said. "She honestly believes she can do a better job than Dad or even Dad and Bertha together."

"Can't she see I'm happy here?"

"She only knows she wouldn't be."

Jocelyn grew thoughtful.

Aleta waited but Jocelyn didn't speak. Finally, Aleta broke the silence.

"Tomorrow you will decide how you want your future to go," Aleta said. "Accept the premise that Mother loves you and she misses you. But remember, she'd terribly manipulative and narrow-minded. She will try to squeeze you into the same mold she squeezed Jayline into."

"I think I'm ready to talk to Stanley now."

"I'm surprised Robert and Bertha aren't back," Aleta commented.

On their way back to Stanley's house, Robert turned off the road and headed for their new house next to his mother's place.

"Are we going to see your mother?"

"No, we're going to decide where to put the nursery."

"I know where. Upstairs next to our bedroom."

"I have another idea."

"You just want to make love," she accused gaily. "You're still on our secret honeymoon, aren't you?"

"Call Stanley. Tell them we'll be late."

The house was dark. The wiring had been completed and the power turned on. The thermostat was turned down to sixty and the two shivered when they stepped through the door. Robert rushed over and turned up the thermostat.

The furnace roared on.

Robert led the way to the small, downstairs room which was earmarked as his study.

"How about in here?" he offered.

"It's your study," Bertha protested. "And I want it to stay that way. That way we're both on the same floor--you working me cooking."

"You need the baby nearby too. You can't walk up and down the stairs all the time."

"Sure I can. It will be great exercise," Bertha returned. "And I can afford to lose a few pounds."

Robert spun her around. "We're not going there. You are prefect as you are."

He whirled around with her in his arms. "And I'm ecstatic! This is the best news ever. And we will set up a crib in the study as well as upstairs. That way I can work and watch her all at the same time."

His hands told him his wife was still following his demand that she wear no undergarments on their honeymoon.

"You do please me," he whispered. He drew her close and kissed her tenderly. Her response told him she felt as he did.

They both felt young again. Aging bodies responded appropriately and the coupling was as fulfilling as each had envisioned. This time the fact that they were on the hard floor didn't matter. The thought of their potential parenthood sent their spirits soaring gloriously.

The knock on the back door came just as they had parted.

"Who could that be?" Robert said pulling on his trousers.

Bertha hastily stepped into her skirt. "Ask who it is."

"Us," came the response.

"My mother!" Robert exclaimed.

"Give me a minute," Bertha whispered.

"Just a minute, Mother," Robert called, tucking in his shirt without buttoning it. He threw the latch and opened the door.

Harriet smiled. "We saw the light and we were worried."

"Everything's fine, Mother."

Bertha appeared at his side. "We were celebrating."

"Where's Claude?"

"At the front door."

It was then Robert noticed the rifle in her hand.

"Mother, you have got to stop carrying that thing!"

"Why? Claude and I are the police in this subdivision."

"Have you told Claude?"

"No."

"I think we should," Robert said.

Bertha hurried to the front door and opened it. "We have an announcement."

"You're married," Claude said.

"You guessed?" Bertha breathed. "How?"

"When Harriet said you two wanted the rest of the day off after the dog show and you asked Aleta because you weren't planning to return until the next morning," Claude explained. "So everyone knew but me?"

"It's beginning to look that way," Robert said. "We had planned to keep it a total secret, but we kept getting caught."

"Like now?" Claude chuckled. "Don't worry. You have a couple of newlyweds here who do understand."

"Well, let me make it up to you," Robert said. "Bertha is pregnant. You're going to have another grandchild to go with your great-grandchildren."

Harriet gasped, "Pregnant?"

"Dr. Chesney confirmed it today," Robert said.

"Whatever made you...?"

"Aleta told us only she denied doing it," Bertha explained. "She said she must have been referring to Teodora, but I felt she was talking to me. There was something strange about how she made the announcement. It bothered me."

"How far along?"

"Five days."

"Isn't that too early."

"Dr. Chesney used one of those home pregnancy tests. In fact, he used two, just to be sure."

"Who knows?"

"Just Jocelyn," Robert said. "Bertha was so worried about her reaction, she wanted Dr. Chesney to tell her."

"How did she take it?"

"He must've done it just right because she did a complete about turn," Bertha replied. "She yelled at her dad for a few minutes and that led to a discussion about why I'd given her a condom..."

Bertha paused.

"To protect her, right?" Harriet said. "Jocelyn hasn't found herself yet."

"Mother, you should have seen her come after me," Robert said, "when she thought I was going to yell at Bertha."

"After he kissed me, Jocelyn settled down and began planning my pregnancy," Bertha chuckled. "It would be funny if it weren't sad."

"We can't legally keep Marian from moving the horse to California," Robert explained.

"And Jocelyn doesn't trust her mother to care for the horse," Harriet assumed. "Can we come to the hearing?"

"It'll be a closed hearing. Even Aleta can't come," Robert said, "but Stanley will be there as Jocelyn's lawyer."

"Who's yours?"

"Hubert. He handled the divorce."

"Even if Jocelyn goes to live with her mother, do you still retain custody?"

"Doesn't work that way."

"So this is a custody hearing?"

"It will probably be the last one," Robert said.

"You asked me to go," Bertha said. "Won't I wind up in the hall?"

"You won't be in the gallery. You'll be sitting beside me as my wife."

"Be sure to wear your rings," Harriet advised. "It's time."

Bertha took her chain from around her neck and handed it to Robert. He unfastened the chain and slipped the ring on Bertha's finger.

She took his chain, removed the ring and put it on his finger.

"After Thursday, we won't have to take them off again," Bertha commented.

"Has she told you about the wedding yet?" Harriet asked her son.

"No, but Dr. Chesney said that she wasn't to ride a horse," Robert said.

"That doesn't mean you won't," Bertha said.

"I'll fall off and break a leg," Robert argued.

"Then Jocelyn and I will go on our honeymoon without you."

Chapter 26

The rain continued on into morning and Aleta who had considered visiting Dennis Middlebourne decided against taking Gerard out. Since Bertha was going to Jocelyn's hearing, she postponed her visit; but told Dennis' assistant that she and Dennis could chat by phone if he liked. Dennis agreed that would be fun. Aleta told his assistant to warn him she might not be able to understand much and the response was, "Let's try."

On the way to the courthouse Stanley reminded Jocelyn to talk only to him.

"If the judge asks you a question you may reply," he added, then he warned her. "Don't anticipate me. We will not leave until everything you want has been requested. There is an order. Don't worry if the judge rules. As long as the court is in session, any ruling can be changed."

Jocelyn nodded.

"Trust Stanley," Aleta had said. "He will protect your horse and you. Even if you don't understand, respect him with your silence."

Still, Jocelyn twisted her hands as they drove. Stanley knew she was in turmoil, wishing her mother would recant and leave her and Yudi here. He knew she was torn between wanting to live with her dad and needing to protect her horse. She'd asked to bring only Yudi from California when she had relocated to be with her father. She'd been willing to leave everything else behind including her college education which, unknown to her, her father had provided for before asking for the divorce wherein her mother had acquired all the family assets.

Her Uncle Paul oversaw her trust fund and had been instructed by Robert to provide generous support for her horse showing expenses.

Yudi was a retired horse. A set of circumstances had made him too unstable for jumping competition. Her mother didn't know that Yudi was no longer Jocelyn's competition horse. Stanley had told Marian about Royal, but Marian had refused to believe he wasn't lying to make the horse seem valueless. It was a ploy she would have used.

The courtroom was small and friendly in Jocelyn's estimation. Everyone was on the same level. The judge sat behind what looked like a desk. There were two tables facing the desk. Her mother and a stranger sat at one. Her father, Bertha and Hubert Praetzel at the other.

Stanley and she didn't sit at either. They took two seats in the gallery. Stanley had explained that she was not a party to the first action and she could only participate from the witness chair. He, however, could stand and be heard at various times from his seat. He was there for her and she could speak softly to him at any time.

Everyone rose when the judge walked in. Jocelyn was disappointed. Judge Norma Jacobi was a short, fat woman with a mass of curly dark hair, large dark eyes, round cheeks and a very Jewish nose. Jocelyn had expected someone that looked like Aleta's mother-in-law, someone distinguished and wise looking.

The judge scanned the paperwork. "Were this merely a dispute over the ownership of a horse, I would have told the parties to work it out without wasting the court's time but the awarding of custody is a serious matter and worth the court's time."

Marian's counsel objected to the presence of Bertha Carlson. "She has no standing in this matter, Your Honor."

Hubert rose. "The former Bertha Carlson is Mrs. Robert Locke. I was personally present at the civil ceremony a week ago yesterday."

Hubert then presented a certified copy of the marriage certificate.

Bertha was allowed to remain.

Marian was first to present her position. She presented a skewed picture of the events of the night Robert Locke requested a divorce from his wife. According to Marian, Robert who had been away for several weeks, returned home, removed his daughter from school and then taken her for a ride in a private plane, allowing her to fly it and promising her lessons. He had brought his lawyer with him, announced coldly that he wanted a divorce and then offered her a generous settlement if she would allow Jocelyn to choose which parent she wanted to live with. She was at the time busy with her daughter Jayline's wedding plans and Jocelyn resented the lack of attention and in a fit of anger chose to accompany Robert to Illinois. He arranged to transport Jocelyn's show horse shortly afterward.

Jocelyn had been given no time to consider her decision. She was kept in Illinois by the presence of her horse. Marian believed that Jocelyn would follow the horse, that the horse was what she had chosen, not her father.

Thus Marian said, since she owned the horse, she wanted him returned to her. She said that now that Jocelyn had had a chance to think, she wanted the custody issue to be reviewed and changed.

Robert Locke gave a different version of the same story. When he told his wife and daughters that he was part Negro, his wife said she would have nothing more to do with him. His daughter Jayline became hysterical and Marian had fabricated a story that when she had learned of his heritage while visiting his mother, she had become so angry that she had had an affair with a white friend and that Jayline and Jocelyn were products of that affair. Jayline believed her mother. Jocelyn trusted her father. He had then settled his entire estate on his wife asking only that Jocelyn's wishes in the matter of custody be left up to her. He'd offered Jocelyn no incentive; however, after she chose him, he had told her he would pay to move her horse with her and had done so. Jocelyn worked for Yudi's board and cared for him personally. The horse was a gift he and his wife had given Jocelyn for her thirteenth birthday. The horse was not considered a marital asset as it had been a gift given to their daughter.

Hubert rose and asked Robert, "Did your wife make any objection to the horse being transported to Illinois?"

"No."

"Was she given ample opportunity to object?"

"Yes."

"How much time?"

"Approximately two weeks. Jocelyn and I flew back to California for Jayline's wedding. At that time the divorce settlement was finalized. She had an attorney who went over everything. After that the horse was transported."

"Was the horse mentioned at that time?"

"We told her we were arranging to ship it. Jocelyn packed her belongings and we left."

"So your daughter had time to rethink her decision?"

"Yes."

"Would you have let Jocelyn change her mind?"

"Yes."

Craig Meyers, an impeccably dressed man, rose and asked, "Where did you live when you first arrived in Illinois?"

"I lived in an RV on my daughter's property. Jocelyn lived with her grandmother."

"That is no longer the arrangement. Why?

"There was an explosion that destroyed her grandmother' house and Bertha Carlson offered a room at her house."

"So you essentially gave your daughter to Mrs. Carlson to babysit; correct?"

"No."

"You mean you both moved into Mrs. Carlson's house?"

"No."

"I believe that's exactly what happened."

Jocelyn squeezed Stanley's arm. He smiled at her and she relaxed.

"Is it not true that the new Mrs. Locke is pregnant?"

Startled, Robert Locke nevertheless replied evenly, "Yes."

"With your child?"

"Yes."

"Did you not marry her hastily in a civil ceremony with your scheduled wedding only ten days away as a cover-up when you discovered your ex-wife planned to sue for custody?"

"No."

Craig Meyers sneered. "Your attorney presented a certificate of marriage dated after Marian Locke arrived in town and hired our firm."

"If you say so," Robert Locke said.

"Why else would you marry Mrs. Carlson ten days early?"

"Jocelyn was going to accompany us on our honeymoon," Robert replied. "We merely wished to spend our first night alone."

"Why would you take your daughter on your honeymoon?"

"She asked us to."

"I suggest that the truth is you'd already been having sex with Mrs. Carlson so you didn't need a honeymoon."

"That is not true."

"Yesterday she was seen leaving the office of an obstetrician. She had just discovered she was pregnant. True?"

"Yes."

"Didn't she know she was pregnant before yesterday?"

"No."

"Why did she make the appointment?"

"For a premarital exam."

"How early in a pregnancy can a doctor tell by examination that a woman is pregnant?"

"I don't know."

"Not in a week," Craig Meyers stated, "unless he is a prophetic."

"He used an over-the-counter pregnancy test."

"Why would he do that?"

"Bertha thought she might be pregnant."

"Why?"

"I don't know."

"Morning sickness, missed period--surely you have some idea?"

"She said Aleta had told her she was."

"Aleta is your eldest daughter, the one who claims to have psychic powers."

"Aleta is a prophet, yes. She hasn't ever prophesied about anything but murder, so we didn't know whether this was a prophecy or not, especially as she couldn't remember saying the words, 'You're pregnant'."

"How convenient for you!" Craig Meyers mocked. "I believe the court can sort through your web of lies and see the truth."

Jocelyn whispered in Stanley's ear in a panic.

"It's not true. None of it is true. Dad never did anything."

"Patience," Stanley whispered back as his father rose.

"Mr. Locke, tell us how you took care of your daughter on a daily basis," Hubert requested.

"Bertha dropped Jocelyn off at school in the morning," Robert Locke started.

"Why didn't you?"

"I was way over in Willow Glen. Bertha lives in Arborville. The Willow Glen high school was on her route to work."

"Go on," Hubert coached.

"Bertha picked her up after school and took her to Aleta's place so she could groom her horse and their horse Sterling. Then she would muck out the stalls which was how she earned Yudi's board. She usually rode him afterward.

At five thirty I came home and we talked. We went over to Bertha's house for supper and afterward I supervised her homework. I left the house around ten and went back to the trailer. Jocelyn was usually in bed at that time."

"What about weekends?"

"Jocelyn spent her time between her friends' houses, football games, riding her horse and working with her trainer. I was mainly a chauffeur."

"One more question," Hubert said. "When is the baby due?"

"The last week in February."

"Nine months from the day you were married?"

"Yes."

Hubert sat down and Robert left the witness chair.

"In the matter of the horse," Judge Jacobi said, "I understand it was a gift; however, as both parties were married at the time it was given and the decision was made jointly that the wife be named owner, I see no reason to set aside that agreement. Mrs. Locke, the horse is yours. Let us move on."

Stanley stood up and was recognized. "Jocelyn Locke asks permission to be heard at this time."

"I was about to call her."

"She would like to speak to the issue of the horse."

"My decision is final."

"She is not going to dispute that. But may she propose certain restrictions?" Stanley asked.

No."

"May I give you a sample?"

"One," Judge Jacobi ruled sourly.

"When she reaches eighteen, she would like the ownership of Yudi to be transferred to her. She suggests that that would complete the gift given her when she was thirteen."

"So ordered."

"She has other requests as well."

"One more," the judge said.

"When the horse was transported from California to Illinois, he did not take the trip well," Stanley said. "She would like permission to personally transport the horse. She believes she can reduce the trauma markedly. This is a show horse, Your Honor, who is currently recovering from an unfortunate incident wherein he encountered a grenade."

Judge Jacobi looked at Marian Locke. "Any objection."

Craig Meyers questioned her ability to drive that long distance unaccompanied.

Stanley replied. "Her father and stepmother will accompany her. Jocelyn owns the horse trailer."

Meyers consulted with his client.

"Your Honor, my client sees this as a delaying tactic. She wants to regain her property without any delay."

Stanley smiled, "Will tomorrow be soon enough?"

"Tomorrow Mr. Locke is getting married."

"They will leave immediately after the ceremony."

"So ordered," Judge Jacobi ruled. "Now can we move on?"

Stanley asked for a moment.

"Two minutes!" she said impatiently.

Stanley leaned over and spoke softly to Jocelyn. She became quite agitated and he nodded.

"Your Honor, she has one more request with regard to the horse."

"It better be important," Judge Jacobi said.

"It is critical," Stanley replied. "Jocelyn would like to be allowed to decide the care the horse will be given. In other words, the food, the accommodations, the vet care and handlers of her horse. She still considers it her horse. She says her mother is not an expert in these matters. She is. May I remind the court that we are talking about a horse trained for competition. They have special needs."

Meyers objected immediately. "She could run up the costs so high Mrs. Locke would be forced to make an unpopular decision."

"My client has a trust fund. She is allowed to use it for the additional expenses that competition entails. However, we assume, Mrs. Locke will provide basic necessities. Jocelyn merely wants to determine that the care will be maintained."

"What does your client think?" Judge Jacobi asked, "Mrs. Locke will stop feeding the horse?"

"Yes, Your Honor."

"Why would she do that?"

"To force my client to do something she doesn't want to do."

"Let's move on," the judge decided.

"Yes, Your Honor. Thank you," Stanley said and sat down. He leaned over and whispered. "She's thinking about your request."

"Miss Locke, will you come up and sit beside me please."

"Mr. Praetzel you may begin," Judge Jacobi said.

"Jocelyn, tell us about your parents, both of them."

"To begin with, Aleta told me to remember that Mother is doing this because she misses me and she loves me. When we left, I was very angry with her for lying and Dad told me that someday I would understand what a tremendous sacrifice Mother had made."

Jocelyn turned to the judge. "May I talk to you directly?"

"Go on," Judge Jacobi urged.

"It's not that I can see this because I can't. She lied to make Jayline feel good. She didn't care about how I felt. She lied because she didn't want to live with the truth. It wasn't a love thing. It was selfish. And now Mother is being selfish again. She got what she wanted in the divorce. Dad didn't divide the money evenly. He gave her everything. And all he asked is that I be allowed to choose who I would live with. That's all.

"After Mother lied about Jayline and me not being Dad's children, Jayline went on and got married and never told Scott she was..."

"Objection, Your Honor," Craig Meyers said. "Irrelevant."

"Noted. Mr. Meyers. I'll decide if it's relative after the child finishes."

"...partly Negro. He never would have married her. Stanley knew. He married Aleta anyway. Aleta won't live a lie. Jayline will. I want to be like Aleta, not Jayline.

"Anyway, Dad didn't know how I'd choose. I believed Mother's lie at the time. He could tell. I got really upset. While Jayline was ecstatic when she was told Dad wasn't her father, I was crushed. I didn't care if I was part Negro or not. I wanted to be his daughter. He told me I was. I didn't believe him. He asked me to trust him. Then he said the money would be Mother's no matter how I chose. That meant that I'd keep the life I had if I stayed with her. Dad was broke and in debt. He did that just to give me a chance to choose. I decided I wanted to live with him."

"Did he offer you any proof?" Judge Jacobi asked.

"No," Jocelyn said. "And I didn't ask. It would mean I didn't trust him, but I know that courts like proof because people lie good, so I brought some."

"What proof?"

"When Mother arrived she told Aleta that Conan Lloyd who was..."

Again Craig Meyers interrupted with an objection.

"Mr. Meyers," Judge Jacobi said, "this is a custody hearing. Everything this child says is relevant."

Jocelyn continued, "Conan was her old boyfriend before Stanley, a real uptight jerk. Mother said he said he was the father of her baby. It was a lie, but Aleta had the baby's DNA tested in case the jerk made a public accusation. While she was at it, Grams and I had her take samples of our DNA. I have the results. The tests show that Aleta and I are sisters and we are both related to Grams. And well she's Dad's mother. And my mother had said that Aleta was Dad's daughter."

Judge Jacobi allowed Stanley to present the results to the clerk and marked them as exhibits.

"Go on," the judge said afterward.

"If I go back to live with my mother, I will be forced to live the lie. It's not as if we tell everyone here, but almost all of Aleta's friends know. While she doesn't lie about it, she doesn't proclaim it either. Grams lived with the prejudice long enough to keep her heritage a secret. Dad didn't know until recently. He told us when it looked as if Grams was going to be exposed. Stanley found out when Aleta did. It didn't bother him at all. They even had a second wedding in Ohio so all Grams Afro-American relatives could come.

"Mother would make me live the lie and say that my dad is not my dad. She would insist I was pure Caucasian when I'm not. And if I didn't do this, she would threaten Yudi somehow."

"I need an example," Judge Jacobi said.

"Not let me see him. He'd feel abandoned. Move him to bad quarters. Cut out his special food. Send him away for harsh training. Even put him down on some pretext or another."

"How does your father handle this heritage thing?" the judge coaxed.

"He makes me be quiet about my heritage too, but to protect me. I guess they both are trying to protect me. Only he doesn't lie about it. And he doesn't insist that I do."

"Continue please."

"Dad and Mom and I are a family. I call Bertha Mom. So does Aleta. She acts like one. So when I say Mom I mean Bertha. I wanted to call my real mother Marian so you'd know which one I was talking about, but Aleta said that would make Mother furious. And Aleta is wiser than I am, but I refuse not to call Bertha Mom. Besides she really is my mom now. Not only that, we're expecting a baby. Dad and I went in to the doctor's office together with her and we were told at the same time, like a family. Dad always includes me. So does Mom, er Bertha. When I asked to go on their honeymoon because I had a vision of my mother taking me when they were gone, it was Bertha who said yes right away. Dad was reluctant. He didn't want me even in the next room when they did it for the first time. Dad would never have done what that lawyer said he did. He is very traditional. And honorable. He didn't regret giving Mother all his money. He said she deserved it.

"Anyway, that's why Dad married Mom a little early. He wanted his first night to be just the two of them. I knew that, but I was so scared I couldn't give them that. And they understood it. Even now Mom, um... Bertha, was the one who suggested they cancel their honeymoon to drive Yudi to California.

"Mother would never have done that. That's the difference."

"Tell me about this so-called vision you had," Judge Jacobi said.

Jocelyn laughed. "You just upset my lawyer."

Norma Jacobi looked at Stanley Praetzel who looked slightly embarrassed. "Are you signaling your client not to answer?"

"No, Your Honor," Stanley replied. "I apologize to the court for my inadvertent reaction. I was surprised. That's all."

The judge still glared at him. Stanley smiled at Jocelyn. "Please answer the judge's query. You are free to tell her whatever you like."

"Why did he say that?" the judge asked.

"Because I don't talk about my ability to prophesy at all. In fact, mostly I deny it. But when I was down south with Aleta and Stanley at a dog show, I had a vision. I saw Mother taking Yudi from Aleta's barn and putting him in a trailer to ship him. Bertha tried to stop them. She was dressed in Dad's clothes. I woke up and Stanley was changing the baby and so I told him about my nightmare. I didn't know that Dad and Mom were married then so I didn't believe my dream. Stanley did and he called Dad and Dad and Mom moved Yudi to a friend's place until the ownership could be decided by the court. Aleta was sure that a gift remains the property of the receiver, but I guess it doesn't, does it? The giver can take it back if it's given to a child. That makes sense to me because kids sometimes deserve to have the gift taken away. I don't think I deserve it, but Aleta says I must respect the court's decision no matter what it is.

"Anyway, the vision turned out to be true. Mother showed up with a horse trailer later that morning. And I found out later that Mom was wearing Dad's sweat suit that morning. They told me about the wedding soon after that. It was a secret, but not a lie. There's a difference, you know."

"Do you think you are a prophet?"

"No. I don't think so. I know I am. But all my prophecies have to do with animals."

"Tell me about another."

"The day our horses were stolen, Aleta knew about that happening because death was involved. She hired a guard. The horses were stolen except for the two that Hubbs moved out of harms way after a phone call from her. I was mad at her because she didn't have Hubbs move Yudi first. Bertha and I went with the police to find Yudi. I had an idea where my friends planned to ride. I told Bertha then that there was going to be an explosion. I told her Aleta told me. Aleta didn't know that part. Just me. And I had told my friends that there was going to be an explosion. I said Aleta had predicted it. I honestly thought she had told me about the grenade exploding. They knew she was a prophet, but they didn't believe me until after it happened. I still didn't believe I had any special powers, but now I do. I knew Mother was coming before anyone else. She hadn't told anyone. I came home from school at lunch and Aleta had company for lunch--by company I mean almost twenty people and I was upset with her for having a party and that's when I asked Dad and Bertha if I could go with them on their honeymoon. I was that scared."

"Does your mother still frighten you?"

"Yes."

"Why?"

"Because she wants to change me and I'm afraid she will. I'm not strong like Aleta. I'm happy here. And I've thought about this for a long time. Last night I told Aleta I would follow my horse back to California so I could take care of him. And my dad and my mom have already accepted this decision. I will be welcomed back when I am eighteen. They will come and get me and my horse. I told myself I could live in hell for a year for Yudi's sake. And that's what I was ready to do last night. And even this morning that's what I would have agreed to do. But after you refused to assure me my horse would be cared for properly, I realized that I really have no power. I can't protect my horse even if I'm there. Then you had me talk about my prophetic ability. When I told you about it, I began to realize that I believe I have it. I'm like my grandmother and my sister and God gives me visions that will protect my horse. If I'm in California, my mother will react badly if I tell her I've had a vision. She will..."

She paused for a long moment. The courtroom remained silent.

Suddenly Jocelyn spoke and her voice rang with an authority it hadn't had previously.

"Judge Jacobi, you are right now thinking that perhaps I should be examined by a psychiatrist before you award custody..."

She paused again. "Oh, you've changed. Now you are thinking you will make it a condition of custody..."

Again she paused. She looked at Stanley. "No wonder you were so upset. You guessed what she would do."

She turned back to the judge and addressed her again.

"That, Judge Jacobi, is intuition and experience. But with me, it wasn't either. Guess work? Not that either."

She stopped as the judge made a movement to pick up her gavel. Jocelyn spoke rapidly. "Please let me at least finish. Then you can have me committed. It would be preferable to going to California. What do I want? I want to stay with my dad. He and Mom and I are family. And we're going to have a baby. And I tell everyone it's going to be a girl because I want it to be a girl, but that's normal. I can't predict what it's going to be anymore than I can predict how you're going to rule."

Jocelyn took a deep breath and went on. "If you tell me I must live with my mother, I expect she will lock me away until I deny my heritage. She will call it a delusion. She will be able to do this because she will have custody. She believes her own lie.

"But I'm taking a chance. I know what I want. I want to live with my dad and my stepmom. I want to go to my sister's boring parties where no one is my age and everyone is into dogs and no one knows anything about horse jumping competitions, I want to be forced to do my homework and muck out the barn and take care of my horses, I want to stay at my friends' houses on weekends and talk about boys, I want to come home to Bertha and tell her all my problems and know she'll understand, but mostly I want to be loved and accepted and supported. That's what I have now, even when I throw a tantrum and pout. Oh, they don't allow me to pout in their presence. Aleta sent me out of the trailer on the weekend until I stopped. My bad attitude lasted two days. Aleta understands me best of all which is another reason I want to live here. I have a big sister and a nephew. My family is here.

"Do I feel sorry for my mother? Yes. Do I love her? No. Do I think I should go and live with her because she's lonely? No. Besides, she doesn't want me. She wants to hurt Dad. She can't stand that taking all his money didn't do it. It would have hurt her. So she's trying to take me. That'll rip his heart out. She's just that mean."

Jocelyn took another deep breath. "If I had one year to live, I would want to live here. My future is here. Please let me have it!"

The courtroom was silent for a few moments.

Then Meyers was on his feet. "We have questions, Your Honor."

"We're breaking for lunch," Judge Jacobi declared. "Court recessed until one o'clock."

The judge went into her chambers and waited. Her clerk joined her as she was removing her robe.

"Tell me exactly what you observed when I left," Norma Jacobi ordered.

"Mrs. Marian Locke fought with her attorney. The girl hugged her lawyer and then her father and new stepmother and her father's lawyer. Her father was crying."

"She's a sharp cookie, that one. Did you see how she pulled the teeth out of the opposition with her closing remark?"

"Yes, I did."

"Be back at one."

Chapter 27

At one o'clock exactly, Judge Norma Jacobi walked back into her courtroom.

Stanley had warned everyone at lunch that this judge's ruling could not be anticipated. It could go either way. He doubted seriously that the judge would make any further rulings on the horse. He was mistaken.

"I have made my decision," Judge Jacobi announced.

"But, Your Honor," Meyers objected, "we wanted to question the child."

"The child is not on trial, Mr. Meyers," the judge replied coldly. "I have heard from both parents and both counsels have had ample opportunity to bring up all arguments at that time. As for me, I do believe I have a clear picture of the situation."

Meyers sat down. "Yes, Your Honor."

"It seems obvious to all of us that Jocelyn and her mother are estranged. It is a sad state. No matter how badly Mrs. Locke may have bungled the job, she has filled the role of mother for sixteen years. Teenage years are tumultuous, at best. Emotions run high. Rebellion is to be expected. I do not like to see a child whisked a couple thousand miles away where all chance of repairing a rift is impaired."

Jocelyn sucked in her breath and held it. Her hand gripped Stanley's arm tight.

I'm going to be black and blue, he thought, and then scolded himself for such an innocuous concern.

"So, it is the order of this court that Jocelyn lives with her mother until she can claim ownership of her horse.

The judge fixed her eyes on Marian Locke.

"Mrs. Locke, you will provide the best of care for this horse and will use the time granted you to reacquaint yourself with the fine young lady your daughter has turned out to be. During this period Jocelyn Locke will not be examined by a psychiatrist or institutionalized. Do you agree to these conditions?"

Marian Locke was nodding happily. Her lawyer told her to respond verbally.

"Yes, Your Honor. Thank you."

Judge Jacobi turned her attention to Jocelyn. "Miss Jocelyn Locke, you will accept the judgment of this court. I am placing the care of your horse in your hands. You will not neglect him because you are not where you want to be. Is that clear?"

"Yes, Your Honor. Thank you for caring about my horse."

"Mr. Locke, are you and your wife prepared to take Jocelyn and her horse to California and to begin your journey by Saturday of this week?"

"We are, Your Honor." Tears welled up in his eyes as he spoke.

To everyone's surprise, the judge wasn't finished.

"Further this court orders that on August sixth of this year, which is Jocelyn Locke's seventeenth birthday, Mrs. Marian Locke is to render the full ownership of Yudi, the horse, to Jocelyn Locke who has proven to this court that she is mature enough to carry such a responsibility.

"Mr. Locke I'm awarding you full custody of your daughter, Jocelyn Locke. Should Mrs. Marian Locke violate any of the terms she agreed to during the court-imposed visitation, you are empowered by this court to take custody of both Jocelyn and her horse, Yudi, and return with them to Illinois."

The three at the table on the judge's right collectively drew a deep breath. The judge continued.

"Mrs. Marian Locke, take advantage of this opportunity given you. Even if Jocelyn changes her mind, she will be returned to live with her father on August 6 of this year. This enforced visitation is not precedent setting. Future visitation will be at Jocelyn's discretion."

"Court adjourned."

After the judge left, the entire group sat stunned for several minutes.

"Did we win or lose?" Jocelyn finally asked.

Stanley smiled. "You won all the way around. It was a brilliant ruling."

Robert approached his ex-wife. "We will leave on Saturday. I've never travelled cross-country with a horse trailer. I think it will take about five days. Jocelyn will call regularly to let you know where we are."

"That will be fine, Robert," Marian said stiffly.

"We will be bringing two horses. Yudi needs a traveling companion."

On the other side of the room, Bertha hugged Jocelyn. "We won't even know what the sex is until you get back. You won't have missed a thing."

"The honeymoon," Jocelyn lamented.

"We'll take another in August. And you can bring a friend--a girlfriend."

"Do you think Aleta will let me take Royal to California? Jack Barton has a great area to practice jumping. It would be good experience for Royal."

"Does Yudi like Royal?" Bertha asked.

"We could take Royal over to fetch Yudi and see if they travel well together."

"We can do that and then decide. We can ask Hubbs. He'll know."

Stanley spoke softly to his father. "It was a better outcome than I expected."

"I could see Jocelyn surprised you."

"Deliberately," Stanley observed. "She's like Aleta."

"Tell me she wants to be a doctor or a horse trainer, not a lawyer."

"I will have Lauren sit her at the tables with doctors and artists and dog trainers and nurses."

"Think that will work?" Hubert asked his son.

"Not a clue."

"Well, at least Robert and Bertha will have their honeymoon. This will be good for them all."

"As I said, a brilliant judgment."

As the group exited the courtroom, they found Claude and Harriet, Aleta and little Gerard sitting on a bench opposite the door, waiting.

Jocelyn rushed up to Aleta. "Can I take Royal to California?"

Stanley whispered to Hubert, "Aleta."

Hubert disagreed, "Harriet."

The two prophets looked bewildered while Hubert and Stanley stood back grinning. Both women glanced up simultaneously and said, "You won."

"I have to visit Mother for two months. I wish my birthday were July fourth."

"What's that got to do with anything?" Aleta asked.

"That's when she comes back," Harriet said. "What about Yudi?"

Jocelyn responded instantly, "He'll be mine! Isn't that cool!"

"Tie!" Stanley exclaimed.

"Harriet guessed the rest," Hubert responded. "I won."

"Aleta's question clued her in."

"Doesn't count."

"Do you two have money on this bet?" Aleta asked.

"A hundred."

She eyed her husband coolly. "Did you bet on me?"

"I always do."

"So now you're going to expect me to pay up."

"As usual."

Hubert chuckled. "No wonder you're such a cheerful loser. Fork over the hundred."

"This is a lot of money, Aleta," her husband said as he pulled a bill from his wallet.

"You want your payment now?"

"You can give me a hundred dollar kiss here?"

"Sit down," she said.

"I'm not sure this is a propitious beginning," he said as he sat.

She placed the baby in his arms and whispered, "Remember my first kiss on our honeymoon just before we conceived him?"

"No."

"I do," she said as she leaned over and brushed his cheek with her lips.

She straightened up. "Now isn't that memory full payment?"

Gerard opened his eyes and stared at his father.

"She's got me, kid. She knows if I say it's not, she'll proceed to part two and that's X-rated."

Marian and her lawyer emerged from the courtroom and silence fell on the group surrounding Stanley.

Bertha broke the silence, "Come over and see your grandson," she urged.

"A baby that young shouldn't be out, especially on a rainy day," Marian snapped.

"I could take a three generation picture of you, Aleta and Gerard with that camera of yours. You could show Jayline. You could even start a collection," Bertha said.

"Jayline and Scott aren't planning a family," Marian sniffed. "They are too busy with their careers."

"Well, Aleta and Stanley are planning more children, so you'll still have a nice collection," Bertha said cheerfully. "He's a good-looking baby."

"Babies all look pretty much alike," Marian retorted.

Curiosity had drawn Marian closer however.

"Hand me your camera and I'll snap the shot," Robert offered.

Marian reluctantly sat down.

"Do you want to hold him?" Stanley asked.

"His mother should hold him," Marian stated.

Undeterred by her sour attitude, Robert took a series of shots.

Afterward Marian rushed into the restroom and washed her hands. When she emerged, Bertha went in, spotted the camera in the trash can, retrieved it and slipped it into her purse.

Marian was still obviously outraged at losing her case.

Bertha arranged to drive Jocelyn home in the second car.

"I need to talk with her a bit," she said.

When they were on the road, Bertha had Jocelyn look in her purse. Jocelyn pulled out the camera.

"This is Mother's, isn't it?"

"Yes."

"Oh, Boy! Is she ever pissed!"

"Develop the photos and send a copy to Jayline," Jocelyn said. "I'll take a set with me. Marian is in every one so maybe she'll let me keep them in my room. I only wish there were one of you and Dad."

"That would be unwise," Bertha counseled.

Jocelyn fingered the camera for several minutes.

"Bertha, I'm scared," she said. "Maybe I won't take Royal after all. I would hate for anything to happen to him."

"Don't plan not to have fun. But let your mother share in your hobby."

"Mother hates horses. She hates the smell of manure around the stable. She hates the rough ground, the dust, and the flies. Besides Mother will plan every day. Having her let me do what I want was just a pipe dream," Jocelyn said bitterly. "I was right. It will be hell."

"Okay don't take Royal. Ride Yudi. Train him."

"It's a waste."

"You'll learn a lot," Bertha said. "Yudi needs more training and calming if I'm going to go riding with you."

"The doctor said..."

"...what Robert wanted him to say," Bertha interjected. "I'd teased your dad by telling him that he might have to ride a horse at the wedding. That scared him. I'm sure he pumped everyone about what kind of wedding I was planning."

"I wouldn't want the baby to be hurt."

"You just concentrate on training Yudi," Bertha advised. "If you don't get to spend much time with him, we'll do it together when you get back."

Suddenly Jocelyn dropped the camera.

"What is it?" Bertha asked. "Did you pinch a finger?"

"I called myself a prophet in court. I didn't mean to lie."

"You didn't."

"I only get pieces, not whole visions."

"And the pieces frighten you?"

"They scare the shit outta me," Jocelyn said.

Bertha pulled over and stopped. She drew the young girl to her and held her. "If you weren't able to prophesy, I'd be scared to death to let you go. Now tell me what you see."

"It's not much."

"It doesn't matter. It will be enough."

Jocelyn began to cry. "All I see is the calendar on the wall and it says July 7. That's all."

"Do you hear anything?   Feel anything?   Smell anything?"

Jocelyn cried even harder.   "Suppose I ask Dad to come out and something happens to him?"

"Where was the calendar?" Bertha said.

"It's the kitchen calendar. It's the kind Mother buys every year. It hangs in the same spot every year."

"So you're at your mother's house," Bertha said. "I'll call Aleta and Harriet and have them come over. Okay?"

"They won't think I'm just bidding for attention?"

"That's your mother speaking. Not any of us."

"Oh my God!" Jocelyn cried, obviously distraught. "I'll never last."

"Your decision warmed your father's heart. You made him very happy."

"Maybe I shouldn't have been so honest," Jocelyn complained. "Look at what I brought on myself."

"What you brought on yourself was a two month visit instead of a fourteen month stay or a life-long sentence."

Jocelyn's manner underwent a change. Some of the tenseness left along with her scowl. "I did, didn't I?"

Chapter 28

The rain stopped in the middle of the night leaving the ground wet. Bertha fretted about it silently.

"We're going to be in a church, Bertha," Robert said hopefully. "Their roofs don't leak."

"Remember, you don't come home for anything. Stanley will give you your wedding clothes when it's time."

"Someone has to pick up Jocelyn."

"I excused her from school," Bertha said. "I need her here. Someone needs to go with Hubbs and Claude and pick up Yudi and Sterling so we can start out first thing in the morning."

"We could leave them there and pick them up on our way."

"Don't bother a bride with changes on the day of her wedding," Bertha barked. "It's a good thing you'll be at work all day. I absolutely don't want you underfoot.

Stanley called from the kitchen. "Breakfast."

Robert looked at his wife questioningly.

She held out her hand. "Give me your ring. I need to give it to the ring bearer."

"We have a ring bearer?" Robert said. "That sounds promising."

"Don't get your hopes up," Bertha said. "You have no idea what awaits."

"Who's cooking breakfast?"

"Aleta."

"She can't cook!" Robert exclaimed.

"I want you to appreciate me."

Robert embraced her. "You have no idea how much I appreciate you."

"Oh I have a little idea. You are still planning on coming to your wedding," Bertha murmured impishly.

"Well, I did surprise you and you were a good sport about it," Robert said. "Only I want you to know I'm praying that I'll survive."

"You'll be wonderful. You always are."

"Most weddings have rehearsals," Robert suggested.

"Just say 'I do' when the minister looks at you."

"So we're having a minister," Robert commented.

"Go eat breakfast!" Bertha ordered.

Robert kissed her and departed.

Aleta's idea of breakfast was cold cereal and orange juice. Robert walked into the kitchen and found bacon and eggs. Stanley was at the stove wearing a large apron.

"Aleta's nursing the baby," he said. "She told me to give you some cereal and orange juice. Is that what you want?"

"I want what you're cooking," Robert replied. "Cold cereal is the limit of Aleta's culinary skills."

"She has other skills," Stanley replied.

"What do you two do when Bertha's not here?"

"Starve, mostly.

"I smell biscuits."

"I dug out some Bertha froze," Stanley said. "I can defrost with the best of them."

"So you'll be alright when we leave?"

"We'll be fine," Stanley assured him. "Now hurry up. We're on a timetable today."

"I'd love to stay and help."

"I'll bet you would."

The office closed at noon so Alice could go home and dress for the wedding. Andrew Jackson and Roland Chin went to lunch with Stanley and Robert and then were sent home to fetch their wives.

Unknown to Robert, an ambulance was sent to fetch Dennis Middlebourne and he came early, was settled in his wheelchair and with his aide enjoyed the last minute scrambling inside the house and watched the outside activities through the picture window. Aleta stopped by regularly to hear his comments. Bertha spoke to him frequently as well.

Ledgewood stopped long enough to tell him he was a client too and his case had been put on hold and then he told him that they'd just won a tough case and ended by saying he'd come to the conclusion these lawyers were worth waiting for. Then he went back to work.

Emerita and Teodora checked on Dennis Middlebourne every hour asking his aide if they needed anything. Aleta introduced them as clients too. When the caterers arrived the two women disappeared.

"Is everyone your client?" Dennis asked when Aleta stopped by to tell him where to position his wheelchair.

"Not everyone," Aleta replied. "But I don't take a client I don't want as a friend. Wait, I take that back. I have served as legal counsel to a true enemy of mine. God chose him."

"Did God choose me?" Dennis asked.

"Yes, he did."

"Well at least I know which direction I'm heading," Dennis quipped. "At least I hope that's what that means."

Aleta smiled. "Until you leave to brighten His day, I'm glad you're here to brighten mine."

"I'm glad you can still understand me. You don't know how good that makes me feel."

"I can scarcely imagine how difficult it is for you," Aleta responded, and then added, "My friends will come up and talk with you. Don't worry about responding. Half of them are lawyers and they love to have the stage all to themselves."

Dennis chuckled.

At five o'clock, Stanley got a phone call. When he hung up, he said to Robert, "We have twenty minutes to dress and ten minutes to get to the site."

"A church?"

Stanley looked at him askance. "Just get dressed. I have to change too."

Robert unzipped his garment bag and called to Stanley. "Who packed this?"

"Bertha."

"There's a swim suit in here."

"Better wear it."

"Did you get one?"

"Nope," Stanley said, "but maybe I'm not going swimming. I've been told you're to wear everything in the bag."

"Oh, hell! I was hoping..." he paused.

"Hoping what?"

"That there'd be no water involved."

"You've been baptized, right?"

"I think so."

"You can't join a Christian church unless you're been baptized," Stanley said. "So were you or weren't you?"

"No one asked," Robert replied.

"Bet Bertha asked your mother."

"You mean I'm going to be baptized?"

"Immersion type looks like," Stanley chuckled.

"Oh Lord, no!" Robert groused.

"Better dress for it. They'll do you naked otherwise."

"I'm going to be publicly humiliated," Robert groaned. "I'm never going to live this down. What if I don't show up?"

"Your wife would never forgive you."

"That's just it. I'm already married. We can baptize me quietly later if it's important to Bertha."

"Just grit your teeth and put on the suit. You'll laugh about this for years to come."

"That's the trouble. Everyone will laugh about this for years to come," Robert quipped.

"We're running short on time. Get a move on."

"No choice?"

"Sure you have a choice. Bathing suit or naked."

"Shit!" Robert exclaimed beginning to disrobe. Stanley went into the bathroom to shave.

As Stanley drove down the driveway with cars parked along the entire length, he handed Robert an envelope.

"From Bertha," he said.

Robert opened it and whooped with joy.

"What did she say?"

"The bathing suit was a ruse. And I'm to do what you tell me to." Robert turned. "You could have told me."

"And get burnt toast for breakfast for a year?"

Stanley stopped the car at the end of the driveway.

Robert stared at the transformation. A tall white canopy was stretched from the house to the barn. Straw was spread over the mud. And Jocelyn stood holding two horses.

"You're riding mine," Stanley said. "He's very calm."

"Just to the barn right?"

"You're getting married on horseback," Stanley told him watching his expression. It showed mild surprise.

"I have to stay on?" Robert questioned.

Stanley noted his lack of apprehension.

"I get the feeling you're prepared," Stanley said.

"I hope I am."

"Did you take swimming lessons too?"

"I worked out at the gym, but there's only so much one can do to rebuild a middle-aged body."

"Mount up," Stanley said, going to Aleta's Appaloosa, sticking his foot in the stirrup and swinging up on the horse in one fluid motion.

Robert, shaking a bit with trepidation, managed to snag the stirrup on his second try. The swing of his leg over the back of the horse wasn't as graceful as Stanley's but it was passable.

He took the reins and Minx followed Shadow down the straw corridor, past the guests standing on either side of the path. As he looked at the sea of faces, he saw nothing but delighted smiles. He began to smile back. This was okay.

The minister rode out on horseback. Stanley positioned Shadow and Robert struggled to turn Minx who wanted to enter the pasture behind the minister. She refused to turn away from the direction that led go it, spinning in place twice to the delight of the guests. Stanley coached Robert to turn one more time and then moved Shadow between the pasture and the recalcitrant horse. Thus Robert finally took his place beside the minister.

Once in place, Robert realized that he was listening to a live string quartet. They played as Jocelyn, dressed in a lovely blue gown, appeared astride Sterling. Evidential his foot was well enough to bear the light weight of his youngest daughter, minus a saddle. A crown of white flowers sat on top of her lovely auburn hair and she scattered flower petals as she came slowly down the path.

Aleta, riding bareback on Yudi, followed. Her gown was a matching one, only in pale green. Her elegance on the horse matched her sister's, and it seemed befitting that she too wore a crown of flowers.

Robert, delighted at the sight of his two daughters astride horses which they rode with uncommon grace, let the tears stream down his cheeks. This alone was worth the anxiety waiting had caused. He heard the saddle squeak as he felt Minx shift her weight. He was reminded that horses once placed are not necessarily stationary.

He thought about the fact that Bertha had used their horses and matched each horse and rider. He knew there was only one horse left, Jocelyn's new highly-prized show jumper, Royal Wedding.

Apt name he thought and realized that that's what probably gave Bertha the idea.

Bertha came from behind the house riding Royal who only Minx matched at fifteen hands high. Royal was wearing a wreath of flowers. Bertha held the reins lightly in one hand, the other carrying a bouquet of the same white flowers that made up the matching crowns.

As she entered the aisle, Robert looked nowhere else. Bertha was the biggest surprise of all. Not only was she radiant, she sat well and rode with an ease that told him she'd been too modest about her ability to ride.

"I'm going to need to take more lessons," he whispered to Stanley.

The ceremony was traditional and Minx had no trouble obeying Robert's direction to turn and face the pasture. Rings were exchanged after Jocelyn managed to figure out how to take them off the chain. The minister pronounced them husband and wife.

Robert looked at the distance between the two horses and said, "Can we do the kiss on the ground?"

The laughter of the group, all of whom were close enough to hear everything indicated that the guests were expecting him to stay on the horse.

He nudged Minx closer, took hold of Bertha with one hand, leaned over and kissed her briefly. Then letting go of his grip on the saddle horn took her shoulders in both hands and kissed her again, this time with the passion and joy he felt. Minx stayed in place.

After the newlyweds turned their horses Robert took Bertha's hand and said, "I have an announcement."

He then told the guests that he and Bertha had been married in a civil ceremony nine days prior for a number of reasons not the least of which was to move up the honeymoon stage.

The group laughed and he went on to say that he wouldn't even have mentioned it, except that that ceremony and the resulting secret honeymoon evidently had God's blessing for it resulted in Bertha conceiving a child.

"We both thought we'd planned the ultimate surprise. We were wrong. God planed the ultimate surprise. Much as we wanted to have a child, we never thought we would be so blessed."

"And I thought I was going to be the big surprise," Paul Locke said from Robert's right.

"As did we!" chorused Bertha's two sons to the left of her.

"Paul, Andrea, Junior, Lettie!" Robert exclaimed.

Simultaneously, Bertha shouted, "Earl! Bob! You came!"

"I'd hug you all, but I barely managed the kiss," Robert said.

"I think you've managed more than that. Congratulations!" Paul said heartily.

"Mom, we're so happy for you," Earl said.

"I didn't hear from you so I thought..."

"You're the one who taught us about surprises," Bob chimed in. "Donna and I wouldn't have missed this one."

"Yeh," Earl agreed. "Imagine surprising a groom! It was Janet's idea to surprise the surpriser."

"And then you come up with this baby announcement!" Bob said. "I told Donna you were the master. Now, at last, she'll understand where I'm coming from."

"Bertha," Robert said. "I am not dismounting in front of everyone."

Bertha laughed. "Be back right after the photographer gets done. I'll never get him back up on that horse, so I have to take advantage."

She chucked at Royal who took off at a trot. Minx followed and Robert hung on with both hands.

"Slow down! I didn't get to the trotting lesson."

He could hear the laughter behind him.

The photographer took a series of photos on and off the horses. In the background they could hear Lauren tell their guests how they were going to be seated.

"I have one more surprise for you," Bertha teased.

"Oh, no," he moaned. "I hope it's a gift."

"It is. It's in the bedroom."

Aleta went into the house to nurse Gerard. Stanley followed after a few minutes and found her in their bedroom, stripped to the waist. Stanley quickly closed and locked both doors.

"I'm tired," she said as she moved to the bed. "Don't let me roll over on him."

Stanley took off his pants and folded them carefully.

"Do you have plans?"

"No, you do."

Stanley removed the remainder of his formal attire and lay down on the bed beside her.

"You're practically undressed," Aleta said.

"So are you."

"What plans do you think I have?"

"You talked to Dr. Chesney."

"I am healed," Aleta told him. "And I need you."

"You're nursing our son."

"He'll be done in a few minutes," Aleta said.

"We can't do it with him here," Stanley protested.

"I don't think he can even see clearly."

"We'll mark him for life."

Aleta giggled. "That's almost prophetic. We'll put him in the bassinet."

Stanley didn't even look around. He'd seen the bassinet when he came in. "Why did you move it in here, by the way?"

"I moved it just in case Robert and Bertha stayed the night."

"They've been here as man and wife for almost ten days," Stanley pointed out.

"But this is their wedding day. We need to stay out of their way."

"They won't know they have the wing to themselves."

"Bertha helped me move the bassinet."

"Are you telling me I was right? You planned this?"

"I knew you'd be aroused seeing me in that dress," Aleta said, "so I arranged an alternative for you."

"I have myself under full control," Stanley insisted.

"Then just kiss me," Aleta whispered, "so I can sleep and have pleasant dreams."

Stanley leaned over and kissed her being careful not to touch the baby still nursing at her breast.

"You will take care of him, won't you?"

"You just sleep," Stanley said. "I'll take care of him."

"And then you'll make love to me," she whispered.

"I won't be in the mood," he said.

"Wanna bet?"

Bertha took Robert into the guest bedroom she and Robert had shared for ten days and locked the door. He was startled.

"We have guests."

"Aleta and Stanley will take care of them. It's their house."

"It's our wedding."

"You're the one who wanted your surprise now."

"Yes, I did."

"Then come over here and unzip the back of my dress."

"I thought you were going to give me a gift."

"I am."

"You didn't get a tattoo?"

"Just unzip the dress and reach in."

"Where?" Robert said as he slowly began to unzip the dress.

"You'll find it," Bertha said. "It's a promise."

"In an envelope?"

"That's for you to discover."

Robert unzipped the dress to the waist and slipped his hands around beneath it. His fingers searched every inch of bare skin until it dawned on him she was wearing no underclothes.

"What does this mean?" he asked as his hands searched again for the envelope he was certain would explain.

Her hands pressed on his from the other side of her dress.

"Does this mean what I think it means?"

"I want us always to be on our honeymoon."

"You feel uncomfortable without undergarments."

"Not anymore," Bertha whispered. "And if you want we can make love before we go back out or we can wait until later."

"Can we do both?" Robert said, gently slipping her arms out of the sleeves.

They heard the baby cry.

"Is he okay?" Robert asked.

"His parents are there."

"Maybe we should check."

"We can't."

"Why not?"

"He's in their bedroom."

"They moved him?" Robert questioned despite the fact that the answer was obvious. The cry wasn't coming from the nursery.

"Aleta and I did."

"He's still crying," Robert said.

"They're busy."

"Doing what?"

"Did you see the way Stanley looked at Aleta?"

"My eyes were on you."

"His weren't."

"But it's our wedding night," Robert pointed out.

Bertha giggled. "Considering where your hands are, I'm glad you remembered."

"You fox, you!" he exclaimed just before he kissed her.

Lauren allowed the teenagers to stay together. Besides Paul Junior and Lettie, Jocelyn's riding group had been invited and the girls all determined they were going to have a wedding on horseback. All of them told Jocelyn how lucky she was to have a stepmother who could ride. Tiffany was still in a wheelchair as a result of the accident, but her parents who'd accompanied her found the guest list far beyond their wildest dreams.

The Patsons were thrilled at the prospect of rubbing shoulders with the county's most notable citizens. Thus when Georgette Patson found herself at a table with Nathan Tobias and Dennis Middlebourne she was upset. She smiled politely at the two wheelchair bound men and looked around to see where her husband had landed. As she was looking around two other women joined the group as did Dr. Chesney. He sat beside Dennis Middlebourne and began chatting with him. Dr. Chesney told Dennis about his late wife and how Aleta had made their last days together wonderful as the stroke had left her unable to communicate.

Judge Davis shook Nathan's hand and sat beside him telling him how lucky she was she finally got to be at a table with him. Georgette Patson looked startled.

Then Harriet Luther joined them saying, "Aren't we the lucky ones. We get two of the most interesting men here to chat with."

"You better have included me in that twosome or I won't deliver your next baby."

Everyone laughed.

"What do you suppose is keeping the bride and groom?" Georgette Patson inquired.

"You don't want to know," Harriet chuckled. "He's madly in love with her and she was a vision today, wasn't she?"

"She was grace and beauty on that horse," Lydia said.

"I can't see Robert resisting," Harriet said.

"Nor Stanley," Lydia said. "Aleta was lovely as well."

"Stanley never took his eyes off her," Harriet said.

"You noticed that too?" Lydia queried. "I thought it was just mothers who focused on their children."

"So, Mrs. Patson," Harriet concluded aloud, "we're in for a wait."

Georgette Patson stumbled over her words.

"I don't understand... that is... you can't mean... I thought Aleta went in to nurse her baby."

"She did," Harriet said, then seeing her discomfort, switched topics. "Tell us, how's Tiffany's leg coming along?"

Georgette brightened at the change in subject. "She'll be on crutches next week, but I'm never letting her on a horse again. And the scar is horrible. I told her she would have to get used to wearing slacks and jeans."

"Did you know Aleta had a horrific scar on her head?" Harriet inquired.

"I'd heard she had brain surgery," Georgette commented coolly. It had obviously been taken care of. It wasn't the same.

"I'm going back to the first scar, the one she got before she got married," Harriet said. "It took out all her hair right down the middle of her scalp. Stanley married her that way. Her mother wanted her to have plastic surgery, but she refused. And Stanley backed her. And on her wedding day her mother wanted her to wear a crown and veil to cover the scar and she refused. Stanley sent her a crown of flowers sewn on a ring of silk fabric. It was soft. She wore that, but no veil. To take the story one more step, when her sister Jayline was married, Aleta had just had surgery on her head again and her head had been shaved. She had both arms in slings and her mother wouldn't let her come to the wedding. Aleta was terribly hurt. We went without her."

"I would never do that," Georgette exclaimed.

"Look over at the table where your daughter is sitting," Harriet said. "Her real friends don't care."

"They'll soon drift apart," Georgette said. "It's their love of horses that keeps them together."

"It's a good bond," Harriet noted.

"But I can't let her ride again!" Georgette declared.

"What does her doctor say?" Lydia asked.

"That she could ride," Georgette said. "But I know her. She'll want to jump."

"Why won't you let her?"

"Because she might wind up like me?" Nathan asked. "Only my injury was the result of an automobile accident, yet I let my son drive."

Dennis mumbled something.

Dr. Chesney said, "I'm not Aleta, but I'm guessing he's telling you she won't catch ALS from a horse."

Georgette glanced over. "Jocelyn is a really good friend. I wish they'd stay friends."

"I imagine they will," Harriet said. "Jocelyn is like that."

"What would you do if she were your daughter?" Georgette charged.

"Let her ride," Nathan declared.

"Let her ride," Dr. Chesney chorused.

"I agree," Lydia chimed in with conviction.

Georgette looked at Harriet. When Harriet spoke her words carried an authority that Lydia had heard before when Aleta prophesied.

"Go tell her now that you're going to buy her a new horse."

"My husband?" Georgette temporized.

"It was your idea to sell Royal, not his," Harriet said knowingly.

"Go!" Lydia urged.

"Go," Dennis mumbled and his aide interpreted his word and added a second word. "Hope."

"She's beginning to despair," Harriet said. "Don't let it happen."

Lydia looked around. Not only was a judge and a doctor telling her to let her daughter ride a horse but a prophet, no less. Why had the knowledge gained from a news article risen to the forefront of her memory at this moment?

She looked over at her daughter. Tiffany had worked so hard in therapy. Her doctor had nothing but praise for the effort Tiffany was expending. Her muscles were so strong the pressure on the bones would be less, he'd told her parents. It would be safe for her to ride soon.

Tiffany had not complained, but she had asked as they were coming to the wedding whether there was any chance she'd be allowed to ride again.

Georgette remembered how definite her no had been.

Now as she looked at her daughter, she could see her wilting as the group became involved in talk about upcoming jumping competitions.

She walked over, kissed her daughter on the forehead and said softly, "Ask your friends to help you find a good horse for you."

Tiffany looked up into her mother's face. Georgette could actually see the joy returning.

Jocelyn had heard the words.

"Hey, Guys, Tiffany's getting a new horse."

"Kevin's selling Spirit," Wade said. "He's a good horse. Kevin never did the right things to get the best out of him. I bet Tiffany could."

"Kevin's horse?" Georgette quavered. "Didn't he throw Kevin?"

"Only Minx didn't rear," Tiffany responded.

"She's the one my dad rode," Jocelyn pointed out. "She doesn't rear, but she's hard to handle. She's got a mind of her own.

"Spirit is a calm horse," Lisa put in.

"He hasn't any big faults," her cousin, Wanda, added.

"And he can stay here," Jocelyn said. "And Tiffany and I can train together. I'll be back in August, Tiffany, and maybe by then you'll be ready to ride. But meanwhile, you can come over and visit him anytime. And say hi to Royal. I don't want him to feel abandoned."

"Could I, Mother?" Tiffany asked, her face bright. "Will you really let me ride again?"

"You've earned the right," her mother said.

"He's a jumper, Mother."

Georgette paled briefly, and then said calmly, "I know."

The two couples emerged from their bedrooms simultaneously. They laughed when they saw each other.

"So you've conceived your next one on our wedding night," Robert quipped.

"Family tradition. Someone had to do it," Stanley retorted. "You jumped the gun. We can't let this day go unheralded."

"We are a raunchy bunch, aren't we?" Robert shot back.

"It's your side of the family," Stanley shot back. "We just find you Lockes irresistible!"

Aleta hugged Stanley. "Saved yourself with that one."

"I wouldn't go announcing another grandchild. Nursing mothers don't ovulate," Stanley said.

"And women in menopause don't conceive children," Robert returned.

"We better go see to our guests," Aleta laughed. "None of them will know what we've been doing."

But Aleta was wrong.

She could tell by all the smirks that everyone had guessed where the four had been.

"How long were we gone?" she asked Stanley.

"It's that satisfied smile on your face that's giving us away," Stanley hissed.

It was Paul who greeted them. "Aleta, I understand you want me to design an addition to your house. I understand you planned your next baby while on the delivery table. So how many rooms do I need to give you?"

"One!" Stanley said.

"Six!" Aleta corrected.

"We already have a nursery," Stanley pointed out.

"Which is going to be another guest room eventually because the children will be in their own wing. You don't want only Gerard alone on the second floor."

"Okay, two," Stanley acquiesced.

"Six," Aleta stated firmly. "And we need the plans soon."

"When do you plan to build--one year, two years?"

"Try nine months from today," Robert said.

"Two babies can share that nursery," Paul remarked.

"But three will crowd it," Robert put in jovially.

"I told you Robert, only your baby is going to be born the last week in February," Stanley claimed staunchly. "Ask Dr. Chesney. He's the expert. Tell him, Bernard. Nursing mothers don't get pregnant."

Dr. Chesney laughed. "They have the same odds against them as women Bertha's age."

Stanley gasped dismayed. "You mean it's not impossible?"

His answer came when the obstetrician grinned and said, "Aleta made an appointment to see me next week."

Stanley groaned. "Oh no..."

The laughter broke what residual tension had been engendered by Paul's open questioning.

The minister leaned over and asked Lauren, "Doesn't he know... you know."

"Stanley loves children," Lauren said. "He's really quite wonderful with them."

"He seems so distressed."

"Aleta knows what she's doing."

"Why is she in such a rush?"

"I have no idea. You might ask her."

"I can't do that."

"I can," Lauren said, standing up.

The minister plucked on her sleeve. "Don't!"

"Your minister wants to know why you're in such a rush to have children."

"And you're curious too," Aleta responded good-naturedly. "All I can say is that God preselected this ova to be fertilized and this day for it to happen. He wants us to have this particular child."

"You said you planned on six," Lydia put forth. "Wasn't this your idea?"

"Oh, Mom. I thought you'd get it. I walk through life with a plan just as you used to walk into a courtroom as a lawyer. And then as I'm walking, I get a bit of insight and I act on it. Fortunately, my overall plan to have six enabled me to be ready for this one. Stanley, on the other hand, simply followed his God-given male instinct and is now surprised at the result. It takes men a while to turn some pages."

"I dare anyone to say they understood that," Lydia challenged.

Aleta grinned. "Dennis did. Do you want to tell them, Dennis? I'll translate."

And for the first time, Aleta's friends witnessed her ability to understand those that couldn't be understood.

Dennis mumbled and Aleta repeated his words exactly as he spoke them. "God gave them a passion for one another. It was ignited by this ceremony. The end result was a renewed consummation of their marital vows and as God blessed their first consummation, so He will bless this one."

The crowd was hushed.

"Okay, Dennis," Aleta coaxed. "You're on a roll. Tell them what Bertha and Robert were doing. You have such a gift of expression."

Again Dennis mumbled and Aleta translated.

"Our newlywed pair had taken vows earlier and had consummated those vows and were blessed by the promise of a child. Today, however, was just as special in their hearts and they went back to exchange a vow too private for our ears and consummated it. They now feel fully wed and committed to their future together. We're gathered here to celebrate this day and that future."

Bertha, tears streaming down her face, went over to Dennis and kissed him lightly on the top of his head. "You blessed man! Thank you!"

Aleta laughed. "He wants a proper kiss from the bride."

Bertha leaned over and kissed him tenderly on the mouth.

"Much better," Aleta said.

"Let's cut our cake," Bertha said. "We can eat while our friends are being served."

"We need to eat the first piece," Robert said.

The cake was cut and a single piece extracted. Bertha broke off a tiny bit and placed it gently in Robert's mouth. Having seen cake shoved in the faces of many grooms, he was surprised. He took a piece and offered it to her. Then they kissed and everyone clapped.

The party lasted long after the cake and Jocelyn's friends told her they'd never had so much fun.

When they left, Jocelyn sought out Aleta who was back in her bedroom breast feeding Gerard.

"I need to talk," she said. "It's private."

"Lock the door," Aleta told her.

Chapter 29

The next morning Andrew Jackson and Roland Chin presented themselves at the Praetzel house at exactly eight o'clock. To their surprise Bertha answered the door.

"Right on time," Bertha said warmly. "Mrs. Praetzel requests that you wait in the study."

"I thought you'd be gone," Andrew said.

"My sons are coming for breakfast and Paul's family is too. You're invited. We eat at nine."

"Do you need help?" Roland asked politely.'

"You can help Robert set up the tables until Aleta is ready to see you."

The two men set down their briefcases and hurried into the family room.

"My wife and I were pleased to be invited to your wedding," Roland Chin said. "We enjoyed it immensely."

"Ditto!" Andrew Jackson said. "I don't remember when I laughed so much."

Bertha glared at him.

"I cried too," he said, redeeming himself instantly.

The tables were up, the cloths spread and the plates and silver in place before Aleta appeared. She went over and kissed Bertha.

"Morning, Mom," she said lightly. "Are the ladies coming here today?"

"They're already here. They're out helping Hubbs clean up the barn."

"Remember it's your honeymoon. Leave the dishes."

"Yes, Ma'am," Bertha said.

Aleta squeezed her shoulder. "Your wedding was a kick. I obviously have overlooked some of your best qualities."

"Aleta, go take care of business. Breakfast is at nine."

"Finally!" Aleta exclaimed. She kissed Bertha again. "Love you, Mom."

When they were in the study, Aleta told her two associates that after breakfast they were going to visit Ed Ornstein. Then they were going to visit Dennis Middlebourne.

"We aren't working today?" Andrew asked.

"I want you to see Ed's office," she said. "I want you to learn not to judge a book by its cover. I know you both think you already do that, but I'm about to shake your world.

"We need to discover a new way to exegete computer data to save our client Gordon Ledgewood from a prison term without accusing the real culprit."

"Why can't we do that?" Chin asked.

"That will be the second of today's lessons. Once you understand that you will be ready to work on Emerita's case."

"I have some thoughts on that," Andrew put forth.

"Hold them for now."

"Why are we visiting Mr. Middlebourne? We met him last night."

"He has something to show you," Aleta said. "Now tell me what you have come up with on his case."

"The Americans with Disabilities Act doesn't directly speak to his situation," Roland said.

"If it did," Aleta quipped, "he wouldn't need us."

"The Fair Housing Act doesn't either--not directly anyway," Andrew said. "And I heard you. That's why he needs us."

"Did either of you study the contract?"

"We looked at it," Roland ventured uncertainly. The young associate suddenly realized that he'd missed seeing a major flaw.

"It's a well-written contract," Andrew stated boldly. "But he is obviously not a man of diminished mental capacity."

"But he falls in the crack nevertheless," Aleta returned. "He's physically incapacitated but capable of ordering his own affairs and support his physical needs with money other than the Center funds. You have half an hour to study the contract before breakfast. Then you'll be somewhat prepared to talk with Dennis."

"Where are you going?" Andrew asked.

"To nurse my baby," she replied. "He likes breakfast in the morning too."

As she closed the door, she heard Roland scold, "You had to ask."

"I thought that's why she was late," Andrew said.

"You got a copy of the contract?"

"Yeh."

"Xerox me a copy."

"What? The mighty Chin came unprepared?

Breakfast was a large family affair. Harriet and Claude brought Lettie with Jocelyn. Paul and his family had stayed at his mother's house. The girls had talked into the wee hours of the morning. Paul Junior had a room to himself and woke up happy.

Bertha's sons and their wives arrived from a nearby motel precisely at nine.

"Men at one table, women at another. Kids over there. Help yourselves," Bertha ordered following Lauren's pattern of separating couples.

Emerita and Teodora served the stacks of pancakes, platters of bacon, baskets of fresh baked rolls and scrambled eggs. They poured fresh squeezed orange juice and chilled tomato juice into tall slender glasses. The children got milk; the adults, coffee or tea.

Bertha sat at the table and was served as a guest. She enjoyed the change in roles. Aleta and Jocelyn called her Mom and soon both of her daughters-in-law who had always called her Bertha switched to Mom too. It seemed so much more appropriate, especially as Lettie had been calling her Aunt Bertha. Harriet soon became Grams to the whole group.

The men, happy to be by themselves, chatted about work, Robert's new truck, the upcoming trip to California and the sights to take in on the way. Robert asked Earl and Bob what their fondest childhood memory was and the women, hearing the subject began sharing theirs.

When more stacks of pancakes appeared at each table, Robert commented, "These are better than your first batch, Bertha."

Bertha gasped, "I've been eclipsed. Hubbs is the second shift cook."

Aleta spun around, "Hubbs?"

"Yes, Ma'am," Hubbs answered poking his head around the corner. "Do you want whipped cream and strawberries on yours?"

"Yes, Hubbs, please," Aleta replied.

Hubbs' pancakes became dessert.

When Aleta left with Roland and Andrew she told Jocelyn that Lettie could borrow Minx if the two of them wanted to ride.

"What about Gerard?" Jocelyn asked.

"We thought you'd want us to baby sit," Lettie explained.

"That's Stanley's job," Aleta said. "You two enjoy your day together."

"Come on, Lettie, let's ride," Jocelyn said with enthusiasm.

"You're working and I'm staying home?" Stanley asked a trifle petulantly.

"Isn't that nice of me?" Aleta said brightly. "I'm giving you a day off. Don't forget that Gerard is with you."

"And if he gets hungry?"

"I'll be home at noon. Entertain him."

"Entertain?" Stanley gasped. "He's only ten days old."

"Should be easy. He's not jaded," Aleta responded gaily. "Jackson, Chin, you're with me."

"Do you want me to help?" Harriet asked.

"Grams," Stanley said, "enjoy Paul's visit. I want to be suffering when she returns."

"You'd better wipe that smile off your face then," Claude said.

"She makes me laugh inside. It just bursts out as a smile," Stanley explained. "She knows I love taking care of Gerard."

"By the way, congratulations."

"We don't know if she's pregnant if that's what you mean. If it's surviving Aleta hanging the family wash out to dry, I'll take it."

"It's both," Claude said. "Women have an instinct about these things. If I were you I'd check the thermometer. My guess is it's been used recently."

"You're betting on science?"

"Yep."

"That little minx!"

When Aleta pulled up in front of the old house with the peeling paint and the lawn with greening weeds sprouting up beside broken stalks from last years crop, the two men looked around.

"We're here," Aleta announced. "At least this is the address he gave me."

"We could ask for directions from the fire house," Roland suggested.

"Or maybe someone at the tavern would know," Andrew added.

"Does this town even have a name?" Roland asked.

"Junction City," Aleta replied getting out of the car. "I'm sure this is it. Let's go in."

"Is he a successful private investigator?" Roland inquired as he carefully made his way down the cracked sidewalk.

"The Tontine uses him all the time," Aleta responded. "Although they haven't had too much work for him lately."

"I can see why," Jackson said. "He needs to brush up his image."

"How would you judge this PI?" Aleta inquired casually.

Roland decided to let Jackson take the lead.

Jackson smiled. "Careless. Not concerned about outer appearances.

"Roland?" Aleta asked.

"Slipshod."

They walked straight into a small office. Ed was sitting behind the same desk he'd sat behind years before in California when Harriet first hired him. It was a wooden desk, scarred and used.

Emma rose from a thick white fleece pad and greeted the visitors with a friendly wag. There were three unmatched folding chairs facing the desk. Each took one.

"Where are we?" Aleta asked.

Ed opened a drawer and pulled out a folder, the contents of which appeared to have been carelessly stuffed inside. "Got copies of the phone records that were used to convict him in court. He's got no alibi. Not for a single instance."

"What does that tell you, Gentlemen?" Aleta asked.

"Tells me he's guilty," Roland said.

"Or framed by someone who knew every time he was alone. That would take someone pretty close," Andrew suggested.

"Hits stopped when he was in the can. Started up when he got out," Ed added.

"How long after he left jail?" Aleta asked.

"Six days."

"Same computer?"

"Yep?"

"The one the wife got in the divorce?"

"Yep."

"You figure the wife?" Jackson asked Aleta.

"The son," she replied.

"The seventeen-year-old?"

"Yep," Ed said.

"That's easy," Roland said. "All we have to do is get the son to fess up."

"Play them the tape, Ed."

Ed's voice came on first. "Why'd you do it?"

"Why not?"

"You know your dad's up on charges."

"Yeh, so?"

"He was convicted."

"Yeh, so?"

"He's gonna go to the pen."

"He didn't do it."

"It looks like he did," said Ed's voice.

"Well, then that's their mistake."

"Will you fess up?"

"No way. I ain't going to jail."

"But you logged onto the sites."

"I ain't going to jail for something everybody does."

"What if I told your mother?"

"She'd say you was lying," the boy said. "Dad's still got his laptop."

The tape ended there.

"Did you talk to the mother?"

"Won't do not good," Ed said.

"Mind if we try?" Roland asked.

"Give them the address, Ed," Aleta said. "You two can go this afternoon. We'll meet back here at three."

"Here?" Andrew asked. "Why here?"

Ed came around the desk, slapped his hand on Jackson's shoulder and shook his hand. "Good luck."

He shook Roland's hand and added, "By the way I got the laptop. He ain't been on it. The computer she's got is the one the kid's using."

Aleta drove through Willow Glen to the Safe Haven Retirement Center on the northeastern tip of the town. It was an area of gently undulating hills and mature oaks.

They exited the cars parked on the curving tree-lined street, walked past weed-free freshly watered lawns leading to flowering bushes tucked under the windows facing the street.

Once inside, Roland and Andrew sat in comfortable chairs and looked around soaking in the cozy dimness of the central room which had no windows, just a skylight. It was the ultimate in privacy. The fire in the fireplace cast a warm glow that was caught by the gold filigree on the bindings of numerous volumes of serious works of fiction, poetry, history, science and philosophy. There were books in three languages represented. The man was evidently multilingual.

The music playing softly in the background was Handel. Both male guests recognized the strains rendered by a famous string quartet.

Dennis Middlebourne greeted them and both politely acknowledged the man whom the night before they had discovered was a man of letters with a poetic bent.

"Well, we're here," Aleta announced. "Let us absorb the pleasantness of this room before we look at the quarters the Center has reserved for you."

The two young lawyers then realized why they were there. The wheelchair moved. Aleta got up and followed Dennis into the tiny walk-through kitchen. The two young lawyers trailed her as ducklings trail a mother duck.

One half the kitchen was an open counter from which one could look into the living room. Dennis stopped the chair in front of a plate of cookies and Aleta looked over the array.

"You remembered what I said were my favorites," she said delightedly. "And apple juice too. How nice! Thank you."

She helped herself to several. Her associates followed her example.

Dennis led the way back into the living room.

After she ate half a cookie, she asked Dennis how he liked the wedding. She laughed periodically as she listened, repeating several choice phrases, but mostly the associates listened as one listens to one side of a phone conversation.

After about twenty minutes, Aleta said, "My colleagues have both concluded we need to break new ground if we are to attack on the basis of either the American with Disabilities Act or the Fair Housing Act."

Dennis mumbled a long string of sounds.

"You have a point. Mr. Middlebourne says if all debilitated persons are treated the same but if that treatment is not the same as non-disabled persons, isn't that discrimination? Think on that please."

More sounds followed. Neither young lawyer could make out a word.

"Yes, I quite agree. I believe we need to attack the contract generally as violating your civil rights."

"We studied the contract before coming over, Sir," said Roland looking straight at Dennis whose head had lolled to one side and thus allowed him to look back from a tilted face.

Roland went on. "Are you thinking that when you read the agreement that gave the power to the Center to move you into their skilled nursing facility that you were envisioning a time when you could no longer direct your own affairs, which time has not yet arrived?"

Aleta laughed. "Spoken like a lawyer, but an accurate depiction of his argument."

Andrew addressed the next question. "Are we to assume-- and not having seen the accommodation that it is not just access to books and music but the ambiance incorporated into this place you call home that you want to enjoy until death comes."

Aleta was sober. "Well put, Dennis says. You two will represent him well. You understand what he is fighting for.

"Now, Gentlemen, not that I believe you need it, but, Mr.   Middlebourne wants you to see the character and atmosphere of the place reserved for him to spend his final days."

With his aide opening doors for him, Dennis led the way out of his apartment, past the small center gardens to a two story square building.   They entered through the handicapped entrance and took the elevator to the second floor.

"You will note," Aleta said, "that while Mr. Middlebourne can maneuver his chair into and out of the elevator, he cannot press a button inside or out to direct it."

On the second floor he led them to a cubicle in which there was a bed, a night stand, a straight-backed chair, a hospital food tray and a small bureau. A television set hung from the ceiling in the corner. It was turned on.

"It's pre-set," Aleta explained. "There is no remote because most patients on this floor can't use one."

"A hospital room is pleasanter," Andrew noted.

"This needs to figure in your argument," Aleta said.

"I need to sit beside a patient for an hour," Roland Chin said. "I need to feel this place."

Not to be outdone, Andrew said, "I don't think I can handle an hour, but let me try for as long as I sat by the fire.

An hour later the two associates were driven back to Aleta's house, picked up their cars and went to lunch.

When she walked into the house, she found Stanley pacing the floor with Gerard who was fussing.

"You and he need to synchronize your schedules better," Stanley griped.

"My timing is off," Aleta admitted rushing toward the bedroom. "House smells great."

"Andrea and Bertha have been cooking all morning."

"I thought Bertha was going to take her sons to see the house and then furniture shopping," Aleta said discarding her blouse and taking the baby.

Stanley closed the door. "Everyone went to see the house. Then Harriet, Donna and Jan went to the furniture store. It seems Jan is a fashion coordinator and has a great eye for color. The three of them are going to pick out pieces for Bertha to pass on later."

"And Paul and Dad?"

"Wandering around, talking. All the dogs are with them. The Pug has become an outdoor dog."

"And Earl and Bob?"

"You need to know where everyone is, don't you."

"Yes," she responded as Gerard began nursing.

"Bertha's sons are also wandering around talking. They haven't seen each other for several years."

"And you've been bonding with your son."

"I've been walking the floor with him," Stanley corrected.

"And how else do you bond with a ten-day-old," Aleta inquired tongue-in-cheek.

"When are you going back?"

"At three. Roland and Andrew have an assignment to complete. I'm meeting them at Ed's."

"They have graduated, you know. They've even passed the bar. They don't need lessons."

"I did," Aleta said. "I still do."

"You're eccentric and you're not even old."

"Are you still upset because I locked you out last night to talk with Jocelyn?"

"A little. Your family kept me company. They understood better than I did. I'm Jocelyn's lawyer, in case you forgot."

"It was one-hundred percent sister talk."

"Is that because it was talk between two sisters, hence it was one hundred percent sister talk."

"You are astute."

"I know you think this is strictly a family affair, but I'm not only family, I'm her lawyer. Not just a lawyer which both you and Robert are, but Jocelyn's personal advocate."

"We may need you--later."

Aleta fell asleep feeding the baby as usual. Stanley left Gerard beside her and joined the rest of the family for lunch.

"She's doing too much," Stanley explained. "She's got to sleep sometime. It's not as if Gerard doesn't have her up twice very night."

"Is she off for the rest of the day?" Harriet asked.

"If she sleeps past two-thirty, she is," Stanley determined. "She has an appointment with Ed at three. Her two associates are suppose to meet her there."

"She won't like it if you don't wake her," Robert said.

"I know. But she needs to slow down," Stanley said. "If she wants to breast feed this baby, she has to slow down. How many times have I made that point?"

Harriet said softly, "None of us needs to be convinced. It's Aleta you need to persuade."

"You guys are easier."

At two thirty Aleta was still sound asleep. The baby was sleeping beside her happily. Stanley called Ed and told him the situation.

"What about Rolly and Andy?" Ed asked.

"Finish the lesson," Stanley directed. "Help me take the load off Aleta."

"Sure," Ed agreed. "Whatcha want me to do with the Ledgewood info?"

"Aren't those two working on it with her?"

"Yeh, I guess so."

"Give them the info."

"It's numbers stuff. Aleta will get it."

"These are bright men," Stanley said. "But you can come to the house later, Ed. You know you're always welcome. I just want to keep Aleta tied down over the weekend. That wedding took the stuffing out of her."

"I'll be by around five."

Chapter 30

At four thirty, Aleta was still asleep and Stanley told the family, she wasn't going out for dinner. Bertha stuck several pot pies in the oven, gave Stanley instructions as to how to bake them and then got dressed. The entire group was heading for Chicago where Harriet had made dinner reservations. They had tickets to a play afterward.

Despite the noisy departure and Ed's arrival and departure, Aleta didn't awaken until almost six when Gerard began to cry and Aleta stirred and rolled toward him. His mouth found her nipple and latched on. He quieted with the first suck and Aleta woke up.

Stanley had come at Gerard's first cry and Aleta looked at him.

"How long's he been nursing?" she asked.

"Just started," Stanley replied calmly.

"I must've dozed while you changed him," Aleta said. "My he's hungry!"

"You didn't doze. You fell asleep."

"What time is it?" she asked still half asleep.

"Six."

"In the evening?" she gasped.

"Gerard wouldn't have let you sleep until morning."

"I had an appointment."

"I cancelled it."

"I needed to get Ed's report."

"He'll be back tomorrow morning."

"We were all going out to dinner."

"The family left at five."

"No one woke me."

"I wouldn't let them," Stanley said. "You had an exhausting morning after a long evening of activity. You needed to recuperate."

"My appointment with Roland and Andrew was important."

"You had two things of greater import to take care of."

"Two things? I know I need my rest to produce milk. What's the other?"

"You're pregnant," Stanley said. "You don't want to miscarry."

"We don't know that I'm pregnant."

"You have an appointment with Dr. Chesney on Monday," Stanley announced.

"Why are you two taking me seriously? I can't predict pregnancy and you know it!" Aleta spit out annoyed. "Besides nursing women usually don't get pregnant."

"Did you have a fever yesterday," Stanley asked casually.

"My temp was up, but only a degree," Aleta said. "I don't have an infection if that's what you think."

"Not unless you consider a fertilized egg an infection."

"It takes a couple days to fertilize an egg."

"Or a few minutes," Stanley said.

Aleta softened suddenly. "Do you really think it's possible?"

"Yes, I do," Stanley said sitting on the bed beside her. "I believed Dennis last night. Didn't you?"

"I didn't dare," Aleta said. "Think how disappointed we would be if what he said was only fantasy."

"We won't be disappointed," Stanley said. "But do you realize that if you are, we need to ease you out of carrying a full load of cases."

"Yes, I realize that."

"For heaven sake, Aleta, I haven't even used one of the arguments I've spent all day working on!"

"Well, they were excellent arguments," Aleta said. "I'm completely convinced."

"I didn't... oh, for Pete's sake... what's the use."

Aleta moved the baby to her other breast. "I slept six hours in the middle of the day and I woke up tired. I can take a hint, especially when it wallops me."

"Let me check on the pot pies," Stanley said. "Bertha insists you must eat. Don't fall asleep."

"I'll come with you," Aleta said rising.

"You're half-dressed," Stanley noted.

"It's more convenient to nurse that way."

"Never mind. I forgot that we're alone."

"Except for three dogs, six horses, two police officers and one groomsman."

"I forgot about Hubbs."

"I'll bet Bertha put three pies in the oven," Aleta commented as she sat down on a kitchen chair.

Stanley opened the door. "You're right!"

"I'm here," came a shout from the back door. "Bertha told me supper was ready at six and not to expect service."

"Come on in, Hubbs. Join us," Aleta called.

Stanley stared at her, but stayed silent.

"Now there's a sight you don't see much nowadays," Hubbs said entering the kitchen. "Used to be common, mothers nursing.

"Bertha said not to forget the biscuits," Hubbs said, sitting down across from Aleta.

"In the warmer," Aleta suggested. "And we could use plates and forks."

"Knives too," Hubbs prompted as Stanley seemed a bit bewildered.

"What's the next one gonna be?"

"Don't know," Aleta responded.

"Bertha's having a girl. Jocelyn told her."

"Jocelyn didn't tell me."

"Maybe she figured you could tell on your own."

"Don't forget my milk, Stanley," Aleta said. "Hubbs do you want coffee?"

"Bertha make any?"

Stanley looked. "Left a full pot."

"She knows me."

"I hear there's a woman who likes you," Aleta said.

By now Stanley was slowly acclimating himself to the fact that his wife was going to stay half naked. She could have excused herself. Instead she engaged Hubbs in conversation.

"Bessie don't want a man."

"Why do you say that?"

"She described Eunice."

"That's because Eunice is the first person she's shared the house with since her parents died."

"You think?"

"I think she was talking about how Eunice fit."

"She did like the stuff I said."

"And didn't they have you over for dinner?"

"It was good."

"Invite Bessie back."

"Where?"

"Have a picnic in the barn. She's a farm girl."

"There's Eunice."

"Pick some time when Eunice is going out with her daughter," Aleta suggested.

"I'm pretty old," Hubbs said.

"You still do a good day's work," Aleta said. "Nobody's horses look better than ours. You're far from done with life."

"Guess Bessie 'n me could picnic. Bet she's got good stories to tell."

"As do you," Aleta responded. "The freezer's full of stuff like fried chicken. Or you can use our kitchen and cook. Sunday would be a good day. Tomorrow we'll all be busy packing off Robert, Bertha, Jocelyn and the horses."

Stanley put the pies on the plates saying, "Aleta, don't you want to put the baby down. These pies are hot."

Aleta smiled up at her husband. He saw the mischievous twinkle in her eye. "He'll be quiet if he stays where he is. I'll manage."

Stanley put the biscuits on the table and sat down.

"Butter one of those for me, Stanley," she said.

He gave in. He was going to have to share the sight of his half-naked wife with his groomsman.

"You gonna have the grandpa name this one too?"

"I think so," Aleta said. "I really like the name Gerard."

"It's a man's name," Hubbs said, taking a forkful of the pie.

"He's got to live with it longer as a man than a boy," Aleta said.

"Girls should have feathery names."

"Feathery?"

"Light," Hubbs said. "Like yours."

"Lydia's a nice name."

"Nope," Hubbs responded definitely. "If you start with family, everybody wants in."

"Do you have a favorite name?"

"Don't everybody?"

"What is it?"

"It's an old-fashioned name," Hubbs said. "It were my mother's. Martha."

"Martha? I like it. What do you say, Stanley? After the woman responsible for us meeting and Bertha and Dad meeting."

"It's a pleasant name," Stanley said. "But only if it's a girl."

"I think this time it will be," Aleta said happily. "And she can marry Lyle's boy--well, one of them."

"Aleta, if she... oh, never mind. You and Lauren can arrange it."

"Don't fret, Mr. Praetzel. She'll marry who she likes, just like you two did," Hobbs observed.

By the time the discussion was done, Stanley had finished his pie. He cleared his plate and looked in the refrigerator.

"No lemon tarts," he said with a faint hope that Hubbs would leave since there was no dessert."

"Pour Hubbs more coffee," Aleta prompted, "and look in the cake tin."

Stanley raised the cover. "Wow!"

He brought the whole array of cookies, brownies and candy to the table.

"Bertha wants me to have a second glass of milk," Aleta surmised picking up a brownie.

"Are you supposed to have chocolate?"

"I'll ask the doctor on Monday. Meanwhile, the answer is: Bertha's a nurse."

Stanley poured her a second glass of milk and gave Hubbs another cup of coffee. He poured himself one as well and settled down and listened to the two chat.

After a while, Aleta rose. "Excuse me, Gentlemen, I need to get Gerard ready for bed. He and I will be taking a shower so..."

"Should you?" Stanley interjected. "I mean he's only ten days old."

"The water will be warm. He'll love it."

The two men watched her leave.

"That lady's got class," Hubbs commented. "Bet that was the first thing you noticed."

"Pretty much," Stanley agreed.

"I'm goin' to Bessie's for supper tomorrow," Hubbs said as he rose to go.

"Sunday the kitchen is yours if you want it."

"Yeh, okay. Be here about ten. After I tend the horses."

Stanley joined his family in the shower. For the first time in his life, he didn't fold his clothes first.

Chapter 31

At midnight Robert and Bertha snuck into the house. They heard the baby cry and Stanley say loudly, "Aleta, if you don't let go, you'll have to change him."

"Let go?" Robert queried softly.

"I'm not sure, but I think it's a part of the anatomy one doesn't just pull away from," Bertha whispered.

"Oh," came the feeble response as Robert got the picture.

"Two cups and a glass. They had company," Bertha said. "Let me just clean up. It'll only take a minute."

"If I don't, you won't settle, so let's get to it," Robert said. "Then I'll expect my pound of flesh."

"You aren't upset I agreed to let Lettie come with us?"

"Two teenagers can't be any harder to deal with than one," Robert said. "Besides I'd like you and her to become friends. But, you realize that this is our last night."

Bertha giggled.

Robert frowned. "It's not funny. Honeymoons aren't supposed to be celibate."

"It won't be," Bertha returned. "You'll think of something."

"My brother will find out."

"Your brother will expect it."

"No he won't."

"I'm finished in here," Bertha announced. "Let's go to bed. I could use a good night's sleep."

Robert wrapped his arm around her waist. "That you'll get for the next five days, but not tonight."

"Promise?" she giggled.

His kiss answered her.

The two were joined when they heard the first shout. Startled, they pulled apart.

"Now!" came the yell. "Buck naked!"

Robert rushed toward Stanley and Aleta's bedroom and threw open the door.

"Press two," Stanley said pointing at the phone which for some reason he couldn't reach.

Robert picked it up, punched in the number.

"Tell her she can't dress," Stanley said. "Neither can Claude. She's to run, put the dogs in the RV. She's to..."

"Hello Mother," Robert said. "Get the dogs into the RV now... Hell, I'm standing naked as a jaybird in Aleta's bedroom..."

"...Give the phone to Claude," Stanley said while Robert was speaking.

"Give me Claude," Robert ordered.

"There are bombs all over," Stanley said.

Robert repeated Stanley's words, adding, "I know you're in the raw. So am I."

Robert heard Claude rout Andrea and Paul and tell them to get the girls to the RV. Stanley could tell what was happening by the satisfied look on Robert's face.

More shouts came over the phone as Claude got Paul Junior out of his room and on his way.

"This does not bode well for my image," Claude grumbled.

"Are you out yet?" Robert said. Stanley motioned for him to put the phone to his ear.

"Nearly."

"Don't put those pants on!" Stanley said. "Just drive!"

The first shot came as Claude was inserting the key in the ignition and Harriet who'd donned a robe was slipping into the passenger's seat.

"Everyone down!" he shouted. "You too Harriet!"

He ducked low as he put his bare foot on the accelerator and the RV moved forward.

Lettie and Jocelyn scooted down the narrow hall and up onto the bed in back of the RV.

"Tell Lettie not to look out!" Stanley shouted.

He heard Claude shout at her. Paul's voice was sterner and more threatening.

The two chastised teens put their heads down and yelled that they weren't going to look. A shot broke the glass and the bullet whizzed over their heads into the wall behind them. Both instantly scrambled backward off the bed and lay trembling on the floor in the hallway.

Lettie began to cry and Jocelyn put her arm around her cousin.

"Aleta never cries 'wolf'," Jocelyn whispered.

"Is Robert really in your bedroom?" Claude asked loudly enough for all to hear. "Naked as a newborn babe?"

"The only one dressed in this house is the newborn babe," Stanley reported.

Claude repeated Stanley's words and Stanley held up the phone so Robert could hear the laughter.

"None of us are ever going to live this down," Robert moaned.

"But we're going to live to laugh about it," Bertha whispered in his ear. "We better dress now. They'll be here shortly. I'll make coffee."

Stanley handed Robert the phone. "Punch 3. It's Milani's number."

"What are you doing?"

"Trying to minimize the damage," Stanley replied. "If I keep my hand on hers she doesn't squeeze so hard."

"So she hasn't let go?"

"I think she needs to hear Harriet's voice. She's terrified."

"Does she do this often?" Robert asked then spoke into the phone. "Chief Milani?"

He clapped his hand over the phone. "Rachael's getting him."

"No, she doesn't," Stanley responded

"After I put my pants on, I'll bring some ice."

"I wish I could do the same," Stanley said wistfully.

"Hey, you're under a sheet," Robert snapped.

"Barely."

"Hi, Chief, Robert Locke. Aleta just had a vision and we evacuated my mother's house. They were shot at as they drove away. Aleta says there are multiple bombs in the house... Yes, everyone will be here at Stanley's... Yes, Stanley's okay... well, sort of... Aleta's in a bad state so he's holding her... er... holding her... No, I don't know if they were followed... They're in the RV..."

When he hung up, he said, "He's going to send more men to escort them here."

"Call Claude back. I need Harriet to come in here right away."

Robert took the phone with him as he headed for his bedroom. He passed Bertha in the hallway and stopped long enough to kiss her.

"You look great in your birthday suit," she remarked, lightly smacking him on the rear.

"You're going to pay for that smack," he threatened gaily.

She laughed lightly. "Well at least we can say we did it once."

"We did it more than once!" he exclaimed.

Bertha smiled as she hurried off. "I just thought you needed reminding."

The Willow Glen police cars escorted the RV straight to the closest spot to the front door. Their flashing lights clued the people in the house that they had arrived. No sirens had been used.

Robert opened the door and was ordered back inside.

"Harriet first!" he shouted.

The officers at the RV door called in the order.

Harriet exited first, barefoot, clutching her robe, grateful she'd left it in the RV. She inched her way along the bare ground, shoeless. The officers made a solid line shielding her from any long distance rifle bullet.

Once inside, Robert hurried her toward the master bedroom buttoning his shirt and explaining as he went.

"Aleta's terrified. She's got Stanley's... well she's holding onto a tender part and she's not conscious. Stanley thinks if she hears your voice, she'll wake up and... er... let go."

"God has a sense of humor," Harriet quipped grasping the robe opening with both hands.

"Mother, I feel for you, believe me," Robert said.

"At least Claude has his pants."

"And you have a robe."

"That's not going to be enough," Harriet predicted.

Harriet rushed around the foot of the bed to Aleta's side. She noticed that Gerard was still nursing. She put her hands on her granddaughter's arm.

"Aleta," she whispered. "I'm here. I'm okay. Are you absolutely certain we have to leave immediately?"

Robert and Stanley stared at each other, bewildered.

"Yes, my dear, I'll go immediately," Harriet replied as if Aleta had spoken. The older woman looked around. "Where's Claude?"

"Here," came a voice from behind Robert.

"We have to fly out of here now," Harriet said, rising, no longer aware that her robe was loose and open.

"You... we have no clothes," Claude protested.

"Take my suitcase," Robert offered. "We're almost the same size. I'll pack another."

As her son was speaking, Harriet opened Aleta's closet and pulled out several blouses and slacks and grabbed a pair of shoes from the rack. She spun around.

"Let's go."

"The dogs?"

"We'll take Stoney," Harriet said. "Robert, drive us to the airport. Claude needs to file a flight plan by phone."

"Why Stoney?" Claude asked.

"Because there are already two uncut males in this house."

"One's a Pug!" Claude objected.

"Babe is coming into season. Stoney is possessive," Harriet said, rushing past him, her armful of clothes covering what the open robe was revealing.

"Mother, where are you going?" Paul asked.

"Aleta will explain," Harriet said rushing through the door with Claude and Robert hurrying to catch up.

Bertha handed Robert a thermos of coffee and a paper bag.

"For their trip," she said. Claude picked up the suitcase by the door that he hoped was Robert's.

"What's going on?" Paul Junior asked. "Where's Grams going?"

The last thing anyone heard was Claude saying, "We need a police escort to the airport."

In the bedroom, Aleta released her hold on Stanley and he rolled away from her and went over to where he'd dropped his clothes.

"Of all the nights to do this," he muttered opening a drawer and pulling on clean shorts.

Paul rushed into the room. "What's going on?"

He saw Aleta on the bed and stammered, "I... I'm sorry... I thought you were both dressed."

"Just keep everyone else out," Stanley said taking a pair of pants from their hanger. "Aleta had a vision that you were in danger. It seems she had a second vision and she sent Claude and Harriet away. They are probably being followed, but the cops are with them. My guess is whoever the person is he is after Harriet for some reason."

"Why? Why would anyone want to hurt my mother?" Paul asked.

"Harriet shot a man dead last Monday," Stanley said pulling on a shirt. "Maybe he has family."

"Will he come after us?" Paul worried.

"No," came the voice from the bed.

Inadvertently, he glanced toward Aleta. She was still lying half-exposed, nursing the baby. Something in the naturalness of her attitude relaxed Paul a little. Stanley noted where Paul's gaze had rested.

"It is a pleasant sight," Stanley affirmed. "Hubbs said it was common in his day."

Stanley recognized Paul's discomfiture, remembering his own. "This has been a wild night. We were all caught with out pants down, or in the case of half of us with our pants off."

Paul chuckled. "Claude apologized all the way over, but we all had our heads buried in the carpet, so we didn't see much, except for Mother, but then she's seen him in the altogether before."

His eyes returned to Stanley's face.

"You know, I went along with the phone call because I was in pajamas, but I don't know if I would have responded as quickly as Claude if I weren't.

"When the house didn't go up right away, I thought he was being foolish. That's when the bullet smashed through the window.

"What I don't understand is why Robert had to come in here and make the call and why he didn't put something on."

"I told him not to," Stanley said. "Seconds counted."

"Wouldn't it have been faster for you to call?"

"My hands were... I couldn't reach the phone."

Aleta looked startled. "Stanley, I didn't..."

"Didn't what?" Paul asked, confused.

"I grab his penis when I'm frightened and I don't let go."

"Ouch! That must hurt!" Paul exclaimed.

Stanley grimaced. "You have no idea."

Aleta sat up, cradling the baby as she did so. Paul found his eyes back on her. If I were a painter, he thought I'd paint her just like this.

"I'm so sorry," Aleta whispered.

Her husband leaned over and kissed her and Paul drank in the scene.

This needs to be painted, he resolved. Could he remember it well enough, he wondered.

"Wait!" Paul cried. "Don't move. Please!"

He grabbed a pad from the night stand that he'd used to sketch some ideas for addition.

"Please, don't move. Please. I need to sketch this."

Stanley smiled and whispered, "I could kiss you forever."

"Do it then," she replied softly.

And they did.

Paul sketched rapidly.

"Hey, Dad," Paul Junior called from behind. "What's going on?"

"Go sit by your mother and be quiet," Paul growled.

The young man backed away.

"Okay. Okay. Just asking. No need to get huffy."

"You are delicious," Stanley whispered.

"So are you," Aleta replied. "And I'm sorry I hurt you."

"The pain is fading rapidly."

"Don't move," Paul admonished. "I have to get the shading just right."

It was ten more minutes before he released them.

"Let us see," Aleta said.

Paul showed them the sketch.

"It's perfect!" Aleta cried. "Absolutely perfect."

"I didn't know you could draw," Stanley said.

"All these sketches of the addition didn't clue you in?" Paul teased.

"I mean... you know what I mean... You captured our feelings," Stanley said. "Can we have it?"

"I'm going to paint from this sketch. You may have that or this when I'm done," Paul promised. "I only wish I could do it here but all my paints are at home."

"Do you have time?" Stanley asked, "I have a friend who's an artist."

"Palettes are personal," Paul said. "So are brushes."

"Do you have time?"

"We were going to tour colleges with Paul Junior, but Andrea could do that," Paul figured. "She thought I might get caught up in working on your addition, so she's half prepared to go on without me."

"You can have the guest room," Stanley said. "Aleta and I would love to have you. Bertha's stocked the freezer, so we'll all eat well."

"I need a room with good light."

"Tomorrow you can check out the family room," Stanley said. "It better be okay. You approved the design."

"The dogs?"

"Can move into the living room."

"I was thinking of their care."

"One of us will be here all the time. We also have Gerard."

Paul laughed. "Of course. How could I have forgotten him?"

"He doesn't have four legs and an inquisitive nose," Stanley responded.

"This would be such a vacation for me!" Paul exclaimed. "You don't mind?"

"If there's one thing you'll discover about us, it's that we're up front."

"I'll go tell Andrea," Paul said happily.

Aleta wore a smirk. "You were looking forward to just the two of us," she accused.

"Did you see that sketch?"

"Rhetorical," Aleta returned, "as I commented on it."

"You can't stop an artist when he had a muse on his shoulder."

"He could stay at Grams," she offered teasingly.

"Too dangerous!" Stanley declared flatly.

"You're just hoping he'll ask you to model again."

"And you aren't?"

Aleta rubbed her mouth. "My lips are numb."

"You're complaining to me?"

"I apologized for that!" Aleta declared annoyed.

She rose in one fluid motion. Stanley marveled at her loveliness anew. It was she he was hoping Paul would sketch again, not himself. As he just had. Discreetly, with only the curve of her back in view down to its very end and her breast half-hidden by the head of her baby. The sheet gathered just above her legs announced her nudity without revealing it. They could display such a work of art.

"Apology accepted," Stanley murmured watching her lower Gerard into the bassinet.

A soft knock interrupted his reverie.

"It's me," said the male voice. "I have your ice."

"Come on in, Dad," Aleta said reaching for her robe.

"You're dressed," Robert said to Stanley.

"Not for long," Aleta announced. "Stanley, take off your pants."

Robert closed the door but not before a titter of laughter made it through.

Aleta took the two ice packs, telling her dad she'd take care of things.

"No one knows," Robert said as he closed the door.

Aleta locked it, knowing Stanley would never disrobe otherwise. Then she let her robe slip to the floor.

"A little more discretion is in order, Aleta."

"We're alone."

"We aren't always."

"I'm aware," she said simply. "Now give me your pants and hop in bed. I'll fold them."

She gathered his trousers and waited for his briefs then insisted he sit. He protested that he couldn't wear a shirt to bed. She stared at him until he sat. While he was arguing, Aleta gently placed ice packs on either side of his sore and swollen penis.

She pulled his shirttail down to shield the area from the shock of the cold packs. He stopped telling her to remove his shirt. The temperature was just right.

She stuffed another two pillows behind him, put on her pajamas, kissed him and left.

He sat in the semi-darkness. If this were anything like last time, it would be days before he would be really comfortable again.

The door opened, and Aleta reappeared with fresh baked coffee cake and coffee. Bertha had used the waiting time to bake.

"Where'd your grandmother and Claude go?"

"To Carbondale, to his old house," Aleta replied.

"They won't be safe there. Will they?" Stanley inquired, his mouth full of cake.

"They only plan to stay the night. Claude says he's too tired to fly far."

"Any word from Milani?" Stanley asked.

"The shot up windows in the RV convinced him the threat was real. We're being guarded like Fort Knox again."

"Where's everyone sleeping?"

"Family room," Aleta told him.

"Robert and Bertha went back to bed, didn't they?"

"Andrea sent them off first thing, reminding them that they had to drive tomorrow."

"So does she," Stanley said.

"She took the cot in the nursery; Paul gets to share the floor with the kids."

"So we are safe," Stanley murmured, pulling the pillows out from behind his back and laying down. "We can sleep."

"For as long as Gerard will let us." Aleta responded.

Chapter 32

Ed walked into the kitchen and saw Aleta at the table nursing her baby. Paul was standing to one side sketching her.

"Ed, the Tontine is hiring you to find out who is after my grandmother," Aleta said.

"Any idea why?"

"She shot that man at the dog show," Aleta said. "I'd start there."

"Milani says he suspects a pro," Ed reported. "The police are already looking into relatives."

"Then you start outside that line—friends, partners, social and business."

"Do I get lunch first?"

"You looked in the refrigerator earlier, didn't you?"

"Bertha's got a sandwich with my name on it in there," he said.

"She knows you," Aleta chuckled. "Paul, do you want to break for lunch?"

"I guess," he responded absently.

Stanley walked into the kitchen.

"Paul, you need to stop. If you keep working, Aleta will feel as if she must."

Paul set aside his tablet and joined the group.

Aleta began digging out the sandwiches, each wrapped and marked.

"Here's mine. She left a prescription with it: 'Eat entire sandwich with one full glass of milk.' My stars! Look at all the stuff she put on it! What does she think I am?"

A nursing mother," Stanley responded. "Let me see it so I know how to make your lunch from now on."

"I'll get fat!" Aleta protested.

"No, you won't. Gerard will," Stanley returned. "Are you done working? It is Saturday, after all."

"I'm done." Aleta said. "Bertha made extra sandwiches, enough for the client in the study and the two associates outside."

As she said that Chin and Jackson entered. Both glanced at Aleta nursing and hesitated.

"Chin, put the sandwiches on a tray. Take them to the study," Stanley ordered. "Jackson, grab the coffee and cups."

"I could do that," Aleta offered.

"You'll get sucked in," Stanley said. "You've done enough."

He followed his two associates into the study. Aleta turned her attention to her uncle.

"Paul, can I see the sketch you did this morning?" Aleta asked.

When he showed her the sketch, Aleta exclaimed, "It's marvelous! We'll buy that one too."

"Buy? I don't consider these good enough to sell."

"A thousand?" Aleta offered.

"Fifteen hundred," Ed said.

"You're going to bid against me?" Aleta laughed.

"Yep," he responded. "It's got me in it. And it'll be worth a hundred times that much some day."

"You bought that painting of Bessie's for two thousand," Aleta recalled. "It's worth two hundred thousand or more today."

"Yep. And you got paid with one. Biggest fee you'll ever collect," Ed shot back.

"But I want this one!" Aleta said.

"What's going on?" Stanley asked, returning for sugar and cream.

"Ed's bidding against me," Aleta complained.

"For what?"

"Paul's newest painting," Aleta said. "It's only a sketch so far, but just look at it."

Stanley looked at the sketch.

"How good are you with oils?"

"Passable," Paul replied.

"Let's find an art store today," Stanley said. "And we'll get your finished painting appraised before you accept a dime. These two won't offer you near what it's worth. But you can bank on their astute art acumen.

"Are you my manager?" Paul asked, smiling.

"Your lawyer," Stanley announced. "Have you paid your models? Not Aleta, of course."

"No."

"Give them the going rate," Stanley said. "We'll get a receipt. I'll get Aleta to word it just right. "

"Why?" Paul asked.

"I'd rather have the painting," Ed remarked.

"That's why," Stanley said. "I'm looking at the future."

"I don't think I'm going to be a millionaire," Paul said.

"I think if you can capture the essence on canvas that you did on your sketch pad, you could make a good living as an artist."

"We can't call an appraiser," Paul said, his doubt forcing him to draw back.

"Okay," Stanley said. "We won't. Suppose I just ask some artist friends to give you their opinion. One of them is coming over now to loan you equipment. She can tell us where to buy supplies."

"Okay," Paul agreed reluctantly. "But nobody else."

"Except Lyle, of course."

"Who's Lyle?"

"My best friend. He's Arborville's police chief."

"That's it," Paul determined. "This is my vacation. And this is a hobby. That's all."

"Hasn't anyone told you how good you are?" Aleta asked.

"No one's seen my work," Paul said. "But I can tell you right now that this is far superior to anything I've ever sketched before. You inspire me, Aleta."

"Wish I did," Ed remarked wistfully.

"Do you really?" Paul asked.

"Yeh. But I ain't got Aleta's face and figure."

Paul took his pencil from his pocket.

"How long can you hold that pose?"

"What pose?"

"Freeze!" Paul ordered.

Inexplicably, Ed did.

Stanley and Aleta stood over Paul's shoulder and watched the fingers create on paper the man sitting at their kitchen table holding a sandwich.

It was twenty minutes before anyone moved. In that time he'd sketched and detailed the eyes and mouth. The rest of the face and body were merely outlined.

He stopped and showed he sketch to Ed.

"I can finish and paint it, but you need to sit a few times for me."

"It makes me look like a nice person," Ed mused.

"It looks just like you," Aleta enthused.

"The real you," Stanley added.

"I can't do just anyone," Paul said. "I've got to know them. I'm afraid I'd never make it as a commercial artist."

"Don't even try," Stanley advised. "Just follow your inspiration. All I want to do for you is protect you so you can paint. I have no agenda, so there'll be no pressure. You can do as much or as little as you want."

"I can't keep imposing on your hospitality," Paul said.

"Stanley!" Aleta charged. "Don't say it."

"You're right. I'm sorry," Stanley said.

Paul looked at Ed.

"What just went on?"

"Aleta did the wife thing," Ed chuckled. "Beatrice does that to me all the time."

"So I am imposing?"

"Stanley's a private person," Ed said. "He thinks he wants privacy, but he don't. He wants Aleta. He weren't happy private, but that ain't quite how he remembers it."

"You are a good subject," Paul said. "I can paint you."

"Sure," Ed agreed. "Nobody will want that one except maybe Beatrice and she can outbid Aleta unless Stanley coughs up the moola."

"Not me!" Stanley said. "I'll pay for just one—the one of Aleta's back.

"Her back?" Ed choked. "I would think you'd want one of her front."

"I have that already," Stanley quipped, eyeing Paul. "Exclusively."

Paul laughed.

"You've got a deal—until you commission me to do a nude of her."

Aleta butted in, obviously irritated.

"What makes you think I'd ever pose nude?"

"And what makes you think Stanley would even ask me to paint you in the nude?" Paul chuckled.

Aleta's manner changed instantly.

"It would have to be a pose I'd choose."

"Aleta!" Stanley shouted. "No!"

Aleta grinned. "Just had to be sure."

Sunday was quiet at the Praetzel house with Aleta deep in research for Emerita Balta's case. She had a solid case for back wages. Aleta wasn't going to give up that claim. Emerita needed to start over. Teodora had a small claim, as well. Aleta was certain that if she won Emerita's case, she'd be able to negotiate a settlement for Teodora as well.

The rapes of the two women would be a he-said-she-said standoff, and she saw the minister's reputation tipping the scales in his favor. He would confess to succumbing to temptation and be forgiven by his congregation. Followers of such dictators forgave just about everything, finding excuses for the behavior that even their leaders hadn't considered.

As Aleta sat at the kitchen table, nibbling on a leftover biscuit, a law book opened in front of her, her baby nursed happily. Paul, who had been working on a large canvas in the family room, stepped away from his task for a moment, entered the kitchen and caught her like that. He quietly picked up his pad. Stanley was in the study working on his own cases.

Paul began to draw the scene in front of him almost stealthfully. He had moved past the sleeping Lab and Chessies who had merely raised their heads when he stole into the kitchen.

The Pug, who might have sounded an alarm, knew that he wasn't allowed to share Aleta's lap with the baby, and so he had already repaired to the study where he had been allowed to settle in Stanley's lap.

Thus Paul sketched happily with enough time to fill in all the details. Aleta tended to let Gerard suck long after he'd emptied her breast. So deeply involved was she in the case studies that she noticed neither that Gerard had been nursing for an inordinately long time nor that Paul had been standing in the kitchen for almost forty minutes.

The two were interrupted by the Pug who came racing out of the study, barking, only seconds before Stanley emerged. All the dogs rose in response. Paul closed his sketch pad.

"You look troubled, Aleta," Stanley said.

Then he glanced at Paul and remarked. "You look guilty. What's going on?"

"Emerita is going to lose Nina to the foster care system," Aleta said. "I have no defense."

"Maybe her compliance is indefensible," Stanley returned.

"I can't go into court with that attitude."

"Then find another one," Stanley charged.

He turned his attention to Paul.

"What's up with you?"

Aleta rose and left the room to put Gerard in his bassinet.

Paul thought about lying, but he realized Stanley would see right through whatever fabrication he thought up. The sketch was everything he'd hoped for. And he'd found the pencil's response to the guidance of his fingers exhilarating.

He looked around. Why hadn't he left the kitchen immediately? Why had he foolishly stood there? Did he want to get caught? He must have or he would have walked away. He had had enough time.

He didn't want to speak, to try to explain to this man that he considered a friend that he'd betrayed his trust.

He flipped back the cover on his sketch pad, paged through the first sketches of people, past his newest rendition of the proposed addition to the house and stopped when he reached the sketch he'd just completed.

Wordlessly he turned it so Stanley could see it.

"You're planning on rendering this in oil, aren't you?" Stanley asked.

"I can't do it without the sketch," Paul remarked preparing to tear it out and hand it to Stanley.

"Bessie said if you finish enough pieces, she'll get her agent to get you a showing," Stanley went on. Paul didn't move his hand.

"Yes, she did."

"Will this one be in the show?"

"Not without your approval," Paul said, beginning to relax.

"It's as good as your first one," Stanley said. "Aleta seems to inspire you."

"Yes, she does," Paul admitted. "I know I promised not to do a nude, but she was just sitting there nursing the baby and studying her law book and nibbling on that roll and doing it with such a casual grace I got carried away."

"This isn't really a nude painting thought, is it?"

"I guess not."

"The arm holding the biscuit is discretely positioned."

"I didn't put it there," Paul said.

"Did she pose?"

"No."

"I believe that. She looks unposed," Stanley observed aloud. His eyes hadn't left the sketch. "It's a real work of art, Paul. I would never destroy such a piece. That is what you'd thought I'd do, isn't it?"

"Yes," came the soft murmur.

"I know at least four of us that will bid on this one."

"You, Mother and Robert. But who else?" Paul asked.

"My parents. It's a true work of art and. And Gerard is their first grandchild."

"It's only a bit of him."

"Will you find time to paint when you get home?"

"I thought I'd take a leave of absence from the firm and really see if this will work."

"You can stay here as long as you need to."

"Andrea will have something to say about that," Paul said.

"There are times when you need to follow your own dream," Stanley said.

Chapter 33

Monday morning when Aleta Praetzel entered the Superior Courtroom of Judge Vincent Walsh, she saw that Dennis Middlebourne had been wheeled into place at the plaintiff's table. His aide was seated beside him.

Aleta put her hand on his as she sat down and said, "Any last thoughts?"

Dennis mumbled something which he knew no one would be able to understand but Aleta. She nodded.

Only one portion of the signed contract was in dispute.

Aleta had familiarized herself with the history and legal mind-set of Judge Vincent Walsh. He had just committed his mother, a woman in her seventies, to a skilled nursing care facility. Parkinson's Disease had not only robbed her of much of her mobility but of consistency of reason. Lucid much of the time, she resented the incarceration, but frequently at night she would rise from her bed and busy herself at tasks both non-essential and at times dangerous without being aware that her actions were inappropriate. His hair had grayed completely as he had struggled with his decision. His wife had insisted that she could not continue to provide twenty-four hour a day care and eventually he gave in to her demands.

Judge Walsh would not break new ground.

Aleta had not planned her presentation to appeal specifically to Judge Walsh. The case was going to be appealed. Her argument was meant for the appeals court.

As she sat at the table, Aleta spoke briefly to Dennis Middlebourne. Stanley sat beside her silently. He knew she was apprehensive.

While Stanley had carried in her briefcase containing carefully selected material, it sat on the floor between them unopened. Stanley knew she was too nervous to write notes or even read any, and she didn't want to appear ruffled.

She appeared calm which caused some in the audience to interpret that she was in control while others saw her lack of last minute prep as the mark of an amateur wanting to give the impression of being in control.

Just before the judge entered, Stanley leaned over and whispered, "If you promise that our sixth won't be twins, I'll argue the case for you."

Startled, she stared at him, and then she smiled. He'd jogged her brain, paralyzed momentarily by fear, into awareness. It stayed that way as she rose to argue the case.

"The Constitution was written by men whose intent was to protect the weak. Unfortunately, just as dolphins are frequently caught in nets intended to trap tuna, people without impaired cognitive abilities are caught in the safety net meant to hold the mentally and physically impaired from dying accidentally by some ill-advised action or inaction.

"In the days when slavery was an accepted practice in our southern states, many men of conscience could only handle subjugating other men by looking upon them as animals, not as thinking, reasoning men. We are not too far removed from those times if we judge a man by his physical impairments to be, by them, unfit to direct his own destiny.

"Despite the fact that Dennis Middlebourne has been able to provide excellent care for himself, he is being forcibly evicted from a home that he bought and paid for on the basis of a clause in a contract that allows another person to

subjugate Mr. Middlebourne.   In this land of the free,
Norman Ipp, Executive Director of the Safe Haven
Retirement Community, on the basis of his interpretation of
the wording of the contract between Mr. Middlebourne and
the Retirement Community, intends to enslave Mr.
Middlebourne until his death.

"The Constitution guarantees every citizen the right to
live freely and pursue happiness. Mr. Middlebourne is doing
the latter to the best of his ability. That he is hampered by
his physical limitations in his quest does not mean he should
be denied that pursuit by anyone, including himself.

"We all sign contracts repeatedly and the law forces us
to live by the promises we make, however distasteful they
might prove to be.

"This contract, however, is an agreement wherein a
person allows that he can be moved to a more restrictive
facility when his powers to care for himself wane to a point
where he needs to be supervised for his own sake. Mr.
Middlebourne is not in that state."

Aleta stopped at that point and sat down.

The first of her two associates took over. Andrew
Jackson produced a series of witnesses who attested to
Dennis Middleborne's ability to communicate his needs to
his staff despite his lack of nearly intelligible speech and
almost no physical ability. Andrew Jackson had prepped the
witnesses and their testimonies were succinct and potent.

Roland Chin then presented a short video of
Middlebourne directing his staff in numerous activities—
activities of which he would be deprived were he moved to
the facility the Center had chosen for him.

Aleta's closing argument was short and potent.

"Yes, it is true, Dennis Middlebourne has almost no
mobility, that he must be fed artificially and that he cannot
speak. He can, however, read a book, enjoy a symphony, and
order his own life. That he has lost many abilities is not a
reason to deprive him of those he still possesses. He is

managing his own life, of which I am the final witness. He was able to hire a lawyer, someone who could speak in a last effort to protect his freedom to die in his home surrounded by his paintings, books and remembrances, listening to music and the voices of friends rather than in a sterile hospital bed bombarded by the sounds of television commercials.

"As you may know ALS usually results in death by asphyxiation and it will happen; however, Mr. Middlebourne's daily activity delays that death. As a living being, we naturally cling to life, no matter how constrained are its parameters. Mr. Middlebourne wants to live as a free man until his death."

That Aleta had seemingly not presented a legal argument as much as an emotional appeal was the first impression of the gallery; however, upon reflection, they realized that she was making a single point and she had made it well.

Judge Vincent Walsh, thinking of his mother's moments of lucidity, felt compelled to pose a query.

"Are you saying that people should be allowed to argue against confinement for their own good?"

"Yes," Aleta said boldly. "People should always be allowed to object to their treatment. It is then up to reasoning men to discern whether that argument is valid or not."

Driven by his personal guilt, Judge Walsh proclaimed, "But the man can't tell anyone he needs help. He needs monitoring day and night."

"While Mr. Middlebourne is not suicidal, he has chosen to enjoy every waking moment rather than lie in a bed listening to his heartbeat and staring at a ceiling in exchange for an extra week of life."

"Then you believe that his life would be prolonged by transferring him to a hospital?"

"Actually, that is the supposition of the opposition. In actual fact, such a move would most likely kill him. If not that, it would shorten his life markedly."

"On what do you base that statement?" Judge Walsh charged, upset because she was attacking his firmly held believe such confinement prolonged life.

"Two factors enter in," Aleta replied calmly. "Mr. Middlebourne would not be moved as much which would promote the onset of pneumonia. In addition, a man with as active a mind as Mr. Middlebourne possesses would find the insufficiency of stimulating activities an anathema. It would crush his spirit and deprive him of his will to live. We are talking about a man with a mind as active as your own, Your Honor, trapped in the prison cell of a non-functioning body, robbed of the ability to communicate his ideas and periodically waking to the fact that he can do one less thing than he could do the day before."

The questioning ended.

The gallery knew that they had witnessed something unusual. Judge Walsh had dared to argue in open court with Aleta Praetzel. That was a first.

There was no jury. The judgment was his alone. Generally, the judge uses his rendering of his decision as a time to proclaim his viewpoint, and while he might question one of the litigators, he would not argue as Judge Walsh had done.

After the judge adjourned the court for the day, Stanley leaned over and whispered, "Stop worrying. You were splendid."

He could tell by her feeble smile of acknowledgement that her mind was still fretting over what she's left out. He wanted to tell her that that very fact proved that she had done well. Only a weak jurist feels he's said all that could be said.

Aleta sat down beside Dennis Middlebourne and listened intently to his mumblings. As she listened, she relaxed a little.

Finally she said, "Yes, I can do that."

After that she left, refusing to make any comment to the press on her way out.

One brash reporter burst through her reserve with an outrageous question.

"You're a prophet.   Are you telling us you can't prophecy the outcome?"

"Yes," she replied. . "I'm telling you I do not know what the decision will be."

When they were on their way home, Stanley asked her what Dennis had requested.

"To continue the fight," she said. "Even it he dies."

"Didn't you already promise that?"

"He wanted me to assure him," she said. "He said if anyone could win this one, I could."

"So he was pleased with your presentation?"

"Yes."

"You're still unhappy," Stanley noted.

"He thinks we lost," she remarked sadly."

"You knew that Judge Walsh would be a hard sell."

"I didn't expect him to be aggressive."

"You were staunch and sharp in your responses."

"I didn't get any feedback at all," Aleta said. "He was too non-committal."

"He had to be. There was more than the usual crowd."

"You mean Superior Court isn't always packed?"

"No, it's not."

"Well, this was an important case."

"This was another Aleta Praetzel show."

"I'm not a freak!"

"I didn't even imply that," Stanley said evenly. "You're exciting and controversial."

"I don't want to lose this one."

"Have you ever tried a case you didn't want to win?"

"But this is more important," Aleta declared.

"We should have the decision in a couple of days."

"Days?" Aleta sputtered. "It shouldn't take that long!"

"He has to decide the case and then support his decision in writing," Stanley responded and then remarked.

"But you weren't asking, were you? You were complaining because you don't want to wait."

"As they were climbing into their car, Stanley got a phone call.

It was the lawyer representing Safe Haven Retirement Community, Anthony Petricelli. He asked for Aleta Praetzel and Stanley told him he was taking her home to rest.

"We want to make a deal," Petricelli said. "I'm standing here with Mr. Middlebourne and he would like to do it now. Three hundred thousand, a rewritten clause in all future contracts allowing for people in Mr. Middlebourne's position to opt out of the skilled care facility option, in return for a promise of no more lawsuits."

'The case hasn't been decided yet," Stanley said, pushing the speaker button on his phone.

"I know. This is a presumptive offer."

"You think we will win?"

"It doesn't matter. Either way Mr. Middlebourne plans to continue."

"You mean if he wins, you presume he will file a civil suit."

"Correct."

"And if he loses, you know he'll file an appeal."

"Correct," Petricelli said. "My client has been receiving such negative reactions to their position that they want this whole matter laid to rest."

At that point, Aleta spoke.

"I will meet you in the conference room on the third floor," she said.

At six thirty that evening, Aleta entered the house.
Stanley was at the kitchen table holding the baby.
"Did Middlebourne settle?" he asked.

"Yes, he did. The change in the contract did it. He said that was what he was after. And I get to write the new clause—for pay!"

"How much?"

"Ten thousand."

"For a paragraph?" Stanley whistled.

"They want a full review of the entire document."

"That's about twenty times…"Stanley began.

Aleta interjected. "I'm expensive."

"I suppose that's in lieu of a cut of the settlement," Stanley said.

"Nope. We cleared two hundred thousand," Aleta responded. "Turns out Mr. Middlebourne is one sharp negotiator.

"Aleta, you did it," Stanley exclaimed proudly. "They never would have settled that high if your performance in court hadn't been brilliant."

"We still don't know if I won."

"But you did win. Mr. Middlebourne gets to live in his home for the rest of his life. On top of that, you're rewriting the contract," Stanley exclaimed. "That's historic."

The fussing of the baby in Stanley's arms brought Aleta's attention to the fact that she had been gone way too long. Stanley noticed her distress.

"Gerard didn't respond well to the formula Emerita said, so I held off on feeding him until you arrived."

"So he's hungry?"

Chapter 34

Early the next morning, Stanley opened the door and greeted a buxom, black woman wearing a white nurse's uniform under a black cloth coat.

"Mrs. Johnson, I am so glad you agreed to come and help care for my wife and baby. Please come in."

"Dr. Cook said that you needed a nurse," the strong voice stated as she stepped through the carved oak door between two stained glass panels straight into a huge room with a stone fireplace separating it from the large kitchen.

"My wife gave birth to our son after a long, precarious pregnancy." He started and then paused and asked, "Didn't we meet at the hospital?"

"Yes."

"As I remember it, my wife really liked you."

"She is a nice lady."

"I couldn't wake her enough to let her know that you were coming," Stanley went on. "I'm sorry about that, but I did tell her several times that I had arranged for a nurse. Dr. Cook thinks that she tried to do too much too soon. She was in court on a big case all day yesterday and at a settlement conference several hours after court. We also believe she is pregnant. That has not been confirmed."

The nurse scowled and Stanley rushed on. Obviously, a pregnancy so soon after giving birth was not appropriate.

Flushing slightly, Stanley rushed on.

"Gerard was able to nurse a bit several times last night. He didn't get much and formula seems to upset his stomach, so I didn't give him any. I believe he will be ready to eat immediately."

"The police?" Nurse Johnson asked, referring to the guard on the door.

"Aleta's grandmother was attacked a couple of days ago. She has since left town. The police are guarding us as a precautionary measure."

"I do not do housework," Jamara Johnson stated flatly.

"Our regular housekeeper is on her honeymoon. One of her new employees, Emerita Balta, will be here at eight. She will have her four-year-old daughter with her. She will feed the dogs. I aired them earlier. She will also make lunch and our groomsman will join you. Aleta's uncle is an artist and he is using our family room temporarily. Please introduce yourself to them. You may call me at anytime. I will be in court this morning; however, I will ask for a recess to answer the phone should you call."

A faint cry told Jamara where the baby was. She took off her coat and hung it on the rack.

"I will be home at five," Stanley said as he put on his overcoat. "Feel free to nurse the baby anywhere that is comfortable. Aleta does."

That last statement changed Jamara's mind about this man. She now liked him.

Later that morning, Aleta heard voices in the bedroom coming from the armchair in the corner. She didn't recognize the woman's voice as being Emerita's voice. She was certain the child was Nina. She lay still and listened, absorbing the child's viewpoint of her life and the people in it.

This stranger had found out more about Nina in a brief span of time than either she or Stanley or the psychologists had with all their determined narrowly defined inquiries. They had all asked the wrong questions.

Suddenly, Jamara spoke directly to the woman in the bed.

"You be right, Mrs. Praetzel. It be me—Jamara Johnson. You be losing your milk because you be doing too much. I be feeding your baby until you can do it again."

Aleta opened her eyes.

"Stanley hired you?'

"Yes, Ma'am. He done that for sure. Dr. Cook be worried too."

"And you remembered the lingo I like."

"It do seem to soothe you."

"Did Stanley go to work?"

"Yes, Ma'am. He be coming home at five."

Aleta rose and went into the bathroom. A few minutes later, Jamara heard the shower running. Then to Jamara's surprise, Aleta slipped back in bed and promptly fell sound asleep.

Stanley came home for lunch at noon. He found Jamara and Nina in the master bedroom. Jamara had just finished nursing Gerard, and the baby lay contentedly in her arms. Aleta had opened her eyes when the front door opened.

Jamara gave Aleta the baby and taking the little girl's hand, told her they were going to go help mommy.

"She calls Emerita mommy now?" Stanley asked.

"I want to be the lawyer in Nina's custody case," Aleta announced abruptly.

"Aleta, I hired a nurse."

"I noticed. I like your choice."

"You are not physically able to spend a day in court without collapsing."

"I didn't collapse. I just got tired," Aleta stated flatly. "I'm allowed. I just had a baby."

"Gerard needs breast milk."

*"And you took care of that," Aleta stated. "Jamara can fill in for me when I'm in court tomorrow."

"I didn't tell you the hearing was tomorrow."

"Isn't it?"

"You can't replace my father." Stanley declared. "He's worked hard on this case as a favor to me."

"I don't want to replace him," Aleta said. "I want to replace you."

Stanley's surprise was complete.

"Me? Why me?"

"Because I know what Nina wants and I know how to present it in court."

Irked, Stanley shot back, "And I don't?"

"No."

"Her flat unequivocal response shocked him.

"Just because I haven't shared all my ideas with you doesn't mean I don't have any."

"You need to step away from this case for the good of the child."

"What on earth are you talking about?" Stanley asked.

"I can't tell you. It's confidential."

"Aleta, we're husband and wife. We're partners in the same law firm. We can share confidences. In fact, it's not only legally allowed, it's morally imperative."

"All that notwithstanding, you must let me be this child's attorney."

"Not without an explanation."

"I will give you whatever you ask for except an explanation."

"I don't need anything from you. You already give me everything a man could possible want."

"I'll go for four children instead of six," Aleta proposed unexpectedly.

Shock made Stanley take a step back. He sat down hard in the chair facing the bed and stared at his wife cuddling their son. It was the biggest sacrifice she could have made. It was beyond comprehension.

He stared at her open-mouthed.

Aleta loved children. One of her main goals was to have a large family. He knew somehow she would wangle a seventh child out of him and now she was willing to cut her desire in half.

Until that moment he didn't realize he was actually looking forward to having at least as many as Lyle who thoroughly enjoyed having a large family. Aleta was naturally loving and he knew theirs would be a happy family. He was looking forward to being persuaded to add to the number.

In addition, he hadn't liked Nina's case from the start. He couldn't see recommending that Nina stay with her biological mother, considering her participation, albeit involuntary, in the molestation of Nina, especially if her legal mother, Dorthea Amend, wanted her. Aleta had not been able to accept his rationale. He felt as if he and she were on opposite sides. He didn't like that.

Aleta had been adamant that Emerita be granted custody. How could he in good conscience hand the advocacy position over to someone who had a pre-determined mindset?

Personally, he'd been torn between the two women. The child appeared to have a positive feeling toward both women. Much as he might like Emerita, it was not apparent that she would be a better parent than Dorthea Amend. Even as he had watched them when Emerita had worked in their home, he sensed that the child felt shut off and alone.

In fact, it wasn't until a moment ago when Jamara took Nina's hand and led her from the room that he'd realized what had been missing in Emerita's relationship with Nina.

"Even though I know how important this is to you," Stanley said. "The answer is no. And I don't ever want another of our planned children put on the auction block again. We are having six and that's that!"

"Six?" Aleta gasped. When did you move to that number?"

"When I decided that I wanted as many children as I could have with you," Stanley remarked.

Aleta beamed.

"Six," she murmured, letting her tongue roll over the word. "Six! You're forgiven everything for the whole month."

"Then forgive me for saying that you are too prejudiced to take over as Nina's child advocate," Stanley ventured."

"Do you believe I will tell you the truth?"

"Of course."

Then listen closely. I can't tell you why but I know that from this moment forward, it would be better if I represented Nina."

"The child trusts me."

"I know."

"I'm experienced."

"I know."

"I'm impartial."

"I know."

"Why then should I step down?"

"Because you trust me and because you know that I can pull a rabbit out of a hat sometimes."

"If you know something I don't, tell me."

"I suspect something. I can extract the truth," Aleta proclaimed.

"Isn't that pretty high-handed?"

"Yes, it is. But it's the truth."

"If you agree to six children and not ever to bargain by lowering that number again, the case is yours," Stanley said.

Aleta smiled as she gazed at her son.

"Did you hear that Gerard? Your dad likes you so much he wants five more."

Stanley rose from his chair. Coming over to his wife, he addressed the baby in her arms, "What I really like is making them, especially with your mother."

Aleta looked up at him and he kissed her.

"It's one of your most appealing traits," she whispered.

Stanley was not to be distracted.

"Now that you have the case, are you going to share with me why I had to give it up?"

"Not until after the hearing," Aleta responded.

"I've done most of the work, you know," Stanley grumbled.

"I called you in because you are the best child advocate in the state." Aleta affirmed.

Still disgruntled, Stanley muttered, "But you think you're better."

"No, I don't. You'll understand when the child testifies."

Stanley drew away.

"Aleta, don't!" he protested. "She's only four years old."

"I know."

"I was planning not to even have her in court."

"Trust me on this," Aleta said, raising her eyes to meet those of her husband.

"Whatever you're going to do, don't do it," Stanley objected. "Not to a child."

"I'm going to protect this child, Stanley. I'm not going to traumatize her."

"You know I can't be there," Stanley said. "The judge will allow only one advocate for the child."

"It's best that you not be," Aleta said rising. "Let's have lunch and tell Emerita that there's been a change in representation.

"What reason are we giving?"

"The truth, of course."

"You mean that I handed the case back to you because I want six children?" he remarked facetiously.

"That's a pretty good explanation," Aleta replied. "I think we'll go with that."

"Aleta!" Stanley gasped. "I was joking."

Aleta eyed him coquettishly.

"Really?"

His grouchiness in full bloom, Stanley shot back, "Are you ready?"

"I will be."

Chapter 35

By the time Hubert Praetzel arrived at the courthouse with Emerita and Nina, Jamara was already seated on a bench outside the courtroom. Aleta had chosen Jamara because she already knew the child's secret and she knew how important this hearing was. At home, in the refrigerator, were two bottles of breast milk for Gerard. Stanley had elected to stay home and take another day of paternity leave.

Andrew Jackson was talking with Jamara when Hubert walked up. Jackson told Hubert that Aleta was dealing with her morning sickness. He assured the elder Praetzel that Aleta would be in court before the judge appeared.

The group stayed gathered around the child while Dorthea Amend entered the courtroom with her lawyer, Nada Parker, a thin-faced woman dressed in a pin-striped suit. Hubert and Emerita entered after Bertram Amend filed in with his attorney Jeff Landrum, well-suited, younger man. Andrew Jackson entered last and sat in the seat reserved for the child advocate.

Andrew saw both Parker and Landrum lean over and whisper in their clients' ears. He hated being taken as an inconsequential force; however, this was a team effort, and if

Stanley could give up the lead position, he decided he could handle his minor role.

Just before the judge was scheduled to appear, Andrew rose and left the courtroom. The bailiff hesitated.

When Aleta appeared and slipped into the child advocate's seat, the bailiff announced the judge. All rose.

After everyone was identified for the record, Aleta asked if the child could answer a short query.

Judge Rosemary Fogle frowned and was about to deny Aleta's request when Aleta hastened to explain.

"Nina is four years old," Aleta said "She is frightened. I have one of her best adult friends waiting outside with her. If she comes in and answers a few simple questions, like her name and age, and then is excused, her wait will be less traumatic. In addition, should we need to hear from her later, she will be less frightened.

"While the explanation was long, Judge Fogle had to agree the reasoning was sound.

Andrew walked Nina down the aisle and handed her over to Aleta. He was told to wait.

"Tell all of us your name," Aleta said.

"Nina," the child replied.

"And how old are you, Nina?"

Nina held up four fingers.

"How old is that?" Aleta asked.

"Four," Nina said.

"You know a lot of people in this room," Aleta said. "Would you tell us who?"

Nina surveyed the people.

"Mommy. Daddy. Emerita."

"You love your mommy, daddy and Emerita, don't you?"

The child nodded happily and shouted, "Yes."

"Thank you, Nina. You did a good job."

Aleta turned to the judge.

"May the child be excused, Your Honor?"

Slightly surprised, Judge Fogle cleared her throat and excused the witness.

Aleta led the child to Andrew, and the two left the courtroom.

When he arrived back in the hall, Jamara looked at him with inquisitive eyes.

"All she did was ask Nina if she loved everyone," Andrew said, still confused as to why the child had been called to testify."

"Is Mrs. Praetzel a smart lawyer?" Jamara asked.

"One of the smartest."

"Then she had a reason."

Hubert Praetzel led Emerita through her testimony slowly and carefully. Emerita's English was better, but still rudimentary. Permission was granted for Aleta to act as interpreter when Emerita appeared confused. She translated the question only. Emerita framed her own answer to the question and the judge was satisfied that Aleta wasn't influencing her responses.

When Jeff Landrum rose to question Emerita, Aleta remained silent, forcing Jeff to frame his queries in the simplest of terms. Surprisingly, her testimony became stronger rather than weaker.

Nada Parker was next. She had learned from her counterpart's mistakes.

"Did you ever spank Nina?"

"Yes."

"Did Mrs. Amend ever spank Nina?"

"No."

"Did Mrs. Amend discipline Nina in other ways?"

Emerita answered as she had been taught, "I don't understand."

Aleta stood and said a single word.

"Emerita nodded and then replied, "Mrs. Amend talked angry. Nina was sad and Nina say she sorry."

"Did you ever scold...er talk angry to Nina?"

"It was my job," Emerita replied.

"Your job was to clean the house, wasn't it?"

"Yes."

"Who taught Nina English?"

"Mrs. Amend."

"Who taught Nina to read?"

"Mrs. Amend."

"Who played games with Nina?"

"Mrs. Amend."

"Since you've been on your own with Nina, what games have you and she played?"

Again Aleta was called upon to translate.

"Emerita nodded.

"Nina taught me game. Fish," she answered.

Nada Parker was surprised enough to pursue a line of questioning without some knowledge as to where it would lead.

"Do you play Fish often?" Nada asked.

"Yes."

"Every day?"

"Yes."

"Do you read to Nina?"

"Yes."

"In English?"

"Yes."

"But you can't read English, can you?"

"No."

"Then how can you say you read books to Nina?"

"Someone read book to me. I remember."

"You memorize books?"

"Yes."

"What books have you memorized?"

"Cat in Hat. Horton Hears a Who. Make Way For Ducklings."

"Children's books," Nada Parker scoffed.

"Nina is child," Emerita stated.

Dorthea Amend took the stand. Nada asked her a series of questions similar to those she had asked Emerita.

When she finished, Hubert began to rise. A signal from Aleta told him not to, so he passed.

Aleta asked the judge's permission to examine the witness on a matter brought to her attention by the child.

"We have ample testimony of Mr. Amend's activities," Judge Fogle said.

"I will not touch on those at this time."

"Proceed."

"Mrs. Amend, I understand that you plan to file for a divorce."

"Yes. I am willing to do that to keep Nina."

"You feel you have a close relationship with Nina?"

"Very, very close."

"Closer even than her biological mother?"

"Yes, I do. Emerita loves her, but I love her more."

"You say you love her more," Aleta began. "Do you hold her in your lap when you read to her?"

"Sometimes."

"So, while you are cool in the presence of her mother, you are warmer when alone with her?"

"I wish to spare her mother's feelings."

"So it would be accurate to say that the woman Nina loves is the warm, loving woman you are when you two are alone?"

"Yes. That would be accurate."

"Are you ever alone with her in any room but your bedroom?"

"No. It is the only room no one may enter unbidden."

"It is the same in my house," Aleta said. "Except lately... Did you know I was breast-feeding my baby when Nina and I first became acquainted? Nevermind. It's not important, except to me. I didn't want to give it up. You'll never know how important that was to me. It establishes a bond between a mother and a child like no other. I imagine you yearned to do that when Nina was an infant."

"Yes, I did," Dorthea Amend said. "But I was able to feed her many times."

"Wasn't Emerita nursing her?"

"I had Emerita put her milk in a bottle so I could feed her too."

"I have stopped producing milk, so I am having Jamara put her breast milk in a bottle so I can feed my baby," Aleta said. "But it is not the same, so sometimes I let my baby suck on my breasts as well. Do you think that is bad?"

"No. Not really," Dorthea Amend responded hesitantly.

"My breast first, then the bottle," Aleta said.

"That is how I would do it," Dorthea Amend remarked.

"In fact, that's how you did do it, isn't it?" Aleta pressed. "You told Nina you had breast fed her as an infant. Isn't that true?"

"I may have said that."

"She was breast fed by Emerita. Isn't that true?"

"Yes."

"Why did you tell her you did it?"

"I wanted her to think of me as her real mother."

"Emerita decided that at two, Nina should be weaned. What did you do?"

"I thought Emerita was wrong. So I kept giving her bottles."

"But you didn't break the pattern, did you?"

"What pattern?"

"Breast first and then bottle," Aleta said. "And you never weaned her, right? You are still nursing her, aren't you?"

"Yes. She still needs it. It comforts her," Dorthea said defensively.

"When you nurse her, you disrobe. Correct?"

"I don't want to wrinkle my clothes."

"And you have Nina remove her play clothes as well."

"They're dirty."

"Then you lay down on your bed, both naked."

"But I do not touch her."

"You are very careful," Aleta said evenly.

"I just let her nurse. That's all."

"Yes, you just let her nurse on empty breasts, but you don't follow that with a bottle anymore, do you?"

"It would make the servants suspicious."

"Is that the reason you hired Rollo Travick to shoot Stanley Praetzel?"

"I didn't hire him! Dorthea shot back. "Bertram did."

"I did not!" Bertram Amend shouted. "You did."

"Order!" Judge Fogle demanded, banging her gavel.

The courtroom quieted.

"He told the police you did," Aleta charged.

"It's a lie!" Dorthea responded angrily.

"You're a liar!" Bertram shouted.

"You goddamn pervert!" Dorthea yelled back. "How dare you touch my baby like that?"

"Your baby? Your toy, you mean." Bertram roared, his deep voice overpowering the judge's gavel as well as her voice. "You're a dried-up, crazy old witch. You were as cold as ice to the child unless she was pawing you like a hungry cat."

"Bailiff, Remove these two!" Judge Fogel ordered. "Contempt of court. One day each."

The bailiff rushed forward and handcuffed Bertram. Two bailiffs rushed in from the side door and took Bertram Amend out. The court bailiff escorted Dorthea Amend through the same door.

"Court recessed until one o'clock," the judge declared.

All rose and stood respectfully until she exited.

"Is it over?" Emerita asked, anxiously.

"We don't know that yet," Hubert responded matter-of-factly. "The judge could decide against you as well."

"Nina stay and I go back alone?"

"Aleta, we need to go see Stanley and get his read on what Fogle might do," Hubert said. "When did Stanley get shot?"

"He didn't. That's why I insisted Jamara come, so he had to stay inside the house with Gerard."

"You said the police..."

"I called Milani. They found Travick in the woods between our two properties."

"Where's Stanley?"

"He's at home with Gerard."

"Then I guess he's making lunch."

"That's okay. Bertha left tons of food in the freezer. Call him and tell him to expect ten for lunch and to stick something in the microwave.

"Ten? There are only six of us here."

"He's got to feed Hubbs and Paul too."

Aleta cut right to the heart of the problem the minute she entered the house.

"Judge Fogle doesn't like her choices. What do we do?"

"She likes lists of recommendations," Stanley responded. "So we give her one."

"Won't the judge be upset?" Aleta asked.

"With you doing your job? No."

"And you know what to put on the list without knowing what went on in court?"

Stanley sighed. "Tell me what went on in court."

When she finished, he plowed right in. "You need to get right to work on the list. Have Alice type it up. Here are your recommendations. Emerita is to be placed on probation for a year with bi-monthly reports required. That'll keep her in the country. Emerita's male boarder is to move out. Nina is to be given her own room properly furnished with appropriate books and toys. Nina is to be enrolled in daycare while Emerita works. Finally, Nina is to see a child psychologist weekly for a year with the Amends bearing the cost. Suggest one of the two psychologists she already has rapport with. Hand me the phone. I'll get Alice started. She knows the form I use."

"Nothing about the Amends?"

"She heard what you heard.   What she has to be persuaded to do is give Nina to her mother," Stanley advised. "Now sit down. Eat."

He handed the baby to Jamara and went into the study and called the office.

"Hello Alice.   Aleta will be over to pick up a recommendation form for the Nina Amend case. Turn on the recorder and I'll give you the list."

When he finished, he joined the family at the table.

"Where's Dad?" he asked.

"He said he had to tidy up a bit." Andrew said. "He said he'd meet us all back at the courthouse at one."

Hubert, however, arrived at the house before everyone had finished eating and asked to see Stanley and Aleta alone in the study.

The three settled down, and Hubert told them that he'd cornered Nada Parker and told her he had a deal for her client. They met immediately.

"I didn't much like having to deal with Nada," Hubert confessed.   "But I knew better than to shut her out completely.

"What did you do exactly?" Stanley asked.

"I made a deal," Hubert said.

"Attorneys don't usually make deals in Juvenile Court," Stanley said. "The judge doesn't expect it, I might add."

"I read Dorthea Amend's face," Hubert said. "She was steamed, I offered her revenge. She was also devastated. I offered her hope."

"What kind of hope?" Stanley charged.

"I told her the record would be sealed."

"Her attorney could have told her that."

"The point is Nada was oblivious to her client's distress. She only saw the anger."

"Go on," Stanley urged.

"Dorthea knew what she was doing was wrong, so she put a limit on her involvement with the child," Hubert said. "It was a strange one, but in her mind it absolved her of true molestation. She forced herself not to touch Nina."

"When they were in bed," Stanley elucidated.

"No. Not ever." Hubert said. "She didn't trust herself."

Aleta broke in, "That was one of the things Nina couldn't understand."

"Go on, Dad."

"I told her Nina would need therapy to help her get over the change."

"What change?" Stanley asked.

Aleta jumped in.

"Why the change from when she was held as a baby and given a bottle to when she went untouched by Dorthea later. Nina noticed the lack of holding as she put it, but she figured that it was because she forgot how to suck the right way. I'm not certain that she didn't comply with the breast sucking to see if she could get Mrs. Amend to hold her like she used to."

"Dad, is that what you told Mrs. Amend?"

"I didn't put it quite that way," Hubert confessed. "I told Mrs. Amend that she had been teaching Nina that she was a failure by having her suck on her breasts with no reward."

"So, what deal did you make?"

"The Amends will pay for a year of psychotherapy, once a week, with one of the therapists Nina likes."

"Anything else?"

"Back wages for both Emerita and Teodora. Our office can calculate them. Minimum wage, but with overtime for the weekends. They were both expected to work seven days a week. Room and board for being on call twenty four hours a day."

"That's pretty much what we expected to get in civil court," Stanley said.

Hubert pushed on.

"Did I mention the fact that Dorthea was steaming?"

"Yes."

"How does nine hundred thousand in punitive damages to Emerita and three hundred thousand to Theodora sound?"

"For the rape trauma?" Stanley asked.

"No, for her turning a blind eye to what was going on." Hubert said. "She says she plans to empty their joint account."

"What about the rapes?"

"Mrs. Amend will testify against her husband. She actually caught him a few times."

"What does she want?"

"Guess."

"No criminal charges," Stanley said.

"But she confessed before a judge," Aleta pointed out.

"That's why you have to address the court and be your usual persuasive self," Hubert said.

"She has to promise never to engage in such acts with another child," Aleta said.

"I told her that would be the price you would exact," her father-in-law said.

"You did?"

"You're as much a child advocate as Stanley," Hubert declared. "And since you weren't going for punitive damages, and I did, we split our one-third evenly."

"We took them on pro-bono," Stanley said.

"I didn't," Hubert returned.

"That's fair," Aleta interjected. "They get to keep all their back wages which in Emerita's case will amount to $83,200 and Teodora will get $49,920. And we will take our one-third out of the punitive award. I gather we have to agree not to sue them in civil court."

"Yes," Hubert said. "That was the agreement."

"I can't get Judge Fogel not to assess punishment when a witness confessed to crime under oath in her court," Aleta declared.

"But the punishment can be suspended or otherwise adjusted," Hubert said. "The record will be sealed."

"But not the decision," Stanley contended.

"I'll take care of it," Aleta said. "I want to get those women that money."

"Aleta, one of the primary rules in Juvenile Court is that the judge is in charge," Stanley said.

"That's true in all the courts," Aleta insisted.

"Then, let's just say that things work differently in Juvenile Court."

"What you're telling me is that Rosemary Fogel won't like me monkeying around with the criminal charges in order to gain a monetary advantage for the women," Aleta said.

"This is not civil court. It is not criminal court. This is Juvenile Court. And the decision before the judge is who gets custody of four-year-old Nina. That's the case before the court."

"I guess I got carried away," Hubert said. "Can she even decide such matters?"

"She has the same power any other judge has," Stanley said. "But she has to be careful how she wields that power. A confession to a criminal matter that involves a child can be dealt with at this time, but the rest can't. The slavery and rape issues are not matters under the purview of Juvenile Court."

"But they're all tied together," Hubert argued.

"I was wrong, Stanley," Aleta said. "You would have been a better advocate for Nina."

"I think that Dad has opened the door for arbitration on the wage issue. We can probably settle that out of court."

"No punitive damages?" Aleta asked.

"The women deserve the money," Stanley said. "But this is hearing is only about custody."

"Doesn't child abuse come under her bailiwick?" Hubert asked.

"Yes," Stanley said. "And I do believe that you can legitimately approach the judge and tell her that Mrs. Amend is contrite and wishes to pay for therapy for Nina."

"Stanley, you're right!" Aleta exclaimed. "I know exactly what to do next."

"Are you going to share?"

"No." Aleta said. "You'll stop me."

"These are the times I want you to share," Stanley said.

"I know. But I want to do this my way."

"I will never turn over another child's case over to you if you don't share your plans for this one."

"You mean that?"

"Yes."

"I accept your terms," Aleta said.

"What terms?"

"Ask your father. I need to prepare my witnesses."

Aleta immediately left the room.

Stanley turned to his father.

"What terms?"

"I think she just promised not to ask you to hand over another child's case," Hubert said.

"We usually don't let her take any on anyway," Stanley returned.

"So, I guess you have no objection to the deal."

"What witnesses?"

"She's your wife."

"She's your partner," Stanley retorted.

"Rosemary won't put me in jail for contempt, will she?"

"All I can say is that people get angry at Aleta and I get shot a lot."

"That's not very comforting."

"I'm not trying to comfort you," Stanley said. "I want you to stop her."

Hubert laughed.

At one o'clock, Jamara was again seated on the bench in the hallway with Nina. That didn't seem odd to Hubert because the judge would be upset if the child weren't available should she order her turned over to Child Services.

After everyone sat down following the entry of the judge, Aleta remained standing.

"I am ready to decide the matter of custody," Judge Fogle remarked.

"And I am going to request that the child be heard before you render your decision. It is important that she have her say at this time. It will aid in her recovery process."

"This is a court of law and not a therapy setting." Judge Fogel stated flatly.

"While I did not tell her that she would testify, it seems that she expected to and it appears that she had prepared to ask for something."

"She did have a chance to speak if you recall," Judge Fogel remarked.

"She has a request to make of the court," Aleta said. "And while she may be only four, this is her life we are deciding about."

"A request?"

"Yes, Your Honor. It is an important request and only you can grant it."

"Bring in the child."

"May her friend accompany her?" Aleta asked. "She is a registered nurse."

"I'll allow it."

The bailiff opened the door and Jamara brought Nina into the courtroom.

Jamara helped Nina settle in the big witness chair and then stood to one side.

"Nina, tell the judge what you want," Aleta prompted.

"Jamara, you tell her." Nina pleaded.

"It's not a bad thing," Jamara said. "Just tell her."

Nina turned to face the judge.

"I want it to be legal to hold me," Nina said. "My mommy says she will be put in jail if she touches me. Emerita says she will be hurt bad if she hugs me or kisses me. Jamara says that's wrong and you can fix it, so will you?"

Children had often surprised Judge Fogel with their honesty and forthrightness. This, however, was a first.

"Thank you for telling me what you want," Judge Fogel said warmly. "I believe I can do what you want."

"Okay, Jamara," Nina said. "We can go now. I'm done."

"The child is excused," the judge said.

Rosemary Fogel frowned as she realized that certain things had inexplicably changed. The list submitted to her clerk before court reconvened needed to be amended. Before she did that she needed to know what had been discussed between counsels. And Aleta Praetzel needed to be involved. As the door had closed, she spoke.

"I understand that there was an agreement reached between some of the parties present in this courtroom. Is that true?"

Hubert stood up.

"My apologies to the court. I am used to dealing in a criminal court where such agreements are par for the course. I was not aware that things are done differently here. I will be representing Miss Balta in both civil and criminal court and the lines got blurred. My apologies to both the court and to Mrs. Amend and her attorney."

"Apology accepted. Chambers. Attorneys only, including the child advocate."

Hubert outlined what had been offered and then Aleta spoke up.

"I know it appears as if Mrs. Amend is trying to buy a lighter sentence; however, I believe a review of the facts will reveal another motive."

"Do you want to put Mrs. Amend back of the stand?" Judge Fogel asked.

"Only if you want her testimony against Mr. Amend on the record."

"I will object, Your Honor," Jeff Lundrum said. "She did not witness any inappropriate sexual act on the part of her husband."

"Then let's go back to court and put everything on the record. There will be no allusion to the offer made by Mrs. Amend," Judge Foley declared. "Mrs. Praetzel is going to dig deeper."

Chapter 36

"Aleta puzzled over the last comment of the judge. For some reason she is expecting me to pull a rabbit out of a hat. But what rabbit?

As soon as court was reconvened, Aleta asked for a ten-minute recess.

"I'll give you twenty minutes," Judge Foley said.

"I need to call Stanley," Aleta told her father-in-law."

"Perhaps I can help?" Hubert offered.

"I think the judge was sending me a message, but I'm not sure."

"About what?"

"Stanley will know."

Stanley, however, was as bewildered as his wife.

"All I can think of is that she's upset about the deal that was made and intends to embarrass you all."

"We overlooked something?" Aleta questioned.

"Possibly."

"It would have to be something blatant."

"That would be my take."

"It would have to be dead on relevant," Aleta said.

"Start with Mrs. Amend," Stanley advised. "I think that she holds the key. I have two questions. Why did she give the Emerita and Teodora such a big settlement? Why didn't she set up a trust fund for Nina?"

Aleta's mind was still pondering those queries when court reconvened.

Aleta followed Stanley's suggestion and called Mrs. Amend to the stand.

"Mrs. Amend, why were you shocked when you found out that you husband had been molesting Nina sexually?"

"Who wouldn't be?" she challenged.

"I'll give you that one," Aleta said pleasantly. "I imagine it was her age that startled you the most, not his proclivity toward sexually assaulting children."

"I knew he liked young girls, but not babies."

"How young was Emerita when she entered your employ?'

"The legal age—eighteen. She had a birth certificate."

"And Teodora?"

"We got her from another family."

"Was she pregnant?"

"I suspected that she was. She suffered from morning sickness shortly after she arrived."

"And you knew it wasn't you husband's child, didn't you?"

"Yes. He is sterile."

"Objection!" Jeff Landrum said. "Irrelevant."

"I'll allow it." Judge Fogel ruled.

"But, he didn't discard her, did he?" Aleta pressed.

"He liked the idea that he would be seen as the father of another child. He is terribly ashamed that he is sterile. He can handle being considered a rapist easier than he can handle having an extremely low sperm count."

"Objection!" Landrum shouted. "Irrelevant. Move that it be stricken from the record."

"The record is sealed," Judge Fogel said. "Overruled."

"Did you witness your husband having sexual intercourse with either Emerita or Teodora?"

"Yes."

"And you didn't report him."

"He said it was consensual."

"And you believed him?"

"They refused to wear the undergarments I provided," Mrs. Amend said. "So, yes, I thought they were leading him on."

"When did you find out Emerita's true age?"

"Just before the hearing."

"How did you find out?"

"Nina told me."

Shocked, Aleta stammered, "Nina?"

"Nina was curious about Teodora being pregnant," Mrs. Amend explained. "She wanted to know when she could have a baby. She said Emerita told her she could have a baby when she was fourteen. I told her Emerita was wrong. I told her fourteen was too young. She went back to Emerita and told her what I had said. That's when Emerita told Nina that she had a baby when she was fourteen."

"And Teodora?

"Emerita referred to her once as her younger cousin."

Aleta stopped her questioning there. She had done what the judge wanted. She had put the entire complicated case in the hands of Judge Rosemary Foley.

That night when Aleta arrived home, she fell into Stanley's arms, exhausted.

"How did it go?" He asked.

"Ask your father," Aleta said. "I didn't do well. I almost goofed up royally."

"I gather you didn't."

"You can thank your dad. His little faux pas turned out to be a brilliant move. Mrs. Amend believed that he would get her off if she helped with the case, and I hardly had to question her at all."

"She's underplaying her role a bit," Hubert said. "Her questions were right on point. I didn't see the age thing, although Rosemary did."

"They were minors when they were exploited by the Amends," Stanley guessed.

"That put everything in Rosemary's court," Hubert said. "Including the back pay issue. Aleta had the numbers at her fingertips. Rosemary was impressed."

Aleta excused herself and headed for the bedroom.

Hubert plowed on. "

"We're fortunate that Emerita is actually nineteen. If she were Teodora's age, she wouldn't have gotten custody of Nina."

"What about Teodora?" Stanley asked, deciding to let Aleta get ready for bed on her own.

"Emerita is her cousin?" Hubert said. "Did you know that? Mrs. Amend mentioned it when she was on the stand."

"What did she think about my recommendations?" Stanley asked.

"She added several more. She ordered therapy for our two rape victims at Bertram Amend's expense. Mrs. Amend pays for Nina's therapy."

"Any punitive award?"

"An interesting one," Hubert related. "An educational trust fund for all three."

"A big one?"

"It will take most of that joint account Mrs. Amend wants to deplete."

"She had a pre-nup, didn't she?"

"A tight one."

"What did she find Mrs. Amend guilty of?" Stanley asked.

"Child abuse in the form of emotional deprivation with regard to Nina."

"That was it?"

"It seems that when Bertram Amend got on the stand, he was so incensed about his wife revealing the fact that he was sterile that he decided to ridicule her. He bragged about fooling her about the ages of the girls. I don't think he meant to, but he saved her from being seen as an accessory. He was very persuasive. I'm not certain Dorthea was as unaware as he painted her, but he was the one who made the girls existence a living hell. She was a hard mistress, but she never physically abused them. She never punished them with anything more than a scold. That was why they didn't wear the underwear, by the way. She would scold, but he would hit."

"Multiple counts of rape of the two teenagers. Sexual molestation of Nina. What else?'

"The fact that Mrs. Amend had agreed before the verdict to give the two the wages due them took slavery off the table. Judge Foley added an interest penalty and they have to pay the Social Security taxes owed. Amend objected vociferously to every dime awarded. Mrs. Amend found that very satisfying."

"How much jail time?" Stanley asked.

"Sentencing is tomorrow," Hubert said. "Will Aleta be up for it?"

"I'm sure all she needs is a good night's sleep," Stanley told his father. "This is her last case for a while."

"What about Mr. Ledgewood?"

"I handed that case off to Chin and Jackson today. I told them that if he wouldn't let them defend him properly, then they could withdraw from the case."

"He won't you know."

"You're right. He wouldn't listen to reason. They told him that his son would not get jail time. He worried that his son's reputation would be ruined. They withdrew from the case."

"Think Ledgewood will react violently."

"He'll react, but he won't hurt us."

The next morning Stanley was going to rue those words.

All the bushes slated for planting were dumped in a heap behind the shed, their pots smashed.

When Hubert arrived to pick up Aleta, Hubbs met him and told him where Stanley was. Hubert found his son surveying the damage.

"Aleta would be heartsick if she saw this," Stanley remarked. "Last night Hubbs saw Ledgewood tossing the plants in a heap and then smashing the pots. Hubbs told the guard to let me handle it. The guard did chase him off the property though. Hubbs called me this morning."

"So Aleta doesn't know?"

"No," Stanley said. "Don't tell her about this. Let me take care of it while you're in court."

"And how are you going to do that?"

"By calling your gardener and offering him free plants and paying him if he'll plant them in a special garden at your house."

"My house?"

"Call it Aleta's garden. She wants to be able to pick flowers in the spring."

"I think she was hoping to have them a bit closer to your front door."

"The children can visit her garden at Grandma and Grandpa's house and pick flowers for her. She'll like that."

"So will your mother," Hubert commented, surprised again at how his son managed to turn a negative happening into a pleasant alternative for his wife.

Hubert would just have had the gardener plant the plants in the holes that were dug, but he realized that Aleta would mourn over every plant that didn't make it. If, however, they died in his garden, his gardener would just replace them. Hubert knew that Stanley would expect him to see to that.

Hubert smiled when he realized that Stanley had, in the end, reaped the reward of the untouched look he loved. That was his garden, the garden he loved as a boy.

He also knew that Aleta would not plant another garden on the farm. Her garden had been planted and would be tended. She would have flowers to pick and so would her children.

Hubert fervently hoped that Aleta hadn't selected any rose bushes.

The Prophet Series

* To be released